SAVAGE URGES

SAVAGE
URGES

THE PHOENIX PACK SERIES

SUZANNE WRIGHT

Published by Montlake Romance, Seattle

www.apub.com

Amazon, the Amazon logo, and Montlake Romance are trademarks of Amazon.com, Inc., or its affiliates.

ISBN-13: 9781503935440
ISBN-10: 1503935442

Cover design by Jason Blackburn

Printed in the United States of America

For Rita, one of my favorite people ever

CHAPTER ONE

Finding an unconscious shifter on your doorstep was a definite buzzkill.

Frowning in surprise, Makenna Wray double-blinked, half expecting him to disappear. Nope, he was still there, which just went to prove that Friday the thirteenth really was an unlucky day.

She gently toed the male body, which smelled strongly of wolf. No response. She squatted beside him, only then realizing he was just a kid. He looked approximately sixteen, but his scent wasn't ripe enough for that age. There was a small pool of blood by his head, but nothing that would indicate an injury he wouldn't quickly heal from, given that he was a shifter. There was also some vomit on his clothes, but it would seem that he'd spewed up elsewhere.

Given all the facts, she suspected that he'd tumbled down the steps that led to her basement apartment. She might have worried that he'd been pushed, but she could scent two other things. Beer and drugs. As such, it was likely that he'd fallen in his drunken, drugged-up state and knocked himself clean out. *Idiot.*

Normally, she'd be unsure of what to do next. Of course, she knew what society dictated she should do: check that the stranger was alive and call for help. Well, she could hear his heartbeat clearly enough, so she could cross the first off the list. As for calling for help . . . that part wasn't so simple.

Packs were insular and private. They understandably didn't like outsiders knowing or involving themselves in their business—especially lone shifters like herself. And Makenna wasn't fond of the idea of having strangers in her home; it was essentially her territory, and she was naturally protective of it.

So yeah, she'd ordinarily be hesitant in getting involved in a shifter pack's business. But as she took in the kid's rumpled clothes, undernourished appearance, and the distinctive musty smell typical of a homeless shifter, Makenna wondered if, in fact, she was looking at another lone wolf.

Of course she could be wrong. In any case, she couldn't leave him out here. This wasn't a good area for unconscious people—hell, it wasn't a good area for *conscious* people. And the truth was she was a sucker for a person in trouble.

Once she'd unlocked her front door, Makenna slipped her arms under the kid's armpits and dragged him through her small apartment to her bathroom, where she dumped him in the shower.

Then she turned on the cold water.

He sputtered to life, shaking his head and coughing. He tried to stand, but his legs buckled. Wild, stunned, bloodshot eyes settled on her. "Who the hell are you?"

"I'm the person who found you unconscious on my doorstep," she replied dryly. "Who the hell are you?"

He squinted. "You did?" The wildness faded from his eyes, revealing an inner turmoil that she could have related to at his age.

Taking pity on him, she turned off the water. "How's your head?"

He touched the back of his head and then winced. "A little sore." His nostrils flared. "You're a shifter. A wolf."

"Yes. And you didn't answer my question. Who are you?"

He regarded her warily. "Zac."

2

"I'm Makenna. Why did you come here tonight?"

"I don't remember how I got here." He ran a jerky hand over his tangled hair. "I was at a party. A fight broke out there, so I left and . . ." He trailed off, slanting her a suspicious glance. "I guess I took a wrong turn somewhere on my way home." He struggled to his feet. "I have to get back. My pack will be wondering where I am."

"You're a loner, aren't you?"

Loners had a bad reputation among shifters and were generally distrusted. Some shifters chose the lone wolf lifestyle, but some had no choice. In any case, it wasn't a pretty fate. They were thought to be on their own because they were banished from their packs for committing awful, heinous crimes. And without the safety of a pack, they became easy prey for other shifters, so a number of them became assassins for hire to earn money and protection. But being in a pack wasn't always a good thing, and it didn't necessarily make a person any safer from harm.

Panic flashed across Zac's face. "No, of course not."

"That party you went to . . . Let me guess, it was Tariq's party."

His mouth pressed into a thin line. "You know Tariq?"

"I know Tariq." He was a shithead who recruited loners to work for him. "You should stay away from him."

Zac bristled. "He's my friend."

"Because he gave you alcohol, drugs, food, and somewhere to stay? That's what Tariq does. He finds loners like yourself, he gives them all those things, makes them feel like part of a group . . . then suddenly he announces, 'Hey, those things weren't freebies. Now you owe me.' Trust me when I say the jobs he'd ask you to do wouldn't be fun."

"How do you know?"

"I've helped a lot of his recruits over the years."

His eyes narrowed in suspicion. "Why would you help loners?"

"Because I'm a loner too. Someone helped me. And now I'm going to help you." Earlier that day, she had helped a ten-year-old loner move to a pack consisting of his extended family—hence Makenna's happy "buzz" that had disappeared on finding Zac on her doorstep.

"How?"

"I'm going to take you to a safe place."

Zac snickered. "There's no such thing."

"I won't ask you to trust me. You have no reason to. All I ask is that you come with me somewhere."

He licked his chapped lips. "Yeah? Where?"

"It's a shelter for loners, you'll be safe there. If you don't want to stay, you don't have to. But if you want food, fresh clothes, and a bed, you'll find all those things there."

"What's the catch?"

"You at least take a shower, because you absolutely reek."

His mouth twitched into the smallest smile for a mere second. He was a good-looking kid. "I don't have to stay there?"

She shook her head. "In fact, you could just stay long enough to eat, shower, and change into clean clothes. But if you go back to Tariq, your life will become worse than anything that ever came before. Believe that, if nothing else."

For a moment, he was silent. "I'll go with you."

"Right decision."

CHAPTER TWO ☉

S talking people was so boring.

At least the view was attractive. Smoky black eyes, a strong jaw, broad shoulders, and impressive abs that she could see right through his dark-gray tee. The angles of his face were hard, rough, and dangerous, matching his menacing frown. He was incredibly hot, if you liked the broody, rugged type, which Makenna *totally* did. Especially when that male exuded strength and confidence with every step he took.

Ryan Conner.

Whenever she found potential guardians for loners, she researched them, scouting the Internet for information and asking questions of her many sources. The guy was a respected enforcer within a powerful pack and was well known for being a seriously talented tracker. All good things. He'd been described as stoic, dauntless, cold. But Makenna often had feelings about people—she was good at reading them, good at seeing past masks and shields—and she had a very good feeling about Ryan Conner.

Since she had a better chance of talking with him in a public place than being permitted on his territory, she'd followed his Chevy Suburban to a small line of stores in town. And now, parked at the far side of the lot, she watched impatiently as he stood by his car talking on his cell phone. Her plan was pretty simple: the moment he put away his cell, she'd approach him, introduce herself, explain the issue, and . . . and now he was walking away.

She grimaced as he disappeared down an alley, out of sight. Crap. Could nothing be simple anymore?

Hopping out of her Mustang, Makenna crossed the lot, traced the path he'd taken, walked into the alley, and—

Where the fuck had he gone?

She moved a little farther into the alley, stepping into the shadows. It was empty. Well, that was totally shit. Now she'd have to—

A large, warm, calloused hand suddenly curled around her throat from behind as a solid body propelled her forward, caging her against the brick wall; the rough surface grazed her palms.

A hot mouth was then at her ear. "Why are you following me?" It was a menacing rumble.

And just like that, at the feel of his breath against her ear and the sound of that gravelly voice, lust slammed into her. The reaction was instant, elemental, and totally unwanted. Sometimes being a naturally sexual creature was very inconvenient. "You know, there aren't many people who can creep up on me. You're good." He hadn't made a single sound. Makenna was good at stealth, but not that good.

For a moment, he didn't respond, and she had the feeling she'd surprised him. He grunted, "Answer my question."

Did he think that gruff tone would scare her? It probably should. Especially since she had well over six feet of untamed power practically curled around her from behind. With her slim build fitting into the groove between his broad shoulders and her head resting just beneath his chin, she felt totally surrounded.

Her wolf should have felt threatened. She didn't though, as she was a little distracted by the dark animal energy that hummed beneath his skin and his delicious scent: rich hazelnut, smoky sandalwood, and a dark sexuality. Makenna could admit it was rather distracting. "Sure thing. But I'll need you to release me first." In truth, she could easily escape his hold. But it would serve her best to let him believe she was helpless.

"I'll release you when you answer me."

"I just need to talk to you."

"So talk." His thumb circled her throat in a movement that was surprisingly arousing.

"Look, I'm on a bit of a schedule here—"

"Who sent you? What pack are you from?"

If she revealed she was a lone wolf this early in the conversation, she'd most likely be sent on her way. "Nobody sent me. I just need to speak with you."

A pause. "You have five minutes."

"I'm gonna need at least ten."

"I mean you have five minutes to convince me not to snap this pretty little neck." He punctuated that with a flex of his grip.

She sensed that he wasn't kidding. Well, of course he wasn't. She was a perfect stranger, she'd been following him, and he had all the instincts of an enforcer. A threat to an enforcer was a threat to their pack. As such, they would never hesitate in eliminating one. "Hey, if you really want me to walk away, fine. But then you'll never know what was so important to make me trail you like this."

He grunted. It was a sound that said, "So?"

"Damian Lewis was your cousin. Correct?" He didn't respond, but she knew she was right. "As I'm sure you know, he died six years ago. His mate died shortly after, unable to survive the breaking of the mating bond, leaving their son to the care of their pack." She licked her lips. "Zac left his pack six months ago, and he point-blank refuses to return. He's been staying at a shelter for loners for the past four months." Ryan still said nothing. "Are you going to let go of me now?"

"No." He circled his thumb over her throat again, increasing the buzz of arousal beneath her skin. "What does this have to do with you? Are you from his pack?"

"No, I'm a volunteer at the shelter."

He growled, "You're a loner?"

As his grip tightened—not enough to hurt but enough to reassert his dominance—Makenna sighed. "Okay, I get it. You're a big, bad, scary wolf, and your proverbial dick is bigger than mine. I'm officially intimidated."

"Really?"

"Yes."

His mouth moved even closer to her ear, until he was almost nibbling on her lobe. "That's a lie. I don't like it when people lie to me. Don't do it again."

As Ryan Conner released her and took a single step back, she turned to face him. Big black-flecked cognac eyes that held a hint of something wild met his steadily; they acted as a punch to his gut and heightened the oppressive, sexual need that struck him the moment he'd inhaled her scent.

She was a pretty little thing. Shiny with all those bangles and dangly earrings. Her slender body was supple, sinuous, and fit just right against his own. He itched to fist his hands in her long, beach-layered waves—a mix of gold, copper, dark red, and a hint of plum purple, making him think of autumn leaves.

While she stood there looking quirky and feminine in a vintage maroon dress that showcased smooth tanned legs he wanted wrapped around him, it would be easy to overlook her strength and keen eyes. But Ryan knew when he was looking at something dangerous. There was something almost . . . untamed about the female in front of him.

Officially intimidated by him? He almost snorted. She'd had a hand wrapped around her throat, an aggressive wolf at her back, and been trapped against a wall. Yet, she hadn't bristled. Hell, her heart rate hadn't even gone up. He doubted much fazed this female at all. He had the distinct feeling that if he were to attack her, she would go crazy on his ass—not come at him with combat moves but with street-fight moves. Scrappers fought dirty and wild.

The fact that she was a lone shifter should have dulled his arousal. They weren't to be trusted—it was a well-known fact. His cock didn't seem to care about that. Nor did the instinct to possess her that was whispering over Ryan like a sensual touch.

The same need for her also rode his wolf. Once, Ryan could have also described his wolf as relatively placid. But after being held captive and tortured by a rival pack many years ago, his wolf had changed. He'd become harder, defensive, and more withdrawn than ever.

One thing had never changed: when the wolf wanted something, he wanted it there and then. He *demanded* it. And at that moment, he was demanding this female. "Who are you?"

"My name's Makenna Wray."

"Why didn't you come to me sooner about the kid?"

"Zac refused to tell me his surname until a month after I found him. It was a further two months before I could convince him to allow me to attempt to rehome him. I needed time to check out his family tree and research each of his relatives—there aren't many. You seemed the most suitable guardian. The Phoenix wolves have a reputation for being dangerous and powerful but also loyal and very protective of their own. Zac needs to feel safe and wanted. Right now, he's convinced that you won't want him."

Of course Ryan would want him. He hadn't been close to Damian and he'd never met the kid, but he was still family. "I'll take him now."

Prepared for an angry response, Makenna said, "Um, it's not gonna work like that." When he growled, she raised a hand. "Easy,

9

White Fang. Hear me out." He just stared at her, his watchful eyes giving away none of the anger radiating from him. It was an unsettling stare, yet it didn't unnerve her. Nor did the menacing vibe he emitted. Instead, she had the sudden urge to poke at him and gain a reaction of some kind. Makenna had to admit she did have an almost pathological desire to antagonize dangerous predators. It was becoming a quest, of sorts.

She went on. "You have to appreciate that although Zac is your family, he doesn't *know* you. He doesn't trust you. And he has absolutely no reason to do so. You're family, but you're *distant* family. You and your pack mates are all strangers to him. His father didn't even speak of you. If I hadn't done a background search on Zac, he would never have known the two of you are related. You need to consider all of that."

Her coolness and formality pricked at Ryan's patience. There was an authority in her voice—the type that came from someone who didn't lead others but who was strong enough to stop others from leading them. Ryan was an enforcer, she was a lone wolf . . . and she was speaking to him as if their statuses were reversed. No, she was speaking to him as though their statuses meant nothing.

He inhaled deeply, seeking patience. And instead filled his lungs with her scent. God, that fucking scent . . . wildflowers, black cherries, and innate sensuality layered with a tint of arousal. He could almost taste it on his tongue. So she wasn't quite as unaffected by him as she seemed.

"He's worried that you'll ask me to return him to his pack," said Makenna. "You should know that I won't allow that."

"What happened to him there?"

"Zac won't speak of it. But he shows all the signs of an abused child, which is why I will do whatever it takes to ensure he never comes in contact with that pack again."

Ryan liked her almost animalistic ferociousness. This was a female who was confident in her ability to protect herself and anyone she considered under her protection.

"I ask that you meet with Zac a few times, get to know him. Then, when he's comfortable enough to do so, he can visit you on your territory and meet all of your pack members. That could be all it takes to make him want to stay with you. However, it may take some overnight visits. It's all about building trust. If you rush this, if you try to take him against his will, he won't feel safe with you. He'll run again."

The same part of Ryan that balked at leaving his relative in a shelter also balked at causing the kid that kind of distress. Ryan wasn't *that* much of a bastard. For the most part. "I'll agree to take this at Zac's pace."

Makenna had to smile at the way he'd said "Zac's pace" not *her* pace. It was a message that she best not think she was in control here. "Good."

"But I want to see him soon."

"Today won't be possible, but tomorrow would be fine. You know Trevon Park, right?"

"I know it."

"Zac and I will meet you there at noon tomorrow."

Ryan didn't like being made to wait for anything. As a rule, he generally didn't deny himself the things he wanted. But it would probably be best to take the time to speak to his pack before meeting Zac anyway. So he nodded. "I'll be seeing you soon, Makenna."

Makenna almost shivered. His words sounded more like a sensual threat than a good-bye, although that was most likely because his voice had that gravelly quality to it. As she walked away, she felt his gaze burning into her back. Her wolf was disappointed to leave him; she liked his quiet, confident, mysterious air. Makenna couldn't deny his appeal. But she'd sure like to.

As she slowly drove out of the lot, Makenna noticed Ryan standing by his Chevy, watching her leave with a deep frown. That natural snarl should have been off-putting, and she couldn't work out why the hell it was far from it.

Chocolate. She needed chocolate.

Passing through the security gates of Phoenix Pack territory, Ryan nodded at Cam, who was manning the security shack. He then drove into the wooded area, taking him onto the rocky trail that led to what his Alpha female called "Bedrock."

Most packs lived in cabins on a large stretch of land—some even lived in one single pack house. The home of the Phoenix wolves, however, was built into a cliff. Deep into the expansive wooded territory, the inconspicuous ancient cave dwelling had been increasingly modernized over time. Even when its arched balconies or windows were lit, they weren't easy to see. As such, it was doubtful that anyone would recognize the dwelling for what it was unless they were looking for it.

Having parked in the concealed parking lot at the base of the cliff, Ryan ascended several flights of steps that were carved into the mountain wall leading to the main entrance. He then walked through the maze of limestone tunnels, taking himself deeper into the mountain, as he headed for the living area. Only as he turned one corner . . .

"Ryyyyyyyaaaaaaaaannnnnn!" A three-and-a-half-year-old came dashing toward him and scrambled up his body like a monkey, wrapping his little arms around Ryan's neck.

Not good with kids, Ryan awkwardly put one arm around the son of his Alpha pair. It was then that he noticed the object in Kye's hand. "Um, I don't think that's yours." Kye's new favorite game seemed to be "let's see what I can steal today."

Tao, the Head Enforcer and Kye's personal bodyguard, rounded the corner and sighed. "That kid is fast." He held his hand out for the cell phone. "Give it back, pup."

Smiling impishly, Kye shook his head.

Tao arched a brow. "What did I say earlier?"

"Don't eat snot."

"What did I say *before* that?"

"Don't pick your nose."

Tao sighed. "Forget it."

Kye snapped his little teeth when Tao tried to detach him from Ryan. "No! I want to stay with Uncle Ryan!"

Ryan cleared his throat as the little boy rubbed his cheek against his. Ryan wasn't good at receiving or giving affection.

Sensing his discomfort, Tao smirked. "Hey, this is what you wanted. When you first heard Taryn was pregnant, you told us you'd be the kid's favorite uncle. You are."

Ryan had said it to needle the other males. He knew little to nothing about kids. He was even worse at dealing with them than he was at dealing with adults. Fisting a handful of Kye's shirt, he dangled the pup in front of him like he often did. As usual, Kye squealed in delight, kicking his legs.

Grabbing the pup by the waist, Tao took him from Ryan. Giggling, Kye squirmed like a cat, stopping Tao from being able to keep a firm grip on him. Then Kye was once again scampering through the tunnels with Tao chasing him.

Ryan continued to the living area, where he found his Alpha pair, Beta pair, and Rhett on the sectional sofa, watching TV. "Rhett, I need you to do a background check on Makenna Wray—she's a lone wolf." Rhett was a talented hacker, and there was very little he couldn't uncover. "And get whatever information you can on Damian Lewis and his pack."

Rhett blinked. "Um . . . sure. Can I ask why?"

"I'll explain soon. Just see what info you can find for me."

As the male left the room, his Alpha female, Taryn, looked up at Ryan. "Who's Makenna Wray?"

"Isn't Damian Lewis your cousin?" asked Trey, her mate. "I mean, *wasn't* he your cousin?"

Ryan nodded at Trey's question before answering the first. "All I know about her is that she's a lone wolf, she volunteers at a shelter for loners, and she's hoping we'll accept my younger cousin into our pack."

Taryn smiled gently. "Ryan, sweetie, I know you're more of a grunter than a talker, but I need some more info here. How did you meet her? Why would the kid need you? What happened to him?"

Settling into an armchair, Ryan gave them a bullet-point version of the morning's events. As his Alpha female had rightly stated, he was a man of few words. Although he was detached and unsociable, he wasn't completely without social skills. He simply didn't care to be what others would define as "social." He didn't believe in fluff talk or that smiling should be his default expression.

People sometimes assumed that he wished he were talkative. That wasn't the case at all. When he was quiet, it was because he simply didn't have anything he wished to share at that moment. But his quiet nature often made people feel uncomfortable, even though not everyone who talked actually *listened*. They wanted to talk mostly to fill a silence.

Having grown up in a house full of drama, he found something about silence very comforting. Words were overrated, in his opinion. They could be used to hurt and scar, and they could easily achieve it.

"I didn't know there was a shelter for loners," said Jaime, the Beta female.

"I suppose it's not something they'd want to advertise, since loners don't have protection from packs," Taryn pointed out.

"Did you know Damian well?" asked Dante, the Beta male, as he toyed with his mate's long sable hair.

14

Ryan shook his head. "I only met him a few times when we were kids. He was my father's first cousin, and my second cousin."

"How did he die?" asked Jaime.

"He challenged his Alpha for the position, lost the duel, and refused to submit."

Shocked, Jaime leaned forward. "He chose to die rather than submit, even though he had a mate and son to take care of?" Her horror was understandable. Shifters often didn't survive the breaking of a mating bond—a metaphysical connection that allowed mates to feel each other's emotions and bolster each other's energy. Damian would have known his death could lead to that of his mate and, consequently, leave his son without parents.

"That's what I heard," said Ryan. At that moment, Rhett returned. "What did you find out?"

Returning to his spot on the sofa, Rhett replied, "Damian Lewis is your cousin, which I'm guessing you already knew." At Ryan's nod, Rhett continued. "He mated when he was in his twenties. His mate gave birth to twins, but one died within hours of being born. His son, Zac, was eight when his father died in a duel with his Alpha. Damian's mate died days later. His pack—the York Pack—is small, extremely private, and resides about five miles from Lance's pack." Lance was Taryn's father, who she didn't have a great relationship with. "Apparently the Alpha, a guy named Brogan Creed, is a tough son of a bitch who runs his pack with an iron fist."

"What about the loner?" Taryn asked. "What did you find out about her?"

"Nothing."

Dante arched a brow. "Nothing?"

"Either Makenna Wray doesn't exist, or someone's erased her proverbial paper trail. There's absolutely no record of her anywhere."

Ryan stilled. He was assuming Makenna had been cast out of her pack, since it was rare for shifters to choose to be a loner. If she'd changed her name, she must have done something so bad that she was in hiding—maybe even had a bounty on her head. Volunteering at a shelter could mean that she regretted her actions and was seeking some form of redemption. Or maybe she was simply using it as a place to hide.

Trey looked at Ryan. "I don't like this."

"Asking you to meet her could be some kind of trap—an attempt to get you someplace, alone and vulnerable," Dante warned.

He was right. But . . . "I have to know."

Trey inclined his head. "So, Dante and I will go with you."

"And me," added Taryn. "You're not leaving me out of this."

Jaime gave Dante a look that said, "Nor me."

Trey pinned his tiny mate with a hard glare that had no effect. "I'm not okay with you being around a lone shifter. They've been hired to breach our defenses and invade our territory many times in the past." He looked at Jaime. "Hell, you were *shot* by a loner."

"So was Roni," Dante pointed out, referring to the mate of their fellow enforcer, Marcus.

"Not all loners are hired guns," said Jaime. "Makenna said she works at a shelter."

"Yeah," Trey confirmed, "but we don't know for sure if that's true."

Taryn raised a hand. "Let it go, Flintstone. Ryan is one of my wolves, and this situation is a tricky one. I intend to be there tomorrow."

"I'm going too." Jaime looked up at her mate when his fingers clenched in her hair. "I won't stay behind, Popeye." She'd given him that nickname due to his very muscular frame.

Of course, Dante—a wolf who valued control as much as Ryan did—wasn't too happy with his mate's response. Apparently he hadn't yet resigned himself to the fact that Jaime would never be someone he could control, because he continued to pressure her to change her mind.

Several futile minutes later, a defeated-looking Dante burst out, "Fine, we'll all go. But if this Makenna person makes a wrong move, we end her."

Ryan's wolf's claws sliced out as the animal released a threatening snarl. The same snarl built in Ryan's throat, and he forced himself to swallow it back. The idea of causing her harm . . . it went against something inside him. The reality that she was a lone shifter and had likely committed an appalling crime against her pack didn't change that.

Ryan always listened to his instincts. And at that moment, they told him that Makenna Wray was going to be a world of trouble.

CHAPTER THREE

H e's not coming."
Makenna looked at Zac. His eyes were darting everywhere as he slouched on the park bench, shoulders hunched, arms folded; he was subconsciously making himself seem smaller, just like prey. "He'll be here."

Zac looked at her, dubious. "What makes you so sure?"

"Because he almost ripped me a new asshole for keeping you from him. I'll warn you, the guy's pretty intense; he seems to have a natural scowl, and you might find him a little intimidating. But I don't believe he's a danger to you."

"Why?"

"He's protective of you." It had been clear in not only his eagerness to meet Zac but his concession to go at Zac's pace. She sensed that protectiveness was a part of Ryan's makeup; that he'd ensure that anyone he classified as under his protection would have whatever they needed to be safe. "Some people have that trait stamped into their very bones—it's in their nature to defend and protect."

"Like you." He shrugged at Makenna's frown. "Even Dawn says you're a natural-born protector." Dawn owned and managed the shelter. It would be more accurate to say she was the heart of the shelter.

Unmated, she'd dedicated her life to the cause of helping loners. Makenna was one of the many shifters that Dawn had helped over the years.

Uncomfortable with the admiration in his eyes, Makenna shifted in her seat. "We're talking about Ryan, not me. He's a dominant male, which means his instinct is to take control of every situation. They're not really into that whole compromising thing, and they like to have their own way. Letting you call the shots shows that he cares about you."

"He doesn't know me."

"You're family; clearly that's all that matters to him."

Zac shook his head. "Even if he does come, he won't want me. I've heard about the Phoenix wolves. They're strong and powerful. I'm weak and—"

"Hey, hey, hey, look at me." Makenna pinned him with her gaze. Voice hard and insistent, she said, "You are *not* weak. I don't know what happened to you, but I do know you were strong enough to get yourself out of that situation. What a lot of people don't realize is that it takes guts to run and take the chance of being caught. But you did it. You braved the lone wolf lifestyle. You survived the streets. You were brave enough to come to the shelter with me when I found you. And you were brave enough to agree to meet with Ryan today. *You are not weak.* You got me?"

Zac swallowed. "Yeah."

She smiled brightly. "Good."

"You're scary."

"Scarier than Madisyn?" she asked hopefully. She was not only Makenna's best friend but another volunteer at the shelter.

He smiled. "She's crazy. I like her. I like you. I like everyone at the shelter, and I like it there. Why can't I stay? I won't get in anybody's way. I'll help out. I'll be good—"

"Kid, you're breaking my heart here."

"I don't want to be in a pack, Makenna. I want to be like you."

"Me?"

"You're strong, and you look out for everyone, and nothing scares you."

"Zac, I'm a single, mostly uneducated, deliberately annoying loner who works evening shifts at a gas station when she's not doing volunteer work at a local shelter. Do not aspire to be like me."

Sadness clouded his eyes. "You want to get rid of me, don't you?"

"Hey, you listen to me. I'll be very sad to see you go, Zac. But I can't claim to care about you and then not do what's best for you, can I? The shelter is a special place, but it can't give you the things that come with being part of a pack."

He scowled. "If being in a pack is so sick, why didn't *you* join one?"

She knew "sick" loosely meant "great," since she'd learned to interpret his slang over the past few months. "I was twelve when I first went to the shelter. Back then, Dawn didn't aim to rehome loners. Instead, she taught us how to integrate ourselves in the human community."

"You're the one who changed it and started rehoming them?"

"Yes."

"But you could join a pack now, right? Why haven't you?"

"Because it's highly unlikely that any Alpha will condone one of their pack associating with loners, let alone volunteering at the shelter. And I like my life exactly as it is. But it still isn't easy to be without a pack. My wolf accepts the situation, but she'll never be satisfied and content. She'll always feel like something's missing, because being a loner goes against our nature." That was why she worked so hard at rehoming lone shifters.

A football came bouncing their way. Makenna caught it and threw it back to the group of human teenagers a short distance away. The park was quite busy, which would hopefully reassure Zac.

After a moment of silence, Zac said, "I didn't think I'd have to meet Ryan so soon."

"And you felt like I was trying to get rid of you in a hurry. No, sweetie. He's really intent on seeing you. I thought it would be best to get the first visit over with quickly. It might placate him a little."

Zac frowned thoughtfully. "Oh." He exhaled heavily. "What if I don't like him? What if he wants me but I don't want him?"

"Then you don't go with him. But you can't make a decision like that until you get to know him. All I'm asking is that you give him a shot."

Zac looked away. "Whatever."

She wondered why that one-word response from a teenager had the potential to make her want to scream. "So . . . do you think stairs are supposed to go up or down?"

He smiled. "Why do you always ask weird questions?"

"You're assuming I do it for a reason."

Chuckling, he shrugged. "Up."

"Okay . . . What about that issue that The Killers raised? *Are* we human, or *are* we dancer? What do you think?"

His shoulders shook. "That lyric makes no sense."

"I know, I don't get it!" Hearing a vehicle pulling up in the small parking lot on their left, she glanced over. She knew that Chevy. "Here comes Ryan." Zac froze. "Don't worry, nothing bad will happen to you. You're in a public place, surrounded by people, and you have me."

Swallowing hard, Zac nodded. "Which one is he?" he asked as a total of five wolves exited the car. "And who are the others?"

"See the broad guy with the snarl and the military haircut? That's Ryan. I'm guessing the others are his pack mates."

"You're not surprised that he hasn't come alone, are you?"

"Loners aren't trusted, so I figured his Alphas wouldn't want him to come without some backup." They approached slowly, their postures nonthreatening—as if they were conscious of not spooking Zac. Everything female in her stood up and paid attention when Ryan's smoky black eyes settled on her. It was pure instinct to irritate him.

"Hey, White Fang. Who've you brought with you?" Her inner wolf was pleased to see him, but not so much his companions. She wasn't always comfortable around strangers.

A mountain of pure muscle cocked a brow at Ryan. "White Fang?"

Ryan just grunted at him, which Makenna translated as "fuck you."

A small blonde smiled at Makenna; there was a hint of cautiousness in her eyes. "You must be Makenna." Her gaze shifted to Zac, and her smile became more genuine. "And you must be Zac. It's good to meet you both. I'm Taryn, Alpha female of the Phoenix Pack." It wasn't said with superiority, just as a statement of fact.

Makenna had heard plenty about Taryn. Mostly that she was plain insane. Makenna could respect that.

"This is my mate, Trey. And these are our Betas, Jaime and Dante."

The strongly built Alpha male inclined his head at Zac before narrowing his arctic-blue eyes suspiciously at Makenna. Jaime, a tall brunette with mischievous eyes, gave Zac a little wave and offered Makenna a guarded smile. Her mate nodded at the kid before studying Makenna intently. Ryan . . . well, he was staring at her again with a crease between his brows.

He looked so indomitable and remote. Again, it should have been off-putting. But his supreme masculinity caused a carnal hunger to slowly begin trickling through her. That hunger intensified as his masculine scent swirled around her like a blanket; it seemed to somehow stand out from the others.

Ryan turned his attention to Zac. His frown didn't ease. "I'm Ryan."

Shifting closer to Makenna so their thighs touched, Zac regarded him as warily as he did the others. "You don't look like my dad."

"You do." Something in Ryan's chest tightened as he watched the teenager's gaze dance around them, as if assuring himself of all possible escape routes. "We won't force you to come with us," he promised the teen. Although, up until that point, he *had* thought about it. He wanted Zac somewhere safe.

As Ryan slid his gaze to Makenna, he noticed the "just fucking try it" glint in her eyes. Yeah, she knew his instinct was to whisk the kid away. And she was prepared to fight for Zac. His wolf loved that fierceness; he wanted to bite her.

She looked just as quirky yet stylish today in colorful bangles, a cropped denim jacket, bold neon-orange top, and low-rise jeans—flashing a diamond navel piercing that had a thin silver chain looped through it. His cock, which had been rock hard since her scent had wrapped around him, throbbed almost painfully. Maybe his wolf's idea to bite her wasn't so bad.

"We just want to talk to you, get to know you," Taryn assured Zac. "Is that okay?"

Zac shrugged one shoulder. "I guess."

All five Phoenix wolves settled on the ground, and Makenna suspected they were hoping to seem less intimidating to him.

Jaime gave Zac a friendly smile. "How old are you?"

He slanted a look at Makenna before replying, "Fourteen."

Jaime's brows arched. "Really? You look older than that."

"Why did you leave your pack?" Trey asked Zac.

He stiffened and his fists clenched so tightly that his knuckles turned white. "I'm not going back there."

Makenna placed a reassuring hand on Zac's arm as they locked gazes. "Hey, no one will make you. I'll kill anyone who tries."

Ryan believed that. She was the image of serenity when she turned back to him and his pack mates, but that wild glint still lurked in her eyes. Her comment and fierce tone might have scared another juvenile, but Zac seemed reassured. He obviously felt safe with Makenna. "I have no intention of taking you anywhere against your will," Ryan assured him. "And I would never force you to go back there."

Zac didn't appear totally convinced, but he nodded once. Ryan took a moment to study him, taking in his appearance. The kid didn't look like a loner. His clothes were decent, he was clean, and he didn't appear undernourished. The people at the shelter had obviously been taking good care of him. "I brought you something."

Zac's eyes widened at the object that Ryan pulled out of his pocket. "A cell phone?"

"The number of every Phoenix wolf is stored in there. If you need anything, if something happens and you need help, you call one of us."

"But . . . you don't know me."

"We're going to fix that."

Slowly, Zac reached out and took the phone. "Um, thanks."

"I have to say," said Jaime, "I didn't know there was a shelter for loners. Where is it?"

"Not far from here," Makenna replied. "The end of Maverick Avenue, near the old church."

Trey's brows lifted. "That's a rough area."

Dante tilted his head as he looked at Makenna. "Where are you from?" He'd spoken casually, but his eyes were sharp. Assessing. Searching.

She was dealing with an interrogator, Makenna knew. "I've lived in a lot of places."

"What do you do for a living?"

"If you mean am I a hired killer, no."

A growl threatened to rumble up Ryan's chest. He didn't like Dante's tone at all. It was the same soft yet predatory one he used when grilling intruders or enemies. Makenna didn't appear to like it much either. But she didn't shrink away. Again, her strength impressed his wolf. He knew it would gain her the respect of the others—even if it were begrudgingly earned.

"One of our pack members is a very powerful hacker. But he didn't find anything on a Makenna Wray," continued Dante. "Not a damn thing. So . . . who are you really? And, more importantly, what did you do that was so bad you were cast out?"

Makenna inwardly sighed. Packs always made the same assumptions about loners. It never occurred to them that sometimes a loner had been wronged in being banished. She'd bristle if she weren't so used to it. "I'm not important here. Zac is."

"You're acting as pretty much a guardian to Ryan's cousin. We have a right to know who you are."

A *right*? Pfft. "You know, my daily horoscope did mention that I'd have a mountain to face today . . . I just hadn't figured it would be an actual living being."

Taryn's mouth curved while Jaime chuckled.

"If you have questions about Zac, feel free to ask them," said Makenna. "I'm not a subject up for discussion." Her tone was firm but not harsh.

With an incline of his head, Dante transferred his focus to Zac. For the next thirty minutes, the Phoenix wolves talked with him about everyday things. They were very patient and friendly toward him. Makenna noticed that although he didn't relax, he was no longer in "flight" mode by the time they returned to her Mustang.

She was just about to slide into the driver's seat when Ryan came to her side. "I'll be one minute," she assured Zac, guessing Ryan wanted to speak with her privately. Zac, who was in the passenger seat playing with his new cell phone, barely looked up.

"What happened to him?" Ryan asked in a low voice after she closed the car door.

She sighed. "I don't know. He won't talk about it. Look, I have to be straight with you. The York Pack has put out a search for Zac, which is why I created a false trail. But if they find out he's with you—"

"Let them fucking come," growled Ryan. "No one will hurt him. I won't allow it."

She nodded. "Good." As Ryan's eyes returned to Zac, she said, "I can understand that your instincts are hounding you to take him. I'm glad of that. But he's not ready yet."

Knowing she was right didn't make it any less frustrating. "I want to see him again tomorrow."

"Good. The consistency will help. We'll meet you at the diner on Lumley Street at noon. He loves the food there." Close to the shelter, the diner was smack bam in the middle of an area that mostly housed loners. Zac would feel safer on what, for him, was home turf.

"That's twice now you've dictated the time and the place that I get to see him."

"Because I know Zac. I know what places make him feel comfortable. I know this must be hard for you in some ways, but his feelings come first to me." Compelled to poke at him, she arched a brow. "Got a problem with that, White Fang?"

"Drop the White Fang."

"Drop the snarl."

"Do you have to be so annoying?"

"There's something freeing about it." She flashed him a farewell smile before hopping into the Mustang.

Ryan wondered how it was possible that a smile could irritate him *and* make his cock twitch at the same time. His little loner was—

Inwardly, Ryan scowled at his mental dialogue. She wasn't *his* loner. But, he mused, he'd found her first. Besides, it was a debate that was only happening in his head, so it made no difference.

It wasn't until the Mustang was out of sight that Ryan crossed the lot to the Chevy. The moment he slid into the passenger seat, Dante switched on the engine.

Jaime was the first to speak. "Well, it would seem that it wasn't a trap after all."

Ryan grunted his agreement. There was no denying that Zac was Damian's son. They looked too much alike.

"He's such a nice kid. Sweet. Polite."

"And scared," added Trey.

"I know," said Jaime. "It was heartbreaking."

"Did you notice he was especially distrustful of Ryan, Trey, and Dante?" Taryn asked Jaime. "Something tells me that whatever happened to Zac happened at the hands of a male."

A growl built in Ryan's chest. Whoever hurt him, Ryan would kill him.

Taryn's voice was sensitive as she asked, "You okay?"

No, he wasn't fucking okay. He hated that a member of his own family was staying with an outsider, especially at a damn shelter. He believed firmly that people should protect their own and take responsibility for their family. Which pretty much made him the exact opposite of his mother. He took pride in that.

"I know it had to be hard to walk away from him," said Taryn, "but yanking the kid out of the shelter would just distress him. I have a feeling he's been through enough already. The last thing you want is to make it harder for him, right?"

Ryan grunted, unable to argue with Taryn's reasoning.

"Makenna will keep him safe," said Jaime. "She's got a wild vibe about her. The kind you'd see from a lioness guarding her cubs."

"I like her," announced Taryn. "And I like that she's not intimidated at all by Ryan's terminator snarl."

"Terminator snarl?" chuckled Dante.

"When we first met, I thought you seemed kind of robotic," Taryn told Ryan with a smile. "But I soon realized that you were so tense all the time because you were always on guard. You've settled a lot since the pack grew in strength. But you're still stoic . . . like a Shaolin Monk Master that's the epitome of cool because he knows he can snap your neck before you blink."

"And it seems to reel females in," said Jaime. "Even though you intimidate them."

Taryn shrugged. "Lots of females like the strong, silent, dangerous type."

Ryan decided not to contribute to what was, in his mind, a pointless conversation.

"When are we next seeing Zac?" Trey asked.

"Tomorrow," replied Ryan. "The sooner he's comfortable around us, the sooner he'll agree to join our pack." Where he'd be surrounded by people who would keep him safe.

"He'll fit into our pack nicely," Trey commented. "But I don't think it will be easy to win his trust. And there's something else that might complicate things."

"What?" Dante asked.

"Zac seems pretty attached to Makenna."

"If she saved him, it might just be a minor case of hero worship," suggested Jaime.

"Maybe," conceded Trey. "I guess we'll just have to wait and see."

CHAPTER FOUR

Hearing a beeping sound, Makenna took her gaze briefly off the road to glance at Zac. He was reading a message on his new cell phone. "If that's Ryan asking where we are, tell him we're literally two blocks away." They were running a little late.

"It's some guy called Marcus. He says he's another Phoenix enforcer."

"Really?"

"The Phoenix wolves have all been texting me to say hi and tell me a little about them."

"Yeah? That means the pack as a whole will definitely welcome you. That's a good thing." And a relief, because it didn't always work that way. "Are they nice?"

"Dominic's pretty fleek"—"fleek" meaning "cool" to Zac— "he keeps sending me jokes."

Something about Zac's tone made her ask, "Dirty jokes?"

"I'm not going to answer that. I'm pleading the seventh."

"You mean the fifth."

"Whatever. I'm pleading."

She laughed. "Fine. But if you—" She broke off at the chiming of her own cell phone. Seeing that the caller was Madisyn, Makenna swiped her finger across the screen and answered, "Hello."

"Shithead's back." Madisyn then hung up.

Makenna swore. "Send Ryan a text, tell him we're going to be even later than what we already are."

"Why?"

"Remy turned up at the shelter." At the next junction, she did a U-turn and slammed her foot on the accelerator. In under a minute, she was pulling up outside the shelter. And there was Shithead, standing at the front door with two of his wolves—most likely trying to coax Dawn into letting them in. Dawn knew better than that. She'd also be busy holding Madisyn back; the feline had a wicked temper that made her easy to provoke. Engaging in a confrontation with a powerful Alpha wolf could lead to many complications, however.

"Zac, wait here. Do not get out of the car until he's gone." Hiding her anger under a façade of calm, Makenna exited the car and strolled toward the Alpha wolf. "Mr. Deacon," she drawled. It wasn't a greeting; it was a warning. But he still smiled, running an appreciative gaze over her.

"Ah, Makenna." The affection and intimacy in his tone pissed her off. He was good-looking and possessed the kind of charisma that probably had most females dropping at his feet. But his beady azure eyes were always cold, and there was never even a hint of sexual awareness there. His flirtations were empty. "You look stunning, as always. And please, call me Remy."

Nah. "Can I help you with something?" Her expression held no welcome, and his smile faltered. His pack mates flanked him. The male gave her a sleazy smile while the female sneered, as always. What-the-fuck-ever.

Remy hummed as his gaze again roamed over her, making her inner wolf bare her teeth despite not sensing any true interest from him. "Curves exactly where a man wants them. Why is it your mouth always has me thinking sinful thoughts?"

Was she supposed to be melting in his arms right now?

"I'm loving that little dress, by the way."

She just stared at him, her expression blank.

"I'm disappointed in you, little wolf, I thought you'd want to play. Okay, I'll get to the point. I wondered if Dawn had given any more thought to my offer."

"She's told you before, Mr. Deacon, she's not interested in joining your pack. That answer ain't gonna change." The extent of his dominance was in his eyes, pressuring her to lower her gaze. She didn't. She met his boldly. He wasn't the only one who was dominant.

"You're strong." Grinning, he cocked his head, lips pursed. "I think you would make a valuable addition to my pack."

A loud, derisive snort popped out of the punk-looking female at his side. Selene was his Head Enforcer and always displayed very possessive behavior toward him. She also liked to refer to Makenna as "Super Bitch," which Makenna considered a compliment.

"It's a win-win situation for everyone, Makenna. If Dawn agrees to join my pack, I'll get more territory, the shelter will have any funding it needs, and all the volunteers will be under my protection."

"It would be impossible for the shelter to work if it were ruled by a pack. You know that any shifters needing help or sanctuary wouldn't go to a strange pack for it."

"All Dawn has to do is name her price."

She blinked. "Her price?" Ballsy fucker, wasn't he? "She can't be bought, Mr. Deacon."

He laughed at that. "Of course she can. Everyone has a price. Everyone has weaknesses—including you, Makenna. Weaknesses that can be exploited."

It was a threat. It was also a pointless one. "Well, since my weaknesses are merely dark chocolate and thrift stores, I'm not sure how that will help you."

His eyes narrowed. "I've heard that many of Dawn's neighbors don't like living among a shelter for lone shifters. Think of our council . . . it wants peace above all else."

"Look, I don't have much patience for the whole 'beating around the bush' thing. Are you going somewhere with this?"

"I'm just pointing out that if the neighbors become more vocal about their issues, it's very likely that trouble will occur. The shifter council won't like that. They would shut this place down to preserve the peace."

"Oh, I see. You think that threatening Dawn with the big, bad council will make her ask just how high you want her to jump." Who would have thought the stupid fucker could be so amusing? "Well, feel free to go to them. I can't promise it'll get you anywhere."

"I already *have* gone to them." He pulled a folded slip of paper from his pocket.

With a bored sigh, she opened it. It was a summons to attend a mediation meeting. The council preferred that shifters attempt to resolve their issues through mediation. If the parties didn't reach an agreement, the disputing shifters had the council's permission to go to war after twelve weeks. The hope was that those twelve weeks would give both parties the chance to cool down and drop their issues. In many cases, it worked. But . . . "We're loners. We can't go to war with you."

He stepped closer, eyes softening. "I don't want us to be at war, Makenna. If you read the summons, you'll see it states that if Dawn and I can't reach an agreement, the matter will go before the council. They'll then decide. Of course . . . we can just avoid all that if Dawn agrees here and now to join my pack and hand over this territory. Surely she'd prefer to be part of a pack. Wouldn't you, Makenna? You know, you'd make a good Alpha female."

This time, both she and Selene snorted. Makenna's wolf wanted to stab a claw in his fucking eye.

He was about to speak again, but then the front door of the shelter creaked open. He smiled at Dawn, who stood in the doorway—chin up, arms folded. Madisyn was behind her, nostrils flaring, looking eager to claw Remy's face off . . . which was no doubt why Dawn was obstructing her path.

"Dawn," Remy drawled. "It's always a pleasure. I was just telling Makenna about—"

"You're not welcome here, Mr. Deacon." Dawn's voice was strong, firm. "It's something you already know. So I'm confused as to why you're here. But if it's to repeat your offer, let me again say that my answer is a resounding no."

A muscle in his jaw ticked. "Do you have any idea what I'm offering you? My pack is large, well known, and powerful. In case you've forgotten, you've got nothing. But I'm welcoming you and your volunteers into my pack. I'm offering to give this place what it needs to keep going and to adequately protect whoever is within it. Surely you want to protect the future of the shelter and all its residents."

The slamming of a car door made Remy's attention snap to a sight over Makenna's shoulder. She would have worried it was Zac if wariness hadn't momentarily flashed in Remy's eyes. Ryan's scent reached her before his body soundlessly sidled up to her, his arm brushing hers, like he belonged in her personal space. His pack mates came to a halt just behind Makenna. Huh. For them to turn up, either Zac had told them about Remy or they didn't appreciate being made to wait longer to see Zac.

"Well, if it isn't the Phoenix Pack." Remy didn't look quite as unaffected by their presence as he sounded. The reasonably small pack of nineteen wolves had a reputation for being dangerous, particularly since Trey's wolf had a tendency to turn feral during battle. "Interesting friends you have, Makenna." The word "friends" had been coated in distaste.

She could sense that Taryn wanted to assert her dominance as an Alpha female and tell the shithead to fuck off. But she didn't, obviously aware that it would make it seem like Makenna couldn't fight her own battles. She appreciated that the Alpha did no more than stand with her Betas. "You should go, Mr. Deacon."

He looked ready to argue, but then his eyes flicked to Ryan. Whatever he saw in the enforcer's eyes made Remy think better of it. "I'll see you soon," he told Dawn.

Selene gave Makenna a condescending wave. "Bye now."

Once Remy and his enforcers were gone, Makenna turned to Ryan. "I didn't need you to step in."

"I didn't say a word."

"Just because you didn't speak doesn't mean you didn't interfere. You came to my side wearing that serial-killer stare"—Taryn snorted a laugh—"making a statement that you'd stand with me against him."

"Making a statement that you're under my protection. I'll kill him if he touches you. It's best if he knows that."

Makenna blinked at the casual way he'd spoken those menacing words. "Not quite sane, are ya?"

Ryan was thinking the same about her. He was actually just as taken aback by his strong sense of protectiveness as she was, but he decided not to overthink it. Self-analysis held no interest for him.

Hearing fast, light footsteps, he looked to see Zac dashing toward them. At the same time, two females—one in her forties, the other in her twenties—stepped out of the basic redbrick building that looked like an old high school and strolled down the path.

"This is Dawn and Madisyn," Makenna told the Phoenix wolves. "Dawn owns the shelter, and Madisyn's a volunteer."

Ryan studied the two females. The plump brunette, Dawn, was as short as Taryn, and strength seemed to radiate from her. This female was a born alpha. He also sensed that she was a cougar shifter. The dark, curvy female, Madisyn, had the sharpest eyes he'd ever seen—Ryan would bet nothing got past her. She was also a feline, but Ryan struggled to sense what kind.

After everyone exchanged greetings, Dawn put her arm around Zac's shoulders as she turned to Makenna. "What's the piece of paper you got there?"

"We'll talk about it inside." She ushered Dawn, Madisyn, and Zac up the path toward the door, intending to tell the Phoenix wolves she'd need to postpone their visit with Zac, but Ryan moved to follow them. Obstructing his path, she arched a questioning brow.

"You said we'd talk inside," he rumbled.

She gestured at herself, Dawn, and Madisyn. "I meant that *we* would talk inside."

"You should have been more specific."

But he made no move to leave. She narrowed her eyes. "This ain't your business."

"It will be."

Taryn stepped forward. "I'll admit, we were all totally eavesdropping from the Chevy before we came over here. We heard a little of what's going on. We'd like to help if we can." It wasn't a request; it was a statement of intention. To Makenna's surprise, the Betas looked just as determined to help. Ryan had resolve and determination etched into every hard line of his face.

Madisyn crossed her arms over her chest. "Why would you do that? We're loners."

"We owe you," replied Taryn. "You helped Zac when we didn't. You've been keeping him safe. If Makenna hadn't contacted Ryan, we wouldn't have even known he needed help. Besides, if you're going to keep Zac here, we need to be absolutely fucking positive in our minds that he's safe. I'll be honest, I'm tempted to pull him out for his own protection."

Zac backed up. "No way! I'm staying here!"

"Calm down," Ryan told him. "We won't force you to leave." Zac would just run from them if they did.

"Too fucking right," muttered Zac.

Dawn lightly tapped his shoulder. "Language, Zac," she reprimanded. She studied the Phoenix wolves closely as she asked, "How is it, exactly, that you wish to help?"

It was Dante who replied. "Any way you need it. But we can't know *what* you need until we know the whole story of what's been happening with Remy."

Makenna saw that Dawn was seriously considering their offer. She couldn't blame her. As loners, they had no protection or resources or alliances, which made them easy targets for people like Remy, and they weren't in a position to refuse any offer of aid. "I don't really know how you can help," Makenna told them. "But if you're serious, come inside and we'll tell you what's been going on."

Seemingly of their own accord, Ryan's eyes dropped to the sway of Makenna's hips as she led them up the path to the shelter. Her pert little ass made his wolf growl with need. The animal was still on edge after the encounter with Remy; he wanted to rip out the bastard's throat for daring to threaten this female.

It had been hard to stay in the confines of the SUV and not immediately go to her side. But instinct had told Ryan that he needed to wait. Remy wouldn't have spoken freely in front of Ryan and his pack mates, and they wouldn't have learned as much as they did about the situation. But there was more to know, and he'd find out what it was. He meant what he'd said to Makenna; he'd make this his business.

They all entered a small, bright reception area. It was like walking into a wall of scents. Lion. Tiger. Cougar. Wolf. Hawk. Falcon. Bear. Fox. Snake. The place obviously hosted various breeds. His inner wolf was wary of the strange scents, unaccustomed to being around such a high and varied number.

A bulky, dark-skinned male rounded the reception desk and came forward. There were lockers behind the desk that Ryan guessed were used by the residents. "I take it he's gone," said the male, who Ryan instantly sensed was a bear. The male's eyes softened a little when they landed on Makenna; the intimacy there made Ryan tense. Were they a couple? Something that suspiciously tasted like jealousy settled on his tongue. His wolf didn't like this situation at all—in fact, he despised the bear on principle.

Dawn nodded before quickly introducing everyone. "Thank you for staying inside, Colton. I know it's hard to resist confronting Remy."

"Why didn't he confront him?" Dante asked Dawn.

"For the same reason Madisyn didn't: Remy would goad him into a fight, and the last thing we want is the residents of the shelter feeling this isn't a safe place. Plus, shifters warring in the street would earn a lot of human attention. The last thing we want is to be on the radar of the human anti-shifter extremists." Dawn took a deep breath. "Anyway, if you want to come any further, I'll need you to sign in. All visitors and residents are required to sign in and out."

While Dante obligingly scribbled down the names inside the book on the desk, Ryan read the "Rules and Regulations" sign on the magnolia wall.

No alcohol.
No drugs.
No weapons.
No violence.
No theft.
No breaking curfew hours.

Dawn presented them all with a bright smile. "Would you like a tour?"

"That would be great," said Taryn.

Dawn talked as she led them down a long hallway. "The building has five floors in all, including the basement. We keep the bedding, food, cleaning supplies, and other such things down there. On this floor, we have the cafeteria, the common room, communal toilets, and some private bedrooms for people with children. Females sleep on the second floor, and males on the third—both floors are like dormitories. I live in the attic."

Ryan frowned as he realized . . . "There's magick here." It seemed to hum in the air.

"Makenna found a witch to imbed protective wards into the walls," Dawn told him. "If someone means harm to anybody in the building, they can't get inside without an invitation."

Such wards couldn't have been cheap. Taking that and her reaction to Remy into account, it was clear that Makenna was emotionally invested in the shelter.

"How long have you been running the place?" Jaime asked Dawn.

"My mother started it thirty years ago. At first, it was just a day center. Somewhere loners could come to simply sit down, have a cup of coffee, talk with others, and eat a good meal. When she got some funding, she expanded it little by little." Dawn opened a door on their right, and everybody inside froze. "This is the common room."

Peeking inside, Ryan noticed that the large space contained a mishmash of things. The sofas were all various colors and styles. Some of the chairs were clunky and cushioned while others were plastic. There was an outdated TV on the wall, some lamps, and a few plants. There was also an old bookcase and boxes of toys in one corner where a few children played. The sight made his chest clench.

One of the children jumped to her feet with a smile of delight. "Makenna!" She ran to the female and hugged her tight.

Makenna smiled. "Hey, Cady."

"Who are they?" She eyed each of the Phoenix wolves with distrust, particularly the males.

"They're friends, Cadence," Dawn reassured her. "Now why don't you go play? Makenna will come back soon."

"Can you read to me when you come back?" Cadence asked Makenna.

"Sure thing, Cady. Be good for your aunt."

A female with hair as thick and dark as the child's smiled at Makenna.

"I'll stay here with the little ones," Zac told Makenna. She knew he didn't fully trust the Phoenix wolves yet and wanted to watch over the kids.

She smiled. "Thanks, Zac."

As they continued down the hallway, Dante said, "Fox. That little girl's a fox shifter."

Madisyn nodded. "Yep. She and her aunt came here six months ago."

Jaime cocked her head. "Why?"

Madisyn smiled wanly. "That's really their story to tell. All I'll say is that her aunt discovered the pack wasn't safe for Cady and so she took her away. They're in hiding at the moment. But Makenna's in the process of rehoming them."

Dawn stopped at a door, pulled out a set of keys, and unlocked it. "This is one of the private family rooms. It's not being used right now."

She opened the door, revealing a very basic room that contained two sets of bunk beds, a cot, and a lockable wardrobe. Although it was clean and bright, Ryan still found it to be a sad sight. Maybe it was the cot. The idea that a baby would be without a pack or home . . . It wasn't right.

As Dawn shut and locked the door, Taryn spoke. "Are all the loners here in hiding?"

"No." Dawn led them farther down the hallway, passing more doors Ryan guessed were also private rooms. "Many are homeless. Some are runaways. Some have been cast out after losing a duel or something similar. And others feel lost after their mate died and just can't function. It's possible to find some lone children wandering the streets, sad to say. Social Services often brings lone children here, just as they brought Makenna and Madisyn."

That almost brought Ryan up short. It hadn't occurred to him that she would have grown up here. What pack would cast out a pup? Just the very idea made his blood boil. It was practically a death sentence. He couldn't imagine that a pup could have committed a crime that led to a banishment. Maybe she hadn't been banished; maybe she'd run away from some sort of abuse. His wolf growled at the thought. The animal's protective streak had shot to life at the sight of Remy threatening her, and it wasn't easing.

"The girls became friends quickly," added Dawn.

Makenna nodded. "Madisyn taught me how to make fire without matches or a lighter."

The feline smiled brightly. "And she taught me empathy."

Chuckling, Dawn rounded the corner. "You were both thick as thieves. Always sneaking out to the local hangouts for teenage shifters." She smiled at Taryn. "They're so good at sneaking, I wouldn't have even known they'd left the building if they didn't always come back covered in bruises after scrapping with the other teens."

"We went there in peace," claimed Madisyn. "There wouldn't have been any fighting if they hadn't targeted us for being loners."

"Yes, well, you both quickly earned a reputation for being crazy. Of course, the teens couldn't complain to their Alphas about you because these hangouts were secret. Their Alphas would have tanned their hides if they knew the juveniles were sneaking out." Dawn stopped and pushed open a door on their left. "This is the cafeteria."

To Ryan, it looked like a typical school cafeteria with all the plastic tables and chairs. People sat around, talking and drinking coffee. They nodded at Dawn, Madisyn, and Makenna, but the sight of Ryan and his pack mates made them stiffen. Ryan realized that Makenna had been correct in what she'd said to Remy: loners would never go to a shelter for sanctuary if it were ruled by a pack. They didn't trust strangers one bit.

As they continued walking down another hallway, Taryn sidled up to Dawn. "Are there any other shelters for loners?"

"Not many, which is unfortunate because the lone shifter lifestyle is a growing problem. There's only one other shelter in California."

Dante abruptly stopped, his gaze on something outside. "There are tents out there."

Ryan looked out of the window, and, sure enough, dome-shaped tents were scattered around the land. Only the children's outdoor play area was clear of them. More children played out there, supervised by a number of adults.

"Some prefer to sleep outside," Dawn informed the Beta male. "Sleeping outside allows mated couples to stay together at night. And there are some people who feel safer sleeping in their animal form, so they choose to stay in a tent or sleep on the surrounding land."

"Do you ever have to turn people away?" Jaime asked as they began walking again.

"Rarely. In emergency situations, we accommodate more by folding up the tables and chairs in the cafeteria at night and setting out some mats and blankets. It's not ideal, but the alternative is sleeping outside in a box or under a bridge. They're just grateful to be warm and safe. Especially the little ones."

Jaime threaded her fingers through her mate's, as if needing his touch for comfort at the idea of children in such need. "What's the average length of stay for residents?"

"Most don't stay long," replied Dawn. "Makenna does her best to get them a place somewhere. If they have relatives they trust, she tracks them down and the relatives then often take them in. There are some Alphas that are willing to foster or adopt loners, even if they're unrelated, so that helps.

"However, some want to remain loners. In those cases, I do my best to get them whatever education, therapy, or support they need to find a home of their own and fit into the human community. In the meantime, I ensure they have a bed, showers, meals, a place to do their laundry, and somewhere to store their belongings. When you're homeless, the simple matter of toilet paper is a luxury."

"I'll bet some don't want to leave," wagered Dante.

Dawn ushered them all into an office. "The isolation of a loner lifestyle is hard for any shifter. Here, they're around people who can understand them and who've had similar experiences to them. They get mighty comfortable and want to stay. Shifters in packs, prides, flocks, or whatever it may be all lean and rely on each other. That's part of what makes it hard for loners to adjust to being on their own. I allow some to stay permanently, but in exchange they have to work for me—whether it's to cook, clean, wash clothes, or something else."

Dante and Ryan leaned against the wall while Taryn, Jaime, and Madisyn sat on an old, faded leather couch. Makenna perched herself on the edge of the desk that Dawn then sat behind.

"You do good work here," said Taryn. "I have to admit, loners have such a bad rep that it never occurred to me how hard it must be for them."

Dawn gave an understanding smile. "It's easy to forget that they're not all bad. Most just need help. I do my best to provide that. But I can't help everyone."

"Must be hard for you." Dante folded his arms. "It has to cost a lot of money and energy to run this place. This is a nonprofit organization, right?"

"Yes. I have sponsors, grants, and private donations. The shifter council only gives a minimal amount of funding, but everything makes a difference. Some people—shifter and human alike—are kind enough to donate blankets, supplies, and food. But some, like Remy, just present us with problems."

Taryn leaned forward. "Tell us about Remy. When did all this trouble with him start?"

Dawn's expression turned somber. "He first came here four months ago. We were scrubbing off some graffiti outside when he came up to us, all charm and smiles. But it's like Makenna says, his eyes are cold. He said he admired what I did but that he'd bet it was hard to run the shelter with no protection. He offered for me to join his pack—said Madisyn, Makenna, and any other volunteers would also have a place, if they wanted it. I declined, and he didn't like it, but he told me to take some time to think about it.

"He came again the following month, made the same speech. Again, I told him no. That didn't faze him. He was back within three weeks. At the time, things weren't great. A human who owns several local businesses had begun a petition to get rid of the shelter; said he's losing business and employees because a lot of humans don't like being close to a shelter for loners. He got other business owners, humans, and the local schools to sign it."

"Bigots," Jaime bit out.

"Yes," agreed Dawn. "Remy said he'd heard about the petition; said he could provide me with the protection I need from this sort of thing, if only I'd join his pack. He's right. If this was officially classified as shifter territory, the humans would have no say. And they wouldn't dare go up against me. But I think Makenna's right."

As Jaime shot a questioning look her way, Makenna explained as she swung her legs—legs that Ryan wanted hooked over his shoulders as he pounded in and out of her—"If you ask me, Remy was behind the petition. He wanted Dawn trapped in a corner so he could be her savior and, in desperation, we'd all fall in line. He somehow got the humans riled up; he may have even given them the idea of starting the petition."

Dante nodded slowly. "I take it the petition came to nothing."

Dawn waved a hand. "The human court dismissed it. I think it likes the idea that shelters help keep loners off the streets, since they often sleep in their animal form because they feel less vulnerable that way. Humans don't want us roaming free like wild animals. And, you know, not all humans hate us. In fact, the majority don't. But those that do hate us . . . well, they can make a lot of noise." Dawn sighed. "Anyway, we hadn't seen Remy again until today."

Dante scraped his hand over his jaw. "I have to say, it's damn odd that the guy wants to expand his territory in this direction. No offense, but this isn't the kind of area that Alphas like to claim. It's rough."

"That's why this makes no sense to us," said Madisyn.

Taryn tapped her fingers on the arm of the sofa. "I'm surprised he hasn't just tried to *take* the territory. You're loners; you can't fight him."

"The land the shelter sits on belongs to me," said Dawn. "It was granted to my mother by the council and she passed it on to me, which makes it my territory. No one can take it without my permission."

"That's probably why he went running to the council." Makenna held out the letter to Dawn. "He presented me with this."

Dawn took the paper from her hand and read it carefully. "Mediation. Says here that if we can't solve this ourselves through mediation, the matter will then go before the council after eight weeks."

"I thought the council typically gave people twelve weeks to sort out their shit," said Madisyn.

"Only in cases where the parties want war," Dante told her. "This situation is different."

"Going before the council could be bad," began Madisyn, "since it wants peace above all else. Right now, the humans who signed the petition are probably all stirred up because it got them nowhere.

The council could see Remy taking over as a way to keep things cool here."

"Remy seems too eager to get ahold of this place to wait for the council's decision," said Makenna. "I think he'll try to put Dawn in a position where she feels she needs him."

Ryan shook his head. "It will never come to that."

Makenna was surprised at the vehemence in that vow. "You heard what he said out there— *'Everybody has a price.'* He was prepared to bribe Dawn" —the feline bristled at the insult— "so I'm thinking he'll try to pay off the mediator, try to make them convince us to give in to him and maybe even suggest to the council that Remy should be given what he wants."

Taryn snorted. "The Californian mediator for shifters happens to be my best friend. Trying to bribe Shaya will achieve nothing. I'm not saying she'll jump on your wagon. She'll remain impartial because it's her job, despite that she'll no doubt totally hate what he's doing."

Madisyn didn't appear completely reassured. "What if he tries to bribe the council?"

"I hope he does," said Dante. "The last time someone did that, they were killed for the insult. When is the meeting?"

"Two weeks from now," replied Makenna. She looked at Dawn. "I'll be coming with you."

"Me too," said Madisyn. Dawn shot them both a grateful smile.

"In the meantime," began Taryn, "all you can really do is stay alert. When you need us, we'll come."

An hour later, after spending time with Zac and an extended tour to check out the basement and upper floors, the Phoenix wolves were ready to leave. Dawn had proudly shown them around while Makenna and Madisyn accompanied her for protection.

Hey, the Phoenix wolves seemed friendly and eager to help, but that didn't mean Makenna trusted them. She especially didn't trust the broad, rugged male who moved into her personal space as if he had every right. Or, more specifically, she didn't trust that his behavior didn't bother her the way it should.

Having said their good-byes at the front door, the wolves then began filing outside, heading to their Chevy. Ryan, however, snatched Makenna's cell phone from the pocket of her denim jacket, keyed in his number, and then just as deftly returned the cell to her pocket. Had she not been looking at him, she might not have noticed. She should have bristled at his boldness, but she was too busy admiring the sneaky move.

"If Remy comes back or there's a problem, call me." It was a rumbled order that brooked no defiance.

A lesser female might have folded under the weight of all that dominance and raw masculinity. "Careful, White Fang. You're pushing."

His scowl deepened, but he said nothing. Just stared.

"Yeah, that whole 'I'll just stare until she gets so uncomfortable she gives in' ain't gonna work with me." His frown remained firmly in place, but there was the *slightest* touch of amusement in those dark eyes. And she couldn't help wondering what he looked like when he smiled. Did his face light up? Did his eyes crinkle? Did he have dimples? Was it a lopsided smile or was there simply a slight curve to his mouth?

It was only right then, when his lips parted slightly, that she realized she was staring at them. She snapped her gaze to his, swallowing as the air became hot and thick. Need began to slowly spill through her veins like warm honey. To evoke this kind of need in her . . . it was power over her. Power that made her anxious. She took a step back. "See ya."

With a grunt, he turned and left. And she indulged in a thorough inspection of his rather epic ass as he stalked down the path.

No sooner had the Chevy disappeared than Madisyn dragged Makenna aside. "I want the details on Mr. Dark and Dangerous."

Of course she did, the nosy feline. "He's Zac's cousin," Makenna replied with a nonchalant shrug. But Madisyn waved a hand, encouraging Makenna to continue. "That's it. There's nothing else to say."

"Why 'White Fang'?"

"You remember the movie, right? The wolf was fierce, morose, and a deadly fighter."

"I guess Ryan does have a savage look about him. I have the feeling that's part of why you're so hot for him."

Makenna frowned. "Who says I'm hot for him?" Madisyn just stared at her. "Okay, I'm hot for him." She liked his hard, dangerous looks and his enigmatic nature. Mostly, though, it was his strength and air of self-possession that drew her. He seemed so solid and steadfast—wolf nip to someone who had never known stability, who had never been able to relax, who hadn't felt safe in a very long time. "But I'm pretty sure that's a one-way street."

Grinning, Madisyn shook her head. "He looks at you like he wants to take a bite."

Makenna blinked. "A good bite or a bad bite?"

"Depends how you define 'bad.'"

"Honestly, I'm not sure I'd know what to do with him. I've never been around a guy as dominant as him before." He wasn't someone who could be handled. "Dominant males are tricky, domineering bastards. Even Colton can't deny that." The dominant bear—who was standing at the reception desk, *totally* eavesdropping—just shrugged, unoffended. They'd once had a short, casual fling, but they'd quickly realized they were better as friends, and there had never been any awkwardness between them. "Still . . . I know Ryan doesn't talk much, but when he does" —she shivered— "I honestly have to wonder if he could talk me into an orgasm."

Madisyn laughed. "You know, I've heard that the quiet ones are always the most vocal in bed. Maybe it wouldn't be so bad to let him take that bite he seems to want."

Maybe. Maybe not. But Makenna doubted she'd be put into a position where she had to decide. She was a loner, which meant he automatically wouldn't trust her around him or his pack. Once he'd won over Zac, she'd likely never see him again. Although the Phoenix wolves seemed genuinely intent on helping with the Remy situation, there was a distinct possibility that they were simply trying to impress Zac and use it to gain his trust. Time would tell.

In the meantime . . . where was the damn chocolate?

CHAPTER FIVE

Eating dinner at the long oak table in the kitchen of Phoenix Pack territory, Taryn informed the rest of the pack of all that they had heard and seen at the shelter. Only four were absent: Roni and Marcus, who were on Mercury territory, and Gabe and Hope, a mated pair that was guarding the gate.

Taryn's expression was pained even though her mate was soothingly massaging her nape. "I have to say, I'm seriously ashamed of myself right now. Whenever I thought the term 'lone shifters,' I thought 'hired guns.' It never occurred to me just how hard it must be for them, or all the different kind of reasons that drive shifters to become loners. It's not always a choice."

Jaime stroked the ugly, loudly purring ginger cat on her lap. "And not all of them have had the luck to get a place in a shelter."

Their resident cook, mother hen, and Rhett's mate, Grace, spoke as she fed chocolate pudding to her infant daughter in the highchair. "The shifters working there are good people for doing what they do."

"Think of what it must cost per person to clothe, clean, and feed the residents," said Jaime. "The animal sanctuary I work at is hard to keep running; it must be way harder to run the shelter."

"What's the interior like?" Lydia, Cam's mate, asked.

Jaime fed some scraps of meat to her cat. "I would have expected a shelter to feel melancholy and hopeless. It didn't, though. There's warmth and comfort there. But also a hint of sadness. It was in the eyes of some of the residents. It made me wonder what they'd been through."

Taryn looked at Grace. "It was absolutely heartbreaking seeing little kids there. Some were just babies—one of them was so little, I think he might have been born there."

Scooping more dessert onto the spoon, Grace said, "I don't want to even imagine how hard it would be to have to live in a shelter with my Lilah. Even though the shelter sounds like a good place, it would still be a sad situation for anyone."

"Not sadder than being on the streets." Jaime sighed. "It's horrible to think that Zac was once in that situation. I wonder how he ended up at the shelter."

Trick, an enforcer, pushed his empty plate aside. "Considering all that's going on, wouldn't it be better to bring him here, out of Remy's reach?"

Taryn shook her head sadly. "I wish I could, but he doesn't feel safe with us yet. And I think Trey's right, parting him from Makenna might be hard. I was pretty suspicious of her and her motives at first, but I totally misjudged her. Dawn said she's been there since she was a kid. I'm guessing that she's changed her name because she doesn't want to be found."

Ryan grunted his agreement.

Dominic, another enforcer, lounged in his chair with his arms crossed behind his head. "I'm looking forward to meeting Zac. Bring him here for a visit."

"He won't come," said Taryn. "Not yet. He knows we'd prefer to have him here for his own safety; he won't trust us not to force him to stay."

She was right, which was why . . . "Remy has to be dealt with."

Dante's eyes snapped to Ryan. "He will be." It was a vow.

"I called Shaya and told her everything," announced Taryn. "Of course, she now thinks Dawn, Makenna, and Madisyn are angels and that Remy needs to jump off a cliff."

Ryan had every intention of attending the mediation meeting. Makenna might not realize it yet, but he would see this matter through to the end with her—even if Zac was part of his pack before the situation was resolved. Since it had shot to life earlier, he'd been unable to shake off the protectiveness or the feeling that it was his *right* to look out for her.

Trey turned to Rhett. "What did you find out about Remy?"

Rhett put down his coffee. "His father died when he was seven, so he was raised by his mother." Most shifters couldn't survive the breaking of a mating bond, but some managed to hang on. "He has a lot of alliances and friends in high places. He became pack Alpha four years ago. Since then, he's been challenging the packs around him to expand his own, spreading over California like a virus. And now he seems to want the territory that the shelter sits on."

Tao, who had Kye sitting on his lap—the kid was playing some kind of game on Tao's cell phone—frowned. "I can't work out why Remy wants that territory. It's a really bad area that's well known for housing loners."

"Maybe it's not the territory he wants," suggested Trick. "Maybe he wants the shelter."

Cam frowned. "But why?"

Trick shrugged. "It could be that he's hoping to shut it down. Being Alpha to Dawn would give him the power to do it."

"But *why* would he want to shut it down?" Cam asked him.

"I didn't say I had the answer. It's just a theory."

Ryan had a theory of his own. "I've been thinking about this . . . and I don't believe this is about the territory at all."

Trey cocked his head. "Why?"

"I once heard a rumor about Remy." A rumor that he hadn't thought could possibly be true—or maybe he hadn't wanted to believe it. But now, with everything going on around them, he wondered if there was something to it. And that made Ryan's wolf want to rip out the fucker's throat. "If it's to be believed, Remy's not into females."

Dante's brows flew up. "He's gay?"

Ryan shook his head. "He likes little boys."

There was a stunned silence followed by a string of curses.

"Are you sure?" asked Taryn.

"Like I said, it's a rumor."

Taryn suddenly looked nauseous. "There were a lot of kids at that shelter."

Dante's hand paused as it stroked over Jaime's hair. "Such kids would be the perfect targets—they don't have a pack to defend them, they don't have anywhere to go unless Makenna rehomes them. If he was her Alpha, he could prevent her from doing so. Dawn said that kids are handed over to them frequently."

Ryan nodded. "He'd basically have access to an endless supply of children." And that was a frightening thought. "He'd have access to Zac. I won't let that happen."

"Our pack as a whole will protect him," Taryn assured him. "Not just Zac, but the shelter. It's doing something good, and that needs protecting."

Greta, Trey's antisocial and pretty psychotic grandmother, raised a hand. "As much as I appreciate what the people there are doing for my Zac"—she hadn't even met the kid yet, but she already considered him hers— "I don't think we should get involved. It's not our fight."

Taryn scowled. "You're suggesting we ignore the fact that those kids could end up in the hands of a pedophile?"

"As Ryan said, it's just a rumor. There are plenty of rumors about my Trey; not all of them are true. The same can be said for most powerful Alphas—there are always people trying to ruin their reputation."

That was part of why Ryan hadn't initially given much thought to the rumors about Remy.

"Yes, but I'm not prepared to take that chance," said Taryn. "Especially since we owe the shelter."

"But we don't owe any of the loners staying there. I'm telling you, loners can't be trusted. One of them shot my Roni."

"So it's totally fine that *I* was shot by a loner?" Jaime asked, amused.

Greta humphed. "Why should I care? My Dante could have done better than you. Just like my Trey could have done better than that hussy."

Greta thought of Trey, Dante, Tao, and all four male enforcers as "her boys" and was having trouble cutting the apron strings. That was why she disliked any unmated females being around them and always did her best to chase them off. It hadn't worked with Taryn and Jaime. Somehow, Roni had tricked Greta into approving of her. The entire pack was still in awe of her for it.

"Back to the subject at hand," said Taryn, "we have to help any way we can with the Remy problem."

Trey cocked one brow at her. "Do I not get a say in this?"

She patted his arm. "Of course you do. Just note that if your opinion is different from mine, it will be disregarded."

"You can't be serious about helping loners!" Greta griped. The word "loners" was spoken in the same tone as someone might use for "Nazis."

The smile that Taryn shot Greta was a little evil. "But just think how much fun it would be to have more unmated females around your boys . . . you know, flirting with them, leading them down the path of sin."

Greta lifted her chin. "I refuse to offer any help to loners."

"And I refuse to accept that someone who is so old she was a waitress at the Last Supper could still be alive, yet here you are."

Hearing a series of beeps signaling that Ryan had received a text message, he took his cell from his pocket. The message was from Zac and mostly in shorthand, but Ryan translated it into: "Thanks for chasing off Remy today. Are you really going to help the shelter?"

Ryan immediately replied: "Yes. The whole pack will help."

It was a promise, and Ryan never broke his word. He wasn't concerned that Greta would change Taryn's mind on the matter. Even if the woman miraculously managed to do so, it wouldn't change Ryan's plans.

Generally, he didn't get involved in other people's drama. Having been raised in a house that was full of it, Ryan avoided it like the plague. But he had every intention of helping the shelter, and he wouldn't be swayed from that course. Once Ryan committed himself to any cause of action, he saw it through to the end. He wouldn't overlook the danger Remy presented to those children and he wouldn't let Zac down.

In truth, the kid deserved a better guardian than Ryan—he wasn't good at giving emotional feedback, wasn't good at bonding, and wasn't good at expressing affection or receiving it. But he could give Zac a home, a sense of belonging, and ensure he was safe. Those were all good things, right?

Spending time with Zac to earn his trust would also mean spending time with Makenna. Ryan waited for discomfort to settle in at the idea of being around a loner . . . but none came. In fact, he realized with a start, he wanted to see her again. Probably because she was a mystery. Ryan liked having all the facts of a situation. He wanted to know who she really was and what happened to her. Moreover, he wanted to know what fucking pack would cast out a pup and just how they could possibly justify it to themselves.

"Where did you hear the rumor about Remy?" Trey asked, interrupting Ryan's thoughts.

"I was at a shifter bar," said Ryan. "The waitress was flirting with him at the other side of the room. One of the barmen—Myles—didn't look happy about it. Then he snickered when Remy dismissed her. He said he wasn't surprised she'd been sent on her way because he'd heard Remy's interests leaned toward young boys."

Dante folded his arms across his chest. "Then I think we need to go and speak with this barman, find out where he got that information."

Later that night, Ryan strode through the crowded bar with Trey, Dante, and Trick. They found Myles at the far end of the bar, flirting with the female he was serving.

He went rigid at the sight of their grim expressions. "What's this about?"

A straight shooter. Ryan liked that.

"We have a few questions," said Trey. "It won't take long."

Myles barked a nervous laugh. "I'd be a fool to walk off alone with four pissed-off Phoenix wolves."

"It's not you we're pissed at," said Trey. "But I have a feeling you can tell us a little about the wolf who *did* piss us off."

Myles pressed his lips together, clearly reluctant. Finally, with a heavy exhale, he rounded the bar and gestured for them to follow him. He led them through a door marked "Staff Only" and into an empty break room. "What do you want to know?"

Trey spoke. "Remy Deacon."

Myles's face scrunched up in distaste. "What about him?"

"Last time I was here," said Ryan, "you told me Remy likes little boys."

Myles shifted uncomfortably. "That's what I heard."

"From who?"

"Some of my pack mates. They were originally members of one of the packs he took over. They switched to ours a few months ago."

"They know this for certain?" asked Dante. "They've witnessed it?"

"No. They said he likes to be around the kids, that he takes them on nature walks and he's adopted all the orphans."

"There's nothing wrong with spending time with pups," said Trey.

"No, but some of the boys have gone missing. And one of the fathers outright accused Remy of abusing his son and then attacked him. Remy killed the father. Since then, some of the families have left—maybe because they believe the rumors or maybe because they're being cautious." He cringed as he added, "I also heard that his extremely possessive mother loves him . . . a little *too* much."

A bitter taste settled on Ryan's tongue. His wolf curled his lip in total disgust. If the latter rumor were true, a person might be tempted to feel sympathy for Remy. Ryan wasn't tempted. Sad and sick as it was, lots of people were abused. They didn't all become abusers.

"We need to speak with your pack mates," Dante told Myles. "We need to know more about Remy."

"I don't think they know anything more."

"Maybe not, but we have to be sure."

Myles scrubbed a hand over the back of his neck. "They're visiting relatives in Canada. They'll be back Friday."

"We'll come to your territory Saturday morning to talk with them," said Trey, his tone nonnegotiable.

Myles tucked his hands in his pockets and shuffled from foot to foot. "What if they don't want to talk to you?"

Trey cocked a brow. "If they believe the rumors are true, I would think they'd want to tell us what they know."

"You'll kill him, won't you?"

"If he's guilty, he doesn't deserve to live."

"No, he damn well doesn't," agreed Myles with a sneer.

By the time Makenna arrived at the shelter the next morning, the residents were just finishing breakfast. They then headed to either work, job interviews, school, or the common room. And that was when Makenna did what she'd been doing each day since Dawn had agreed for her to remain in the shelter many years ago: she began her designated chores.

Aided by some of the staff, she cleaned the kitchen, wiped down the cafeteria tables, and mopped the floor. Following that, she checked on each of the new residents, making sure they were settling in and asking for names of any family they would trust to take them in.

After a light lunch, she headed to Dawn's office to use her computer. There, she ran searches on each of the names that the new residents gave her, hoping to electronically track their whereabouts. She was halfway through the list when Colton called the office phone. "Hello."

"We have visitors. They're asking for you."

Curious, Makenna left the office and made her way to the reception area. Colton and Madisyn were there, watching curiously as three unfamiliar females studied the décor while chatting among themselves. Several boxes were at their feet. Makenna cleared her throat to get their attention.

They each pivoted, smiling. They didn't look at all alike; one was tall and slim, the second was a very curvy brunette, and the third a peroxide blonde who was rather tan-tastic. Submissive wolves, she sensed.

The tall one smiled brightly. "You must be Makenna. It's great to meet you."

The brunette nodded. "We've heard a lot about you."

Confused, Makenna said, "Um . . . I'm sorry. Who are you?"

Putting a hand to her chest, the tall one replied, "Oh, I'm Lydia"—she put a hand on the brunette's shoulder—"this is Grace, and that's Hope. We're from the Phoenix Pack. We're here to help."

"Help how?" The door opened as Dante and two other males filed inside carrying boxes, garbage bags, and . . . "Paintings?"

Lydia's smile turned even brighter. "I thought it would be nice to spruce up the place. Give it some color. Jaime was right, the place has a lot of warmth."

The burly male with claw marks on one side of his face inclined his head at Makenna. "I'm Trick."

The hot blond beside him with a hint of mischief in his eyes flashed her a flirtatious grin. "Hey, I'm Dominic."

Makenna nodded. "Ah, the enforcer who sends Zac dirty jokes."

"Actually, I'm a freelance gynecologist. When was your last checkup?"

"Dominic," chastised Grace.

Makenna's chuckle cut off as the door again opened and Taryn, Jaime, and Ryan entered. The very second Ryan's eyes found hers, a tingle of pleasure shot down her spine. The raw need building inside her was live and electric. In spite of herself, she wondered how it would feel to have him in her, over her, taking her. She would bet all his natural intensity translated into hard, rough, demanding sex—the best kind, in her opinion.

"I brought some clothes to donate," said Hope. "They're from everyone in the pack. Some of them don't quite realize yet that they've donated, but I'm sure they'll notice soon."

Trick's brow furrowed. "What exactly have I donated?"

"We had some extra food," Grace told Makenna.

She called those three boxes *extra*? Like the stuff had just been lying around? "Extra food," repeated Makenna. "Right."

Nostrils flaring, Dominic sidled up to Madisyn with a frown. "What are you?"

The feline got that a lot. Most shifters didn't sense what breed she was. And Madisyn kind of liked it that way. She very rarely revealed the truth, since she found joy in dicking with people. "A woman," Madisyn replied.

Dominic rolled his eyes. "Yeah, but what type of shifter are you?"

"A cat."

"What kind of cat shifter?" he pressed, impatient.

"A rare one."

Lydia did a little clap, overriding Dominic's growl. "Well, let's get to work."

It quickly became clear to Makenna that Lydia was quite artistic and had a flair for interior design. She recruited some of the shelter's volunteers and residents, even the children, to help with improvements. Paintings were hung up, potted plants were brought in, colorful blackout blinds replaced outdated curtains, and stylish light fixtures were added.

The common room was completely transformed. The old carpet was replaced by laminate flooring and then covered with a beautiful, coffee-colored rug the same shade as the blinds. The upholstery was changed with matching sofas and cushions, and white faux-leather covers were added to the plastic chairs.

The children painted pictures on the walls of the outdoor playground, which was further improved by a playhouse, sandpit, basketball net, and trampoline that the Phoenix wolves had brought with them. Apparently, they were the things the Alpha pair's son was no longer amused by, but Makenna wasn't so sure she believed it was old stuff.

Madisyn, too, had her suspicions. Dawn . . . well, Makenna hadn't seen her that happy in a long time. The woman was thrilled with all the other things the wolves had donated: bedding, clothing, footwear, sleeping bags, hygiene supplies, books, toys, towels, a microwave, a toaster, and a kettle.

The wolves claimed the stuff had been just "lying around." But as Makenna gazed at something hanging on the common room wall, she said to Ryan, who had rarely left her side, "I refuse to believe you had a wide-screen TV just lying around."

"You'd be surprised. We have a lot of guest rooms, but they're rarely used."

"Guest rooms?" She would have thought he'd say "guest cabins." "Does that mean you guys all live in one big pack house?" Picking up some of the garbage bags at her feet, she headed toward the side exit; Ryan did the same.

"In a sense," he replied as they stepped outside into the side alley. Like Makenna, he slung the garbage bags into the trash. "Who is Colton to you?" Ryan blurted out, unintentionally abrupt. He inwardly winced. By nature, he was curt and straight to the point. Which meant he often came across as rude and intolerant.

"He's a volunteer and a friend." She was panting with exertion after all the hours of hard work, but Ryan hadn't even broken a sweat. She'd resent him for it if it hadn't been so pleasurable watching all those muscles bunch and flex.

"Friend? He walks into your personal space like it's his right."

"So do you."

Yeah, well, they weren't talking about him. "Are you two dating?"

"Why? Are you interested in him? Because I don't think he swings that way." She grimaced as a crow landed nearby. "Well, that's not good."

Blinking at the sudden change of subject, Ryan glanced at the bird. "What?"

"Seeing one crow on its own is bad luck." She didn't add *obviously*, but it was in her tone.

Ryan looked from her to the bird, feeling compelled to point out, "It's just a crow."

"Come on, you've heard the rhyme. 'One for sorrow, two for mirth, etc. . . . '"

Yes, but still . . . "It's just a crow." And that was just a rhyme.

"You're not at all superstitious?"

"You mean do I have completely illogical beliefs? No." He'd expected her to be offended. She actually smiled, looking curious.

"So you don't believe in luck?"

"No."

"But you believe in fate."

"No."

She gaped. "How can you not believe in fate? You're a shifter. We have predestined mates."

"That doesn't mean our lives are written out like a script." *He* dictated his fate, no one else.

"But it would suggest that some things are set in stone. There's a female out there who was pretty much made for you."

"That doesn't mean my fate is to spend my life with her." It was simply a possible path his life would take . . . if he *chose* that path.

"Okay, that's true," Makenna conceded. He could fail to find his mate, or one of them could imprint on someone else. Shifters who weren't true mates could still come together and form a mating bond through the process of imprinting. It was just as strong and true as a bond between predestined mates. "Are you rejecting the notion of fate because you don't *want* to find your mate?"

"No." Ryan had never feared mating, never feared the commitment. He'd played around, knowing that once he found his mate he'd attach himself to her and that would be that. Simple. He really wasn't sure why other people found the matter so complicated. "I just don't believe our lives are dictated by luck or fate or that mating bonds are cosmic, magical things."

He was so stoic and serious, she mused. Always in enforcer mode. She posted a memo on her mental corkboard to remind her to make Ryan smile at least once before they parted for good. "All right, then what do you think bonds are?"

"Evolutionary measures to ensure procreation."

That sure surprised her. "You think it's a genetic thing?"

"Shifters can't procreate with anyone other than their mates. In that sense, mating bonds ensure the continuation of the shifter races."

"So you think the bond is some kind of trap?"

"No. I just don't think it's anything other than an evolutionary measure, that's all. Why does that make you smile?"

She shrugged. "Your mind is so practical. It's fascinating."

He was certain no one had ever referred to him as "fascinating." Cold, yes. Merciless, yes. Emotionally sterile, yes. Fascinating? No.

"Well, *I* believe there are such things as fate and luck. Madisyn is one of the luckiest people I've ever met; she's always winning and finding stuff. And take Zac. I found him unconscious on my doorstep, pumped up on alcohol and drugs. In that state, he could have ended up in a number of places; he was hurt and vulnerable. But it was *my* doorstep he found his way to—a person who could lead him someplace safe. That right there is an example of a higher power at work."

His mother's voice was suddenly ringing in Ryan's head . . . *"I should have waited for my true mate! This is my punishment from fate for betraying him by imprinting on your father!"*

No, his mother was miserable because of *her own* choices—something she'd never taken responsibility for. She'd blamed fate, the universe, his father, everything and everyone but her. "There's no such thing as a higher power," Ryan insisted. People were in charge of their own destinies. If they fucked up their lives, it was their own fault and they needed to own it. "Zac could have still ended up here at some point. How did *you* end up here?"

"That doesn't matter."

Pissed by those words in a way he couldn't explain, Ryan closed the small distance between them. "You've been living as a lone wolf since you were a kid . . . and it doesn't matter?"

"My life is good. I have friends, an apartment, a job, a car, and my own money."

"But not a pack, not pack mates, and not a real territory. Don't tell me that doesn't hurt you or your wolf." He narrowed his eyes. "What's your name?"

She blinked. "You already know my name. Did you hit your head?"

"But it's not your real name."

It was possible that he was right, but Makenna didn't know. As she had no intention of explaining that, she simply said, "It's the only name you're getting."

"Are you in hiding? Is someone looking for you?"

"Ryan, let it go."

The door swung open as Dante and Dominic came outside with more trash. Dante's brow creased. "Everything okay here?"

Ryan grunted, urging her inside with a hand on her lower back.

"He thinks you should mind your own business," Makenna told the Beta, translating the grunt.

Dominic cocked his head. "You understand his grunts?"

"You don't?"

"You got 'Mind your own business' . . . from that one sound?"

She lifted her chin. "I thought it was crystal clear."

Dominic turned to Ryan. "Marry her."

Ryan grunted again before heading for the door.

"What did he say?" Dominic asked her.

"Fuck off," she translated.

"Hey!" Dominic moaned at Ryan, following him back inside.

By the time the Phoenix wolves were done giving the shelter a makeover, dinner was being served. Due to the residents' discomfort around packs, it was decided that the Phoenix wolves would eat outside with Dawn, Madisyn, and Makenna. They all settled on the benches near the children's playground.

Once they had finished their meal, Dawn spoke. "I can't thank you enough for everything you've done."

"You really didn't have to do this," said Makenna.

"You're uncomfortable with all the help," Taryn observed.

Makenna shrugged. "It's not that I don't appreciate it. The shelter needs whatever help it can get. But a lot of the stuff you brought here is new."

Dante nodded. "But like you said, this place needs whatever help it can get. On another note, you might want to know what we discovered about Remy." He told them everything Rhett had uncovered and the rumors surrounding Remy.

By the time Dante was done, Dawn had paled considerably. "So it could be that what he really wants is access to the children?"

"As sick as it is, that makes more sense than anything else," the Beta replied.

Stomach twisted with disgust, Makenna placed her half-empty plate at her feet. She'd picked up that something wasn't quite right about Remy, but she hadn't considered this. And now she felt true fear. If he got what he wanted, the children in the shelter would suffer. She wouldn't be able to protect them because the first thing he'd do would be to get rid of Dawn, Madisyn, and Makenna. He wouldn't want any obstacles.

Her wolf, who was just as protective by nature as Makenna, wanted to hunt him down and tear him apart. Makenna approved of the idea. Sick fuckers like him didn't have the right to exist—it was really that simple. But getting onto his land, bypassing his wolves, and getting the opportunity to end his life . . . *not* so simple. That didn't stop her from fantasizing about it.

As she looked up, her eyes collided with Ryan's all-too-perceptive gaze. He knew what she was thinking. She wondered if he knew just how little it would bother her conscience to take Remy's life, wondered how hard he'd judge her for it. She decided she didn't want to know. "We can't tell Zac about this. We can't tell anybody in the shelter. Many of them are here to escape abusive environments. They'll run if they find out this rumor about Remy."

"I agree," said Madisyn, cheeks flushed with anger. "They need to feel safe here."

"Has Remy tried to bribe your mediator friend?" Dawn asked Taryn, her voice shaky.

Taryn shook her head. "But I strongly suspect that he will. It won't work."

"Do you think he'll try to pick a fight at the meeting?" Madisyn asked.

Taryn snorted. "Not if he likes breathing. Ryan will be there."

Makenna had to have heard wrong. "I'm sorry, what was that?"

"I'll be at the mediation meeting," Ryan rumbled.

Was he high? "You can't go. You don't work for the shelter."

"No, I don't," he conceded, "but I can be there as part of Shaya's security team." Mediators always had bodyguards.

Jaime nodded. "That would work. Our pack and Shaya's are closely allied with each other through a blood bond—we even share enforcers. It wouldn't be considered strange for him to be there."

Before Makenna could say that Ryan shouldn't get so heavily involved, Dawn smiled at him and said, "Thank you, Ryan. I'll feel better knowing that my girls and I will be safe in the event of a fight."

Ryan gave a "you're welcome" grunt in response.

Taryn glanced at her watch. "We should get back. My son is probably driving the others crazy, especially my mate."

Dawn chuckled, though her eyes still glinted with worry. "You get back to your mate and pup."

Ryan rose to his feet. "I want to see Zac first."

"Of course you do. He'll be glad to say good-bye." Dawn once again expressed her thanks to the Phoenix wolves for their help as she and Madisyn then led them back into the shelter.

As he turned to go inside, Ryan noticed that Makenna hadn't moved from the bench. "Not coming to protect Dawn from us?" Her head whipped to face him. Oh yeah, he knew she didn't fully trust them. He even understood it. His wolf didn't like it, though; he wanted her trust, believed it was his due.

"Madisyn's with her. That girl's tougher than I am."

He doubted that.

"Have a safe journey."

The dismissive comment rubbed him up the wrong way. "You still haven't told me your real name or how you ended up here." Okay, those words came out snappier than he'd intended. There was his lack of tact again.

"Because it's not your business, White Fang."

Ryan stood in front of her, meeting her bold "I fucking dare you to push me" gaze that for some perverse reason, caused his body to tighten. "I'm making it my business."

Bristling, she cocked a brow. "Oh, is that fucking so?"

It was fucking so. "No pack has the right to cast out a pup. They should pay for it."

Her suspicions were right, reflected Makenna. Protecting and defending were imprinted in his bones. "They will. Karma will see to that."

Yeah, *he'd* be the karma she was referring to. "Just give me the name of your pack."

"You're a stubborn son of a bitch," she said without heat. With anyone else, she might have thought he was pushing this merely because—like most dominant males—he didn't like to be told no. But she sensed it was more than that. It was almost like he had this *need* inside him to be productive, to be useful, like he had something to prove to either himself or others.

"Just concentrate on Zac," she told him. "Right now, he needs you." A long moment of silence passed, but there was no way to tell what was going through his head. She'd never before met anyone who was such an expert at controlling their emotions. There was little of it in his voice, eyes, words, or outward demeanor. His body language was reserved; he never fidgeted, never evaded eye contact, never rambled or stammered. Hell, she had more success understanding his grunts.

Sensing that she wasn't going to budge, Ryan decided to bide his time. He'd get his answers eventually. "Remember to call me if there's a problem." With that, he left.

CHAPTER SIX

*T*he crack of a whip on his back. Rope abrading his wrists. White-hot pain as claws stabbed deep in his side. Rage and hatred pumping through his veins. The burn of the hot iron rod. Voices questioning, laughing, taunting. Ice-cold water hosing him down. The drill going through his hand. The sting and burn of salt and red pepper being rubbed into his wounds. The smell of sweat, blood, anger, corruption, and—

Ryan bolted upright in bed, panting and caught up in the fury that had clouded his thoughts all those years ago. His wolf, who had woken with a bestial growl, finally settled in his pacing as he realized it had been no more than a nightmare. Ryan didn't have them often anymore. Once every six months, at most. They were always the same: broken, distorted snapshots of memory.

After Trey had gotten into an argument with the Alpha of a rival pack, Ryan had been kidnapped, kept prisoner, and tortured by them for information that he didn't give.

Although the Linton Pack had plenty of questions, Ryan didn't believe their need for information had been the primary reason for the torture they had inflicted on him. They had done it because they got off on it. The Alpha, in particular, had been a sadistic bastard.

It hadn't been just the torture that pushed Ryan so near to the end of his endurance. It had been the sense of helplessness, of being out of control and unable to defend himself. His wolf had been chomping at the bit, furious that he'd been injected with drugs that prevented him from shifting and tearing his captors apart.

Ryan had known that his only chance of escaping would be to cross over the knife edge of feral, giving his animal total control. He'd known that the extra speed and strength would enable him to fight the fuckers. But he'd also known that if he did that while he was so enraged and no more than an animal in mind and heart, he could possibly turn rogue.

As such, he'd hesitated for over two weeks, hating the idea that going rogue would force his pack to track and kill him. But the more the Linton Pack had hurt him, the more they'd fed his need for freedom and vengeance.

Drugged, tired, hungry, enraged, and in utter agony, Ryan had finally given in. Completely feral and out of control, his wolf had lunged to the surface in spite of the drugs—and had escaped and ripped apart his captors. Ryan didn't remember much about it; there had been so little left of him that felt human.

After that, his wolf had fled to his territory. By then, he'd calmed enough that Trey and Dante were able to call him back from the edge. The only words Ryan had spoken had been to say that the small Linton Pack had caught him, and they were now dead. They hadn't pushed him for more information—maybe sensing there would be no point. He'd been so emotionally numb, yet so close to the edge.

Time around his pack had helped him heal, and he was about as functional as could be expected. Being a member of a tight, supportive, loyal pack could heal many wounds. That was why he believed his pack would be good for Zac. He just needed the kid to figure that out for himself.

•••

Zac glanced through the glass door of the shelter's entrance. "Ryan said in the message that he's coming alone today."

That surprised Makenna. "You sound relieved."

"I like the others. It's just that, you know, there's a lot of them, and . . ."

And a group of strong personalities could be intimidating. "I get it."

Zac licked his lips. "Why do you think they're not coming with him?"

She could practically see his worry flashing in neon lights on his forehead. "It's not because they don't like you."

Colton nodded. "It was obvious that they want you in their pack. Maybe Ryan doesn't have enough tickets for the game." He patted Zac's shoulder. "Don't worry so much."

"Don't worry so much," the three-year-old little girl hanging from Colton's neck repeated, which is why she earned the nickname "Parrot." All kids loved Colton. Beneath that muscular build was a complete marshmallow.

Hearing his cell beep, Zac said, "That might be Ryan." Swiping his thumb across the screen, Zac smiled devilishly. "It's Dominic."

Makenna arched a brow. "Do I want to know what it says?"

"Nope."

Colton looked at her, eyes smiling. "You thought any more about Madisyn's suggestion?"

She knew he was referring to the feline's idea that Makenna should let Ryan "take that bite he seems to want." Makenna personally wasn't convinced he was attracted to her. Even if he was, and even if it didn't matter to him that she was a loner . . . "I don't have the time or ability to handle this particular individual."

He snorted. "You handled me just fine. I pushed you too hard, too often. You pushed right back. Never took any crap from me." He bumped her shoulder with his. "I just want you to be happy. There's more to life than the shelter."

"Hmm." She peeked through the glass door just as a familiar Chevy pulled up. "Here's Ryan." Her stomach clenched and her wolf sat up, pleased. "Let's go." By the time she and Zac reached the bottom of the path, he was opening the front passenger door. "Hey, White Fang. No pack mates to protect you from me?"

Ryan grunted, taking a swift inhale of her scent. And he scowled. There was a slight whiff of Colton there. His wolf raked his claws at Ryan, demanding he challenge the male. It was tempting.

Body unnaturally stiff, Zac shyly tipped his chin at him in that way teenagers often did. "Sup?"

Ryan gave him a brief nod before his attention darted to the car lurking a short distance from the shelter. The two males inside the vehicle looked everywhere but at them, pointedly avoiding his gaze. They had done the same thing the previous day. It would seem that Remy was having the shelter watched.

"Zac, why don't you ride shotgun?" suggested Makenna. "That way, you guys can talk."

Once they were all in the Chevy, Ryan put the car in gear, pulled away from the curb, and scowled at Remy's wolves as he passed. Then a silence fell. For the first time that Ryan could recall, he found silence uncomfortable. Knowing he had to talk to Zac, get to know him, was the kind of pressure that made him edgy. And the more minutes that passed, the edgier he became.

What did fourteen-year-old boys like to talk about? What interested them? His mind came up empty. Zac had seemed to hit it off with Dominic. What would *Dominic* ask him? Probably nothing suitable for a fourteen-year-old to talk about.

What Ryan wanted to know most of all was what had happened in Zac's pack to make him run. He wanted to know who'd hurt him—or, more to the point, who needed to get their fucking throat ripped out for doing so. But until he'd earned Zac's trust, he'd have to keep his questions casual or the kid might close down. He needed him to relax, but Ryan wasn't exactly a relaxing person to be around.

Shit, he should have taken Zac somewhere else so his pack mates could have come along. It had been Jaime's idea to take Zac to the game. She thought the only way Ryan and Zac could truly get to know each other would be if they didn't have lots of company. Ryan would do what came naturally and say very little to Zac if his pack mates were there and asking questions *he* should be asking. Yeah, okay, she was right. But this was awkward as fuck.

"You know," said Makenna, breaking into his thoughts, "I think I'd have a decent shot of surviving a zombie apocalypse. What about you guys?"

And just like that, the tension melted away.

"She does that a lot." Zac chuckled. "Ask weird questions, I mean." He twisted slightly in his seat to reply, "Um . . . yeah, I think I could." Then he looked at Ryan. "You?"

Ryan opened and closed his mouth three times. "I don't know how to involve myself in this conversation." It was totally pointless. But if she'd been aiming to ease Zac's nerves—though he had the feeling it was simply that her brain shot into weird directions—she'd succeeded. And yeah, okay, Ryan had also lost some of his edginess. Enough that he could think of a decent question. "Are you a big fan of football?"

If the way Zac's eyes lit up was any indication, it was the right question to ask. "Hell, yeah. The Grizzlies are the best." Grizzlies being a bear shifter football team that was playing in the game they were going to watch.

"Who's your favorite player?"

Makenna listened as the boys bonded over football. It was almost cute how hard Ryan found it to simply have a casual conversation. He was the epitome of socially challenged. But she liked that he didn't wear a social mask—too many people did, too many people said and did what they thought others wanted them to. It was difficult to build a friendship with someone based on falsities.

As she watched Ryan push past his comfort zone in order to get to know Zac, she saw just how important the kid was to him, which made her smile. Ryan Conner, she thought, was a good guy. But not a well mannered, safe, comforting kind of good. No, Ryan was hard, dominant, and dangerous—someone who wouldn't hesitate to kill if the need arose. But he had strong pack values and a solid sense of duty that she admired.

By the time they arrived at the stadium, the boys were much more relaxed with each other. She remained silent—except when it came time to order food and drinks, of course. She noticed that a lot of females were ogling Ryan and even sending him welcoming smiles. *Tramps.* Harsh, yeah, but it wasn't like Makenna had said it aloud, so she figured it didn't count.

Ryan led them down to their row and ushered her and Zac to move along first . . . but she came to an abrupt halt as she reached her seat.

"What's wrong?" asked Ryan.

"I can't sit in this seat."

"Why?"

"It's number thirteen." And he wanted her to sit in it? Was he crazy?

Ryan spoke slowly, like he was talking to a mentally challenged person. "Yes, like you said, it's a number."

"An *unlucky* number."

"There's no such thing as luck." Ryan shook his head, resisting the pointless urge to argue with her over the subject. She was clearly insane, and he should just accept it. "I'll take that seat, you have mine."

Makenna almost felt bad placing him in danger by swapping seats. Almost. Leaning back, she soaked up the expectant atmosphere. The crowd was hyped, ramping up the anticipation. She sipped at her Coke through her straw. "Damn, it's hot."

Wedged between them, Zac grinned. "Dude, these seats are fleek. How did you get such good tickets so late?"

"I already had them. Dominic and Trick were going to come with me." They hadn't been too happy to lose their tickets and had pointlessly complained. Ryan had stared at them until they had thrown their hands up and walked away. "Are you any good at football?"

"I'm all right. I play with Colton and some of the other guys at the shelter sometimes."

That name made his wolf growl; he viewed the male as a rival. Personally, Ryan didn't believe Makenna was dating Colton. That didn't mean he wanted to hear about him.

"Makenna used to come along and watch . . . but they banned her from the games."

Ryan blinked. "Banned?"

Makenna adjusted her sunglasses. "It was totally unwarranted."

Zac laughed. "You punched the ref, and that was before the game even started."

"He told Cady she couldn't play because girls were too fragile for football. I was merely proving to the chauvinist asshole that not all females are fragile."

There was genuine outrage in her voice, and Ryan was getting the impression that Makenna was a female who would stubbornly stand behind any key causes that she believed in. He liked that.

Originally, he'd suspected that she was using the shelter as a place to hide or to seek redemption. But now he was thinking . . . "Supporting the shelter is your way of fighting for loners, isn't it?" Those shifters had no rights, no protection, and had a terrible reputation—it was an injustice that the Makenna he was coming to know would despise. Maybe because nobody fought for her.

Makenna didn't like that he'd read her so well. She gave him a breezy smile. "The shelter's pretty cool, right?"

She was good at evasiveness, Ryan acknowledged. It was irritating. "Do you often answer a question with a question?"

"Do you think I do?"

He barely fought the urge to grind his teeth. Instead, he bit into his hot dog.

"Makenna told me you're a tracker," said Zac. "Where did you learn to track?"

"One of the enforcers in my old pack taught me when I was a kid."

"A kid?"

"I spent a lot of time with the enforcers." At first it had been because his mother frequently dumped him on them—wanting his father, who was a trainee, to care for him. Ryan hadn't minded. He'd been fascinated by it. So they had given him the same training, taught him to fight, to hunt, and—later—to kill. Those enforcers had given him the skills and confidence he had today as well as a talent he could take pride in. At home, he'd felt like an inconvenience and a burden. Being around the enforcers had given him a sense of belonging, made him feel useful and worth something.

"Do you like being one?"

"Yes." It was all he'd ever wanted to do.

Zac scoffed down a few pieces of popcorn. "What's it like?"

"Hard. Grueling. Rewarding. Long hours." Although, to be fair, he worked longer hours than most. "This morning, I was up at six a.m.—"

"Seriously? Dude, I don't even know what six a.m. looks like."

Makenna smiled as Zac listened avidly to Ryan's bullet-point description of a typical day for an enforcer. She couldn't help but notice that Ryan didn't include any of his feelings on his position or the responsibilities. It didn't even seem he was being evasive or bottling his emotions. It was as if it didn't occur to him that people would care to hear about his feelings on matters.

She wondered if it had anything to do with his parents. When she'd researched Zac's family, looking for potential guardians, she'd learned about Ryan's parents. His mother was a selfish, chronic complainer and his father was a retired enforcer who had a big fondness for whiskey.

Growing up around such emotionally absent, self-absorbed parents would certainly lead a kid to believe that their feelings simply weren't relevant. The thought of a small Ryan being overlooked and emotionally isolated made her ache. Her wolf growled, protective of Ryan. Makenna could admit that she, too, felt a little protective of the surly male. She didn't bother questioning why—her thoughts often made no sense. Besides, she didn't have time to think on it any further, because the stadium announcer's voice suddenly blasted through the speakers.

Although Makenna wasn't necessarily a big fan of football, she found herself enraptured by what was happening. The game was pretty intense. Like most of the crowd, Zac cheered, gasped, cursed, yelled advice, and complained about penalties. Ryan remained as reserved as always. Sometimes he would grunt or shake his head, and his eyes would twinkle whenever a touchdown was scored.

Zac spat a particularly loud curse when the ball went wide, zooming in the air toward the crowd, and—

She winced as it bounced off Ryan's head, almost making his neck snap back. Damn, that had to have hurt. "Wow, are you okay?"

His scowl harsher than usual, he grunted before throwing the ball down to the field. By the time the game ended and they were leaving the stadium, he had a goose egg on his fucking head.

Riding shotgun, Makenna simply couldn't resist pointing out, "You know . . . if you hadn't sat in that seat—"

"Don't say it."

"—the ball would never have hit you."

Ryan flexed his grip on the steering wheel. He'd known this was coming. "It hit me because the player hurled it in my direction, it had nothing at all to do with the number of my seat. If the ball had sailed just a bit in your direction, it could have hit you."

"No, it couldn't have. I have my rabbit's foot on my keychain."

He did a double take. "What?"

"It wards off bad luck."

"You really believe that part of a dead animal's limb protects you?"

"Obviously, jeez. Don't you know anything?"

"Tell me you're kidding." Because he didn't want her to be beyond help.

"It's common knowledge."

"It's not knowledge, it's superstition—otherwise known as utter bullshit."

She huffed. "You can be so irrational sometimes."

"*I'm* irrational? I don't have part of a dead animal on my keychain!"

"Maybe if you did, the ball wouldn't have hit you!"

Struggling with a response, Ryan shook his head. "I can't do this. I just can't have this totally illogical conversation."

A deep laugh burst out of the teenager behind them, who was struggling to sit upright. "You two are funny."

Ryan exchanged a look with Makenna before frowning at Zac in the rearview mirror. "I'm never funny." He sincerely doubted that the word had ever before been—and would ever again be—used to describe him.

"You are when you lose it with Makenna."

Ryan's frown deepened. "I never lose it."

The kid held his hands up, smirking. "My mistake."

But it wasn't a mistake, Ryan begrudgingly admitted to himself. She had a way of getting under his skin. Yet, he still wanted nothing more than to take her home and fuck her to sleep. That just increased his frustration.

Ordinarily, Ryan was impervious to external distractions. But Makenna Wray was a walking, talking, and completely illogical distraction that drew him. Technically, she shouldn't. She was whimsical and unpredictable, she asked unusual nonsensical questions, believed her rabbit's foot charm warded away danger, and she seemed to genuinely enjoy provoking him. He was very good at analyzing people, but it was impossible to read someone who didn't react normally.

In short, she made no sense to him. Ryan was all about logic and reason; he liked things to make sense in his world. Yet, he found himself a little fascinated by her. His wolf, too, found her intriguing; he was constantly hungry for the female with the mouthwatering scent and the wild spark in her eyes.

Quite frankly, it pissed Ryan off. He prided himself on being an extremely disciplined person. He didn't have problems resisting temptation, he didn't have cravings, and he didn't obsess over anything. But Makenna . . . she made him fucking ache.

Finally, Ryan pulled up outside the shelter and parked just behind her Mustang. "Wait here." Sliding out of the Chevy, he scanned his surroundings as he circled around to the other side of the car. Satisfied that there were no signs of Remy or his pack mates, he opened both passenger doors.

Zac hopped out with a smile. "Thanks for taking me to the game. It was pretty awesome. Except for the part where you hit your head."

Ryan might have bought the kid's sympathetic comment if laughter wasn't gleaming in his eyes. So Ryan just stared at him, daring him to say more.

"And now I'm going to go." Clamping his lips together to hold in a laugh, Zac jogged to the entrance.

Makenna waited until he was inside before she turned to Ryan. "He enjoyed himself. It was a productive day." She wanted him to know that pushing past his comfort zone had paid off. "You did good."

At her genuine compliment, Ryan's irritation left him. She was hard to stay mad at. Especially when she was standing there looking pretty and approving, and smelling so damn good. That wild scent had kept his cock hard and heavy all day. "I can't see Zac tomorrow." He was meeting with Myles's pack mates. "But I'll arrange something for the day after."

Makenna nodded. "Text him with the specifics when you have them."

She turned away, and Ryan found that he couldn't let her go yet. "Farrah Grove."

Slowly twirling to face him, she searched her memory for the name and came up blank. "Should I know her?"

"She left her pack when she was twelve. Some say she vanished, some say she ran away. She fits your description."

"Oh, I see." He thought she could be Farrah. Nope. There were a lot of things Makenna didn't know about her past, but she knew enough to be certain that she wasn't Farrah Grove—particularly since she was younger than twelve when she left her pack. "You think I'm her?"

Actually, now that she was in front of him . . . no, Ryan didn't. She didn't look like a "Farrah." She looked like . . . well, a "Makenna." "If you're not Farrah Grove, who are you?"

"There are these things—you might not have heard of them—they're called 'boundaries.' That means that if there are things I don't want to share, you need to respect that. And let's not forget that it ain't your business, White Fang."

Before he knew it, his hand had shot out and fisted in her hair. Tugging her close, he said, "You are my business." That she'd say differently . . . it offended some part of him. The same part of him was urging Ryan to taste and bite her mouth.

Makenna swallowed hard, disturbingly turned on rather than pissed by his dominant, possessive hold. "You should let go."

"Why? I want you." Ryan almost winced at the gruff words. He probably shouldn't have just blurted it out like that, but he'd never been smooth. Still . . . "And you want me." She looked ready to deny it, so he tightened his grip on her hair. "It's in your scent, so don't lie to me."

"My body wants you. That doesn't mean that I do."

He spoke against her mouth. "I said, don't lie to me." Punishingly, he bit her lip. Her mouth opened on a shocked gasp, and he drove his tongue inside. Fuck, her taste was as addictive as her scent. Sweet and almost bubbly, like sparkling Champagne. Unable to get enough of her, he ate at her mouth, sipping, licking, nipping, and biting hard enough to leave prints of his teeth on her lower lip. His wolf growled his approval at the mark as Ryan soothingly laved it with his tongue.

"You bit me," said Makenna in pure wonder, her heartbeat racing.

"I did." As he stared down at that mark, masculine satisfaction thrummed through his veins, filled every part of him, and settled into every cell and bone. And that was when he knew the truth. There was no denying it, because nothing else made sense. Nothing.

Ryan didn't question his thoughts, actions, or urges. But it didn't take self-reflection to conclude that this female was his true mate.

"Mate" . . . the word felt right to both him and his wolf. Like a puzzle piece sliding into place.

It would explain all the primal feelings that had been taunting Ryan since he first caught her scent: the urge to possess and own, the *right* to protect and defend, and the obsessive hunger that just kept building and building. It didn't matter that Ryan couldn't feel the tug of the mating bond. The facts spoke for themselves.

"Makenna . . ." But he didn't have the words to explain his thoughts. Hell, he never did. Instinct told him that blurting out his belief with his usual lack of tact wouldn't work out well. He needed to think about this. He needed to come to her with the right words, make a case she couldn't argue against . . . because she *would* argue against it. Instinct told him that too.

He took a moment to breathe her in, to take that scent deep into his lungs. Then, with one last lick over the mark, Ryan released her and stepped back. It was hard. Damn fucking hard. Now that he knew—and he *did* know, he was sure to his bones—that she was his mate, walking away from her . . . it felt wrong.

"Be safe for me, Makenna." Because he'd lose his fucking mind if anything happened to her. Her forehead crinkled—most likely in confusion at his choice of words—and he smoothed it out with his finger. "Remember: if there's a problem, call me."

As Ryan slid into the driver's seat, he took one last look at Makenna. It was a mistake. Because the sight of even that small distance between them pissed him the fuck off. His wolf paced angrily, wanting to return to Makenna. Wanting to take, and bite, and own.

They'd claim her, he assured his wolf. There was no chance Ryan would give up this one good thing he could have. She was his mate, she was born for him, and she'd never get away from him.

When the Chevy disappeared into the distance, Makenna took a steadying breath. The guy certainly knew how to mess with a girl's equilibrium. He kissed the way he did everything else—dominantly, confidently, and with enviable skill.

And then he'd bitten her.

Part of her had bristled at the possessive act, but she'd been so damn shocked that she'd done nothing more than state the obvious and stare at him in dismay. Well, Madisyn *had* warned her that he looked at her like he wanted to take a bite. Makenna just hadn't thought he'd actually do it.

That little interlude had confirmed what she'd already suspected; he was a pushy motherfucker who she'd be completely unable to handle. So why did she want him? Because all that strength, confidence, and animal energy was like a damn aphrodisiac for Makenna. So now she was wet and aching for more . . . and the fucker had driven away. She might have been offended, might have suspected that he was put off by her being a loner, if it hadn't been for his parting words.

"Be safe for me."

Why? And why had he seemed reluctant to leave her?

Shaking off the matter, she headed into the shelter. Madisyn and Colton were chatting near the reception desk. Madisyn slowly came toward her. "Everything okay?"

"Yeah," sighed Makenna. "I'm just tired."

"Oh." Madisyn patted her shoulder. "Guess it was that kiss that drained you, huh. Don't growl at me, Wray."

"Fuck off, feline."

Colton laughed as Madisyn began singing, "Ryan kissed Makenna, Ryan kissed Makenna, Ryan kissed—*ow, let go of my hair, heifer!*"

CHAPTER SEVEN

S ome people got utter joy from teasing others. Trick was one of them.

His attempts to irk Ryan very rarely worked. When they did, it wasn't so much that the things he said bothered Ryan; it was that Ryan lost his patience with the whole thing. Still, the majority of the time, Ryan simply drowned him out. Or stared at Trick until he stopped. It depended on his mood. Today, though, his efforts to rile Ryan were paying off.

"I was just making the very obvious point that Makenna's hot," said Trick, who was riding shotgun. "No need to snarl."

And how had Trick made his point? By complimenting her body— her eyes, her mouth, her breasts, her ass, and her legs.

Dante locked gazes with Ryan through the rearview mirror, looking curious. "What's wrong with you? You're gruffer than usual."

Ryan didn't respond. All he wanted was to get this meeting with Myles's pack mates over with. He'd had a shitty night's sleep, having spent hours simply lying there, deciding what he'd say to Makenna. He wanted to see her. Touch her. Inhale her scent.

He hadn't yet told his pack mates about his belief that she was his mate. It seemed wrong to do it before he'd had the conversation with her.

"I don't suppose you know if Makenna's dating anyone, do you?" Trick asked.

Ryan growled at the interest in his voice—it came from both him and his wolf.

Trick grinned. "If I'm not mistaken, there was some possessiveness in that growl."

"You're different with her, Ryan. I mean, you talk to her," Jaime marveled. "And I don't mean in monosyllables. You actually converse with her."

"And she talks to you," added Taryn. "Dominic said she can interpret your grunts."

"I hope she's single," said Trick. "It's been a while since I've been with a female who—"

Another growl rumbled out of Ryan. "Don't say it."

Trick's grin widened. "Ho, ho, ho, Ryan's finally showing some real interest in a female."

Leaning forward, Trey smacked Trick over the back of the head. "Ignore him, Ryan."

Sounded like a good idea to him.

Before long, they were at the border of Myles's territory. The wolves on guard waved them through, showed them where to park the Chevy, and then escorted them into a large pack house. In the dining area, a mated pair rose to their feet—identifying themselves as the Alphas. Travis Bradwin was a big man. Tall, broad, and muscular. His mate, Elise, was just as tall. If they were nervous about having six strange wolves on their territory, they didn't show it.

According to Rhett, Travis had been an Alpha since he was twenty-one. He'd mated a year later and had four pups. He mostly kept to himself, not interested in politics or making alliances; he was much like

Trey, in that respect. Trey hadn't bothered to form alliances until just before he mated Taryn, when he'd been a target of an ambitious asshole.

Travis inclined his head at Trey. "Coleman."

"Bradwin," said Trey.

It was a simple greeting, but their tone was polite and respectful.

Travis introduced his mate, Betas, and two enforcers before introducing the two wolves they had come to see—Rosa and Fenton. Trey introduced each of the Phoenix wolves, and then everyone took a seat. Except for Ryan, who stood with his back against the wall, watchful.

"Myles tells me you need to speak with two of my wolves," said Travis. "Your high-handedness isn't appreciated. You should have contacted *me* and requested a meeting."

Trey didn't appear to take offense. "I figured you'd contact me if there was a problem. But you didn't. Why? Why not refuse us entrance?"

"Because the subject is Remy Deacon. I have pups of my own, so if the rumors about him are true, I've no problem being of assistance to anyone who wishes to end his life."

Good, because it was very likely that was exactly what would happen.

Elise bit her lip. "Are they true?"

"That's what we're here to find out," replied Taryn. Because Trey had a way of inspiring fear in people, she'd insisted on coming along, strangely thinking that her presence would be reassuring. The presence of another female, sure. Not Taryn, considering she had a reputation for being just as unbalanced as her mate.

Trey looked at Rosa and Fenton. "As you know, we have some questions about Remy."

Rosa licked her lips. "May I ask why you're interested?"

"I can't go into the specifics. But I can tell you that he may soon be in a situation where he has access to a lot of shifter children."

Fenton visibly recoiled and Travis uttered a low expletive.

Rosa swallowed. "What is it you want to know?"

Taryn leaned forward, bracing her elbows on the table. "I want to know what kind of Alpha Remy is; I want to know about his personality. What five words would you use to describe him? I don't mean things like 'dominant' or 'domineering'—we've figured that much out for ourselves."

Rosa thought about it for a moment. "Charismatic. Neat. Well mannered. Determined. Short-tempered. But I've never seen him blow a fuse. They're more like hot flashes of anger."

"He's a good Alpha," said Fenton. "More ambitious and greedy than most, but not negligent. He's protective of his wolves, and he keeps the pack organized and strong."

Trey spoke then. "From what Myles said, you think his mother sexually abused him. Is that right?"

Rosa seemed to struggle for words. "Their relationship . . . it's not healthy. She doesn't like other females around him."

Taryn's mouth curved slightly, and Ryan imagined she was thinking about Greta. "Maybe she just can't cut the apron strings."

Rosa shook her head. "You'd have to see them together to understand. She touches him all the time—lingering touches, not the way a mother touches her son. It made my skin crawl. Deanne's possessive of him the way a shifter would be possessive of their mate. She constantly accuses him of sleeping with females of the pack. To my knowledge, he hasn't slept with any of them. I know some females who would have been happy to crawl into his bed—not everyone believes the rumors."

"What about Remy?" asked Taryn. "How does he react to Deanne's behavior?"

"I wouldn't say he's receptive to her touch, but he never pushes her away. He doesn't like her possessiveness and they argue something fierce about it. But then she cries and says he doesn't love her or he wouldn't yell at her like that. Then he stops and comforts her, saying of course he loves her." Rosa rubbed her upper arms. "Like I said, you'd have to see them together to really understand. But I'm telling you, no mother should touch her son like that."

Trey draped an arm over the back of Taryn's chair. "I understand Remy spends a lot of time with the children."

Fenton nodded. "Mostly the boys. He keeps them close to him."

"You sure that he's not protecting them from Deanne?" Taryn shrugged. "I mean, if she abused him, he could worry she'll abuse them."

Rosa twiddled her fingers. "It crossed my mind, but . . ."

"What?" Trey pressed.

"Again, it's something you'd have to see." Rosa's gaze turned inward. "The way he touches them is innocent, almost reverent. Just little strokes on their head, light pats on their back, and fingering their hair. But I once saw a child flinch away from his touch, and Remy backhanded him so hard he fell to the ground. The boy didn't flinch the next time."

Ryan bit back a growl. It was like Remy was grooming them, getting them used to his touch.

Dante linked hands with a pale Jaime. "How many boys went missing?"

"Three," replied Fenton. "Two were orphans."

"How old were they?"

"I think two of them were seven and the other was eight, but I'm not certain."

"Do you think Remy killed them?"

"That, I don't know. It's hard to imagine him doing such a thing. He's very protective of all the pups, even if it's for the wrong reason."

"Maybe they fought the abuse or threatened to tell someone," suggested Jaime. "Remy wouldn't have liked that."

Ryan grunted his agreement. Remy would get rid of them not just to protect his reputation but to show the other children what would happen if they put up any sort of struggle.

"Myles mentioned that one of the males within the pack accused Remy of abusing his son," said Trey.

Fenton nodded. "I wasn't there, but Rosa was."

"That was an awful morning. Vance was a dominant wolf, but he wasn't the confrontational type. He was a very laid-back male, hardly ever lost his temper. But that morning, he tracked Remy down and looked ready to kill him. Vance said that his nine-year-old son, Clay, claimed that Remy touched him inappropriately when they went on one of their nature walks. He called him sick and perverted and a bunch of other names. Then he just flew at Remy, shifting into a wolf midair. He fought well, but Remy won. Vance's mate didn't survive his death, and Clay was nowhere to be seen. Some think Remy killed him, but most think he just ran off."

Ryan had a question. "How many actually suspect he's a pedophile?"

"Not many," replied Fenton. "We talked about it. We thought of grouping together and confronting him. But most of us were submissive wolves—we didn't have a chance against Remy, even as a group, especially since he has his Beta and enforcers to protect him."

That much was true. They would have simply gotten themselves killed, which wouldn't have helped anyone.

"And after seeing what happened to Vance, we were all afraid," added Rosa. "By killing him, Remy showed the pack exactly what would happen to anyone who voiced their suspicions. And that's all they are—suspicions."

"But that Clay kid accused Remy of abusing him," Trick reminded them.

"Yes," allowed Fenton, "but as Remy pointed out, Clay was a troubled pup who was always lying and stealing."

The perfect target, in a way, since it was unlikely that his accusations would be believed.

"Yet, you didn't stay there." Dante tilted his head. "I'm surprised he let you leave."

"That's the thing about Remy," said Fenton. "He *is* a good Alpha. He treats his wolves well. That's why it's so hard to believe he could be guilty of those things. But we have kids; we weren't prepared to take the chance."

Neither was Ryan, which was why he had to ensure that the shelter was never handed over to Remy. And if it turned out that the rumors *were* true, Remy would have to die.

Makenna was serving a customer when the door of the gas station opened and a specimen of untamed masculinity stalked inside. Her wolf sat up, fascinated as always by Ryan's immense confidence and forceful presence. As his dark, brooding eyes met hers, raw hunger flared through Makenna's body. It was a need that viciously clawed and bit at her day and night. She'd dreamed of him the previous night, his teeth dominantly locked around her shoulder as he fiercely hammered into her.

Dragging her gaze away from him, she smiled at her human customer and handed him his change. It was almost amusing the way he regarded Ryan nervously, as if expecting to be leaped on. Ryan didn't spare him a glance; he was staring right at Makenna—focused on her with the intensity of a jungle predator. And the memory of his kiss shoved its way to the forefront of her mind. All day, she'd tried not to think about it. Tried not to think about how he'd overwhelmed her senses and taken her mouth like it was his right. Tried and failed.

Once he was finally alone with Makenna, Ryan said, "We spoke with Myles's pack mates." He'd half expected his words to be guttural. A ferocious hunger was building inside him, tightening his body and causing an animalistic growl to build in his chest. He frowned as he saw that the mark on her lip had faded. "They had a lot to say."

After he told her all he'd heard, Makenna blew out a long breath. "A small part of me actually feels bad for Remy, but none of what happened to him could ever excuse what he's doing. He can't get his hands on the shelter—"

"He won't," Ryan promised, voice filled with resolve. "I won't allow that."

It was impossible not to believe him. "Well, thanks for keeping me updated."

As she released a tired sigh, Ryan noticed the dark circles under her eyes. A growl trickled out of him. "You haven't been sleeping."

Stress tended to keep her awake. Unable to resist poking at Ryan, she merely said, "So?"

"So I don't like it."

"Is that a fact?" She chuckled.

"You like to see me agitated."

"I'd rather see you smile. I'm working on that."

Warmth filled Ryan. He couldn't recall anyone ever caring whether or not he smiled. Makenna Wray, or whatever her name was, had to be his mate. He placed his hands on the counter. "Bonnie Phillips."

"Another missing person?" Makenna rolled her eyes. "Why can't you let this go?"

Ryan's eyes dropped to her lower lip—a lip he couldn't stop thinking about marking again. "I want to know your name."

"I'm Makenna Wray, a loner who's a gas station clerk and does volunteer work at a shelter. That's who I am."

"It's who you are now. But who were you before that?"

"Your cell's ringing."

It was, but he ignored it. "Are you afraid that if I find out who you're hiding from, I'll contact them?" Midsentence, his voice faded into an offended growl. He would never betray her.

She cocked her head. "You know, if you're not frowning, you're growling, or both."

"And you're avoiding my question. You do that a lot." Ryan leaned forward, bringing his face close to hers. She lifted her chin, refusing to be intimidated. His wolf fucking loved that. "Why won't you tell me, Kenna?"

The abbreviation of her name made her blink in surprise. "It's *Ma*kenna. And we've talked about this, White Fang. You need to respect my boundaries."

"Maybe. But I won't." The wild glint in her eyes sparked for a second. It was most likely wrong that her anger made his cock throb. But all that wildness . . . it was something that spoke to his wolf, something that Ryan would bet made her just as wild in bed. He wanted to find out, wanted to be balls deep in her with her pulse beating between his teeth.

"Stop looking at me like that," she hissed.

"Why would I do that?"

"Look, I'm going to be straight with you. I don't have a lot of free time, so I don't do relationships. But I don't do the bed-buddy thing either; bed buddies tend to want exclusivity." Something dark and dangerous flashed in his eyes—a rare display of emotion that made her tense.

"No one but me will touch you." His tone was even but implacable.

She cocked an impervious brow at him. "Oh? And why, pray tell, is that?"

"For the same reason I asked you to be safe for me. You're my mate, Makenna."

Her mind went blank for a moment. He was kidding, right? He had to be. Only . . . he didn't look like he was. She cleared her suddenly dry throat. "Why would you think that?"

"I don't think it, I know it. The facts are there."

"What facts?"

"Since day one, all I've thought about is being balls deep in you. Your scent drives me insane. My wolf hates being apart from you. You're an outsider, a loner, but I'd fucking kill to protect you. And I'd kill to possess you. I'm not a possessive person, Makenna. But I'd like to string Colton up by his intestines for touching you."

Not for a single second would Makenna have guessed that he'd been feeling that way. He was too damn good at hiding his emotions. Her wolf was uncharacteristically quiet. Surprised? Alarmed? Curious? Makenna couldn't tell.

Returning his honesty with her own, Makenna said, "I won't say that the attraction is only one way. I admit, I don't like it when females are mooning over you. And I don't like the idea of you in danger. And my wolf . . . well, she feels the same way. But if we were mates, we'd *know*. We'd feel the pull of the mating bond."

"Not if the frequency is jammed by mental barriers or anxieties about mating." Wanting—no, *needing*—to touch her, Ryan shackled her wrist, circling her madly beating pulse with his thumb. "What do you fear, Makenna? What about mating makes you afraid?"

Her spine snapped straight. "Who says I'm afraid of mating?"

"I've watched you. A lot. You're not easy to read. Mostly because you don't act or think normally." Why she looked proud of that, he wasn't sure. "You put a lot of time and effort into helping others. But you don't let many into your life. You step into their life, but you don't let them step into yours."

There was more truth in that than she was comfortable with.

"Maybe it's because you don't want them to know your secrets. Maybe it's because you once lost someone important to you."

Flushing, she tried to yank her hand away; he held it tight. "You can stop analyzing me now."

"Those sort of issues would jam a mating frequency."

"Did you ever consider—assuming we *are* mates—that maybe *you're* jamming it, not me? You can't tell me you don't have issues of your own."

"I have issues. But I haven't let them blind me to the truth."

As his eyes roamed over her face with a fierce possessiveness that made her stomach clench, she said, "You're absolutely positive about this, aren't you?"

"We wouldn't be having this conversation if I wasn't."

"How long have you believed this?"

"Since yesterday."

Well that explained the odd behavior he'd displayed. He'd probably felt as shocked as she was feeling right now. Honestly, Makenna had never imagined herself mating. Ryan was right; she didn't know how to be open with people. A part of her had shut down after her mother died. For as long as she could remember, it had always been the two of them against the world—Fiona Wray had been everything to Makenna, her rock, her safe place.

Then she'd died, and Makenna had been lost.

So lost she'd sought sanctuary in her wolf form, desperate to escape the pain and grief. Her wolf, just as guttered, had turned half feral. When she was placed in the shelter by Social Services, Dawn and Madisyn brought her back from that state and forced her to grieve like a human. But even back in her human form, she'd remained half feral for a while, a state that had amplified those feelings tormenting her.

Dawn and Madisyn had offered her a shoulder to cry on, but Makenna hadn't taken it. Hadn't shared her grief with anyone. Instead, she'd turned inward, become her own rock. She didn't rely on others for anything, and she liked it that way. A mate, however, would never accept that. As such, Ryan's claim scared her.

Still, that bone-deep loneliness inside her reached out to him, wanted it to be true. Being independent gave her strength and a sense of security and control, but it also made her feel very alone. She'd accepted that, though. She'd thought she could handle it. It wasn't until this very moment that she realized she felt as incomplete as her wolf—maybe even more so.

Still, Makenna didn't know if she wanted to let anyone be her rock again. Ryan's strength and air of self-possession drew her. It would be so very tempting to lean on him. But what if she tried that, what if she let herself hope, and it turned out that he was wrong? Makenna didn't want to ever be that lost again.

Her wolf wasn't caught up in any of Makenna's issues, too elemental in her way of thinking. The animal didn't recognize him as her true mate, but she wasn't fussed by that. She saw a strong, dominant, reliable, loyal male who would make an excellent partner and give her what she wanted, including a pack.

"Tell me what you're thinking," said Ryan. "I've been very honest with you, Makenna."

She inhaled deeply. "I can see that you're one hundred percent certain we're mates, Ryan, but . . . I can't say the same, I'm sorry." The lonely part of her was sorry about that too.

His wolf snarled at the rejection, but Ryan simply said, "Okay." He released her wrist to cup her chin. "But can you say that you're one hundred percent certain that we're *not* mates?"

She swallowed. "No."

He gave a short nod. "That's enough for now." She was open to the possibility on some level, and that was something Ryan could work with. It was also more than he'd hoped for. But he didn't like the weird look that surfaced on her face. "What is it?"

"Don't get offended and growly, but we need to keep this to ourselves."

"No."

"For Zac's sake. If he thinks that I—someone he trusts—might join your pack, it could sway him to do the same. He has to join for his *own* reasons, not because he thinks I might be there to protect him." Particularly since there was a high chance that Ryan was wrong about them being mates. "Besides, he needs to feel that your attention is on him, that he's your priority. Once you have his trust, it will be a different matter. But for now . . ."

Ryan was a contrary mixture of both pissed and proud. He did not like the idea of keeping his mate a secret. But she was right about Zac, and he was proud of how she was willing to put the kid first. It was typical Makenna, putting others before herself, and while that irritated him . . . "I agree that we should concentrate on Zac. For now."

But his pack wasn't stupid. They'd see that he was different with Makenna; they'd form their own conclusions. Hopefully, Makenna would soon form that same conclusion. He doubted she'd fully believe they were mates until she felt the tug of the bond. That meant he'd need to smash down whatever was jamming the frequency.

To do that, he'd need to gain her trust, get her to open up to him, and share all those secrets that acted as a wall between them. Only then would he be able to step fully into her life and become a part of it.

It wouldn't be easy. Ryan was severely disadvantaged when it came to getting to know people, since he wasn't really a talker. He wasn't the type to confide in people, and he mostly kept his own counsel. But he couldn't expect Makenna to open up to him if he didn't do the same.

Another problem was that relationships required skills that Ryan simply didn't have. He lacked pretty words and didn't know how to make people feel good about themselves. He wasn't very tactile or affectionate. Hell, he didn't even know how to accept affection. What's more, he could be pushy, abrupt, and overbearing—which weren't exactly winning qualities.

However, he was also relentless and focused—which were traits that would help him achieve his current goal. And he *would* achieve it. Ryan never settled for anything less than what he wanted. And right now, Makenna Wray was the thing he wanted most. Nothing could make him walk away. Not her fears, not his faults, and not even her doubt that she was his mate.

CHAPTER EIGHT

Mediation meetings were typically held on the territory of whichever mediator was dealing with the case. As such, Makenna found herself on a corner of Mercury Pack territory two weeks later. She and Madisyn sat on either side of Dawn at a long table, and all three stared boldly at the Alpha male opposite them.

He'd been looking especially smug since entering the clearing. His smirk had faltered somewhat when he caught sight of Ryan among the security team, which consisted of three other males and one female. Makenna was guessing they were Mercury wolves, much like the slim redhead sitting at the head of the table who was both an Alpha female and mediator.

Makenna could feel Ryan's piercing gaze fixed on her with absolute precision. It always was. Despite the grave circumstances, his unbridled attention was heating her blood. He was still utterly convinced they were mates. "The facts speak for themselves," he often said. That was something she agreed with, but she saw a different set of facts.

One, there was no mating bond.

Two, her wolf didn't recognize him as her mate.

Three, mates completed each other—she had the kind of personality that would annoy Ryan rather than fit with his. Yes, he claimed to have been possessive, protective, and attracted to her from the start. But it was worth noting that those things hadn't been enough to tempt him until he found himself convinced they were mates. Only then had he begun his pursuit.

If she was honest, though, she hadn't tried very hard to push him away. In a world where she was surrounded by jaded people who'd suffered loss, betrayal, and pain, Ryan—with his loyalty and honor—was a breath of fresh air. He might not be sensitive or particularly empathetic, but he was *good*. Each time he stepped out of his comfort zone for Zac, each time he donated things to the shelter, and each time he swore to Dawn that he'd never allow Remy to take the shelter from her, he chipped away at Makenna's defenses. And he damn well knew it.

Zac was totally won over by Ryan. They saw each other almost every day. After only a week, Zac had felt comfortable enough to go on day trips without her as an escort. Sometimes it would be him and Ryan alone; other times they would be joined by other members of the Phoenix pack. They had taken him to an amusement park, a bowling alley, and another football game, among other things.

Zac thoroughly enjoyed their contact, and he was always eager to see them. Nonetheless, he remained undecided about joining the Phoenix Pack. She knew it galled Ryan, and she could sense his eagerness to take Zac. But the kid had learned very early what it was like to be betrayed by those who were supposed to take care of him. He wasn't going to risk that happening again by rushing into this situation.

Given how intense Ryan was and the danger that surrounded him like a cloak, she'd been surprised by just how comfortable Zac was around him. He actually preferred Ryan's company to that of the other pack members—although Dominic was a close second. Maybe it was *because* of how strong and dangerous Ryan was. Ryan's level of dominance most likely made him feel safe. Zac talked about him constantly . . .

Ryan said he'll teach me how to track.

Ryan's going to show me some combat moves.

Ryan promised me an iPad if I stop laughing at Dominic's jokes.

Words like "fleek" and "awesome" were used a lot when describing Ryan. She was glad Zac had found a new role model, because she was far from a good one.

Pulling Makenna out of her reverie, the Mercury Alpha female cleared her throat. "I'm Shaya Critchley-Axton and I'll be acting as a mediator in this dispute. I'm here to help this be a productive meeting by guiding the discussion, so you can communicate and explore your issues. Be aware that both parties are free to leave at any point. If you do so, a decision won't be made in your absence. Now, starting with the applicant, could each party please introduce themselves?"

Remy slanted a look at the mediator that glinted with annoyance—that may have been because, according to Ryan, Remy had in fact tried to bribe Shaya. "Remy Deacon, Alpha of the Cedar Pack," he said with supreme arrogance. "On my right is my Beta, Killian, and on my left is my Head Enforcer, Selene. Behind us are my five enforcers."

Apparently it was supposed to be an intimidating sight. The fact that he felt the need to intimidate three females only served to confirm that he was in fact an asshole. Makenna was so tempted to question him about the rumors, but Dawn was right—he'd only cry "slander" to the council. It would work in Dawn's favor if she were seen as a victim and he was perceived to be a bully trying to snatch the shelter from beneath her.

Shaya looked at Dawn. "As the respondent, can you now introduce yourself and your companions?"

"Dawn Samuels, owner of the shelter that Mr. Deacon seems to want, for a reason I can't fathom," said Dawn impatiently, as if Remy was a child asking for something he knew he couldn't have. "Sitting on either side of me are two of my volunteers, Makenna and Madisyn."

"Thank you," said Shaya. "Next, you both need to outline the issue as you see it without interrupting each other. We'll start with the applicant."

Remy shrugged. "You know what I want, Dawn. We've discussed it before. The situation is very simple. I want to expand my territory by including the land your shelter sits on. I think we can agree that I've gone about this reasonably. I haven't been confrontational, I haven't made any threats, and I'm not proposing war. In fact, I'm offering you and your volunteers a place in my pack. That will give you protection, pack mates, and whatever help, support, and funding your shelter needs to keep running. It's a beneficial situation for all concerned."

Shaya spoke then. "Dawn, as the respondent, what's your viewpoint on this?"

Dawn lifted her chin. "You say this is a beneficial situation, Mr. Deacon. And that confuses me. You see, I can understand an Alpha wanting to expand his territory, but there are other directions you can go in. My shelter is just a little spot on the map—it's not what anyone would consider a prize. I don't have alliances that could be useful to you, and the territory isn't a beautiful stretch of land. Given all that, I really don't see how you would benefit from this at all."

Remy ground his teeth. His smug smirk had disappeared. "It's true that there are other pieces of territory. But I believe your shelter is a good thing, and I wish to protect it. I have a high regard for you. Not many people out there would provide such a service. You have to admit that it would run more efficiently if you had the support of a pack."

"It runs efficiently now. Why fix what isn't broken?"

"How many people do you have working for you? Not many, I would think. I have the means to improve and expand the building, add more staff, and make it so that you can provide better care for the residents. There is no downside to that."

"Actually—"

"And you can't deny that trouble sometimes comes your way. Only recently there were humans petitioning to have the shelter shut down. Now, if it was considered shifter territory, the humans wouldn't have the right to do any such thing. I don't understand why you—why all three of you—wouldn't want protection."

"Yes, you do," interjected Makenna, "because I've already explained it to you. Loners come to the shelter because it's run by a loner. They would be too fearful to go to a pack for help."

Madisyn spoke then. "And you're either forgetting or ignoring that only Makenna is a wolf. Dawn and I are both felines. We wouldn't feel comfortable in a wolf pack."

Dawn nodded. "So . . . taking everything into account . . . no one at all, not even you, Mr. Deacon, would benefit from us agreeing to what you're asking for."

A muscle in his cheek ticked. "I'm sorry you see it that way. But I have to wonder, do you *really* see it that way, Dawn? Or are you being pressured and influenced by your two 'volunteers' here? Not for one moment do I believe they merely do volunteer work. In a sense, they are your enforcers. Maybe they like the power that gives them. Maybe they don't want to give it up, and so they are trying to convince you to turn down my offer."

"Or maybe you're just talking out of your ass," said Makenna.

Dawn's smile was brittle. "Let me assure you, Mr. Deacon, that I have a mind of my own. Now, I've made my feelings on all this clear. I think you understand my point of view."

His eyes darkened. "You don't want me as an enemy."

Makenna gave a false shiver. "Ooh, that almost sounded like a threat. Didn't it, Madisyn?"

"Yep. And here I thought he was smart—well, sort of."

There was a snort of amusement that may have come from the female wolf in the security team.

Selene snarled. "Remy, I don't understand why you would want them in our pack, especially Super Bitch over there."

Makenna smiled. "Aw, I do so love your pet name for me."

"One day, you and me are gonna have a one on one," growled Selene.

"I am *so* looking forward to that day," said Makenna.

"I'm assuming, then, that an agreement can't be reached between the two parties," said Shaya. Remy grunted his assent while Dawn nodded. "Remy, do you wish to withdraw your application?"

"No," he bit out. "I want that territory." He leaned forward slightly, eyes drilling into Dawn, Makenna, and Madisyn. "And I *will* have it. Think very clearly about whether you really want this to go further. I can promise all three of you that you'll come to regret it if you don't agree, here and now, to give me what I want."

Makenna pretended to consider it. "Nah." She looked at Dawn, who shook her head. "Madisyn?"

"No, I'm not feeling better about Remy," the feline replied.

Shaya leaned back in her seat. "Okay, then. In eight weeks this matter will go before the council. Unless, of course, both parties come to an amicable agreement within that time frame." She rose from her seat. "And that concludes the meeting. Remy, you and your pack mates will leave first. After ten minutes, the respondent and her companions will leave. This is protocol to prevent confrontations from occurring between parties." Selene appeared disappointed.

Remy slowly got to his feet, eyes narrowed at Ryan. "I'm not sure why you're here."

Ryan just gave him what Zac referred to as "the look."

"He's part of my security team today, as you can see," said Shaya.

Remy ignored her, adding, "Seems to me like whenever I want to talk to Makenna, *you* turn up. I don't like that."

"Then don't talk to her," said Ryan, glaring at the fucker and enjoying the angry flush that stained his cheekbones. The male grated on every nerve Ryan had. His wolf was pacing, itching to surface and lunge at the prick. Ryan was sorely tempted. His muscles hurt with the strain of holding back. The only thing that kept him in place was the knowledge that attacking an Alpha, particularly one of a very large pack, would bring problems to his own. Remy would pay for what he'd done. Just not yet.

After a moment of strained silence, Remy glanced at Dawn, Makenna, and Madisyn. "I'll see you all in eight weeks . . . if not before." The latter words held a threat that made Ryan tense. He didn't react, though, as he knew it was exactly what Remy wanted.

When the Cedar wolves were finally gone, Shaya puffed out a long breath and spat, "What a fucking dick. He needs to fucking choke on his own fucking balls, assuming the shithead has any."

Makenna smiled. "I think I'm going to like you."

"She uses bad words like an expert," said Madisyn.

Shaya chuckled. "Thanks."

"Taryn speaks highly of you," Dawn told Shaya.

Shaya flushed a little. "Let me introduce you to these guys over here. We have my Beta, Derren, and three of my enforcers, Bracken, Roni, and Marcus. Marcus and Roni are mates; we share them with the Phoenix Pack, since that's Marcus's original pack."

All of the guys were tall, hot, and exuded dominance. Roni was tall, though smaller than the males, dominant, and had a lethal vibe that Makenna liked.

"You're the expert in these situations; what do you think will happen next?" Dawn asked Shaya.

"Taking into account Remy's vow to have the shelter and his parting words, I'd say he'll do his best in the next eight weeks to create a situation in which you need the protection and support he's offering."

"They'll never need him," Ryan vowed.

Shaya smiled apologetically at the females. "I'd love to give you the support of my pack, but I can't. As the mediator—"

"You need to remain impartial and can't get involved in disputes," finished Makenna. "We get it."

"The last thing we want is for you to lose your job," added Dawn, and Madisyn nodded.

"Don't worry so much about Remy," advised Marcus. "You have the protection of the Phoenix Pack, and that's no small thing."

Ryan glanced at his watch. "I need to leave. I'm picking up Zac in an hour."

After everyone said their good-byes, Ryan remained close to Makenna as he escorted her, Dawn, and Madisyn to the Mustang. He knew his stance was both protective and possessive, but hell if he could stop it. The amount of time he spent around Makenna hadn't gone unnoticed by his pack. They assumed that he and Makenna were having a casual fling, and he allowed them to believe it, although it galled the possessive streak in him that he couldn't declare the truth.

"Where are you and Zac going today?" Dawn asked him as they reached the vehicle.

"I told him I'd let him choose."

"You've made a lot of progress with him."

Not enough. "He won't accept a place in my pack."

"Yet. That's not something you should take personally. Zac's probably having more trouble trusting his own judgment than trusting you. And if my suspicions are right and he was abused in some way by the people who were supposed to care for him, his hesitancy to put his safety into the hands of another is only to be expected."

"He trusts you three," Ryan pointed out.

"We helped him, so he associates us with safety. Be patient. You'll soon have him in your pack."

When the females slid into the Mustang, Ryan braced his hands near the open window. "Call me if you have any problems," he told Makenna.

"You say that a lot," she said impatiently.

Dominant females liked to take care of their own shit, but this was a lot of shit to shovel. Rather than saying that, he sneakily added, "It's not just your safety at risk." He knew she'd accept his help for the sake of those under her protection. He pushed away from the vehicle, *almost* smiling as she grumbled under her breath before switching on the ignition and driving off.

She made him *almost* smile a lot, he mused as he hopped into the Chevy and headed for the shelter. She wasn't afraid to ignore fashion trends—in fact, she carried her whimsical dress sense with confidence and dignity. She felt absolutely no shame about her differences or quirks. And she seemed to believe that rational people were the quirky ones.

What he liked most of all about her was her strength. It was a quiet thing that manifested in her bravery and resolve to make a difference for the loners she met in the shelter.

What he didn't like was that she still hadn't shared any of her secrets with him. Although she'd told him some things about herself, they were shallow and superficial. None of it gave him much insight into her or what had happened to her. But if she thought he'd give up, she didn't know him at all.

Pulling up outside the shelter, he beeped his horn. Zac immediately dashed outside and jogged over to the car. Inside, he tipped his chin. "Sup?"

Ryan nodded. "Where do you want to go?"

"You're letting me choose? Sweet. Um, how about we go for pizza? I'm starving." He gave directions to the restaurant he had in mind. Once Ryan began driving, Zac asked, "How did mediation go?" He rolled his eyes at Ryan's grunt. "Dude, I'm not Makenna. I can't understand your noises."

"Remy asked them to join his pack. They said no. It'll go before the council in eight weeks."

Mouth twitching into a smile, Zac shook his head. "I shouldn't have asked. Storytelling's not your thing."

Ryan just grunted again, which made Zac laugh.

After they'd settled in a booth at the restaurant and placed their orders, Zac spoke. "I've heard little things about your pack. Did Trey really almost kill his father when he was fourteen?" He flushed, looking apologetic. "You don't have to tell me."

"Yes, I do. You're a Phoenix wolf now." He had a right to know.

"I haven't said yes to your offer."

"Doesn't matter. Wherever you are and whatever you decide, you're a Phoenix wolf." He could see that his answer touched Zac, and Ryan was glad of it. "To answer your question, it's true. Trey beat his father, who was also the Alpha, in a duel." But the sick, abusive bastard had deserved it.

Once the waitress placed their Cokes in front of them before disappearing once again, Zac continued, "Was Trey really banished?"

"Yes." By rights, Trey should have been appointed as Alpha—it was protocol for someone who defeated an Alpha to then replace them, but some of the pack had come together to instead drive him out. However, Ryan decided not to add on that part, since challenging an Alpha was exactly what Zac's father had done. Ryan didn't want to dredge up bad memories.

"Was that when he joined the Phoenix Pack?"

"No. When he was banished, the people who disagreed with the decision left with him. Together, they formed the Phoenix Pack."

"You were one of them?"

Ryan nodded. "Trey's my friend, and he hadn't deserved what happened to him."

"Did your family leave too?"

"They were happy to see Trey go." His mother was just as happy to see Ryan go.

"Do you see them much?"

Ryan shook his head. He liked it that way.

The waitress reappeared with their pizza. Once she was gone, Zac said, "I have one more question. Does Trey really turn feral during battles?"

"Yes. But he's never hurt anyone from our pack. And Taryn pulls him back from that state quickly." He took a swig of his drink. "There are a lot of rumors, and some have truth in them. But our pack is a good one. We take care of our own. The dominants would fight to the death before they would let anyone in our pack come to harm. Let me take you to my territory tomorrow—just for the day. You can meet everyone, explore the land. It will just be a daytrip."

Zac frowned thoughtfully. "Okay. Just for the day. But I want Makenna to come."

Ryan inclined his head, though it galled him that Zac didn't fully trust his pack not to force him to stay.

"You want her, don't you? Makenna, I mean."

Ryan veiled his surprise. "Yes."

"So why aren't you doing anything about it?"

"I'm concentrating on you right now."

Zac chewed another chunk of pizza. "Well . . . it would be cool with me if you asked her out. Just . . . don't hurt her, okay? She's been hella good to me. She helped me when I wouldn't help myself. She's a good person."

Yes, she was. Her actions were driven by a good heart and a pain she strived to hide. In the beginning, he hadn't trusted her level of compassion and empathy. He hadn't seen how it could be real . . . because he'd never before known it.

"I think she likes you too. So she'd probably say yes if you asked her out."

Ryan narrowed his eyes. "If I didn't know any better, I'd think you were playing matchmaker."

Zac just smiled.

CHAPTER NINE

As Ryan drove through the gates of Phoenix Pack territory the next morning, he stopped beside the security shack. Cam strolled toward the car with a "Hey."

"This is Zac and Makenna," Ryan told him.

"And you're Cam, Lydia's mate," said Zac, riding shotgun. "You were in a selfie that she sent me." The Phoenix wolves often sent him photographs.

The baby-faced wolf smiled at him. "It's good to finally meet you, Zac." His smile shrunk a little as he nodded at Makenna. He was uncomfortable having a loner on his territory, and Ryan doubted that she would blame Cam for that.

"I'll see you when your shift ends," Ryan told Cam. Putting the Chevy in gear, he then proceeded to drive them deeper into his territory. As they neared the mountain, he said to Zac, "Look carefully at the front wall of the cliff. What do you see?"

Leaning forward, Zac studied it intently. "Holy shit," he breathed. "I mean . . . wow," he quickly corrected. "Makenna, do you see the windows and doors?"

"I see them." Makenna was truly awed. She'd never before seen anything like it. "You live inside the mountain?" How cool was that?

The wonder in her voice pleased Ryan's wolf. He wanted her to like his territory, as it would soon be her home. "Yes."

"Did your pack build it?" asked Zac.

"No," replied Ryan, entering the concealed parking lot where he whipped the Chevy in his usual space. "It was once an ancient cave dwelling. It's been modernized over the years." He led Zac and Makenna up the smooth stairways that were carved into the face of the cliff. Zac's excitement grew as he noticed the arched balconies and glanced down at the surrounding land.

Reaching the main entrance, they found the Alpha pair waiting. Trey inclined his head in greeting while Taryn smiled and said, "Welcome to Bedrock."

Zac chuckled. "This place is seriously awesome."

Makenna nodded. "Very impressive."

Taryn's smile widened. "The interior is even better. Come on, everyone's waiting."

With Zac and an overbearing enforcer on either side of her, Makenna followed the Alphas through what turned out to be a network of tunnels. The walls were light-cream sandstone and looked so smooth that she ran her fingers across them, half expecting them to be soft. Her wolf, always curious, was especially intrigued by her surroundings and wanted to explore by taking the occasional turnoffs.

"We'll give you a tour soon," said Ryan.

Zac's eyes lit up even further. "Sweet."

Finally, they reached the living area, and Zac halted after taking only one step inside the room. At the same time, he shuffled closer to Makenna and she understood why. It was one thing to know that people were waiting to meet you, it was another thing to see an entire pack crowded together in one space with their attention totally focused on you.

Easing the tension, Dante, Dominic, Marcus, and Trick came forward and greeted Zac with fist bumps and light slaps on the back, treating him as "one of the guys"—something he seemed to love.

"I know everyone's been sending you pictures, Zac," began Jaime, "so I'm guessing the others don't really need to introduce themselves."

Zac rubbed one of his hands on his thigh. "I recognize them."

An older woman stepped forward wearing a wide, affectionate smile. "It's great to finally have you here, sweetheart." She pulled Zac into a hug. "I know my Trey sent you some pictures of me with little Kye."

"You're Greta."

"That's right." Greta's attention shifted to Makenna, and her expression lost its warmth. "You must be the loner."

Wow, the latter words were like blades. Jaime had laughingly told Makenna all about Greta's issues, had warned her that the psychotic woman would see her as a threat to her unmated "boys."

Taryn quickly came to Makenna's side with a little boy balanced on her hip. "This is my son, Kye." He gave Makenna a shy wave. "Greta here is Trey's grandmother; feel free to ignore her."

Sounded like a good idea.

The wolves who hadn't yet officially met Zac then came forward to chat with him. He didn't move from Makenna's side, but the tension had left his body by the time the introductions were all done.

Taryn then offered to give them a tour. Jaime, Ryan, and Kye came along, since the kid had latched on to Ryan's neck and wouldn't let go. The little boy was a mini version of his father but with Taryn's hair, which was made up of several different shades of blond.

Zac's excitement returned as they explored the first floor where the living area, kitchen, laundry room, game room, poolroom, and office were located. It was also where the Alphas, Betas, Tao, and the enforcers slept.

The second floor featured many en-suite bedrooms—some belonged to pack members, others were for guests—a small kitchenette, and a laundry room.

"There are two other floors, and they're all the same as this one." Taryn stopped at a particular room on the second floor. "This, Zac, will be your room." She opened the door wide, revealing a large space that had been decorated perfectly for a teenage boy. Undoubtedly, Lydia had had a hand in the design.

"My room?" he echoed, voice hoarse.

Ryan spoke. "You can use it for overnight visits." When Zac darted a panicked look at Makenna, Ryan added, "Makenna could come along. We have plenty of guest rooms."

Swallowing, Zac forced a nonchalant shrug. "Okay. Sure."

Ryan nodded approvingly. "Good."

After the tour, Taryn led them all out of the caves and down to the surrounding land. Makenna smelled the food before they reached a lake where a large patio table, chairs, and a BBQ was set up. There was also another table on which finger foods, cakes, and other typical party foods were laid out. Dante and Grace were grilling meat on the BBQ while others lounged around, lazed in the lake, or played football—or, in Dominic's case, repeatedly threw a ball at Tao's head until the guy snapped and lunged for him.

Zac was practically dragged into the game of football; Kye and Ryan joined him. Taking a seat at the patio table, Makenna watched the Phoenix wolves interact. Watched them all laugh, play, and tease each other. Watched the mated pairs snuggle each other and make a fuss of the pups. The pack was like one big family.

This . . . this was what a pack should be like. This was what she'd never known. Oh, she'd been around packs before; she'd visited many when rehoming other loners. But she'd never spent so much time around them, and they had never relaxed enough around her to be themselves. Not that she believed the Phoenix wolves trusted her. No, they trusted one another to watch their backs.

This place was special, and it would be a place where Zac could heal and thrive. Going by the joy on his face, it was only a matter of time before he accepted their offer to join the pack.

Despite how special it was, Makenna didn't feel comfortable or relaxed. Being surrounded by such a tight-knit group of people had a way of making a person feel very alone. But Makenna was good at being alone. Leaning on others was alien to her.

"Zac's a cute kid," commented Jaime, watching him with a smile.

"He is," agreed Taryn. "He'll break many female hearts when he's older. We asked Rhett to find out what he could about the kid's old pack. They're still looking for him."

Yes, and that worried Makenna. Zac would run if they came close. But he wouldn't run to the Phoenix Pack, because he didn't fully trust he'd be safe here. He'd just disappear. "I erased his trail as best I could and even laid down a false one. But if they're determined to find him, my efforts won't be enough."

"I'm going to be straight with you, Makenna. If they come too close, we'll take him—even if it's against his will. Yes, he'll hate us at first, but I'd rather that than him be back in their hands."

Makenna liked the Alpha female's fierce protectiveness. It was something she could relate to. "Good, because if you don't, he'll run again and be out there all alone. He doesn't deserve that." Taryn nodded—it was a deal.

Roni cocked her head at Makenna. "What pack are you originally from?"

"Not one worth discussing."

"What did you do to be cast out?" asked Greta.

Unable to resist taunting the woman, Makenna replied totally straight-faced, "I was caught having a foursome with the enforcers."

Greta gasped in horror while Taryn, Jaime, and Roni did their best to stifle a smile.

"The Alpha was quite pious and believed that shifters should only give their virginity to their mates."

Greta spluttered. "He's right. Foursome? Disgusting."

Taryn puffed out a breath. "Well, Greta, looks like she really could lead one—maybe even all four—of your unmated boys down the path of sin."

"Path of sin?" repeated Makenna.

Jaime leaned into her and explained quietly. "Taryn likes to tease her with how you and any other females at the shelter might seduce one of her boys."

"What are you whispering about?" demanded Greta.

"I was just asking her what the foursome was like," replied Jaime, eyes twinkling.

Makenna grinned. "Hot. Really, really hot."

"I don't want her around my Zac!" Greta burst out. "He needs people who are a good influence. You're a hussy through and through, even worse than *her*." She slanted a look of distaste at Taryn.

The Alpha female blinked. "Wow. I didn't think there'd ever come a day when you hated anyone more than me."

Makenna said, "I do try to beat world records."

Greta scowled at Taryn. "Why aren't you throwing her out? She has no business being here and corrupting my Zac."

Makenna tilted her head, helplessly amused by the antisocial woman. "If you had a part in raising Ryan, it would explain why he's not quite sane."

"Something tells me you're a little crazy too," Taryn said to Makenna, chuckling.

"I didn't say it was a bad thing."

As Dominic approached the table, dripping wet after being pushed into the lake by Tao, he grinned flirtatiously at Makenna. "Fancy a dip in the lake?"

"No, thanks."

"Why? Are you scared of water? I'll keep you safe; I'm a great swimmer." Mischief glinted in his eyes. "Would you like me to demonstrate the breast stroke?"

She laughed. "Oh, you have 'trouble' written all over you."

"He has a habit of saying dirty lines." Taryn sighed. "We still haven't worked out why."

"Don't you flirt with *her*," Greta told Dominic. "She was cast out of her old pack for having a foursome with the enforcers."

Dominic's smile grew to epic proportions. "Makenna, we absolutely *have* to get to know each other better."

When Dante called out that the steaks were ready, Ryan turned to Zac. "Come on, let's eat." Dropping the football, the teenager followed him.

"You played well," praised Trick as he jogged past with Marcus and Tao.

Marcus glanced over his shoulder with a smile. "Welcome to the pack, kid."

The words made Zac come to an abrupt halt that only Ryan noticed. "What's wrong?" There was a fair amount of distress on the teen's face.

Zac spoke only loud enough for Ryan to hear. "My old pack will be looking for me. Makenna didn't say it, but I know they are."

Ryan's claws sliced out, making Zac jolt in surprise—thankfully not in fear. "If they come here and cause trouble, they'll die."

"You don't even know what happened in my old pack."

"So tell me."

"If I do, you won't want me."

"Whatever happened to you is not your fault," snapped Ryan. He winced at his gruff tone, wishing he had more tact. "Many of the shifters at the shelter have suffered at the hands of others. Do you blame them? Do you think less of them?"

Zac jerked backward. "No."

"Then there you go." Ryan sheathed his claws. "You're one of us now. If whoever hurt you comes here, we'll kill them." The words probably would have spooked another juvenile, but Zac seemed to find strength in them. "Come on."

Tao sidled up to Ryan as they approached the buffet. "Quick question," the Head Enforcer asked quietly. "What would happen if I asked Makenna out?"

With a calm he didn't feel, Ryan said, "I'd rip out your throat before the last word escaped your mouth."

Tao nodded. "Thought so."

Ryan and Zac plated some food before joining the others at the patio table. Zac took the seat on Makenna's left, and Ryan sat on her other side—forcing Dominic to move. "Here." He put a plate of food in front of her, remembering from their conversations what she liked.

She looked from him to the plate and then flashed him a wide smile. "Thanks, Ryan. You're a sweetie."

Um, no he wasn't. His pack mates' expressions told him they were having the same thought. He didn't fail to notice Taryn and Roni whispering to each other with a conspiratorial glint in their eyes as they watched him and Makenna. If they were planning on doing some matchmaking, he wouldn't be opposed to it. He needed whatever help he could get.

As they ate, Ryan listened to Makenna talking with Jaime as they compared the workings of the animal shelter and the loner shelter. Greta directed some snide remarks at Makenna, but his mate ignored them with total ease. She truly didn't appear at all bothered by them, and he wondered if it was because—as a loner—she was used to such verbal abuse. In any case, Ryan didn't like it. "Greta, don't."

"You didn't hear why she was banished from her pack."

If Taryn's smile was anything to go by, Makenna had merely been toying with Greta. Ryan could easily believe that, given her antagonistic streak.

"This day is for Zac, Greta," interjected Trey. "You will *not* spoil it for him."

He'd taken the words right out of Ryan's mouth. As he reached for the ketchup, Ryan accidentally knocked over the salt. Makenna quickly pinched some of the spilled salt between her thumb and index finger, and then offered it to him. Not understanding, he just looked at her.

"Throw it over your left shoulder."

Ryan blinked. "Why?"

"You knocked over the salt."

And apparently that was supposed to mean something to him. At a loss, which was often the case when it came to Makenna, he said nothing.

"You have to throw some over your left shoulder to keep away bad luck."

He looked at his pack mates, surprised to see that the females—including Greta—all nodded, as if her words made perfect sense. Hell, even some of the males seemed to agree with this totally irrational claim. "It's just salt."

"But you knocked it over," persisted Makenna.

"I don't believe in luck, good or bad." She knew that already.

Makenna shook her head sadly. "Don't say I didn't try to warn you." Like he'd made some kind of fatal decision.

"It's just salt."

"*Spilled* salt. There's a difference."

"I don't care."

"You will when bad luck comes your way. *Again*."

His jaw hardened. "Nothing bad is going to happen to me."

"Now you're tempting fate. Quick, knock on wood."

She had to be fucking kidding. "Knocking on wood will keep me safe? You truly believe that?"

She lifted her chin and sniffed. "I don't care for your tone."

"I don't have a tone."

"Not usually," she conceded. "But you sure do have one now, White Fang."

"I told you to drop that."

"And I'm astonished that you thought I'd obey you."

With a muffled curse, Ryan turned back to his food, only then realizing that his entire pack—other than Zac, who was silently laughing his ass off—was staring at him in shock. He knew why. Nothing much ever provoked him. Although he could be rude and surly, he wasn't one to lose it . . . except when it came to Makenna Wray.

"Please don't stop," said Dominic. "Watching you two interact is seriously fascinating." When Ryan grunted, Dominic asked Makenna, "What did he say?"

"He called you an asshole."

Dominic feigned hurt. "Dude, that was mean."

Focusing on his burger, Ryan ignored him. He ignored the curious glances that his pack mates were shooting him. He ignored the vibes of amusement coming from Zac. He ignored the delusional female at his side, who—

Okay, he *tried* to ignore her. In truth, Ryan's mind, body, and wolf were intensely conscious of her, of her scent, her movements, her words, and her innate sensuality. The fact that he had his mate with him, on his territory interacting with his pack mates, gave him a deep sense of satisfaction.

He was aware of just how fortunate he was to have found his mate, since many shifters didn't. It was hard not to claim her, not to make it all public and official. Holding back agitated his wolf; he didn't understand any of Makenna's issues. But Ryan did, and he'd give her the time she needed. He just hoped it wouldn't be too much longer.

"I'm curious, Makenna," began Grace. "You spend a lot of time trying to rehome loners, and you're obviously good at it. Why haven't you found yourself another pack?"

"I seriously doubt any Alpha would condone one of their wolves associating with loners, let alone volunteering at the shelter," replied Makenna. "That's a job I refuse to give up."

Ryan would ensure that Trey didn't force her to do so. Whether she trusted the situation or not, the fact was that she was his mate, and that automatically made her a Phoenix wolf.

Grace popped a grape in her mouth. "Do you keep in touch with any of the loners you rehome?"

Makenna felt Zac still beside her. "If they're okay with that, yes." She liked to be sure that the placement was working out for them, and that they were happy and safe.

Dominic nudged Zac. "So, you staying over tonight? I figured you'd want to try out your room."

Wide-eyed, Zac glanced around the table and swallowed hard.

"Come on," urged Dominic, "it'll be fun. Makenna can stay over too."

"But . . . I don't have any stuff with me," Zac pointed out.

"Actually, the guys bought you some new clothes," said Taryn.

Ryan grunted. "You'll need stuff of your own when you move here, so we got you some."

"I can lend Makenna some sweats to wear for bed," offered Jaime. She cocked her head at Zac. "So, what do you say?"

As Zac looked at Makenna, seeming torn, she asked, "Would you like to stay over?"

He swallowed. "You'll stay too?"

"If that's what you want."

Zac turned to Dominic. "Okay. I'd like that."

Makenna smiled. It was a big move for Zac. A step in the right direction that—

Crack.

Before Makenna could wonder at the sound, Ryan sort of disappeared from her peripheral vision. Blinking, she looked down to see that one of his wooden chair legs had broken, and he was now awkwardly wedged between her and Trick.

"Damn, you okay?" asked Trick, shoulders shaking.

Not at all impressed with the situation—or with Dominic and Zac for laughing so hard they couldn't seem to breathe—Ryan got to his feet and shoved the chair away. He glared at Makenna, who was wearing an "I told you so" look. "Don't say it."

She held her hands up, averting her gaze. "I wasn't gonna."

They both knew that was a lie.

Later, when the BBQ was over and the sky had darkened, everyone cleaned up and then filed back inside the mountain. Jaime lent Makenna some clothes, and then Ryan and Dominic escorted her and Zac to the second floor. Stopping outside Zac's door, Ryan pointed to a room at the end of the tunnel. "That's where Makenna will be staying." Ryan would prefer to have her in his room, but he knew Zac would feel better if she were close by.

"Whoa, wait," Dominic said to Zac. "You're not going to bed yet, are you? Come play pool with Trick, Tao, and me."

Zac turned to Makenna, who gave him a look that said it was his decision. He shrugged at Dominic. "Sure." The two males disappeared down the tunnels, talking and laughing.

Ryan led Makenna to her room, opened the door, and moved aside for her to enter.

She walked inside, admiring every inch of the space. "Nice." Hell, the guest room was nicer than her apartment. It was like a luxurious hotel room, complete with a balcony and an en-suite bathroom.

Hearing the door shut behind her, she turned in time to see Ryan turn the lock. The raw hunger in his dark eyes tightened her nipples . . . and told her exactly what his intentions were. That hunger called to hers, pulsing in the air like a living thing. Even though she knew this wouldn't be a good idea, excitement burst through her, making her heart pound and her mouth dry up.

She forced a breezy smile. "Zac's clearly having a great time. Your pack's been very welcoming, which really put him at ease. His room's perfect for him, by the way. I'm betting Lydia designed it. You know, I think you've got a good chance of making Zac join your pack sometime soon. I mean, he—"

"You're rambling," said Ryan, stalking toward her.

"I'm not rambling."

"You're nervous, so you're rambling."

Shit, she was. "Why would I be nervous?"

He backed her against the wall next to the balcony door. "Because you know exactly what's going to happen." He was going to fuck her again and again, until neither of them could walk. He buried his face in the crook of her neck, taking her scent inside him where it belonged. It was spiced with arousal, making his wolf growl.

Makenna shook her head as his warm hands settled on her thighs possessively. "You'll try to claim me." Her voice came out embarrassingly breathy.

Loving the feel of her soft skin, Ryan slowly snaked his hands under her dress and up her inner thighs. "I'm not going to claim you until you're positive in your mind that I'm your mate." Otherwise, it would have no meaning. A claiming was a sacred thing, and he would never disrespect it or her that way. "But I *am* going to fuck you."

Gripping his T-shirt, Makenna gasped as his thumbs slid just under her panties and idly stroked the outer edges of her folds. Her pussy clenched. She was already wet and he'd barely touched her. But then, Ryan never needed to touch her to reduce her body to a puddle of need. It always responded to him, had done so since the first moment they'd met.

Yet, as he'd pointed out, Makenna was nervous. She liked sex; she was no stranger to it. But this . . . it felt *different*. Maybe it was because she was used to one-night stands and short, shallow flings. It was different with Ryan because she respected him, admired him, and he appealed to her on a level no one else ever had. Not to mention that he thought she was his mate. "Ryan . . ."

"If you really want me to leave, all you have to do is tell me." He sipped at her lips, lazily breezing his thumbs along her outer folds. "Tell me to go, Kenna." But she didn't, so he slid one thumb between her slick folds and pressed down on her clit. Gasping, she bucked her hips, seeking more, but he didn't move. "Say it, and I will. Tell me to go."

She should. She didn't.

With a growl, Ryan took her mouth. Feasting and dominating, licking and biting. His body *hurt*. Ached. Demanded her. She gave as good as she got, fed him cock-torturing little moans and sucked on his tongue. Her taste and her scent tantalized his senses and ate at his control.

He peeled off her dress and groaned in appreciation when he saw she wasn't wearing a bra. Her body was fucking beautiful—graceful and lithe with delicate curves, flawless ivory skin, and high, perfect breasts. He cupped and shaped them possessively as he closed his mouth around one nipple. The taste and texture of the taut little bud made his cock throb.

Fuck, he needed to be in her. He needed to be in his mate, possessing her the way he'd been imagining since the second he first saw her. Nothing else would feel right. Next time, he'd go slow, savor and gorge on every inch of her. Right now, he had to have her.

He snapped off her panties and thrust one finger inside her. And groaned. She was hot and tight and . . . "All mine." He didn't go easy on her; he fucked her hard with his finger. "You're going to come for me, Kenna." He added another finger, stretching her, readying her for him. "Then I'm going to fuck you so hard you scream for me."

Makenna had never been a fan of foreplay; it was overrated, in her opinion. But, shit, Ryan was good with his hands. Every expert thrust of his fingers hit her G-spot just right, building the friction inside her. Needing to touch him, Makenna tore open his fly and fisted his cock. Just as she'd suspected from the glimpses of the bulge she'd often seen in his jeans, he was long and thick. She wanted him in her, filling her to the point of pain, wanted—

Teeth sank into the curve of her breast, and Makenna made a strangled moan as waves of pleasure shook her body. Her pussy clenched as Ryan withdrew his fingers, leaving her feeling painfully empty.

With a growl, Ryan cupped her ass and hoisted her up. "Wrap your legs around me," he rumbled. "That's it." He angled her hips just right, holding her gaze. "You're mine, Makenna. You can fight it all you want, but you belong to me." He slammed into her. *Fuck.* Ryan groaned against her neck as her slick pussy tightened and rippled around him, so tight and hot it was almost too much, almost hurt. He was finally balls deep in his mate, exactly where he needed to be. He resisted the urge to pound into her. For all of two seconds.

Makenna held on tight as he savagely powered into her, feeling the bunch and flex of his muscles beneath her hands. Every thrust was hard, rough, possessive, and deep enough to hurt. That pain only heightened the pleasure. She'd known it would be like this. Known all his natural intensity would make him this ruthless and demanding. And she absolutely loved it.

Feeling his mouth clamp around her pulse, teeth grazing the skin, Makenna probably should have been nervous. But Ryan had said he wouldn't claim her, and she trusted him to keep his word. Still, the way he possessed her body *felt* like he was claiming her in his own way—it was primitive, aggressive, and left her in no doubt of exactly what he considered her to be: his.

Ryan knew he was hurting her, and he would have dug for the strength to slow down if he hadn't been sure that she liked the bite of pain. It was clear in her hoarse moans, the demanding prick of her claws, and the way her hot pussy pulsed and contracted around his cock. She was his match. Made purely for him. No one would make him think otherwise.

He sucked on her pounding pulse, making her pussy tighten around him and bathe his cock in a rush of cream. His wolf was urging him to bite her hard, to draw blood and claim her. It was tempting, so fucking tempting, but Ryan would never do it without her consent—even though the drive to claim was like a drumbeat in his chest. No, he wouldn't claim her. But he'd sure as hell fucking mark her so she knew whom she belonged to.

Feeling her release start to creep up on her, Makenna clawed at his nape. "Ryan, I need—" She cut off as he shifted her hips slightly, so that he was now hitting her G-spot with every brutal, territorial thrust. "Fuck."

Meeting her glazed eyes, Ryan reached between them and found her clit with his thumb. "Come for me."

The power and authority in his voice hit her deep in her core, sending her tumbling into a climax so vicious it tore a scream from her throat.

Ryan snarled as her claws sliced into his back, branding him, just as her pussy clamped down on his cock, rippling and spasming. It was too much. Sinking his teeth into her throat, he rammed himself deep and exploded, shooting jet after jet of come inside her. Soul-deep satisfaction settled deep in his gut. He might not have claimed her officially, but he'd claimed her in his own way with his body, his teeth, and his come. For him, at least, it was binding.

Makenna Wray would never be free of him.

CHAPTER TEN

S taring at herself in the bathroom mirror the next morning, Makenna sighed. *Hell.* She was covered in brands that pretty much broadcasted "Ryan has been here." There were little bites on her neck, shoulders, and breasts. There were claw marks on her hips, stomach, and upper arms. And there were fingerprint bruises on her hips, ass, and thighs.

She wished she could say they pissed her off. They didn't. Nor did the fact that she was sore and tired. She felt taken, sated, and very well fucked.

She *had* been well fucked. Ryan had taken her in the shower, on the floor of the bathroom, and from behind as she braced herself against the wall. Then—while she'd been limp as a noodle—he'd bathed her, ate her out, and put her to bed. In the middle of the night, she'd woken to feel him fucking her slow and hard.

Their first time had been so wild and frantic that she'd missed what the next few rounds with Ryan had shown her—the guy had a big thing for control. Not to the extent that he expected her to be submissive. No, he *liked* that she was defiant. He even liked that she made her own demands . . . he just ignored them.

Hell, the night itself had branded her.

Her wolf liked wearing his marks, liked that he'd felt the need to display such possessiveness. What she *hadn't* liked was the amount of scars on his body.

It hadn't been until they showered together that Makenna saw them. They weren't battle scars. No. The scars, lesions, and burns told her that he'd been subjected to horrific torture. And she fucking hated that. Her wolf had lunged to the surface with a growl, making Makenna's eyes turn wolf. Ryan had kissed and licked her neck, soothing the animal and calming her. Makenna had wanted to ask about them, but it didn't seem right to do it while he had three fingers buried in her. There was a time and a place for conversations like that. It was—

A flicker of movement in her peripheral vision alerted her that she wasn't alone. Ryan was in the doorway, staring at her, eyes inscrutable as always. Naked, he was a sight to behold with all those sleek, hard muscles and a set of fantastic abs. She met his gaze through the mirror. "You do realize I look like the victim of an assault, right?"

Moving to stand behind her, Ryan cupped her hips possessively, eyes roaming over her brands. "I don't think my back looks much better than your front."

Recalling the amount of times she'd clawed him, she'd have to agree with that. She'd also bitten his shoulder a few times. "We need to learn some self-control."

Ryan usually had that in abundance. He was rough during sex—it was the way he liked it. But he never lost control. Except with Makenna. "You need another bath."

Makenna made a show of sniffing her armpit. "I don't smell that bad."

He ignored that. "Even though you had one last night, you still have to be sore."

She shrugged one shoulder. "I don't mind." It was a reminder that he'd been there, a reminder of their night of endless hot sex.

"You should still have one."

His gruff voice made her smile. He was trying to take care of her. "I need to eat first." As if to express its agreement, her stomach rumbled.

"Then we eat."

Despite how hungry she was, Makenna wasn't at all looking forward to breakfast. The Phoenix wolves were bound to say something about the brands, since her T-shirt wasn't going to cover all of them. Not one to procrastinate, however, she got washed and dressed.

On the way to the kitchen, they knocked on Zac's door. A grumpy, sleepy voice called out, "Go away."

"Zac isn't a morning person," Makenna warned Ryan as she picked Zac's lock with a hairclip. Swinging the door open, she shouted, "I hope you're not naked, kid, because I'm coming in."

"Ah, Makenna, it's early," he slurred. They found him in bed, curled up under the quilt. Makenna opened his curtains, and Zac shrunk away from the daylight like he was a vampire. Dragging the covers over his head, he whined something incomprehensible.

"If you don't get up, you'll miss breakfast."

"Grace goes all out," added Ryan. "There'll be bacon, eggs, toast, biscuits and gravy—"

Zac shot up in bed and peeked at them out of one eye. "Biscuits and gravy?"

Ryan nodded. "But Marcus is here. He never stops eating, and he loves biscuits and gravy. If you don't hurry, there'll be none left."

It was almost comical when everyone did a double take at the brands on Makenna's neck and upper arms when they walked into the kitchen ten minutes later. If their shock was anything to go by, Ryan hadn't been lying when he said he wasn't usually the possessive type. Zac hadn't seemed that surprised by the brands; he'd merely smirked.

The Phoenix wolves recovered quickly enough from their shock, greeting Zac warmly and behaving fairly amicably toward Makenna. As they took their seats, no one made any teasing comments about Ryan's display of possessiveness, although it looked as if Trick was eager to say something. Maybe he was holding back because Zac was present—she wasn't sure. In any case, it meant that the meal wasn't the uncomfortable affair she'd expected. Until Greta spoke.

"How could you, Ryan?" The old woman slammed her mug on the table. "What were you thinking, branding a loner? *Her* I expect this behavior from, considering why her pack banished her. But you . . . I raised you better than this."

Looking at her blankly, Ryan grunted.

Jaime whispered to Makenna, "What did he say?"

Just as quietly, she replied, "He thinks she has way too much time on her hands."

Jaime snickered into her coffee mug. "She does."

"Whispering again?" griped Greta with a sneer.

Makenna nodded. "Try it sometime." She jumped as Dominic started choking on his toast. Trey seemed to take delight in thumping him on the back. These people were strange.

After breakfast, many of the pack accompanied Makenna, Zac, and Ryan to the parking lot. While they made a fuss of Zac and said their good-byes, Taryn linked her arm through Makenna's and said, "Walk with me a little."

Makenna dug her heels in after three steps. "Um, I'd rather not."

Taryn laughed. "I sure do like that you're direct."

"I know exactly what you'd like to say: that you've noticed all the brands, that you can see something's going on between me and Ryan, and that you'll come after me with a pitchfork if I hurt him."

Taryn pursed her lips. "I wouldn't have chosen a pitchfork."

"The thing is . . . I would have had to then respond that what goes on between Ryan and me is our business, that you shouldn't think I'm an easy target, and that if you come at me you should do it with everything you have because I won't submit. So I guess it's a good thing that this is just a hypothetical conversation."

A smile slowly spread across Taryn's face. "I can see why Ryan likes you. And I think you'll be good for him. So, yes, I am going to ask you not to hurt him. But I'm also going to ask you to be patient with him, because he could easily hurt you even though he won't mean to." She seemed to struggle for the words to explain. "He hasn't been involved in any serious relationships. The females he's had fun with all said the same thing—he's emotionally stunted, he doesn't feel anything, which isn't true. Ryan just doesn't share what he feels.

"I assume you saw his scars, so you can guess what happened to him. He's never once spoken of it. I wasn't part of the pack at the time, but I was told that when he came back, he was a physical mess and had to be in absolute agony . . . but to look in his eyes, you would never have known it."

Makenna could believe that. Ryan was a closed book.

"From what I heard, Ryan was always quiet and self-contained. But after that he became harder, withdrew even further. That was why everybody was so shocked yesterday when he argued with you," continued Taryn. "That kind of emotional engagement isn't normal for him. He likes you a lot more than any of us suspected. He might look like a guy who's too tough to hurt, but I don't believe that's true. He's vulnerable in his own way. So I'm asking you to be careful with him, and to not be upset if he doesn't give you pretty words."

Her wolf bristled at the warning, not liking another female interfering in such a way. But Makenna was glad that his pack mates were so protective of him. That was how it should be. He was a good guy. He deserved that protection.

Said guy then approached, glancing from her to Taryn. "Ready to go?"

"Yep." Makenna gave Taryn a short nod. "See ya."

When Ryan drove out of the lot with Makenna in the backseat and Zac riding shotgun, he asked her, "What was that about?"

Makenna smiled. "Are you always so nosy?"

His hands clenched around the steering wheel. "You're answering a question with a question again."

"Am I?"

Ryan ground his teeth so hard it was audible, which made Zac laugh. The teenager seemed to find genuine joy in watching Ryan and Makenna spar. Ryan had to admit that he sometimes found their sparring sort of invigorating.

As Ryan finally pulled up outside the shelter, Zac grinned. "I had an awesome time. Your territory is seriously cool." A pause. "Dominic said I could go again tomorrow."

"It's your home, you can come whenever you want." Was the kid not getting that?

Zac's eyes clouded. "I could just bring trouble to your door."

"We already talked about that."

Makenna leaned forward and placed a hand on the juvenile's shoulder. "Zac, if your old pack comes looking for you and causes any trouble, it won't be *your* fault. No one would blame you. Every Phoenix wolf will do whatever they can to protect you whether you're living at the shelter or not. Staying here won't save them, if that's what you're trying to do."

Ryan wanted to kick himself. *Of course* that was what Zac was doing. Ryan would have done the same. "Take tonight to think about it. I'll be here at nine in the morning. If all you want is to spend the day there, I'll return you here later."

"I'll think about it. See you in the morning." Zac opened the car door. "Later, Makenna."

Watching him run to the shelter's entrance, Makenna said, "I think he'll say yes."

Ryan looked around. "Where's your car?"

"Getting an oil change."

"I'll take you home." She rattled off her address, but Ryan already knew it from conversations he'd had with Zac. "What were you and Taryn talking about?" he asked as he headed to her apartment.

"She wasn't confronting me, if that's what you're worried about. She asked me, in the nicest possible way, not to hurt you. It's a good thing that your pack's protective of each other."

"They're good people."

Makenna nodded. "From what I've seen, yes, they are." She didn't much like Greta, but she appreciated that the woman was protective of Ryan.

"They're also smart. They'll guess that we're mates. We should just tell them."

"Ryan—"

"You said yourself that Zac will probably agree to join tomorrow. We don't have any other reason to keep quiet about it."

"You mean apart from the fact that you could be wrong?"

"I'm not wrong."

She twisted slightly in her seat to better look at him. "How can you be so positive? I mean, I agree that us being mates would explain a lot of things. But how can you be so sure when there's no mating bond pulling at you?"

"I just am. But if you need to feel the bond to believe it, you need to clear the frequency."

You need to share your secrets and fears, he didn't say but she clearly heard. He was right, and that put her on the defensive. "I don't ask you to share all your shit. Whenever the topic of your parents is brought up in even the most casual sense, you change the subject. I've never called you on it."

She was right, Ryan realized. He did do that. But it was more out of habit than anything else.

129

"And have I asked about your scars, even though the sight of them makes me want to fucking kill somebody? No. I respect that you might not want to talk about painful things in your past."

Given the soft heart beneath all that armor, he'd expected compassion or pity—both of which would have cut him deeper than any of the implements used on him. But no. She was absolutely enraged. It made him want to smile. "It was a long time ago."

"That's not the fucking point. No one had the right to hurt you like that. *No one.* Tell me the fuckers are dead."

"Every single one of them," he verified.

"Good." Her wolf strongly agreed.

"You have a bloodthirsty streak, don't you, Kenna?"

"My name is *Makenna.*"

"No, that's the name you hide behind. You've created an alternate identity, so your past, your pain, and your secrets can't touch you. But it doesn't mean they're not there."

She shook her head. "You think you know me, but you don't have a fucking clue."

Parking outside her apartment building, he switched off the engine. "Don't I?"

"No."

"Then stop holding it all in."

"You know all you need to know."

Was it really so awful that he wanted to know who she really was and what happened to her? "Trust me, I will make sure that whoever is looking for you never finds you. I will keep you safe. Just tell me."

Her blood seemed to bubble in her veins as anger unfurled inside her. It was the promise to keep her safe that did it. The last person who'd said that to her had been Dawn when she first arrived at the shelter . . . because she'd been all alone—lost and half feral. She hated to think about that time in her life. "Just let it go."

"You know I won't."

"It's not your—"

"Don't tell me this isn't my business. Everything about you is my business."

She clenched her fists. "Just leave it."

Ryan cupped her nape. "Tell me, Kenna. Trust me to keep you safe."

There was that promise again. *"I don't know!"* She practically leapt out of the door and marched toward the building.

Sure he'd heard her wrong, Ryan got out of the car and went after her. "What?"

At the top of the stairs leading to her apartment, she pivoted on the spot. "I don't know, okay," she said through her teeth. "I can't give you the answers you want because I don't have them."

Ryan followed her as she stomped down the stairs, unlocked the door, and went inside. He watched her warily as she dumped her purse on the coffee table before heading to the kitchen, where a mug and coffee machine bore the brunt of her anger. "Makenna . . . I don't understand."

Taking a steadying breath, Makenna dragged a hand through her hair. "I just don't remember any of what happened. My mother and I were banished. She told me I was just a toddler at the time, so maybe that's why I have no memories of the pack or what happened. If my birth name *is* different, it was changed long before I was old enough to remember. The answers to all your questions died with my mother when she was attacked by a group of falcon shifters, *for fun*."

Her pain echoed in every word. Ryan felt something in his chest tighten as he looked at her standing there, eyes blazing with anger and hurt. Before he knew it, he was moving toward her.

She backed away. "No."

Ryan cupped her nape and pulled her against him, holding her there. He'd never been good at giving comfort, but he couldn't just do nothing. Her pain pulled at him, made his stomach churn. He stroked a hand over her hair. All this time he'd thought she was keeping secrets from him; he hadn't for one moment guessed that she'd held back because it was too painful to admit that she simply didn't know the truth. "I can find them, Makenna. Give me everything you do know about the pack, and I'll find them."

"I don't want to find them."

She'd shocked him again. In her shoes, he'd want the whole story— all the facts. "You deserve to know where you come from. You deserve to know why you and your mother were banished."

Stepping back, Makenna shrugged. "If she'd wanted me to know, she would have told me."

"She never mentioned the pack?"

"Once." It had been the time when they were evicted after her mom lost her job. "She said that we didn't deserve this, and she hoped those bastards paid for it."

"What about your father?"

Pain lanced her chest. "I asked about him once, and she started crying. I never asked again." Fiona Wray had been a strong woman who hardly ever cried. It had been disturbing to see. And it had made Makenna feel like total shit. "I'm not interested in knowing what happened. Who I was before doesn't matter."

Bullshit. "I think it does matter to you."

"Oh, really?"

"There are lots of different ways you could help the shelter. What do you do? Rehome loners. You track down their families and you reunite them. On some level, you *do* want to know about your past." She sucked in a sharp breath, looking as if he'd slapped her. "I'm not trying to hurt you. I would never purposely do that."

Recalling Taryn's words, Makenna nodded. "I know. And I appreciate that you want to help. But I'm asking you to let this alone. Okay?"

"You deserve to know the truth, Kenna. And they deserve to pay."

That dark, dangerous rumble made everything in Makenna still. There was vengeance in his eyes—the uncharacteristic display of emotion made her swallow hard. "They will. Karma's a bitch." She pressed a kiss to his jaw. "Let it go."

He didn't say anything, just held her. But Makenna didn't believe for one second that he'd acquiesced. He was a determined male driven by the need to protect and defend. There would be no changing his mind if he was set on tracking down the people he believed wronged her. *Hell.*

Makenna was running late when she left her apartment the next morning to head for the shelter. She stopped dead at the sight of a middle-aged female standing beside her Mustang, jaw clenched, wearing the glare from hell. Approaching, Makenna cocked a brow. "Is there a problem?"

"I have a problem with my son involving himself with lone wolves."

Makenna blinked, wondering what the fuck the woman was talking about. Then she noticed the beady azure eyes she'd seen somewhere before. "You must be Remy's mother." A depraved, twisted bitch who had molested her own child.

Her wolf wanted to lunge, rip off the bitch's ear, and spit it into her face. Creative, but Makenna knew better. Hurting this female would have grave consequences. As a loner, Makenna didn't have the support and protection of a pack. Oh, she didn't doubt that Ryan wouldn't do all that he could to defend her, but that would bring trouble to him and the other Phoenix wolves. Remy's pack was large and he had many alliances. There was every chance that if it came to a battle, the Phoenix Pack would lose . . . and all because she couldn't just play this smart. Besides, she didn't need to physically harm the woman to piss her off.

"Yes, I'm Deanne Deacon." Like that made her special. "I know he's been sleeping with you. Don't deny it. Selene told me he's been flirting with you." And apparently to Deanne, that meant Remy had most definitely fucked Makenna. Well *someone* was a little paranoid.

Suspecting that any denials she made wouldn't be believed, Makenna simply said, "Really?"

"No doubt you think you can convince him to take you as his mate and become our Alpha female." Her mouth tightened. *"Over my dead body."*

The latter sounded good to Makenna. "I thought he was exaggerating. He warned me you were freakily jealous and a little unbalanced. But I thought to myself, 'Surely not. What kind of mother would be almost incestuously possessive of her son? She'd have to be a pretty sick bitch.'"

Baring her teeth, Deanne said, "Remy is my son—"

"But not your mate. Or your lover. Right?"

Deanne's flinty eyes narrowed to slits. "You will not touch him again."

"Oh? Why is that?"

"Do not test me, loner."

"Remy actually wants me in your pack, so it's possible that I won't be a loner much longer."

"He doesn't want you or your friends in our pack," scoffed Deanne. "He wants the shelter and the land it sits on—nothing more. He's using you, trying to soften you up and win you over so that he'll get what he wants. You're *nothing* to him."

"If you're so convinced of that, why are you here warning me away from him?"

"You're a loner; that's enough of a reason."

But it was more than that. Makenna suspected that Deanne saw every female who existed on even the periphery of her son's life as a threat. She was no longer secure about her place in his life. Maybe it was because of the power and authority he now had. Maybe she was unable to control him the way she once had, now that he was older. Or maybe she doubted her ability to sexually attract him. Well, if the guy had an interest in young boys, he definitely wouldn't find his mother's body all that exciting. She'd have to sense that disinterest; she'd have to worry on what it meant for her.

Once again, Makenna almost felt sorry for him. But being abused didn't give him the right to inflict such abuse on others. He could have become someone who protected others from such harm. Instead, he'd chosen a path that robbed children of their innocence, despite knowing how much that hurt.

Figuring it would be best to get this perverted bitch out of her sight before Makenna was tempted to act on the violent fantasies swirling around her head, she forced a smile. "Well, it's been great talking to you. I don't want to keep you, so . . ." She flicked her fingers.

"You think you can *dismiss* me? You think I'm weak?"

"I think you're twisted and evil and you fucked up your child's head so badly he's now just as sick and depraved as you are."

A flush stained Deanne's cheeks. There was no shame or remorse in her expression, just anger. She didn't deny her actions or defend herself, which was confusing as fuck. Could she genuinely not believe she'd done anything wrong? If so, that made her as chilling as it did warped.

"Just stay away from my son." She marched off, head held high. Someone needed to kill that bitch. Hopefully karma had some interesting things in store for Deanne Deacon.

Hearing her phone chime, Makenna scooped it out of her pocket and swiped her thumb over the screen. "Hey, Madisyn."

"Makenna, please tell me you're on your way here. Something weird is going on."

CHAPTER ELEVEN

S tanding in Dawn's office, Makenna looked at the feline in disbelief. "I'm going to need you to repeat that."

Dawn rubbed her temple, shoulders curling forward. "Four of our biggest sponsors pulled out." As news went, that was extremely bad. The shelter couldn't afford to lose sponsors—big or small. The grants Dawn received were helpful, but they didn't cover the full cost of the shelter's upkeep or fund the other services Dawn provided, such as therapy, education, and substance abuse projects. Those services were important. They helped the residents have what they needed to move on and start afresh, thereby making room for other loners to stay at the shelter.

It wasn't until Makenna felt her nails digging into her palms that she realized how tightly she'd clasped her hands. Forcing them to relax, she asked, "Did they say why?"

"One claimed to be unable to offer any further financial aid. The others gave no explanation at all."

"Either Remy paid them off or intimidated them into withdrawing their help."

"I should have seen it coming." Dawn sighed, her gaze unfocused. "It's such an obvious way to make it difficult for me to run the shelter."

"That's not all," said Madisyn, sitting on the sofa, her expression hard. "Some of the residents were fired from their jobs."

Makenna blinked. "Fired?"

"They were posing as humans," Madisyn said. "Their superiors were 'alerted' that they were shifters, and apparently those particular humans don't want our kind working for them."

Restless with manic energy, Makenna began to pace. "Remy had to have exposed them."

"But how would he know their names or where they work?" asked Dawn.

Madisyn bit her lower lip. "We know he has people watching the shelter. Maybe he also has people following the residents who leave each day for work, learning everyone's patterns."

"But why have them fired?" Dawn shook her head. "It seems such an indirect form of attack for someone so angry with us."

"It is indirect," agreed Makenna. "So much so that you're thinking it probably has nothing to do with him. That makes this extremely smart. Think about it, Dawn. A huge way that you make a difference is by helping loners get a job so they can financially support themselves. Without that, they can't afford to move into accommodations of their own. Ask yourself what would happen if a lot of the residents couldn't afford to leave."

Dawn swallowed. "The shelter would become too full at some point, and I'd have to turn people away—especially since I no longer have as much funding as I did before."

"Exactly. That would mean the number of lone shifters living on the streets would build and build. The shelter wouldn't seem to be making much of a difference anymore. Also, loners living on the streets tend to stay in their animal form so they can better defend themselves. The humans would notice wild animals roaming around, and they wouldn't like it—particularly the people who started that petition not so long ago."

"The council wants peace. If Remy can present himself as the answer to my problems and the end of any trouble, they may very well agree to give him what he wants."

"And we could accuse him of being the one to cause the problems," said Madisyn, "but he's attacking the shelter in a way that doesn't actually look like an attack. The council would ignore the claim."

A knock at the door made Dawn's head snap up. "Come in!"

Zac strolled into the room. As he took in their solemn expressions, he blanched and every muscle in his body tensed. "They've found me, haven't they?"

"No, sweetie," Makenna assured him. "This isn't about you. Remy's playing games." She noticed he was carrying a small bag. "What you got there?"

He cleared his throat. "My stuff. Ryan will be here any minute. I told him on the phone that, um, I've decided to join his pack."

Dawn brightened. "That's fantastic news!"

Madisyn did a little clap, but her smile was strained. "Zac, that's great! And *totally* the right decision."

Doubt crossed his face. "Yeah."

Makenna put an arm around his shoulders. "Don't second-guess yourself. I know you think it's selfish because it could bring your old pack to their doorstep, but it's not. Being there for each other is a pack thing. The Phoenix wolves consider you one of theirs. Ryan won't let anything happen to you."

Zac nodded. "I know. I trust him."

She smiled. "I'm proud of you. It's not easy to trust another person when you've been betrayed by those who are meant to look out for you." Trusting Dawn and Madisyn had been hard for her in the beginning, but they had earned that trust with their kindness and patience. The truth was that she also trusted Ryan. She just didn't trust the situation. She didn't trust that smashing the barriers between them would reveal anything other than that Ryan was *not* her mate. Then what? He'd leave her life, and she'd likely never see him again.

Her chest tightened at just the thought. But if it turned out that they weren't mates, it was exactly what would happen. Her wolf didn't worry about that; she saw him as a permanent fixture. But Makenna knew how loyal Ryan was. He could view choosing another female over his mate as betrayal . . . and there was a chance that Makenna simply wasn't his mate.

It would be fair to say that that didn't mean Ryan would leave her. There was the whole imprinting option. But she knew from her research into his family that his extremely unhappy parents had imprinted on each other, that they'd always had a turbulent relationship. Such a thing could make a person determined to wait for their true mate, couldn't it? And she just couldn't shake the feeling that his true mate simply wasn't her.

Ryan entered the shelter with Jaime and Dominic close behind, and his eyes immediately found Makenna near the reception desk, talking with Dawn and Colton. His wolf bared his teeth at the male, and Ryan struggled not to do the same. He crossed to Makenna, sliding into her personal space and dropping a kiss onto her mouth. Yes, he was marking his territory, but so fucking what. He didn't spare Colton a glance. The guy was insignificant, and he needed to know it.

Makenna smiled, recognizing the possessive gesture for what it was. "My day is improving." She gave Jaime and Dominic a quick greeting. "Zac told me he's accepted his place in your pack. You must be thrilled."

Ryan narrowed his eyes. "What do you mean, your day is improving? What happened?"

She sighed. "Remy, the bastard, is . . . well, being a bastard."

Dawn briefly explained the situation before adding, "The residents who were fired are upset. If more sponsors pull out, we'll have a real problem on our hands."

Ryan seriously wanted to gut Remy. "He wants you to feel unsafe and vulnerable so that you'll fall in line and seek his protection." Colton nodded his agreement, but Ryan ignored him.

"Well, it's working," said Dawn. "And it has the residents fretting. Don't forget that some are in hiding. They worry that if Remy discovers their identities, he could contact the people they're hiding from."

Makenna pursed her lips. "I don't think we'd have to worry about that. For one thing, they don't leave the shelter. For another, he's clearly trying to be subtle. If he exposed those seeking sanctuary, several shifters would come knocking. A load of trouble hitting the shelter—a place that's never had any real trouble before—all at one time wouldn't be subtle. It would look suspicious."

Taking a steadying breath, Dawn nodded. "That's true. But I think some still want to leave."

"If they decide to leave, where will they go?" Jaime asked.

"The foxes will probably agree to join the relatives they've been gradually getting to know," said Makenna. "The bear cub might do the same with his godparents. As for the other three . . . I know an Alpha who might willingly take them in on a temporary basis."

"If at any point they choose to leave, they can stay with us until the Remy situation has been resolved," said Ryan.

Makenna's brows flew up. "Seriously?"

"Do I ever joke?"

"Not on purpose."

"You'd really be prepared to do that, Ryan?" asked Dawn. "Why? They're not your problem."

"It would be the right thing to do. And it would help Makenna. I don't like it when she's stressed."

Makenna's breath caught at his matter-of-fact words. He put so much time and energy into helping her . . . and she might not even be his mate. Could anyone blame her for not wanting to lose him, for not being in any rush to crash through barriers that might just lead to him disappearing from her life?

Dominic turned to him with a grin. "Aw, dude, I didn't know you had a romantic streak."

Romantic? Ryan scowled. "I'm being honest, not romantic."

Jaime patted his upper arm. "But admitting something so sweet is romantic."

Ryan grunted. Turning back to Dawn, he said bluntly, "Do you want the help or not?"

"Now *that's* the Ryan we know and love." Dominic chuckled.

"There are other ways we can help," said Jaime. "We can find you more sponsors. Have you set up an online sponsor form?"

Dawn blinked. "No. Is that possible?"

"Sure," said Jaime. "We can get Rhett to set it up for you. We will *not* let Remy win."

Makenna tilted her head. "I wonder if he knows about his mother's decision to visit me earlier."

Ryan growled, "What?"

"She came to my apartment to warn me away from her boy. I'm telling you, after the way she spoke and the jealousy that was rancid in her words, the rumors about her are definitely true. My wolf wanted to kill her. And I wasn't at all opposed to the idea."

Ryan folded his arms across his chest. "Tell me exactly what happened." By the time she was done, he was ready to throttle her. "You thought it necessary to antagonize the woman?" A female sick enough to abuse her child was a dangerous thing.

"Necessary? No. Entertaining? Yes. I could have told her the truth, but it wouldn't have made any difference to that paranoid bitch. Her twisted mind was all made up. She would have just thought I was lying to placate her."

"Remy won't like that you toyed with her," said Jaime. "That thought makes me smile."

Makenna chuckled. "I can't go and confront him over what he's done because none of it can be traced back to him. So I'll settle for causing some ill will between him and Norma Bates."

Ryan opened his mouth, ready to lecture her on antagonizing dangerous shifters and not calling him when shit went down. But he resisted, supposing he should resign himself to the fact that his mate was always going to make him crazy, one way or the other.

"Oh, here comes Zac," said Dawn.

Dominic fist bumped him. "Hey, Zac, ready to come home or what?"

Zac smiled. "Sure."

"Is that lipstick on your cheek?" asked Makenna.

He scrubbed at it, flushing. "It's Madisyn's."

"Give me a hug." Dawn held out her arms. "I'm going to miss you."

Grumbling under his breath, Zac accepted the hug. "I'll, um, I guess I'll miss you too. Maybe."

Chuckling, Dawn gently shoved him toward Makenna, who draped an arm over his shoulders.

Zac frowned up at her. "Why are you saying good-bye? I'll see you all the time, since . . ." He looked from her to Ryan. "Wait, have you guys broken up?"

"No, we haven't," said Ryan. It was the first time he'd verbally acknowledged their relationship to others. It would ensure that Colton understood the way of things.

"I was just going to say that I'm happy for you," Makenna told Zac. "That's all."

Zac's shoulders relaxed. "Okay. Sweet."

Makenna and Dawn walked Zac to the Chevy. Makenna didn't fail to notice Remy's guard dogs in their usual parking spot, but she chose to ignore them. Dawn gave Zac one last hug before he hopped inside with Jaime and Dominic.

Ryan cupped Makenna's chin and dropped a kiss on her mouth. "Call me when you're done here." She nodded, gave Zac a final wave, and returned to the shelter.

As Dawn went to follow, Ryan spoke. "Can we talk a minute?"

Dawn raised her brows. "Of course. Is everything all right?"

"Do you know anything about Makenna's old pack? She told me that she was banished as a toddler and has no memories of it."

Dawn looked at him with a probing gaze. "It's true, she remembers nothing."

"I never asked if it was true. I asked if you knew anything."

"Why should I tell you?"

"Makenna says it doesn't bother her that she has no idea where she comes from. You and I both know that isn't true." Apparently that wasn't enough to convince Dawn to talk. "It hurts her that she doesn't even know her mother's real name. I don't want her to hurt. But I don't want to push her to look for answers if the truth is something she's better not knowing."

"You really do care about Makenna, don't you?"

He grunted. He would have thought that was obvious. People said that actions spoke louder than words, but they didn't seem to take clues from the behavior of those around them.

Dawn let out a long breath. "I don't know much about Fiona. She was found dead in a park. When the police went to her apartment, they found Makenna; she'd been alone for two days. Fiona had several fake IDs. There were no personal or sentimental items that might hint at her roots. But there was one thing . . . I don't know if it will help uncover her history, but it's strange."

Ryan took a step closer. "What?"

"The image of a salamander had been burned into the flesh of her back. Like someone had branded her with a hot iron."

The image tickled his memory. He'd heard of such a thing before, but where? The answer slipped away the second he reached for it.

Dawn sighed. "Deep down, she wants to find them, and she wants to understand what happened. Most of all, she wants to confront the people who ordered the banishment because Makenna hates injustice—or maybe that's *why* she hates injustice. But I think she convinces herself they don't matter, because then she doesn't have to be hurt by what they did and they have no power over her."

Ryan could understand that. Makenna had a soft, compassionate, bruised heart. Facing her past would mean potentially facing more pain, so she chose to live in denial instead. It was a primitive defense mechanism that most people used to some degree in their lives, and sometimes it was the only thing that helped a person function. What Makenna wasn't seeing was that closure could go a long way to helping her heal.

Giving Dawn a nod of thanks for her honesty, Ryan slid into the Chevy and drove to Phoenix Pack territory. Once Zac was settled, Ryan retreated to his room and dialed a familiar number. "Garrett, I have a question."

"Well, hello to you too, son."

Ryan inwardly sighed. Garrett was the Head Enforcer of his old pack and had taught him how to track. He'd also been more of a father to Ryan than his true father had. "You know I don't like pleasantries."

"Yes, I do." Garrett chuckled. "What's your question?"

"You ever heard of any wolves having a salamander branded into their skin?" Ryan didn't intend to track Makenna's roots until after the Remy situation was over. But it bugged him that he was sure he'd heard of the salamander brand before.

"I once heard of an Alpha who likes to brand his wolves. He apparently thinks of it as an honor. A symbol of his favor. But to brand a shifter the way they brand their mates is the ultimate exertion of dominance, nothing more."

"What's the Alpha's name? What pack does he run?"

"It was a long time ago that I heard about it. I don't remember any of the specifics."

Disappointment welled up in him.

"Why the interest?"

Ryan's lips tightened. "I can't say. It's not my secret to tell."

"Fair enough. You should visit us sometime soon."

Be in the general vicinity of his parents? Not an appealing idea. "I'll think about it."

Garrett snorted. "No, you won't. But I understand why. Take care, son." The line went dead.

Returning his cell to his pocket, Ryan wondered if he should feel guilty for going against Makenna's wishes. She'd shared her secrets, only asking that he'd let them alone. But how could he? How could he ignore something that hurt her? The answer was . . . he couldn't. When she hurt, he hurt—an amazing phenomenon, given that he wasn't particularly empathetic. Apparently, she was rubbing off on him.

That night, Ryan lay on his bed with Makenna snuggled into his side, her head on his chest. Both were naked and thoroughly sated. As he played his fingers through her hair, he sensed she was on the verge of sleep. He should have let her rest, should have simply said good night. Instead, Ryan found himself blurting out what he'd wanted to say all day. "We should tell people we're mates."

Makenna exhaled heavily. "I told you, I don't want to say anything until we know for sure."

His hand clenched in her hair. "We're mates, Kenna. I know it. You know it."

She peered up at him. "And if you're wrong?"

"I'm not wrong."

She rolled her eyes. "Let's pretend for just a moment that you're a mere mortal and make mistakes like everyone else . . . What if you're wrong?"

The anxiety that very briefly flickered in her eyes surprised him. "You're mine, Kenna. Nothing will change that."

Makenna wished she could believe that. She wanted to, wanted it more than she'd wanted anything in a very long time. But she couldn't envision Ryan ever imprinting on someone.

He rolled onto his side and lapped at a bite on her neck. "Tell me about your childhood."

"What do you want to know?"

"Everything." Obviously.

"If you think my childhood was awful, you're wrong. My mom was a very fun, positive person who was extremely superstitious." He didn't look surprised to hear that. "Fiona Wray always saw the bright side of everything. She could lift anyone's spirit. She taught me never to give up, to never let the lone shifter lifestyle beat us, that life itself was a gift and that I was living proof of that for her. So it didn't matter to me whether we were in a hostel, a B & B, an apartment or living in our wolf form. I was happy as long as I had her."

Ryan traced her collarbone with his finger. "But then you didn't have her anymore."

"You know what's sad? She was a really special person . . . but I was the only one there to mourn her. Others didn't realize just how great she was. She didn't make her mark on the world."

Ryan stroked a hand over her hair. "Tell me more."

"Why? I'm sure you found out plenty from Dawn." She'd just been calling his bluff, but the way he stilled ever so slightly made Makenna smile. "Ha, I guessed right, didn't I? You went to Dawn."

"Why would you think that?'

146

She snorted. "Because you're a tenacious bastard who has to always be in possession of the facts." She grazed his chest with her nails. "Tell me about your childhood. I confess, I know a little about your parents from when I was checking out Zac's family tree."

"You ruled them out as suitable guardians."

"I was told they had a strained relationship."

That was somewhat of an understatement. It wasn't a topic he ever discussed, but this was Makenna. "My parents imprinted on each other when they were seventeen. A year later, I was born. Gwen was an immature eighteen." The woman was still immature.

"Imprinted at seventeen and then parents at eighteen? That was fast."

Ryan nodded. "Too fast for them. Neither was ready. It was harder for Gwen because she was alone a lot. My father, Galen, was training to be an enforcer, so he spent a lot of time out of the house. She did the night shifts, the day shifts, the diapers, the bottles, everything. It had to be an overwhelming responsibility. She resented the effect it had on her social life. And she resented losing some of Galen's attention and time."

"So the stress took its toll on their relationship."

"Yes." The house had been a place filled with tension, fights, silent arguments, things thrown, and angry sex that never resolved anything. Some of the arguments had been about Ryan: that she had no life because of him, that Galen gave him more attention than her when he *was* home. "All the fighting made Galen spend more time away from the house, which made Gwen worse. To be fair, she had no life."

Pissed by that, Makenna snapped, "Yes, actually, she did. She had a son and a mate—things that some never have. She should have appreciated what she had instead of moaning about what she didn't have. And your dad . . . he should have been there for you. Your parents let you down big time."

"They're not bad people. They just don't make good parents. She told me many times that she wasn't like that until I was born. From what others have said about her, it's the truth."

"Just because she wasn't ready for a baby didn't give her the right to make her child feel like he came second. You are not at fault for their fuckups."

"I know that."

Maybe, but Makenna would bet he'd blamed himself as a child. She'd bet it was why he was so serious and withdrawn. She suspected it was also why he bottled his emotions and didn't share much of his thoughts or feelings. Having parents who were all about themselves would have made him feel like his own needs weren't important, that he had no right to have his own feelings and, as such, giving away his pain was pointless.

Slipping an arm around his back, Makenna burrowed closer against him, wishing she could also hug the solemn little boy he'd once been whose parents had made him feel of little importance. It explained why he had this need inside him to be productive; he was proving to himself and others—maybe only on a subconscious level—that he was more than a burden who ruined someone's life and his parents' relationship. He deserved better.

She was comforting him, Ryan realized. He would have found it awkward to accept that kind of tactile contact from anyone else. But not her. Everything was different with Makenna. Ryan didn't crave physical contact. He couldn't remember there being a time when he ever had. But he needed to touch her, just as he needed to breathe her in and be around her.

If anyone had asked Ryan what he thought his mate might be like, he wouldn't have even come close to a description of Makenna. He wouldn't have thought he could relate to someone so empathetic and compassionate. Nor would he have thought he could genuinely enjoy the company of someone so zany and superstitious.

It wasn't a case of opposites attracting, though. They were similar in some ways. They both had strong convictions, refused to be people pleasers, and found it hard to reveal their vulnerabilities to others. They fit.

But she didn't see it.

She didn't see what they were to each other, and it made him and his wolf crazy. Tangling his fingers in her hair, Ryan tugged her head back. "I'll only give you so much time. It's almost up."

Makenna didn't need to ask what he meant. "It's not that simple."

Sure it was. "Your secrets are out. All that's left jamming the bond are your fears about mating. Say them out loud. I'll make them all go away."

His arrogant comment made her smile. "You can't chase away someone's fears."

"Let's test that."

If she confessed them and then found that there was no bond waiting, something in Makenna would just . . . go. Die. Leave her with another hole and no Ryan in her life. It was her own fault, really. She should have protected herself by pushing him away. She hadn't. He'd been right in what he once said: she didn't let people step fully into her life. But she had let him in. She didn't want him to go. "You never really answered my question. What if you're wrong?"

"I'm not."

"That's not a real answer. *What if you're wrong?*"

It wouldn't change a damn thing. "I'm not going anywhere." He curled a lock of hair around her ear. "Why do you find it so hard to believe we're mates? The facts—"

"—speak for themselves, yeah. You obsess over facts. But what about how you *feel?*"

"You know what I feel."

"Possessive, yes. But that doesn't mean we're mates. Protective, yes. But that trait is part of your personality. Attracted to me, yes. But that's just sex. Those things aren't feelings, Ryan. They're instincts." She placed her hand on his chest. "What do you feel?"

He was quiet for a moment, caught off guard by the deep question. "I don't know."

He sounded so confused and vulnerable. "What I'm asking is . . . Do I matter to you? Not because you think I'm your mate. I mean me, Makenna, do *I* matter?"

Ryan wished he could be better at articulating how he felt, but he suspected that would never happen. "You're important to me." He brushed his thumb over a bite on the curve of her breast. "I don't like being away from you. And sometimes . . . you make me want to smile."

God, the guy did things to her insides. *Good* things. Turned her to mush. She hugged him tight. "You know, that's probably the nicest thing anyone's ever said to me."

Ryan smoothed a hand up and down her back. "Are you telling me I actually said something right?"

Looking up at him, she chuckled. "Yep."

With his hand spanning her throat, he kissed her. Slow and deep. Drinking her in, making her rub up against him like a cat. He ended the kiss with a sharp bite to her lower lip. "Sleep."

She fisted the cock that was now hard and ready. "But you want me again."

"I always want you."

"Prove it."

If she insisted. He rolled her onto her back, hiked up one leg, and plunged deep inside her.

CHAPTER TWELVE

Having finished his midday perimeter check, Ryan was about to return inside the caves when he found himself suddenly surrounded by Taryn, Jaime, Shaya, Roni, Grace, Lydia, and Hope—all of whom looked sober and determined. Marcus stood behind them, pinching the bridge of his nose. Now what?

Taryn took a step toward Ryan. "We should talk."

Talk?

"Don't worry." Jaime gestured to herself and the other females. "*We* will do the talking. You just need to listen."

Sighing, Taryn placed a hand on his arm. "You know me, Ryan, I don't like to interfere in other people's business"—he almost snorted at that—"but I'm making an exception here."

"We wouldn't poke our noses in if it wasn't necessary," claimed Lydia. Again, Ryan almost snorted. The females in front of him were all nosy and meddlesome. Well, except for one. He arched a questioning brow at Marcus's mate.

Roni raised her hands. "I didn't really want to get involved. But I like you. And the girls are right. You're missing the truth."

"By a mile," added Hope.

Shaya nodded. "You've left us no choice but to step in."

"To be honest, Ryan, I'm surprised that we have to," said Grace. "You're a smart male, you listen to your wolf, and you have extremely sharp instincts. You shouldn't need us to point out what's so damn obvious."

Having not even the faintest fucking clue what they were talking about, Ryan looked at Marcus.

The male enforcer sighed. "They think Makenna's your mate."

Oh. "So do I," Ryan said simply before heading for the cliff steps.

Taryn hurried after him. "Wait, you do?"

He grunted.

"Why haven't you told Makenna?"

"I have."

"And?"

He halted, turning back to the females. He wasn't going to be able to escape this conversation. It would be best to get it over with. "She's not convinced."

Jaime cocked her head. "But *you* are, aren't you?"

"I know she's my mate. I don't need the pull of the mating bond to tell me that." His wolf growled his agreement.

Frowning thoughtfully, Grace tapped her fingers on her cheek. "Something's obviously blocking the bond. Do you know what it could be?"

"She fears mating," replied Ryan. "She hasn't explained why."

"It's not uncommon for people to fear it." Lydia sighed, a grim twist to her mouth. "But I think, having watched you two together, that she does want it to be true. Has she said as much?"

He shook his head. But he believed that Makenna wanted them to be mates.

"Maybe she's afraid to hope in case it turns out that you're wrong; she might worry you'll then leave her." Marcus slanted Roni a meaningful look. "Some females can get dumb ideas like that."

"I'm not wrong," Ryan stated.

"But if you were, would you leave her?" asked Hope.

"No." Ideally, he would have preferred to avoid imprinting on anyone. But if that was what it took to bind Makenna to him, fine. "She's mine and nothing will change that." It had been two weeks since he'd first spoken those very words to her. He'd said them again early that morning when he dropped her off at the shelter. She'd looked no more convinced then than she had the first time. But she'd looked like she *wanted* to believe him.

Marcus slid an arm around Roni's waist. "Yeah, but does Makenna know about your parents? If she did a background check on your family when looking for guardians for Zac—"

"She knows," Ryan confirmed.

"Then she'll probably find it difficult to believe that you'd consider staying with someone who wasn't your true mate," said Marcus.

Ryan inwardly stilled. He hadn't thought of that.

Frowning, Taryn shook her head. "No, she knows Ryan cares for her." She raised a brow at Ryan. "You *have* told her that, right?"

When Ryan didn't respond, the females all sighed, shaking their heads at him.

"A big problem is that you and Makenna haven't really had quality time as a couple," said Shaya. "Both of you have been putting most of your energy into Zac, the shelter, and fighting off Remy. Everything's been intense and stressful, which doesn't exactly go hand in hand with a budding relationship."

"You need to take her on a date," said Hope.

Shaya's eyes widened. "Ooh, yeah! You should take her out to dinner."

"Or for a boat ride," suggested Lydia.

"Or ice skating," said Jaime.

"Or on a picnic." Grace pointed at him, stern. "Make sure you take her flowers."

"And maybe write her a poem," said Shaya.

Taryn blinked at the redhead. "Oh, I'm sorry, is it 1953?"

Shaya ignored that. "You could even take her star gazing. Nick did that with me once."

"Willingly?" asked Ryan.

She swatted his arm. "We're trying to help you."

Marcus stepped between the females. "Your suggestions are good ones, ladies, but they're not exactly Ryan-type activities."

"I actually already had something in mind," said Ryan.

Lydia's brows flew up. "You did?"

"Really?" asked Taryn.

They didn't have to sound so astonished. He grunted.

Grace waved a hand, impatient. "Well, what is it?"

"Makenna said she'd always wanted to go to an outdoor movie festival," said Ryan. "There aren't any local ones so I thought I could set something up here on our territory. We have a projector and a white screen and speakers. I could do a campfire and toast marshmallows and . . ." And why were they now smiling dreamily at him?

Jaime put a hand on her chest. "I think Makenna would really love that."

"I think *I* would really love that," said Taryn.

Grace's manner turned abruptly businesslike. "Leave the planning of this to us, Ryan. We can set this up. Bring her here at seven. Everything will be ready by then. I don't think that girl's had much fun in her life. If she wants an outdoor movie festival, she'll get one."

"Wait," began Marcus, "it won't exactly be a date if they have our entire pack hanging around."

"If they went to an actual movie festival they would be surrounded by people," Lydia pointed out. "The same would apply if they went out to dinner or bowling or something."

"Making this a pack event will be a good thing for Makenna," said Grace. "She's never quite relaxed here. Like she doesn't feel she belongs."

Ryan had noticed that. It was understandable, since she had grown up without a pack.

"She needs to feel like one of us," Grace went on, "which is exactly what she'll be when she and Ryan finally mate." She patted Ryan's cheek. "It will happen, sweetie. You just need to find out what's blocking that bond and smash it into teensy-weensy pieces."

Easier said than done, but Ryan would accept nothing less.

When Makenna left the shelter later that day, she found Ryan waiting for her, leaning against his Chevy. Having spent much of her day with a malnourished and frightened pup that had been brought to the shelter the previous night, she felt sad and weary. All of that seemed to leave her at the sight of Ryan whose mere presence seemed to send feel-good endorphins through her body.

Similarly, her wolf lost her tension and did a very languid stretch. He was like hot chocolate, a steaming bath, a happy movie, and a pillar of strength all rolled into one. "Hey, White Fang."

The bright smile she gave him went straight to his groin. "I told you to drop that." Splaying a hand on her lower back, Ryan pulled her close and kissed her. Her sparkling taste never failed to make him groan. He inhaled deeply, taking the scent of his mate inside him. It was tinted with coffee, feline, and . . . "Colton." It was a growl. The male's scent was barely there. Nonetheless, everything in Ryan bristled and possessiveness gripped him hard. His wolf snarled.

Sensing his mood shift, she nuzzled his chest. "I worked with him a little today, that's all."

Sliding his hands around Makenna's neck, Ryan kissed her again. Harder and more dominantly than before. He took and tasted and demanded, stroking her tongue with his until she was pliant against him. The spicy scent of her need rose up, blanketing those other foreign scents until all he could smell was her. He hummed his satisfaction. "That's better."

A little disoriented, Makenna double-blinked. Walking on shaky legs had its challenges, but she managed not to embarrass herself as she hopped into the Chevy. Five minutes into the journey, she realized . . . "We're not heading to my apartment. Why are we not heading to my apartment?"

"Because we're going to Phoenix Pack territory."

And there went Makenna's buzz. She liked the Phoenix wolves well enough, she just didn't enjoy feeling like a spare part. They were all so close and tight that it made her feel even more like an outsider than she normally did. Well, she'd get to see Zac—that would be good. "Oh, okay."

If Ryan didn't know her well, he might have bought her perky smile. But he sensed her disappointment and discomfort. He thought about telling her she had no need to feel awkward around his pack, but the night's events would quickly teach her that.

When they finally arrived at his territory, the sky had begun to darken. With so few clouds, it was a pretty sight. He parked the Chevy and then led Makenna into the woods, which made her frown. "We're not going inside?" He didn't respond. "You're being more mysterious than usual. If your plan is to drag me someplace private and have your wicked way with me, I'm totally on board. Just thought I'd throw that out there."

Ryan almost smiled.

"I smell fire. And food. What's going on?"

Stopping, Ryan turned to her. He couldn't remember ever feeling so awkward. "I wanted . . . I wanted to do . . . something nice for you. I remembered you talked about an outdoor movie festival and . . ."

The guy was turning her insides to mush again. He looked uncharacteristically self-conscious, and it was just adorable. Makenna slid her arms around his waist. "You didn't have to do anything for me. But thank you." Her wolf was charmed by it.

He scowled. "You don't have to thank me." She was his mate. *Obviously* he'd do things for her.

Smiling, she rubbed her nose against his. "So grouchy. Come on, I'm hungry."

Threading his fingers through hers, he led her through the tall trees. "The clearing's up ahead."

The closer they got, the more scents hit her: fire, popcorn, beer, marshmallows, nachos, and sausages. Stepping into the clearing, Makenna was surprised to see some unfamiliar wolves. She guessed they were from the Mercury Pack, since Shaya and some of her security team were also present.

"That's a lot of people," said Makenna. Some were gathered around a hissing, crackling campfire where Trick and Gabe were toasting marshmallows and sausages while Dominic whined that he wanted a turn. Some sat on fallen tree trunks, chatting and drinking. Others were settled on the blankets that were sporadically laid out with pillows and cushions; all faced a large white screen that Kye and a little girl with blonde curls were sniffing and poking.

Spotting Makenna, Zac hurried over, eyes gleaming. "What do you think?"

She smiled. "I think you guys must have had a really busy day."

Jaime and Shaya appeared, wearing huge welcoming smiles. Then they both pulled Makenna into an unexpected hug as they greeted her.

"I'm so glad you're finally here! Let me introduce you to my mate." Shaya linked Makenna's arm and went to lead her away . . . with absolutely no success. Ryan held Makenna's hand tight, scowling at Shaya.

The redhead rolled her eyes at him. "Can't you spare her for just a few minutes?"

Ryan yanked Makenna to his side. "No."

"I'm sure you'll find this great news," said Jaime, smiling, "Greta won't come. She said she won't be part of an event that's being held for 'the loner.'"

Makenna's mouth pursed. "That's funny, because she's right over there by that tree." Arms folded, the old woman was huffing and humphing and snarling at the whole setup.

Shaya snickered. "She probably came because she's scared of missing anything. What a shame."

"Ryyyyyyyyaaaaaaaaaan!" Kye ran to the enforcer and scrambled up his body. "Look what I've got."

Ryan frowned at the object in Kye's hand. "I don't think that's yours."

Shaya sighed. "That's because it's Nick's." She held her hand out, but Kye didn't give her the wallet. Just as she opened her mouth to speak again, a little blonde toddler crashed into her leg. "Hey, angel." Shaya scooped her up. "This is my friend, Makenna. Makenna, this is my daughter, Willow."

Makenna lightly tapped Willow's cheek. "Hi, cutie." The toddler smiled, the image of her mother.

"And the blond with Trey who's heading for us is my mate, Nick." Shaya smiled at him as he draped an arm over her shoulders and kissed Willow's hair. "Nick, this is Makenna."

Nick inclined his head. "Nice to meet you, Makenna. I've heard— Hey, that's mine! Hand it over, pup." Kye just stared at him. "Stop trying to outstare me," Nick ground out, which made Trey chuckle.

"This again?" laughed a brunette with almond-shaped green eyes.

"Makenna, this is Ally, Derren's mate," said Shaya. "She's a Seer." Which meant she had visions of the future and was very empathetic.

Ally smiled. "It's nice to meet you. I've heard about the work you do at the shelter. I think it's awesome. I came very close to choosing the lone shifter lifestyle myself once. Fortunately, the Mercury Pack gave me sanctuary."

"And now we won't let her leave," said Shaya.

Ally snorted. "If I wanted to go, I totally could."

Derren came up behind Ally and wrapped his arms around her. "Nah. I'd never let you." He nodded at Ryan, who grunted.

Tired of sharing Makenna, Ryan handed Kye to Trey and then guided his mate to the collection of blankets. He chose one that was near a thick oak—far away from the blanket that Greta had claimed while no one was looking. He sat with his back against the tree and Makenna snug between his legs. "Comfortable?"

She burrowed deeper into him. "Yep."

Brushing her hair aside, Ryan licked a mark he'd left on her nape. It had almost completely faded. He'd have to fix that. Later.

As Grace and Lydia passed around snacks, Makenna asked him, "What are the funniest famous last words you've ever heard?"

Lost, Ryan just stared at her. Why did her brain constantly spit out nonsensical questions?

"Fine, be boring." She turned to Jaime, who was sprawled on the neighboring blanket, and repeated the question.

"Lightning never hits the same spot twice," said Jaime. Everyone laughed. "You know any?" she asked her mate.

"Pull the pin out and count to what?" said Dante.

Dominic plopped himself on the ground next to Zac. "I got one: Hold my beer while I do this."

Taryn raised her hand. "Hey, what does this button do?"

"This doesn't taste right," said Marcus.

Bracken, a Mercury Pack enforcer, spoke. "It's just a flesh wound."

Ally offered, "No, dummy, that's a dolphin fin."

"What's that red dot on your forehead?" said Makenna.

Amused in spite of himself—it was, after all, a completely pointless conversation—Ryan kissed her temple. He remained mostly silent while everyone talked about various things, and he noticed that his pack made a point of involving Makenna in conversations. The tension soon left her, satisfying both him and his wolf; they wanted her to be relaxed and happy here.

It pained Ryan that she had been a loner for so long. Pack should be everything to a wolf, and he wanted Makenna to have that. Wanted her to feel as secure and safe with these people as he did.

Grace clapped, getting everyone's attention. "Right, let's get this movie started."

Since Kye and Willow were present, the movie had to be something "age appropriate." So everyone munched, drank, and laughed as they watched Disney's *Toy Story*. Dominic seemed to be enjoying it the most. Ryan couldn't claim to be all that stimulated by talking toys, but then he'd never really been stimulated by normal toys. Still, he wasn't bored; he was content to be with his mate—holding her, breathing her in, and listening to her laugh. It was a soft, melodic sound that played over his skin.

When the movie was over, the fire was put out and everyone cleaned up, packed things away, and headed back to the caves. Fingers knotted, Makenna and Ryan then walked to his room. "Tonight was a lot of fun," she said as they reached his door. "I didn't realize how much I needed to wind down until just now. Tha—"

"Don't thank me," he growled, drawing her into the room and closing the door.

"Why does my gratitude offend you?"

"I don't need it." He nipped her lower lip. "What I need is you beneath me."

"I'm totally down with that plan."

He backed her against the wall, sipping at her mouth. "Then open for me." The second her lips parted, Ryan thrust his tongue inside, sweeping it against her own. She responded instantly, nails digging into his shoulders. The kiss was hot and hungry. *He* was hot and hungry. Drunk on the taste and scent of her.

Bunching the bottom of her dress in his hands, Ryan peeled it from her, revealing every luscious inch of the perfect little body that was all his. A body he'd soon be possessing. His cock was thick and full and hurting like a motherfucker. Cupping her breast a little too roughly, Ryan took her mouth again. He claimed and consumed it with his tongue and teeth as she clawed off his T-shirt.

Makenna tried to pull back, intending to tell him to take off his shoes and jeans, but he wasn't having any of that. A growl rumbled into her mouth as one hand spanned her throat. The dominant move didn't ruffle her wolf in the slightest. Maybe it was that the animal trusted him, or maybe it was just that she was in a good mood. Makenna, however . . . her natural defiance rose up fast.

She bit his lip, breaking the kiss. But before she could order him to release her, he snarled and reclaimed her mouth, squeezing her throat just enough to be uncomfortable but not enough to choke her. Then, his mouth still on hers, she was turned and forced to take backward steps to the bed.

"Lay down," he rumbled.

In general, Ryan's tone never changed. But in bed? That was a whole other matter. Right now, his tone was authoritative and brooked no argument. But she *liked* to argue. Another male might have engaged in a battle of wills with her. Ryan? He just pushed her down and pinned her there with his hold on her throat. She should *not* like the way he just maneuvered her where he wanted her.

Sliding his hand down to palm her breast, Ryan grazed her throat with his teeth. One day, he'd leave his irrevocable brand on that very spot. "I'm going to lick your pussy until you come on my tongue, Kenna. Then I'm going to fuck you. Come inside you. Mark what's mine."

Growling at the proprietary comment that dared her to object, she went to fight him.

"Don't move."

161

That assertive rumble made her freeze. Which pissed her off. Since when was she so submissive? Makenna bared her teeth. "For someone who doesn't like talking, you're awful fucking chatty in bed." The bastard blew over her nipple, making it tighten painfully. Then he flicked it with his tongue before latching on tight. Her eyes fell closed.

Ryan licked his way down to her navel and flicked her belly button ring with his tongue. "I want your eyes, Kenna." They opened, blazing fire at him.

"You want a lot."

He slipped off her shoes and then snapped off her panties. "I want everything. I won't accept anything less than everything you are and everything you have to give." He took a step back and grabbed her thighs. "Everything, Kenna." He tilted her hips toward him and then swiped his tongue between her slick folds. Her taste exploded on his tongue. She made that sound. God, that fucking sound. It was throaty and breathless and held a hint of demand.

Makenna fisted the sheets as he licked and ate at her pussy like it was his job. Lapping and nipping and pumping his tongue inside her. The friction built, winding her tighter and tighter. When his fingers dug into her thighs so hard she knew she'd bruise, that bit of pain sent her over. But Ryan didn't stop. Merciless in his assault, he threw her into a second orgasm. Still, he didn't stop. Her clit was sensitive enough to make her wince, but the friction still built once more. And when he pulled his wet finger from her pussy and pushed it into her ass, she came again. It was like her body didn't belong to her anymore. It was giving Ryan what he wanted. She felt powerless, vulnerable. And she didn't like it.

"Ryan, stop." His head very slowly lifted, his features savage and predatory. She froze at the danger there. "I want to be on top." The position would give her some measure of control. He was taking it all from her. Her libido was quite happy to roll over and show its belly.

"No." Ryan suckled on her clit.

"It's too sensitive." He ignored her. So, in one swift, sneaky move, she pulled one thigh free and kicked his chest hard. Not that it appeared to have hurt him, but it did make him stagger backward.

"You kicked me," Ryan growled. "That wasn't nice." She slid off the bed and onto her knees, tackled his fly and pulled down his jeans—which took him off-guard for two reasons. One, she seemed pretty pissed with him. Two, dominant females weren't quick to deliver oral sex. They took their sweet time about it. When her eyes flicked to his and he caught the calculating glint there, he understood.

Fisting a hand in her hair, Ryan held her head in place before she could put her mouth on him. "No. You don't want to suck me off, you want to take control." He slowly shook his head. "Not happening. When you *want* my dick in your mouth, you can have it. Until then, you'll wait."

She snarled. "Who says you get to be in control?"

"I do." He never ceded control. "Get up." She just stared at him defiantly. "Get up, Kenna."

The power and dominance in his tone made her pussy quiver. She relented and stood . . . but she licked his cock from base to tip as she did so. Makenna winced as he tightened his hand in her hair hard enough to make her scalp prickle.

"Careful, Kenna. Or don't you want to be fucked?"

She licked her lower lip. "Do it."

Releasing her hair, he slid his hand down to close around her breast. "Do what?" Her eyes narrowed, once again glinting with a defiance that made his cock throb. "If you want me in you, you have to tell me." He punctuated that with a pinch to her nipple.

"You know I want you in me," she ground out.

Ryan sucked on her earlobe and lightly tapped her ass. "Turn around and bend over. I want your head down." Ever so slowly, she obeyed him. The graceful arch of her spine made him groan. "Good girl." He kicked off his shoes and jeans, and shoved them aside. Splaying one hand on her back, Ryan slowly sank into her, groaning. She had the tightest pussy he'd ever fucked. It was hot and wet and rippling around him. Balls deep, he flexed his cock. "See how well I fit? That's because you were made for me." He thrust hard. "Only for me."

Makenna gripped the sheets as he rode her hard, caught up in the sensations. His fingers biting into her hips. The burn of his cock, full and thick and long, stretching her pussy. His balls slapping against her ass.

She hissed at the sharp prick of his claws, but he didn't sheathe them. "Claws," she reprimanded. He paused and withdrew them, which made her frown. Ryan wasn't so easily handled.

"You don't want my claws branding you?"

It was a casual question, but something in his tone made the hairs on her nape rise. "No."

Ryan covered her body with his, sliding his hand around to possessively cup her breasts. "Such a little liar." Locking his teeth around the fading bite on her nape, he brutally hammered in and out of her. Because he could. Because she was his. Her pussy squeezed him tight, showing him she loved it. His pace was feral and unrelenting, and she pushed back to meet each ruthless thrust. He growled his approval.

"Ryan, I'm going to come." The feel of his teeth digging harder into her skin sent her tumbling into an orgasm. She screamed, arching against him as her pussy clamped down on him. He slammed into her one final time and pulsed deep inside her again and again and again.

Ryan laved the fresh bite on her nape. "You're mine, Kenna. You're running out of time to accept it." Panting and shaking beneath him, she raised a hand. And flipped him the finger. He almost smiled.

CHAPTER THIRTEEN

A few days later, Makenna woke to the sound of voices. Lots of them. Shouting. Chanting.

She groaned, wondering if the noise was responsible for her pounding headache. Forcing her eyes open, she saw that Ryan was gone from what had become his spot on her bed. She wasn't surprised. Sleeping over at her apartment didn't stop him from rising at the crack of dawn to go begin his enforcer duties. His scent lingered, tickling her senses and pleasing her wolf.

Rolling onto her back, Makenna stretched. And winced. Ryan had been exceptionally rough with her the night before. Not that she was complaining. She didn't mind those little aches that reminded her he'd been there.

She *did* mind all those damn voices.

God, she needed some Advil or something.

With a huff, Makenna slid out of bed and pulled on her robe. In the bathroom, she opened the cabinet. No painkillers. Fucking grand. Turning on the faucet, she jerked back as the pipes groaned and water spluttered out in three short bursts. Then nothing. "You've got to be kidding me!"

Silently, she grumbled as she brushed her teeth—which was *not* a pleasant experience when she had no water to dilute the toothpaste. And when she dropped the roll of toilet paper into the toilet, she was more than a little pissed. Her wolf found it kind of amusing.

By the time Makenna returned to the bedroom, her headache was worse and she was seething. *And those voices were still yelling.* She marched into the living area. Halfway to her tiny window, she halted. She didn't need to look outside to know what was happening. Not when she could now clearly hear the words they were chanting.

"We won't be an animal's mate. Exile all shifters before it's too late. In the name of God, we stand and yell, 'Shifters must return to hell!'"

Her wolf's good mood fled. Oh, fuck. Anti-shifter extremists. Not just any extremists, but the religious nut jobs—better described as people who'd been deprived of oxygen at birth and turned loco as a result. They were completely unhinged. Religion had nothing to do with why they did what they did; it was simply something they latched on to and used as justification.

Could her morning get any worse?

It couldn't be a coincidence that they were outside a building wherein a lone shifter lived. Someone must have tipped them off to the whereabouts of a local loner. Prejudiced humans often sold the identities of loners to extremists.

She doubted the extremists knew what apartment was hers or they would have smashed her tiny windows by now—maybe even have tried to get inside. A few months ago, she'd chased off a lone shifter who had been bullying a human female outside the building. That meant that some of the human tenants knew she was a loner. If the extremists offered enough money to them, one might be persuaded to point the extremists in her direction.

One thing was for damn certain: she needed to get out of there.

She could try just walking out. If she were casual enough, they wouldn't suspect her . . . unless they had a photograph or physical description. *Crap.*

The only other option was to use the fire exit. It was a small window, but she'd be able to slide through it. While there could be some extremists covering the rear of the building, it was only a matter of time before they found out which apartment she lived in, and Makenna didn't see any other option.

She thought about calling Ryan and asking him to collect her, since she had no way of reaching her Mustang. But she couldn't risk the extremists spotting her with him. They would take his license plate, find out what pack he was from, and then switch their attention to the Phoenix wolves. She couldn't allow that. For the same reason, she couldn't call Madisyn. She'd have to slip away alone and then call someone when she was a safe distance from the building.

Plan in place, Makenna pulled on a tank top, jeans, her denim jacket, and her side purse. She opened the fire exit window and slid out into a small space that was covered by a white hatch. For a moment, she didn't move as she listened for voices or movement outside. Picking up none, she unlocked and lifted the hatch slightly. The small communal garden—if you could call a cluster of weeds a garden—was empty, which, to be honest, she found a little suspicious. Still, she didn't have the option of sticking around.

Fully opening the hatch, Makenna quickly and quietly climbed out before closing it shut. After merely six steps, she halted. She scented them before she saw them. Several humans came out of the shadows, wearing long hooded robes. Some were holding small wooden crucifixes. Makenna sighed at the ridiculous spectacle. If her wolf could have snickered, she would have.

"Move no further, demon!" ordered one of the robed figures.

Yes, they insisted that shifters were a form of demon. Makenna didn't see the point in correcting them. It wasn't possible to have a rational conversation with these people. Whatever you said was hit with a quote from the bible and branded "words of the devil." They were right, you were wrong, they were good, you were bad, they were on the righteous path, and you were on a descending elevator heading to the fires of hell.

"Child of the Devil, you shall be—!"

"Look, guys, I've had a really rough morning." And now *this*. The basic message Makenna was getting from the universe today was: just go back to bed. She would have done just that if it weren't for the noise these bastards were making.

"Renounce the Devil!" he shouted as they spread out and began to loosely circle her. "Confess your sins! Repent!"

"I swear I'm not jealous that God only talks to you, okay. In fact, I think it's unfair that when a person talks to God it's called 'praying' but when he talks to them it's called 'schizophrenia.'"

"We refuse to stand aside and allow your practices of bestiality, infanticide, violence—"

"Can I just point out the bible says something about turning the other cheek and loving thy enemies?"

"Silence, demon!" He held his hands up toward the sky. "In the name of Jesus Christ, we condemn you!"

Oh for the love of . . . well, God. Could this get more ridiculous?

Muttering prayers, they each produced little bottles and slung the contents at her.

Apparently, yes, it could.

Holy water. Fan-fucking-tastic. She wiped some of the water from her eyes with her fingers. "Okay. This has gone far enough. You need to—" She tensed as one of the humans produced a black rope net from behind his back. Worse still, the leader took a large knife from inside his robe. A chill came over her, and her heart slammed against her ribs. She'd underestimated them when she'd caught sight of the little crucifixes. It hadn't occurred to her that they would be armed. Stupid, stupid, stupid.

"Ever seen one of these knives?" asked the leader, eyes swirling with calculation, as he moved a little to her left. He was trying to take her attention off the net, she realized. She shifted slightly, angling her body in a way that allowed her to keep both threats in her peripheral vision.

"It's pretty, don't you think?" he continued. "It's called a wasp knife. Have you ever heard of them?"

No, but it sure didn't sound good. Her wolf coiled, raring to strike.

"Many sea divers and hunters use them to defend themselves against predators. They have a cylinder of compressed gas in the hilt. Do you know what that means?" He was so confident and at ease, so sure of his power, that she suspected they had done this many times before. "That means that when a person stabs the animal and presses this little trigger, the gas is injected deep into the wound, freezing their organs."

How fucking charming. Makenna licked her lips, giving the net holders a sidelong glance. They hadn't moved. But they would; she knew that. She didn't doubt that she could claw her way out of the net, but being pinned down for just a few moments would leave her helpless against them.

She had no combat training. She was more of a scrapper than a fighter. And she was outnumbered and facing fanatical nut jobs complete with a net and a knife. Not exactly a positive situation. That didn't mean she'd roll over and take this shit.

"I used it on a bear shifter once. It took him a few minutes to die. But smaller shifters like cougars and foxes tend to die in under a minute."

She clenched her hands into fists as her stomach sank. *Bastard.*

"I'm wondering just how long *you'll* take to die." But he didn't move to find out. Just stared at her with a cruel twist to his mouth. If he was trying to taunt her with anticipation, he was doing a good job.

Her peripheral vision alerted her to movement. The net holders were edging behind her and—

The leader charged at her. The others all lunged forward . . . catching the net as it flew over her head and pulling it down. It was heavier and thicker than she'd expected; the weight of it combined with the strength of the humans took her down to her hands and knees, trapping her. It happened so fucking fast. And here was the damn knife.

Chanting a fucking prayer, the leader tried stabbing her through one of the square holes. Makenna moved with the enhanced speed of her kind, rolling onto her back and dodging the knife. The leader stumbled and almost lost his footing. Taking advantage, Makenna clawed at the net. It took a few slashes to slice through the rope to create a big enough gap and—

And now the knife was coming at her again.

Faster than the human could ever hope to be, Makenna lunged upright and grabbed the wrist holding the blade. "Looks like God didn't hear you." She yanked his wrist hard, twisting it until something snapped. Merciless, yes, but who gave a shit?

With a loud cry, he dropped the knife. It grazed her thigh as it fell through the hole in the net and hit the ground with a clang. Hyped on adrenalin, she barely felt the sting.

In one swift movement, Makenna leapt to her feet, came up behind him—twisting his broken wrist behind his back in the process—and curved her free arm around his front, pressing her claws to his throat.

Everyone froze.

"Now we're all going to calm the fuck down," snapped Makenna. Her wolf flexed her claws, not *at all* interested in calming down. "Boys, back away from the net—I don't think I have to explain what will happen to your leader if you don't." The humans slowly edged back. "Wise decision." The next thing on her agenda was getting away from this net. "Church Boy, we're going to take a few slow steps forward." She half expected him to try something. He didn't.

As soon as they stepped off the net, she kicked it aside. "Now—"

The fire exit hatch flipped open, and a head popped out. Eyes wide, the male yelled, "She's out back! She's got Jeff!" The human toppled clumsily out of the hatch.

"Jeff," drawled Makenna. "Is that your name? Not the kind that strikes fear into the heart of a person, is it?"

The leader sneered, "I do not converse with demons."

The sounds of running footsteps made her tense. It was more like a stampede. "Looks like your other friends are joining us." Sure enough, they all hurried out of the side alley . . . holding stakes? She snorted at Jeff. "Stakes? Seriously?" He actually flushed.

They slowed as they took in the situation, seeming confused as to what to do. That told her that Jeff was their leader too. He'd probably stationed them outside the front of the building as a decoy, forcing her to leave through the back—exactly where he'd be waiting.

"You might want to tell them to stay the fuck away."

Instead, Jeff's mouth curved into an ugly smirk as he spread his free arm out wide. "Do your worst," he dared Makenna. "Charge!" he hollered at the humans, shocking the shit out of her. The crazy bastards did. With a roar, they came at her with their stakes.

"Fuck." She could run, she could stand and try to—

They halted. Just stopped dead, casting wary glances at something over her shoulder. She inhaled deeply. *Ryan.* Relief surged heavily through her and her wolf. Makenna didn't think she'd ever been so glad to see anyone in her life.

He came to her side without making a single sound, radiating fury and danger. And for once, his emotions were evident in his expression and body language. It was only then that she heard other noises . . . footsteps, light and agile enough to go undetected by most. She inhaled deeply again, picking up other scents—Jaime, Dante, Tao, Trick, Dominic, Marcus, and Roni.

With one glance, Ryan took in the scene—took in the open hatch, the gathering of humans, the clawed net, the knife glinting beneath it, and Makenna's hostage. It was easy enough to read what had happened. "They used a net on you?" rumbled Ryan as the other wolves fanned out around them.

"I could be wrong," said Makenna. "But I don't think these humans like me very much. Not that I'm complaining, but what brought you here?"

"The extremists attracted a news crew. I saw them on TV outside your building." And Ryan had almost lost his fucking shit. "You didn't answer my calls." That was when he *had* lost his fucking shit. Panic had seized his body, taken over his mind, and sent his wolf insane. His pack had managed to calm him just enough to instill some rationality into him. But now, as it became obvious just how much danger Makenna had been in, the rationality began to slip away.

Makenna inwardly winced at his words. She'd forgotten to take her phone off "silent" mode when she woke up. Even so . . . "I was a little busy here with Jeff and his buddies."

"I wonder if these little photos will feature on the news," said Jaime. That was when Makenna noticed she had her cell phone out, snapping pictures of the net, the knife, and the humans.

"I remember when Derren once uploaded a video of violent extremists on YouTube," said Roni. "It upset a *lot* of shifters."

Dante nodded. "Those humans had to disappear for a while. Come to think of it, I don't think they ever reappeared."

Ryan growled as he smelled something. Blood. *Makenna's* blood. "Where are you hurt, Kenna?" The words came out sharp and clipped.

"It's just a gash on my thigh. It's almost healing." She watched Ryan take slow, deliberate, predatory steps as he moved to stand in front of Jeff, his eyes cold, hard, and menacing. Ryan always looked unnerving. Right now, he looked downright terrifying.

"Was it *you* that made her bleed?" Ryan asked Jeff.

Makenna shivered. Ryan's normally bland voice vibrated with the need to *hurt*.

Jeff sneered. "Our Lord protects us. Your kind can do us no harm." His words were confident. His tone wasn't.

"Wrong," rumbled Ryan, edging into Jeff's personal space. The human stank of corruption, hatred, and a little bit of fear. "Very, very wrong."

"If you know about shifters," began Marcus, "you know how protective we are of our mates. You know we'll die for them, kill for them. That guy right there wearing the glower from hell . . . he's the mate of the female you targeted. I wouldn't like to be any of you right now."

Makenna started at that. Clearly Ryan had shared his belief with his pack mates, her wishes be damned.

"When the members of The Movement see you on the news and look at our photos, they won't be happy bunnies either." Dominic shook his head. He was referring to a band of shifters that protected their kind from the extremists. Not at all subtle or diplomatic, The Movement returned violence with violence—conveying that there would be repercussions for such prejudice and unprovoked attacks. That was most likely why the humans here all blanched.

"Yep," agreed Tao. "The Movement will match a name to every face, will find every one of you. I'd say 'God help you and your families,' but not a thing will save you from them."

"You didn't answer my question," Ryan growled at Jeff. *"Was it you who made her bleed?"* He barely sounded human. In truth, he didn't feel all that human either. With the exception of his time in captivity, Ryan never lost control; he never snapped, and he never lashed out. One thing he never, ever did was show his pain. He was always calm and controlled in emotionally intense situations. Emotions got in the way. But this was Makenna, and that made everything different.

She'd once asked him if she mattered to him—not as his mate, but as *Makenna*. At the time, he hadn't properly understood the distinction she was trying to make. Now he knew. It was one thing to panic because your mate was in danger and a whole other thing to panic because that person was so important that losing them would fucking destroy you.

"Yes," hissed Jeff. "I stabbed her. The sound the knife made as it sliced through her skin was—"

As Ryan's claws sliced out, his eyes glowing with anticipation, Makenna burst out, "Ryan, no! He's lying. He wants you to hurt him."

"I'll give him what he wants." With absolute fucking pleasure.

"Ryan, look at him. I mean *really* look at him. He's smiling. He's a freak who believes in 'his cause' that all shifters are evil and can't be allowed to live. He will happily die right here at your hands if it means it supports his argument that we're violent and dangerous. Don't give him what he wants. This is about more than just me, Ryan. More than about you. It's about our kind."

Maybe so, but that didn't matter to Ryan right then. The consequences didn't matter. Only she did. Only that she was hurt and could have been taken from him. Adrenalin and rage were pumping through his system, feeding his need for vengeance. The scent of her blood, the sight of the net, and the thought that he could have been too late—all those things were taunting him. He could hear pounding in his ears, his muscles were so tight they hurt, and his jaw ached from clenching his teeth so hard.

"She's right, Ryan." Dominic exhaled a disappointed sigh. "We can't kill him yet."

"I say we give him to Ally's *friend*." Roni was talking about Ally's foster brother, Cain, who was a member of The Movement.

"Good idea," said Trick. "Jeff here is a leader. He'll know a lot of important things, a lot of names."

Ryan was supposed to care about names and information? He glared at Trick. *"He. Hurt Her."*

"Yes," said Jaime. "Which is why she needs you right now."

Makenna did need him right then, which should have pissed her off but didn't. She was fast heading for an adrenalin crash. She needed Ryan to be as solid and steady as he normally was. But he didn't look inclined to calm down. That worried her. She'd never before seen him without his infamous control.

"He won't get away with what he's done," Dante assured Ryan. "He'll get all the pain he deserves. Just not here and now."

Yeah? That wasn't good enough for Ryan. He wanted to kill this fucker, wanted to see and smell his blood. Wanted to be the cause of his pain and fear and misery.

"He's just a pawn anyway," Tao pointed out.

Jeff frowned. "What do you mean, pawn?"

Tao gave him a cruel smile. "I mean that there's a very good chance that the person who sold you Makenna's name did it because they wanted you to kill her. And that that person was a shifter. If I'm right, it wasn't God's work you were doing today. It was the work of the very thing you loathe."

Makenna wouldn't put it past Remy to sic extremists on her.

"Trick, go get the SUV," Dante said before taking slow steps toward Ryan, as if conscious that trying to take Jeff away could prompt Ryan to pounce on the human. "Ryan, I know it's hard, but you have to step back."

No, Ryan didn't have to do that at all. It would be so easy to end the pitiful human's life. So effortless. All it would take was one claw to slice open Jeff's jugular. Just one single swipe, and he would be dead. But that was too quick. Almost merciful, really.

"Ryan," drawled Dante.

He could stab his claws right into the bastard's stomach, could slit him from groin to sternum. All the while, Ryan would watch the excruciating agony flash in Jeff's eyes. It would be so very satisfying. His wolf agreed, reminding him that his pack mates wouldn't be fast enough to stop him.

"Ryan," Dante repeated.

Or Ryan could do what his wolf wanted most: shift into his animal form, rip out the bastard's throat, and toss it at his friends. His wolf could then claw open his belly and—

"Ryan."

That soft voice penetrated his daze. He looked into his mate's cognac-brown eyes. "He hurt you. I recognize that knife." He'd seen wasp knives before. "I know what it can do. He would have killed you."

"But he didn't. I'm here. I'm safe."

"*They* would have killed you." She couldn't have fought off a mass attack.

"But you got here in time."

Barely. A minute later, and she could have been dead. His wolf growled, lashing out with his claws.

"You saved me." She smiled weakly. "And now I'd really like to hand this asshole over to Dante and just get out of here. I could do with a hug too."

If he weren't looking right into her eyes, Ryan would have thought she was just trying to distract him. But he could see the sincerity there—along with exhaustion and worry. She didn't need his anger right now.

Sensing Ryan's capitulation, Dante snatched Jeff from Makenna. The human flailed, struggling to get free. It was a fruitless attempt. Tao moved to Jeff and whispered something in his ear. Ryan had no idea what the Head Enforcer said, but Jeff stilled and blanched.

Makenna placed her hands on Ryan's chest. "You okay?"

Ryan wrapped his arms tight around her, burying his face in the crook of her neck. A hard exhale shuddered out of him. Feeling her pulse beat against his mouth helped ease the fear that had gripped him with iron jaws. He let her comfort him. Let her scent, touch, and voice smooth over him, settle his heartbeat, and thaw the cold rage that had iced his veins. His wolf, too, took comfort in her presence and warmth.

"I need to take a look at your leg." But Ryan didn't release her, just kept breathing her in.

She kissed his throat. "It's healing fast."

The SUV pulled up, and Dante quickly tossed Jeff into the trunk. The Beta then smiled at the other humans. "We know how much you all must love Jeff, so if any of you would like to come along and meet the members of The Movement, say so now."

It wasn't a shock when none of them said a word. They might be fanatical and prejudiced, but they had a sense of self-preservation. Or, at the very least, they had way too much fear to follow their leader into what would effectively be hell.

Dominic rapped his knuckles on the top of the trunk. "Did you hear that, Jeff? Me neither. There's nothing but blessed silence. Your disciples aren't as devoted to you as you thought, huh. That's gotta hurt."

Makenna sure hoped it did.

CHAPTER FOURTEEN

R eally, I'm fine," Makenna assured Madisyn, who had her on speakerphone so that Dawn and Colton could join the conversation. Suspecting they would see the news coverage soon enough, Makenna had called as soon as she reached Phoenix Pack territory to assure them she was okay.

"Give the Phoenix wolves our thanks," Dawn told her. "We owe that pack more than we'll ever be able to repay."

"You should have called me!" whined Madisyn. "I would have come! I would have helped you!"

Makenna smiled, touched by her friend's protectiveness. "I know you would have, which is exactly why I didn't call you." Madisyn hissed, not so touched by Makenna's protectiveness. "My boss called a few minutes ago; he said extremists turned up at the gas station this morning too. They did some marching and shouting outside."

Dawn hissed. "Let me guess. You no longer have a job."

"Good guess." It wasn't because she was a loner or that her boss was prejudiced against shifters. He simply couldn't afford to lose the business that extremists would chase off.

Madisyn bit out a curse. "Where's that Jeff fucker now?"

Dante had dropped Jeff off at Mercury Pack territory on their way here, certain that Ally's foster brother would come for him soon. But since Makenna promised Ryan she wouldn't reveal Ally's connection to The Movement, she simply said, "He's no longer a problem."

"How's Ryan doing?" asked Colton. "Not so well, I'm thinking."

From her position in the tunnel, she glanced into the kitchen, where most of the pack was gathered for lunch. Ryan was staring at her with his usual frown. His eyes weren't as wild now, but he was far from calm. "He's been better."

"Is Zac settling in all right?" asked Dawn.

Makenna smiled. "Yes, he's got the biggest crush on Hope. It's super cute. He's very happy here."

"I think you will be too."

"Huh?"

"Don't play with me, Makenna Wray; I've known you since you were a child. I know you better than most."

"Not better than me," snorted Madisyn.

"And I've seen the way Ryan looks at you," continued Dawn. "That male cares for you, just as you care for him. He might look like a menace to society at first glance, but he's an honorable person. He's a keeper. At your age, being alone might not be so bad. But at my age, when you realize you'll probably grow old alone and even die alone, it hurts. Don't be like me. If he offers you more than something casual, take it."

Chest tight, Makenna said, "I didn't realize how much you hurt inside, Dawn. I'm sorry." She should have seen it.

"Don't be sorry, sweetheart. There are many good things and many good people in my life. I don't have . . . what do you call them, Madisyn? Oh, pity parties. I don't have them. But a person can be happy and sad at the same time."

As Grace and Hope began to lay food out on the table, Makenna said her good-byes and ended the call. Ryan had saved her a seat between him and Zac. She slid into it with a smile, watching as both males piled food on her plate. Taking care of her, she knew. "You two are sweeties." Both males scowled at her, indignant. She laughed.

"I picked up too much stuff, so I dumped some of it on your plate, that's all," said Zac with a shrug.

Taryn smiled. "Don't let him fool you, Makenna. He was seriously worried when he saw the news footage of the extremists outside your building. We all were." The Alpha female jumped as she dropped her knife.

"Ooh, you're going to have a visitor," Makenna told her. At Ryan's look of confusion, she added, "She dropped her knife."

Ryan blinked. "Dropping a kitchen utensil symbolizes an upcoming visit?"

Makenna waved a dismissive hand. "You don't have to believe me, White Fang."

"I told you to drop—" He inhaled deeply. "You know what? Forget it." He'd already resigned himself to the fact that his mate wasn't totally sane.

"Jaime said your boss called on the drive here," Grace told Makenna. "Did he really fire you?"

"Yeah, but I can understand why. I'm not pissed at him; I'm pissed at the extremists." Because how was she supposed to afford her rent without a job?

"If the humans traced you to the gas station," began Gabe, "can they trace you to the shelter?"

Makenna shook her head. "I'm not listed as an employee there. There's no paperwork to link me with the place."

"Unless Remy tips them off," Tao pointed out. "Just like he told them your name and address."

"Dead men can't do anything," rumbled Ryan.

Meeting his gaze, Makenna found vengeance reigning there again. "Don't go after him, Ryan."

He grunted.

"You can't. Think about it. If you go to see him, he'll twist it around. He'll argue to the council that Dawn sent packs to intimidate him and spread lies about him. And then there's the other thing."

"What other thing?" asked Marcus before stuffing a forkful of food into his mouth.

"It might not be him."

Roni blinked. "Why would you think that?"

"All his attacks have been indirect and nonviolent."

"So maybe he's stepping up his game," said Tao.

"To the point that extremists are knocking at my door, attracting a news crew?" Makenna shook her head. "It's a really big escalation."

Tao shrugged. "Maybe he got pissed that his other attacks weren't having the desired effect."

Makenna tilted her head, allowing that.

"Who else could it be but Remy?" asked Dante.

Makenna smiled. "Dear old Deanne."

Ryan's frown deepened. "Remy's mother?"

"I pissed her off real good," she reminded him.

Taryn adjusted Kye's position on her lap. "You met her?"

Makenna took a sip of her Coke. "Ryan didn't tell you?"

Taryn snickered. "Ryan? Share stuff?"

Okay, the female had a point. Makenna gave a brief version of what happened. "What better way for her to get rid of me and away from her son than to sic the extremists on me?"

Trey tapped his fingers on the table. "There is a chance it was her. But there's also a chance he did this because he was majorly pissed at you for what you said to his mother."

Makenna pursed her lips. "He doesn't strike me as the impulsive type. He's too smart for that."

"Maybe. But, in any case, he's still a suspect when you consider what's going to happen now that you have the extremists' attention."

"What do you mean?"

It was Ryan who explained. "The extremists from today will probably skulk away in fear of The Movement. But it's likely they'll pass on your name and address to other extremists. You're on their radar now. Remy will expect you to lie low and hide out somewhere. Think of what that would mean for the shelter."

"It would leave Dawn short a staff member," Makenna realized.

"Not just any staff member," interrupted Trey, "but the staff member who rehomes the loners. He wouldn't want the children going anywhere, would he?"

Makenna cursed silently. She hadn't thought of that. It had seemed most likely to her that the culprit was Deanne. Now, she wasn't so sure. "No one will keep me away from the shelter." She'd find a way to get there without leading any watchers there. "I won't be forced into hiding either."

As much as part of Ryan wished she'd step back from the shelter, he knew it wouldn't be right to ask that of her. It wasn't in Makenna's nature to sit back and watch the people she cared for struggle. She wouldn't leave them when they needed her most. To ask her to do differently would be asking her to be someone she wasn't. If she wanted to keep volunteering at the shelter, he'd go along with her and keep her safe.

"You're not going to go back to your apartment, are you?" Zac said to Makenna. "I mean, more extremists could be waiting."

"My stuff is there."

"It's probably been trashed," Roni warned her. Sadly, she was most likely right.

Zac looked at Taryn. "Can Makenna stay with us for a while?"

"She's staying," Ryan firmly stated.

That definitive answer pissed her off a little, but Makenna decided not to snap at him. He was still freaked out and it wasn't the time to push him. Still, she had to point out one thing. "If the extremists somehow find out I'm staying here, it could turn their attention to you," Makenna warned. Some of the wolves snorted. "What don't I know?"

"Both our pack and the Mercury Pack had a run-in with them once before," Trey explained. "The people who invaded our territory mysteriously disappeared. The extremists have stayed away from us since then. They won't come here."

Greta spoke. "You're wrong. The extremists aren't smart enough to stay away. I'm telling you, we'll have trouble on our hands again." She threw Makenna a dirty look. "Surely there's somewhere else you could—"

"She's staying here," Ryan told the old woman.

Cheeks reddening, Greta said, "How can you want that hussy, Ryan? I told you why she was banished from her old pack, and you're still with her! You're worth more and you deserve better!" She smacked the table with her hand. "She's a danger to us, and you *swore* to protect your pack!"

Hiding her amusement, Makenna shrugged. "Sure, but it's not like he signed anything." Wow, Greta looked like she wanted to lunge down Makenna's throat.

"You might want to know," began Jaime, stifling a smile, "that Rhett uploaded my photos onto his blog. There have been a lot of comments from shifters and humans. They're outraged by the extremists' behavior. I mean, a net and a wasp knife . . . that's beyond cruel."

"I agree," said Dante, glancing at his cell phone. He looked up. "Taryn, Gabe just sent me a message; he said your uncle's here to see you."

Ryan's jaw tightened at the amused smile on his mate's face. "Don't say it."

She raised her hands. "I wasn't gonna."

He grunted, not the slightest bit convinced.

•••

Later that day, Makenna was sprawled out on the warm grass, enjoying the sun on her skin . . . and cursing inside her head. All in one day, she'd been attacked, lost her job, and been *evicted*. Her landlord had called ten minutes ago with that delightful bit of news. She'd argued that it wasn't legal to throw someone out of their home when they hadn't done anything wrong. He'd said that he needed to know his tenants were safe, that he couldn't guarantee that if she were there.

He was right. And so she didn't fight his decision. But it meant she had no home. Still, things could always be worse. Remy or Deanne had wanted to cut her off from Madisyn and Dawn—the only family she had. That would have hurt like nothing else could.

Hearing a slight rustle in the grass, she looked up to see a magnificently beautiful wolf. His fur was pure black, with the exception of the fur on his face, neck, and the inside of his ears, which was a creamy blond. *Ryan,* her senses told her.

He'd left her an hour earlier, told her he needed to do a perimeter check. But she'd suspected he wanted some time alone in his wolf form. Wanted the calm and solace that came from it.

The wolf padded over to her and licked at her jaw. She petted the dark, thick fur of his flank, making him release a satisfied growl. Smiling, she playfully shoved at his muzzle, expecting him to pounce in an equally playful move. Instead, he just looked at her.

Makenna rolled her eyes and sat upright. "So you're as serious as Ryan, huh?" Her wolf would make him play, but her wolf would also brand the shit out of him—something that wolves shouldn't do unless they were mates. Makenna needed to be 100 percent certain that Ryan was hers before she laid any such claim on him. Otherwise, it wouldn't be fair to him.

The wolf nuzzled her throat, so she lightly shoved him again and wagged her finger. Again, he just stared at her. "I want to play." After the shitty day she'd had, she needed some downtime. Playing with her favorite wolf would definitely give her that. "If you're not going to play, you have to leave."

He growled, eyes flashing human. Ryan—unlike the wolf—understood her words.

"Grouchy." She dived at the wolf, wrestling him to the ground. He squirmed and struggled free of her grip. Righting himself, he looked startled. Confused. A little lost. She shoved at his muzzle with a playful snarl. He swiped at her shoulder, claws sheathed. Ooh, progress. She lunged again, knocking him to the ground. He got up, looking exasperated. That was better than him looking lost.

"I need to up my game here, huh." Makenna jumped to her feet and took off. The wind whipped her skin and the branches abraded her cheeks and arms as she ran through the trees, the wolf fast on her heels. Birds and other wildlife scattered.

Sensing the wolf closing in on her, she put on a burst of speed—racing into a clearing, where she spun to face him with a growl. Skidding to a halt in front of her, he bared his teeth. She snapped hers. And . . . he wagged his tail. "That's it."

They tussled, wrestled, and pounced until Makenna flopped to her back, out of breath. The wolf stood over her, triumphant. Bones cracked and popped as his body shifted shape, and she then had a very naked Ryan on top of her. She wound her arms around his neck. "Your wolf played with me. He's fun."

"Only with you."

She moaned as Ryan kissed her, twining his tongue with hers. Within moments, she was just as naked, and he was giving her exactly what she needed, pounding into her at a feral pace that soon had them both exploding.

In the aftermath, she snuggled into his side as he lay on his back. Sated and riding her post-orgasm buzz, she said, "This territory is pretty awesome." Her wolf was utterly relaxed, surrounded by the scents of

Ryan, pine, grass, and sun-warmed earth. The only sounds she could hear were those of wildlife and water trickling in the near distance.

Cupping her chin, Ryan lifted her head to meet her eyes. "Then why do I hear a little sadness in your voice?" He didn't like it. Wanted to fix whatever was wrong.

"There must have been countless times in your life when you've roamed your territory and found a cozy little spot where you feel safe. My wolf . . . she never had that. I never had it."

"You can have it, and you know it," he said a little too sharply. This place was her home. She just had to step forward and claim it. His wolf was just as frustrated by her failure to do so. Others would have been surprised to see his wolf—always so serious and gloomy—playing with her. Ryan wasn't. The animal adored her, he considered her his own; there wasn't a thing he wouldn't do for her.

"So, you told your pack that you believe we're mates."

"They guessed. They agree with me. You're the only one that doesn't."

He looked so hurt by that, like she was rejecting him. Makenna snuggled closer. "I would be proud to be your mate. You're the full package. Loyal. Strong. Hot. Honorable. A born protector who never lets people down. That's—What? What did I say?" Because he was averting his gaze. "Ryan?"

"I let you down today."

She frowned. "How?"

"I asked you to trust me to keep you safe. I promised I would. But I wasn't there for you today." If there was one thing Ryan was good at, it was keeping people, under his protection, safe. But his mate had been in danger, and he hadn't been there. That fact had tormented him and his wolf all day long. "I should have stayed with you this morning."

"That's ridiculous. You have a job, a very important job."

"If I'd been with you earlier, you would never have ended up tangled in a net." Like an animal.

"For someone so practical, you can be seriously dumb sometimes." Her wolf totally agreed. Makenna propped her chin on his chest. "It's not that *you* should have been there. It's that they *shouldn't* have been there. They were the ones who were in the wrong place, *not* you. And the person who's most to blame for all of it is Remy." Assuming it wasn't Deanne.

"He'll pay for it." His wolf growled, fully supportive of that idea.

"But not yet. After the meeting with the council, sure. Until then, we don't rise to whatever he does. Okay? Okay?"

No, it wasn't okay at all. It *especially* wasn't okay that she was right— the practical side of him couldn't deny that. "You need to understand something. I know we need to be smart in how we handle this situation. So I'll hold back." Even though it was killing him. "But if Remy hurts you, if he even *tries* to harm you, I'll kill him."

Makenna rubbed her nose against his. "Can I watch? I'll bring popcorn. We'll make a day of it."

Ryan almost smiled. "Insane." Still, he'd never want her to be anything but exactly who she was. She hadn't been in his life long, but she'd already brightened and refreshed it. If the extremists had had their way today, his life would have been dark and bleak.

She cocked her head as his expression hardened. "What's wrong?"

"You could have died today."

"I did worry for a minute when I noticed there were some magpies." At his baffled look, she explained, "You know, 'one for sorrow, two for luck, three for a wedding, four for death.' At first, I thought there were four, but then I realized there were only three. I wonder who's getting married. Why are you scowling at me?"

He just grunted. This was what insane people did, and he'd just have to get used to it. Besides, she'd said she'd be proud to have him as her mate, so there wasn't a lot that could upset him right then—especially since he had her here at his territory for good. If she thought it was temporary that was her mistake. "Do you need someone to go to your apartment and see if there's anything to salvage?"

"Actually, it's no longer my apartment. I've been evicted."

"Evicted?"

"My landlord said he'll box up my stuff." At Ryan's growl, she said, "I thought you'd be happy about it. We both know you want me staying here indefinitely."

"He's being unfair to you." Ryan would never be happy about something like that.

"But not unfair to the other tenants. He's doing right by them."

It was typical of her to put the safety of others before that of herself. It irritated him. He knotted a hand in her hair. "You didn't call me for help earlier because you thought you were protecting me. I get that. But don't do it again." It was his right to protect her.

Both Makenna and her wolf balked at his words. "Like you, I protect the people who matter to me."

His breath almost caught in his throat. "I matter?"

"You damn well know you do."

With this grip on her hair, Ryan pulled her closer and took her mouth. Took it with an intensity and possessiveness that reminded her she was his. Would always be his. The sooner she accepted that, the happier they'd both be.

As usual, Ryan woke at six a.m. Seeing Makenna naked and warm beside him, he was tempted to stay where he was. He pressed a light kiss to her throat. She grumbled something unintelligible and rolled onto her side. Being a deep sleeper, she didn't wake as he washed and dressed before—with a kiss to her shoulder—he left to do his morning perimeter check.

Outside, he picked up Zac's scent. It was too strong to come from the night before. Ryan frowned. The juvenile was never up this early. Following the scent, he found Zac just past the fringe of the forest sitting on a fallen tree trunk, dark circles under his eyes. Looking up, he tipped his chin in greeting.

Ryan took a seat beside him. "Everything okay?"

Zac twisted the blades of grass in his hands. "I had a shitty dream, that's all."

"Do you have nightmares a lot?" The kid just shrugged. Ryan detested the idea that Zac was hurting, but he didn't know how to get him to talk.

What had Makenna once said? *"Zac feels like we'll judge him because we can't understand what he's been through."*

Ryan, however . . . maybe he did understand. Sort of. Maybe if he made Zac see that he could relate to him in some ways, the kid would open up. But he couldn't expect Zac to expose such a deep wound unless Ryan was prepared to do the same for him. So Ryan did the one thing he'd sworn he'd never do: he shared what had happened to him all those years ago. "I was once taken by a rival pack." That made Zac's gaze snap to his. "They tortured me for weeks. Kept me drugged so I couldn't shift. Tied me up so I couldn't free myself."

Zac swallowed. "Trey and the others came for you?"

"They didn't know where I was."

"How did you get out?"

"I gave control over to my wolf. Feral, he had enough strength to shift and get free. Then he killed them, ripped them to pieces. They died too quick, in my opinion." That probably wasn't the most comforting thing to say to the kid, he mused with irritation. "My point is that I know what it's like to have people do things to you—hurtful things, humiliating things. I know what it's like to feel helpless. I hated that, I hated them, and I hated myself for not being able to stop it." Just thinking about it made fury bubble inside him. Still, he kept talking. "I know what it's like to have to relive those moments at night in your sleep. It's hard to move past something that you have to relive over and over. I'm the last person who'd ever judge you. Was it the Alpha who hurt you?"

Zac was quiet for so long, Ryan thought he wouldn't answer. Finally, the kid said, "It wasn't just him."

"Who else?"

"The pack healer."

His wolf snarled. "What did they do?"

"The healer, David, took me in after my parents died. I was okay with it. He was always nice to everyone, you know? Kind." Zac looked down at the ground. "But it's not real." A long pause. "They're like Remy."

"You mean abusive?"

Zac nodded. "The Alpha's the worst. He likes to see people in pain. David always healed me so there was no evidence."

A growl rumbled up Ryan's chest. He wanted to know every detail, but he knew from personal experience just how hard those details could be to share. "Did you think people here would judge you for not being able to defend yourself against someone bigger and stronger than you?"

"Not for that." Zac met his eyes then. "I wanted to run for a long time. But . . . I was scared. The night I left, David came into my room, said he was taking me to Brogan, the Alpha. My wolf . . . he just lost it. Like he couldn't take anymore. He took control, and I shifted, and my wolf went crazy on his ass. He killed David."

"Your wolf went feral. In dangerous situations, people can lose control of their wolf."

Zac shook his head. "You don't get it. I didn't try to stop him when he attacked David. I didn't try to pull my wolf back. I just watched. The only thing I did was urge him to run when I heard people coming. That's it. David is Brogan's brother. He's dead because of me. When I say they'll come for me, I mean it."

"They'll die if they do." It was a vow. "I'll end them. I won't allow them to hurt you again. You got me?" He needed Zac to believe that.

"I got you." The words were low but strong.

"Good. It was brave of you to share what happened. Is it okay with you if I give the basics to the pack?" They needed to be prepared for the inevitable battle ahead. "They will not judge you."

After a moment, the kid gave a curt nod. He looked a little lighter. Maybe opening up had helped him in some way. Ryan hoped so.

When he returned to his room, it was to find Makenna dressing. He shared Zac's story with his mate, not at all surprised when she paled and sank onto the edge of the bed.

"No wonder he's so sure they'll find him," she said. "If he killed the Alpha's brother, they'll never stop until they do."

"As I told Zac, we'll kill them if they come."

Makenna nodded. "I know. That's why, on some level, I hope the bastards do."

CHAPTER FIFTEEN

Ryan had just finished a training session with Dante, Tao, and the other enforcers when his cell phone rang. He was surprised by the identity of the caller. "Garrett," he greeted.

"One day, you could try saying *hello*."

"I could." But he probably wouldn't.

"I'm calling about the salamander brand."

Ryan stopped in his tracks. "You remembered something?" It had been over three weeks since he'd mentioned the matter to Garrett.

"No, but you know I don't like unanswered questions, so I looked into it. Asked a few people. The Alpha of a wolf pack in New Zealand made a point of branding each of his wolves. His name was Conrad Griffin. He was a sick bastard."

"Was?"

"He's been dead for seven years now. From what I've heard, the new Alpha's nothing like him."

Ryan would decide that for himself after he'd done some research. "Thanks, Garrett." Ending the call, he went to his room, took a shower, and then pulled out his laptop. He could have asked Rhett to do the research, but it wasn't right to share any of this without Makenna's permission.

Two hours later, Ryan's head was swimming with information. He wanted to share it with her, and yet he didn't. Some of it would hurt her; he didn't want that. But she was already hurting, wasn't she?

Torn, Ryan spent the rest of the day debating what to do. Makenna deserved to know her past. But she'd already told him she didn't want to know. The thing was, he didn't believe that. Not for a minute. And neither did Dawn.

That night, as they lay in what had become their "spot" in the forest, she braced herself on one elbow and said, "Okay, spill it." She jabbed a finger at him. "Don't blow me off. Something's been bothering you all day. I gave you the chance to tell me, you didn't. So now I'm asking, what is it?"

He played his fingers through her hair. "You'll be mad at me."

Makenna stilled as various bad scenarios ran through her head. "What?"

"I couldn't let it alone, Kenna. Not when it hurts you."

Just like that, she knew what this was about. "What have you done?"

"I haven't killed them, if that's what you're asking." He rolled onto his side to face her. "You have a choice to make: you can ask me to share what I've discovered about your past, or you can tell me to keep it to myself and we'll never speak of this again."

She ground her teeth. "I trusted you with my secrets, Ryan."

"I haven't shared them with a soul."

"All I asked was that you let it lie."

"I'll never overlook something that hurts you." Ever. She tried to stand, but he curled an arm around her waist and pulled her close. "I can tell you about your pack. About your father. I can tell you what your real name is, what your mother's real name was." He raked a hand into her hair. "If you don't want those facts, I'll drop this forever. I just wanted you to have the choice." He rested his forehead against hers. "But I'm sorry if I've hurt you."

She knew he was; knew he never meant to hurt her, so she couldn't stay mad at him. She'd always thought she didn't want any answers. It should have been easy to tell him to do as he'd promised and drop it forever. But now that the answers were close, now that curiosity was biting her, it was hard to let it go. There was no harm in asking at least one question, right? "What was my mom's real name?"

Ryan had suspected she'd want to know that, if nothing else. "Sinead Gannon."

Makenna frowned. The name wasn't bad, but it didn't suit her mom at all. She shouldn't ask. She should drop it, but . . . "And mine?"

"I don't know about your first name. Your surname would have been Gannon-Paxton."

Makenna's nose wrinkled. "Why couldn't you find out my first name?"

"You weren't born in the pack. It's a long story."

That made absolutely no sense. She inhaled deeply, unable to resist asking, "What's the story?"

"You're from the Geraint Pack in New Zealand. When the old Alpha, Conrad, was in charge, it was very cultlike. He was controlling and oppressive. He branded each of his wolves as a symbol of dominance and ownership. He had a tattoo of a salamander, which was why he used it as a symbol for the pack. No one complained. They saw him as their savior."

"Savior?" she repeated, incredulous.

"The prior Alpha was even worse. When Conrad stepped in and killed him, the pack was grateful. He rebuilt the place, gained them more land, found them a healer, and brought order. In doing all that, he bought their loyalty and took control. They felt indebted to this person who convinced them that everything he did was for the good of the pack. They were devoted to him."

"Why did he banish my mother?"

Ryan slowly skimmed a hand up and down her arm as he spoke. "Your parents weren't true mates, but they cared for each other and asked Conrad's permission to mate. There were no unsanctioned pairings. He arranged every mating, whether those wolves were true mates or not, whether they cared for each other or not."

"But that would be sabotaging the future of his pack. Only true mates or imprinted couples can develop mating bonds, and only mated couples can have pups. He had to know that."

"It's said that he wasn't altogether sane. Maybe that blinded him. Maybe he didn't want his pack to expand because it was easier to control a small one."

"He didn't give my parents his permission to mate, did he?"

Ryan shook his head. "But imprinting can happen without a couple's control. They probably tried to hide it at first. But once their scents mixed it would have been impossible. Conrad was furious. Especially since it was obvious by your mother's scent that she was in the early stages of pregnancy. He wanted to publicly execute them as an example to the others. But your parents were able to escape. Probably because Conrad wouldn't have ever expected them to dare try."

"Wait, *both* of them escaped?"

"Conrad sent his enforcers after them, but they were smart. They disappeared."

Her mother had told her that she and Makenna were banished when she was a *toddler*. If Ryan's info was to be believed, Makenna had never known her pack at all. "But . . . my father."

"Nobody knows what happened to him. I couldn't find out, Kenna, I'm sorry."

"Why would my mom lie and tell me we were banished? Why wouldn't she tell me the full story?"

"Maybe the truth was too painful for her to talk about. Maybe she intended to tell you what really happened, when you were older."

Maybe. "You called Conrad 'the old Alpha.' He's dead now?"

Ryan nodded. "Which means I can't kill him." And that was terribly disappointing. "The new Alpha seems to be a good one. He's also your mother's younger brother. He's been looking for you and your parents for a long time."

Makenna puffed out a long breath, overwhelmed. The answers she'd fooled herself into believing she didn't want were much worse than she'd expected. *So* much worse. Her Alpha had not only been a traitorous bastard but a twisted one. He hadn't banished her mother, he'd refused to allow her to mate and then he'd hunted her—forcing her into hiding. As for her father . . . Makenna still had no idea what happened to him. She did know one thing. "My parents didn't deserve what happened to them."

"Neither did you."

"I don't really know what to do with all that information right now." It was too much for her to process while she felt so raw. And, honestly, she didn't want to process it. She didn't want to lie there dwelling on how different things could have been. She just wanted to let her mate hold her and comfort her.

Not liking that she was retreating inward but understanding why she would wish to, he said, "You don't have to do anything with it." He dabbed a light kiss on her mouth. Gripping his nape, she tried to take over the kiss—to make it rough, wild. He didn't let her. He kissed her soft and slow and deep, skimming one hand up her thigh and under her dress to cup her ass.

As Ryan possessively dug his teeth hard into her throat, she hissed in warning. He growled. "Mine to bite," he reminded her. He expected to see a spark of defiance in her eyes. Instead, there was sadness and longing. "Tell me your fears, Kenna. They're the only things left jamming the bond."

Makenna worried her lower lip. His words weren't coaxing; they were a pure demand. Her time had run out, just as he'd warned her it soon would. She couldn't really blame him for his insistence on the truth, especially when he believed it would be the answer to their problems. Unlike her, he didn't see it as a risk or as something that could lead to the end of what they had. He truly believed that the mating bond was waiting for them to clear the path. She didn't have that same faith, and she didn't want to gamble and lose him.

The truth was, she loved him. But that wasn't an excuse to hold her to him like this by dragging her heels. And that was exactly what she was selfishly doing. If there were a female waiting for him somewhere—her wolf snarled at the very thought—he deserved to know and be free to find her. Rising to her feet, she folded her arms over her chest and took a deep breath. "Okay. Fine. Let's find out once and for all if you're right."

Ryan got to his feet, not liking her defensive body language or the distance she'd placed between them. He also didn't like the way she was looking at him. Sad. Regretful. Moments went by, but she said nothing. "Tell me, Kenna."

She straightened her shoulders, trying to ignore the anxiety curdling in her stomach. Her lungs seemed to hurt with every breath. She wasn't ready to let him go yet. But her instincts told her that it was exactly what she'd have to do. "You'll want me to rely on you." Swallowing the emotion clogging her throat, she admitted, "I don't think I can, even though I want to."

"Because you lost the last person you did rely on." He understood that. It was a fear Ryan could easily chase away. "You won't lose me, Kenna. I'm not going anywhere."

"Yes, you are." Her smile was sad. "Because there's no mating bond." There was nothing at all there. But she would *not* cry. Even though her throat ached, her chest was painfully tight, and her world was fucking falling apart, she wouldn't cry in front of him. She wouldn't guilt him into staying with her. He didn't deserve that.

"That's because you're holding something else back."

Cold all of a sudden, she hugged herself as she shook her head. "No, Ryan, I'm not. That's the only fear standing in the way of me ever accepting a mate."

Ryan advanced on her, gripping her hips when she tried to back away. "If that had been the only thing jamming the frequency, the mating urge would have kicked in by now."

"Only if we were true mates."

"We are," he growled.

"There's no mating bond, Ryan. I don't feel it, and neither do you. *There's nothing there.*"

"Then something else is jamming it."

"There is nothing else! You were wrong!" She shoved at his chest, but he didn't budge an inch.

"I know I'm not wrong. If I was, we'd be at least partially imprinted by now." The vulnerability in her expression made him want to punch something. "Look at the facts, Kenna. Imprinting can happen without the conscious decision of the couple. I've never wanted anything as much as I want you. I told you before, I'd kill to have you. When I say you belong to me, I fucking mean it. Nothing and no one will ever take you from me. You can't feel that way about someone who isn't your mate and *not* imprint on them unless you mean nothing to them." He didn't know what Makenna felt for him, but he believed she felt something.

"Imprinting would never happen for us. Not given your feelings about it."

He frowned at her, not understanding.

"Growing up, you saw how it can go wrong. Your parents made themselves and you miserable. If they had just waited for their true mates—"

"Their relationship isn't bad because they're not true mates. It's because they didn't work at it. Instead of trying to fix their problems, they constantly lashed out at each other. Gwen blames just about everything and everyone for her unhappiness. She constantly tells him she wishes she'd waited for her true mate. Galen just laughs and dares her to leave, even though her words hurt him. They poisoned their own relationship."

Ryan could see that his answer had knocked her off balance. Apparently, Marcus was right: she'd thought his past would stop him from ever imprinting on someone. He rested his forehead against hers. "There is a mating bond. We just can't feel it." He didn't understand why. Maybe he was the one jamming it. But he believed with every breath in his body that it was there. When he saw that she was about to object, he said, "Even if I'm wrong, it doesn't change that you're mine and I'm keeping you."

He kissed her, pouring his hunger and resolve into it so she'd feel and taste his sincerity. She kissed him back, but there was a hesitance to it. His mate was holding herself back from him. He'd never tolerate that. Collaring her throat, he hardened the kiss, dominating and consuming and owning. Claws pricked his arms, warning him not to push too far. Ryan growled. He'd push as hard as he damn well had to until she understood and accepted that she was his.

Makenna told herself to pull back, to walk away. She'd gambled and she'd lost. He wasn't hers to kiss or touch. In objection, her wolf raked Makenna with her claws. Well, the wolf could fuck off. There was no changing the situation. If there were a mating bond, they would have felt it by now. It was as simple as that.

Was she surprised that Ryan argued against her point? No. He was too freaking stubborn to admit he was wrong. So stubborn that he'd continue to hang around for months and months, waiting for the non-existent bond to make an appearance. That wasn't fair to either of them. It was possible that all that time together would spark the imprinting process—the selfish part of her wanted to grab that opportunity with both hands. But she couldn't shake the feeling that she would be stealing him from what fate had in store, from someone better suited to him.

Yet, she didn't fight him when he took her to the ground and draped himself over her. She didn't object when he pushed up her dress and settled between her thighs. Didn't tell him to stop when he snapped off her panties and slipped a finger between her folds.

Once more, she told herself. She'd have him once more. Then she'd let go what was never hers to begin with.

Ryan should have been relieved when she suddenly threw herself into the kiss and arched into his hand, but it felt wrong. He'd been balls deep in Makenna more times than he could count. She could be defiant, mischievous, and wild in bed. But the way she clung to him now . . . there was something desperate about it.

"This isn't a farewell fuck, Makenna." Her eyes turned glossy with unshed tears. "Don't cry," he growled. He couldn't be sensitive or patient right then. He was pissed at her for being willing to walk away. Pissed at the bond for being just out of his reach.

"I'm not who fate gave you."

"You think I give a fuck about fate? I make my own decisions. I choose my own path. I choose *you*." To punctuate that, he drove a finger inside her. He grunted as her claws dug into his back.

"You wouldn't find that so easy to say if you weren't convinced we were mates."

Yes, he would. Ryan didn't care about her because she was his mate; he cared about her because she was Makenna. Strong, brave, protective, loyal, playful, and a little crazy. She was under his skin, and there would be no getting her out. "You and me . . . There's no going back, Kenna." He twisted his hand, rubbing her G-spot. Bucking, she gasped into his mouth. "You don't get to walk away."

She bit down on her lip as he shoved a second finger inside her. Despite the topic of conversation, she was wet and aching for him. That didn't surprise her. Her body always responded to him, was even turned on by being pinned down with his body weight. "It's you who'll walk away."

"Why would I walk away?" He tugged down the top of her dress just enough to bare her breasts. The material bunched up beneath them, raising them to his mouth.

Her breath caught in her throat as his tongue curled around her nipple. "When you realize you're wrong, you'll—"

"Makenna, you're not fucking hearing me." This had nothing to do with whether he was right or wrong. "No matter what, you belong to me." Withdrawing his fingers, he pulled off his T-shirt and snapped open his fly. His cock sprang out, heavy and throbbing. He needed to be in her, dominating her, driving home the truth. Ryan grabbed her hips and eased a little of his cock inside her. "Arms above your head."

She narrowed her eyes. "Why?"

"You don't get to touch what's not yours." He almost smiled at her growl. "You're mine, Makenna. Make no mistake about it. I own you. I'm going to take what I own. Are you going to accept that? Are you going to accept that I'm yours?" She didn't respond. "Then put your hands above your head." She did as he ordered—but very, very slowly.

"Good girl." He lapped at a mark on her neck as he moved in and out of her with slow, deep thrusts. She felt so fucking good. Smelled so fucking good. Every one of his senses was filled with her and drunk on her. "Can you feel how tight your pussy squeezes me, Kenna?" He nipped her throat. "Like it never wants me to leave. That's what scares you, doesn't it? That I'll leave." He hiked one of her legs up higher, allowing him to go even deeper. "I told you I won't. Don't you trust me?"

She fisted her hands in the grass. "I know you'd keep your word if I asked for it."

Ryan got it then. She worried he'd find out they weren't mates but stay with her anyway . . . merely because he'd sworn he would. He could understand that. He wouldn't want her to be with him for the wrong reasons. He was about to say as much, but then she tried to move her arms. "No."

That one word vibrated with authority and power. It impressed her wolf. And it triggered that defiant switch in Makenna's brain. She snarled, "I want—"

"I know what you want." For him to fuck her rough and fast. "But you can't have it."

So Makenna fought him. She kicked, shoved, and struggled to be free, but the bastard pressed more of his weight on her and collared her throat. The dominant hold was firm and tight, but not tight enough to hurt. Just tight enough to remind her who he thought was in charge right then. It was instinctive to freeze. "Let. Go."

He thrust hard. "What's wrong, Kenna? Is this too slow for you? You want it faster?" She just grunted her assent. "Tough. I'll fuck this pussy however I want. Because it belongs to me." He lunged deep once, twice. "Now . . . hands above your head."

Not at all intimidated, Makenna fought him again. Well, she *tried*. It was kind of hard to fight someone when you could barely move and there was a strong hand wrapped around your throat. But she didn't give up—biting, scratching, and squirming. His grip on her throat flexed just enough to make her wheeze a little. When she stilled, his thumb drew a soothing, almost rewarding circle.

"Stop fighting me, Kenna." Ryan punched his hips hard, and her pussy tightened almost painfully around his cock. "You're mine, and I'm yours. Accept it." Another punch of his hips. "Fucking accept it."

Makenna bit his chin. Not breaking skin, just cautioning him. "There's no mating bond. Accept *that*."

He had to admire her spirit. "Maybe there isn't." Of course, he didn't believe that for even a second. "But we'll be mated, Kenna, one way or the other." If that meant imprinting, fine. He didn't give a damn how they bonded just as long as they did. He refused to give her up. "Or are you going to lie and tell me you don't want that?" He licked and sipped at her mouth. "Lie, Kenna. Do it. I dare you." She didn't, and he rewarded her with two hard thrusts. "See, we both want the same thing. All you have to do is reach out and take it."

He made it sound so simple. And so very tempting that Makenna felt herself wavering, especially while her wolf was urging her to claim him. If he wanted to take the chance and forsake his mate, that was his choice, right? It wasn't like she was taking advantage of someone naïve and dimwitted. He was a big boy, quite capable of making his own decisions. He fully understood the choice he was making and all the issues around it. He wasn't impulsive, which meant he'd thought this through. Still . . . "You have to be sure. You have to be one hundred percent positive that I'm who you want, no matter what."

Ryan slid both hands into her hair, pinning her with his gaze. "You're all I want. All I'll ever want." He circled his hips. "You're mine, and I'm yours. Say it." He thrust with an impatient growl. "Fucking say it."

Makenna inhaled deeply, tired of fighting him—tired of fighting herself and her wolf too. He'd made his choice. Fuck fate. "I'm yours, and you're mine." Triumph, satisfaction, and naked possessiveness glinted in his rarely expressive eyes. Then all thoughts were sucked from her brain as he began to violently hammer in and out of her. "Fuck." She held tight, claws digging so deep into his shoulders that she drew blood. A growl of approval rumbled in his chest. So she raked her claws over his back deep enough to leave permanent brands.

Ryan paused only long enough to hook her legs over his shoulders, and then he was pounding into her again—deeper this time, so deep he knew it hurt her a little. Her pussy tightened, bathing his cock in cream, and she arched into every thrust.

Fisting her hair, he yanked her head aside to expose her throat. He licked and sucked at the spot on her neck he'd chosen, letting her know what was coming. Then he bit. Sank his teeth down hard, tasting blood. Makenna's pussy squeezed and fluttered around him as she came, screaming. All the while, he licked and sucked at the bite, making it a definitive brand that would be recognized for exactly what it was—a claiming mark.

Ryan grunted as Makenna reared up and bit the crook of his neck. No, she wasn't just biting him; she was marking him. Claiming him right back. That knowledge threw him right over the fucking edge. Tightening his fist in her hair, he jammed his cock deep and exploded inside his mate.

Boneless, Makenna lay with her eyes closed as her body was racked by little aftershocks. Ryan was irrevocably hers now, and that knowledge warmed every part of her. Still, the whole thing was bittersweet, because there was no bond to accompany the claiming. The absence of it was a physical ache. The only thing that eased it was the knowledge that the imprinting process would now surely begin.

Letting her legs slide from his shoulders, Ryan licked at the fresh bite as his now-relaxed wolf rumbled in satisfaction. It was higher on her neck than most claiming marks were. He wanted it to be the first thing she noticed every morning; wanted everyone who looked at her to know she was taken. "Now you can't ever again argue that you belong to me."

She frowned. "Actually—"

"Don't dare even try it," he warned her. But she was laughing. He nipped her jaw.

"Hey!"

He rolled onto his back, taking her with him so she sprawled on top of him. "Then don't tease me."

"But it's fun."

He grunted.

"Yes, it is. You have to admit, you wouldn't want me any other way."

Ryan frowned. "Actually—"

"Fuck you, White Fang." She chuckled. Then she gave her wolf what the animal had wanted for a long time.

The woman could shift fast, thought Ryan as he suddenly had a beautiful silver wolf standing over him. He stroked her neck as she licked his jaw. A butterfly flew in their direction, snatching her attention. The wolf chased it, trying to swat it with her paw. Apparently she was easily distracted. That assumption was proven when the sound of a bee had her whirling, searching for the insect. Ryan almost smiled. His wolf lunged for the surface, wanting time with his mate. Ryan retreated and gave it to him.

Seeing that her mate had shifted, the female playfully snapped her teeth and bounded away. The male raced through the trees, following the scent of his mate. She was fast. But he was faster. Could track her anywhere. Soon she was in his sight. The male wolf knew there was a stream ahead. Knew she would have to turn. He took another path; came at her from the front.

The female didn't halt as her mate neared. Didn't try to skirt him. She pounced with a bark, knocked him to the ground. He got to his feet. Alert. Still. She didn't like that. Her snarl was a taunt; she wanted to play. She'd teach him how.

The male followed her lead. They wrestled. Tumbled each other to the ground. Playfully bit, licked, and clawed. Then he mounted her, biting her nape. Claimed her as his mate just as his human had. The male wolf understood there should be a mating bond. Was confused that he didn't feel it. Urged his human half to find it.

As Ryan and Makenna returned to their human skin, sprawled side by side, he promised his wolf he'd clear whatever jammed the frequency of the mating bond. Nothing got to stand between him and his mate. Nothing.

CHAPTER SIXTEEN

Ryan wasn't on duty the next morning, but he still woke at his usual hour thanks to his internal clock. And there was his mate. She always looked young in her sleep. Deceptively harmless.

The claiming bite on her neck caught his eye, filling him with a masculine satisfaction he doubted could ever be equaled. It was official now. Makenna Wray was no longer the person he was trying to convince was his mate; she *was* his mate. There was no going back, only forward.

It bothered him that she still didn't believe they were true mates. But nowhere near as much as before, because it meant she'd *chosen* him—not because fate paired them, but because she cared. From Makenna's perspective, she'd forsaken her true mate to be with Ryan, to claim him and allow him to claim her in return. A person wouldn't do that unless they cared deeply.

If the situation were reversed, he would have done the same. Like he told her, she was all he wanted, all he'd ever want. He couldn't imagine anyone else fitting him the way she did.

He wasn't lacking in self-insight. He knew he was so emotionally disconnected that he depended too much on facts. He knew he could be much too serious and didn't know how to enjoy himself. Makenna balanced him out. Made him see the emotional connotations of situations, allowing him to look at things from different perspectives. She forced him to play, to joke, and to not take things too seriously.

Just the same, Ryan balanced her out. Makenna could be so blinded by emotion that she didn't always consider things from outside the box. By pointing out the facts, he pushed her to do so. Also, although Makenna's playful and mischievous nature wasn't a bad thing, those traits manifested themselves into a need to provoke and antagonize whenever she was annoyed. Ryan made her consider the consequences of her actions—the lesson was slow going, but he had hope.

Additionally, whereas Ryan felt little empathy, Makenna felt *way* too much. So much so that she put others first, living more for the shelter than she did for herself. Ryan would never allow that. He would force her to see her own worth, just as she taught him to see his. He'd always felt like he had something to prove, that he needed to earn his worth. She never made him feel that way. Never complained about how tactless he was or how few pretty words he gave her. Nor did she criticize or judge him for being so emotionally disconnected.

They complemented and strengthened each other, fit too well to *not* be true mates. The rest of the pack agreed. They hadn't been at all surprised when he and Makenna went for dinner last night, claimed and mated. But they had been shocked as all shit to hear there was no mating bond. It was fiercely bothering the females.

Makenna's eyelids fluttered open, and it was only then he realized he'd been circling her claiming mark with his thumb. "Didn't mean to wake you."

She snuggled closer to him and pressed a kiss to his collarbone. "Go back to sleep."

Ryan slid his hand down to rest on her ass. "Can't." But he'd stay with her, watch over her while she slept.

"Sure you can." The words were whispered against his skin as she petted his chest. "Try. For me."

Purely to indulge her, he closed his eyes and enjoyed her petting and stroking him. Her hand soon went limp and her breathing evened out. Ryan just lay with her, content and relaxed while he had the scent of his mate in his lungs, her skin beneath his hands, and her—

His eyes snapped open. He'd almost dozed off. Actually, if the bedside clock were to be believed, he *had* dozed off. For over two hours. He rolled onto his back, grabbed his cell phone from the small cabinet, and checked the time. It seemed the clock wasn't lying.

Makenna hummed, having woken at the loss of his warmth. "What's wrong?"

"It's eight o'clock," he said, disbelieving.

She frowned. "So?" Realization then dawned. "You fell back asleep? That's good."

He grunted, returning to her.

"And it's nice to wake up and find you here. You're usually gone."

Something in her voice made Ryan frown. "That hurts you."

"Hurts? No, I know your job is important. But imagine if every time you woke up, I'd already left. It would be nice to have me here for a change, right?"

Ryan scowled at the thought of her gone each time he awoke. He liked that she was the first thing he saw when he woke up each morning. Liked being able to kiss her before he left, even if she were asleep. "I'll change some of my shifts around."

Makenna blinked, sure she'd misheard him. "Say what?"

"I don't need to do the early perimeter run six days a week. I'll reduce it to two."

"I wasn't trying to guilt you into changing your hours."

"I'm doing it because I want to." And because anything that even minutely upset her wasn't acceptable to him. "Just like you're going to reduce the amount of days you work at the shelter a week. You don't take a single day off."

She narrowed her eyes. "We talked about this already. The shelter is important to me."

"It should be. And it should be part of your life. But it shouldn't *be* your life."

"Says the person who works longer and harder than the other enforcers." It was more than that, though. She'd come to realize that his job was all tangled up in who he was. Probably because he'd started training when he was just a child. "I'm not complaining. I'm just saying you're being a little hypocritical here."

"I've just said I'll change some of my shifts around." His mate slowly raised a brow at him. "You don't think I will?"

"I think you'll go stir crazy having spare time on your hands."

He kissed her. "I won't if you're with me." It was the truth.

She twisted her lips, pondering the idea. "I'll take one day off a week."

"And you won't stay late each night just because you don't have to work at the gas station anymore."

"*You* work late hours."

"I'll stop if you stop."

She searched his eyes, which was pointless, of course, as they rarely gave anything away. "You honestly think you can?"

"I want more time with you."

How could she say no to that? She rubbed her nose against his. "Okay. As it happens, I won't be working at all today. I need to go shopping." Dante and Trick had picked up her things from her landlord yesterday—there hadn't been much left undamaged. Most of her clothes had been slashed with her own kitchen knives. She'd been more upset to hear that her Mustang now looked like a heap of scrap. It would seem the extremists had had some fun with it.

"I'll come with you."

Makenna blinked. "You heard what I just said, right? That I was going shopping?"

"Yes."

"I really don't see you having the patience for a shopping trip. You're a tracker; you have a hunter-type personality. I'll bet you treat shopping like military missions: you go inside, retrieve the item, and then leave just as fast."

Yes, that was exactly what he did.

"Me . . . I'm a browser." She kissed his chin. "I will drive you insane."

Then it wouldn't be much different than any other day. "I'm coming with you." Until the Remy situation was over, she wasn't going anywhere alone.

She exhaled heavily. "If you're sure."

"You're not going to argue that you don't need my protection?"

"I never did understand those book and movie heroines who insist on facing danger alone. There's being capable of protecting yourself, and there's being plain stupid. In a one-to-one fight, I wouldn't need you to step in. But against a group of extremists, I could do with a little help." Their prior attack on her had quite clearly shown her that. "And I know being away from me while I'm a target would make you crazy. I don't want to do that to you."

She understood him well.

"And, hey, maybe we could pick you up some stuff too." His "no thanks" grunt made her smile. "I've seen your wardrobe. It's comprised of three brands at most, and you wear the same stuff over and over."

"Because I know they fit and they're comfortable." That was all Ryan required from the things he wore.

"But you only wear dark colors."

"I only like dark colors."

"Whatever. It's clear that you can't be helped. Now, are you positive that you want to come along? Because you *will* be bored, and you *will* become exasperated, and you *will* want to cry. I could ask Jaime and Taryn to come along instead; then I wouldn't be alone."

"I want to go with you."

"All right, but don't say you weren't warned."

Four hours later, Ryan was fast losing the will to live. At first, shopping with his mate hadn't been so bad. He liked seeing her enjoying herself, liked seeing her relaxed and carefree. Also, he'd foolishly thought that she wouldn't take too long, even though she'd told him she was a browser. Why? Because just before they left, he'd caught her scribbling things on a sheet of paper. When he'd asked what she was writing, she'd replied, *"I always make a list of the things I need. Then I promise myself I won't deviate from that list. It's stops me from buying shit I don't need and then spending too much."*

The practical rule had surprised and impressed him. What he hadn't considered was that her determination to not waste money would make the shopping trip even longer. If she were on the fence about anything, she'd leave it. If she weren't 100 percent happy with the color, texture, fit, and price, she wouldn't buy it.

So off they'd go to another store. And he was the mule.

He'd quickly learned that his mate loved bargains. If there were a sale on, she was right there. Not that she bought things just because they were on sale. No, she didn't buy something unless she would have bought it if it *hadn't* been a bargain. That didn't stop her from checking every rack, every shelf, and every floor. And where did she get all these coupons?

Then there were the times she asked for his opinion. Didn't she understand he didn't have the credibility to comment on clothing that all looked the same to him anyway? Didn't she see the sweat building on his forehead at the prospect of saying the wrong things and hurting her feelings? And why ask his opinion when it was clear she'd already made up her mind on what she wanted?

There were no guarantees that she would buy something even if she *were* 100 percent happy with it. No, she'd check a comparison price website on her cell phone. If the item were cheaper elsewhere, she'd drag him to that store instead.

She tried on everything. And she wasn't fast about it either. What irritated him was that when she finally walked out of the fitting rooms, it was often to tell him she didn't want the damn things or that she'd come back at the end-of-the-season sale and get it cheaper. Ryan never tried on anything. He just bought it and took it home. If it didn't fit, he'd hang it up in his wardrobe even though he'd never wear it.

As such, he was now hungry, thirsty, bored, and tired. But he couldn't be pissed at her. He'd brought this on himself. Makenna had warned him. Several times, in fact. She also regularly suggested he should go home.

When she finally announced she was done, Ryan couldn't help but burst out, "Thank God."

She laughed. "Come on, let's go eat."

It was the best idea she'd had all day. Fearing that his stomach was eating itself out of desperation, he pretty much hauled her into the nearest restaurant. Just as they were finishing dessert, her cell phone rang.

Makenna smiled as she greeted, "Hey, Dawn, how are you?"

"I have good news and bad news."

As a sense of foreboding came over Makenna, she put down her spoon. "Hit me with the bad first."

"One of our sponsors called to report that a wolf tried blackmailing him into withdrawing his funding."

Makenna cursed, and her wolf snarled. Ryan, who would be able to hear every word, didn't outwardly react, but she knew he would be pissed. Then something occurred to her. "Wait, you said 'tried.'"

"That's the good news." There was the slightest smile in Dawn's voice. "Not only does he refuse to be intimidated, he's agreed to testify about the blackmail attempt to the council."

That really was good. They would need whatever help they could get to convince the council that Remy was responsible for all the trouble happening around the shelter.

"It was nice to have some good news, especially after what happened last night."

Makenna frowned. "Last night?"

"The computer crashed. Seems someone sent a virus that messed up the whole system. If it wasn't for you insisting on me keeping backup files on the memory card, I'd have lost everything."

As a strong possibility occurred to Makenna, cold invaded her limbs. "Motherfucker."

"What?"

Dread a heavy weight on her chest, Makenna replied, "Remy sent the virus. But what if he managed to hack into the system first? He could have all our files." She shot a questioning look at Ryan, hoping he'd contradict her.

Frown deepening, Ryan said, "It's possible. There are some viruses that are used as ploys to gain access to whatever information is in the computer hard drive."

Fuck, fuck, fuck. "Think what that would mean."

Dawn gasped. "He'll know the names of the loners who are in hiding. He could expose them. Makenna, we have to get them out of here."

Her stomach churning, Makenna dragged a hand through her hair. "If he got the files last night, we don't have much time. Personally, I doubt he'd expose all of them at once. He won't want the shelter damaged in a war of any kind."

Dawn took a calming breath. "That's true. But I don't think we should risk it. It's better to be safe than sorry."

Makenna fully agreed, which was why she and Ryan headed straight to the shelter. On the drive there, Ryan called Trey and explained the situation. He told them he would send some of his wolves to meet them at the shelter very soon.

When Makenna entered the building, she found a manic-looking Dawn talking animatedly with Colton. Catching sight of Makenna, her shoulders seemed to lose some of their tension. She drew Makenna into a hug. "Honey, thank you so much for coming." Pulling back, Dawn looked at her neck and smiled a little. "Someone's been claimed. I'm glad you both finally accepted the inevitable. Congratulations."

Ryan accepted her words with an incline of his head. Colton also passed on his congratulations. Ryan ignored him and moved closer to Makenna. Anyone who didn't know her well probably wouldn't sense how on edge she was. Ryan could see that she was doing her best to stay strong for the others—as usual putting other people before herself. His wolf wanted to nuzzle her, comfort her.

The door opened, and Ryan turned to see Jaime, Dante, Trick, Dominic, and—what the fuck?—Zac enter.

At Ryan's scowl, Dominic quickly said, "I seriously doubt these loners are going to be happy about leaving with perfect strangers—especially since you look like a serial killer, Trick has that scary scar, and Dante's so big he has his own zip code. But they know Zac. If they see he's fine and well, they might be more comfortable coming with us."

Ryan couldn't deny that he made sense, but he didn't have to like it. Makenna didn't appear to like it much either.

"How many need to relocate?" Jaime asked.

"Originally, there were nine," replied Dawn. "Now there are only three."

Ryan asked, "Are they children or adults?"

"One adult, two children. None of them are wolves. Would that be a problem?"

Jaime shook her head. "Our pack has agreed to give them refuge, no matter what species they are."

"Thank you. You don't know how much I appreciate this. They're in my office with Madisyn."

Makenna was glad that Ryan stayed at her side as they headed to the office; the simple contact of his arm brushing hers was somehow soothing. She was pissed, she was worried, and she wanted to burn shit down. The shelter was supposed to be a safe place, a sanctuary, and Remy had ruined that.

"Do you think they'll agree to leave with us?" Ryan asked Makenna.

"They might for the simple reason that Zac trusts you all. But honestly, I'm not sure. Riley is . . . well, you'll see."

As they entered the office, the scents of cheetah, snake, and raven hit Ryan all at once. His wolf stilled, already on edge due to Makenna's anxiety. Madisyn rose from behind the desk, and the other adult female planted herself in front of two small children. He'd seen the three from afar during one of his visits.

He doubted they were at all related. The adult female was small and had dark iridescent hair typical of a raven shifter. The little boy had a mop of blond curls and was crouched behind the raven, ready to pounce. The second child, who coiled herself around the raven's leg, had caramel pigtails and golden eyes that didn't once blink as she took in the strangers with a solemn expression.

Zac held up his hands. "Guys, it's okay; this is my cousin, Ryan, and my pack mates, Dominic, Jaime, Dante, and Trick."

The little girl tried to dash to Makenna, but the raven barred her way with her arm.

Dawn sidled up to the loners. "Riley, you can stand down. They won't hurt you or the children. In fact, they've offered to give you all a place to stay. They're good people. We wouldn't have let Zac join their pack if they weren't."

"But like Zac said, one of them is his cousin," said the raven, cutting her eyes briefly toward Ryan. "Just because they're good to him doesn't mean we should trust them."

"They wouldn't expect your trust, Riley," said Makenna. "They just want to help."

Riley's keen gaze studied the Phoenix wolves. "Why would you want to help us?"

"It's the right thing to do," replied Jaime. "Every child—human or shifter—should be protected. You're clearly willing to protect them, but you'll have a problem doing that all by yourself if someone comes for them. I don't know what your story is, and I'm not asking. All I'm asking is that you let us help. For their sake."

After a long silence, Riley glanced briefly at Dawn. "We'll come. But just until this all blows over. This is Savannah, who's four, and Dexter, who's two."

Dominic got down on his haunches, smiling at the children. "I'm pleased to meet you." Zac squatted too, and both he and Dominic told the children about the pack and their territory, about how much space they would have to run and all the local wildlife. Savannah and Dexter listened intently, gradually relaxing.

Makenna leaned into Ryan as she said in a low voice, "Dominic's good with kids. I didn't expect that."

Jaime snorted. "Dominic can charm anyone . . . although sometimes that charm is a little twisted." Ryan grunted.

"We parked the Chevy near the side alley," said Dante. "It should be easy enough to smuggle them inside. The windows are tinted, so they don't need to worry about being seen. Trick and Dominic will be staying behind at the shelter. From now on, there will always be two Phoenix enforcers around. If Remy's done what you suspect, there will be trouble at this door soon. The protective wards will stop them getting inside, but magick won't stop them from causing a huge fuss or damaging the building."

"No offense," said Makenna, "but if that happens, two enforcers won't be able to take them on."

"No," agreed Jaime, "but it will knock them off balance."

Trick nodded. "If any of those assholes come here, they'll do so expecting to be able to easily break into the building and take whomever they've come for. They won't anticipate loners having the protection of a pack. When they realize that their actions will mean taking on our pack, they'll be careful how they proceed."

"Our pack might not be as huge as Remy's," said Dante, "but it's one thing that his is not: respected. The fact that we're also strongly allied with the Mercury wolves—a pack that's equally respected—makes us people that most shifters hesitate to fuck with."

Makenna rubbed the back of her neck. "You're right in what you say, and having some enforcers around here can only be a good thing. But if your pack is seen to be helping us, someone could guess that you're the ones hiding those that need sanctuary."

"Not if we tell them how Remy's just trying to sic people on the shelter to make it easier for him to claim this territory." Trick shrugged. "It's not the complete truth, but it's not a lie. I doubt they like him much anyway, since he's constantly taking over packs and increasing the size of his territory. Shifters won't like that because it can make him a threat."

Ryan wondered if Remy had considered that if he were seen as too powerful, there would be shifters who would unite to take him out. That would be a really good day.

Minutes later, Jaime, Dante, Zac, and the loners exited through the side door of the building and headed to the Chevy. While Dawn and Makenna briefed the remaining residents on Remy's actions, Ryan, Dominic, and Trick did a thorough patrol of the shelter's territory. Satisfied that no strangers were lingering around the border, they headed back to the building.

Dawn was waiting near the children's playground, rubbing her hands together anxiously. "Did you find anything?" Ryan shook his head, and she let out a sigh of relief. "We told the residents what happened. They're understandably worried, but none of them wish to leave. In fact, many of them expressed their intentions to defend the shelter if any trouble came. Ryan, you'll find Makenna in the basement, taking note of the supplies."

Giving Dawn a nod, he walked inside the building and tracked his mate to the basement, where he found her checking off boxes on a clipboard.

She flashed him a smile. "Hey. Any signs of intruders?"

"No." He closed the distance between them. "We're alone now."

She glanced around. "That's true."

"It means you can stop pretending you're okay."

Makenna thought about brushing off the comment, but that would only insult him. He didn't deserve that. "I'm just pissed at myself."

"At yourself?"

She hugged the clipboard to her chest. "I thought these people were protected, Ryan. I thought the wards would keep out any danger. But Remy still found a way to invade the place. I should have considered that, but I didn't. Dawn is so devastated, feeling like she let the residents down, when it's my fault."

Ryan curled a stray lock of hair around her ear. "Are you done being irrational?" That wild glint in her eyes sparked.

"Excuse me?"

He took the clipboard and slid it onto a nearby shelf, not liking that little barrier between them. "You are not responsible for another person's actions. There's such a thing as cause and effect. Remy's the cause, and these are the effects. You do not enter that equation."

His matter-of-fact tone probably should have rubbed her the wrong way, but Makenna found it soothing. When something was on her mind, she'd find herself obsessing over it until she drove herself crazy. Ryan's practical, no-nonsense manner had a way of calming the chaos in her head.

He cupped her face with both hands. "The blame belongs solely to him. You put everything you are into this shelter. No one here would ever blame you for what's happening." He slid his hand around to her nape and pulled her to him. With a sigh, she rested her forehead on his chest. He rubbed her back until she relaxed against him. "I hate the stress he's causing you. And I hate that I can't do anything to help." Makenna's happiness was most important to him, and it tormented him every second of every day that he couldn't eliminate this threat. It was his practical nature that held him back. As Makenna said, they needed to play this smart.

"How can you think you've done nothing to help? Seriously, Ryan, if it wasn't for you and your pack, we'd be on Shit Street right now."

He kissed her. "No, you wouldn't. You'd have found a way to protect the people here." And he fucking adored that about her. He kissed her again, savoring the taste of his mate. Needing it. Loving it. And wondering yet again why the fuck their bond was out of his reach.

CHAPTER SEVENTEEN

That evening, as Ryan drove with Makenna through the gates of his territory, he asked, "What are the stories of the loners we're hiding?" He gave Gabe, who was in the security shack, a curt nod as they passed him. "We can't adequately protect them if we don't know what or who might come for them."

Makenna agreed, but she couldn't break their confidence. "Riley shared her story with me, trusting I wouldn't repeat it. I can't violate her trust like that. But I can tell you about Savannah and Dexter. As you might have sensed, Savannah is a snake shifter. A viper. She was abandoned as a baby, left outside a church. Social Services mistook her for a human. When she started displaying strange behavior—hissing, biting, and climbing just about everything—her human adoptive parents took her to be tested. When it transpired that she was a shifter, they didn't want her anymore. Social Services passed her on to Dawn."

His wolf snarled at the idea of a child being deserted not just once but twice. "Why do you think she needs to be hidden?"

"I did some research on viper nests, trying to track her origins. Vipers are rare, so it wasn't hard. Did you hear about the nest from Arizona that was wiped out by a cougar pride that swore it would see every last viper within the nest dead?"

"Yes. The Alpha wanted revenge when his son died after being poisoned by a female viper."

"We think Savannah was part of that nest. The ruling pair reportedly had a baby daughter that was nowhere to be found when the nest and pride went to war. The cougars searched for her. Our best guess is that her parents abandoned her to protect her."

"The Alpha wanted to kill their daughter as a tit for tat," Ryan concluded.

She nodded, a grim twist to her mouth. "Hopefully Remy doesn't make the connection between Savannah and the war. She may *not* be from that nest, but the cougars would still come to find out for themselves. I wasn't going to take any chances."

"What about Dexter?"

"He was also brought to Dawn by Social Services. We have no idea what pride he's from. He'd been living wild on the streets. He was found by human kids who tormented and prodded him with sticks. A passing stranger recorded the incident with his cell phone . . . so I watched as Dexter's claws sliced out and he attacked the kids to defend himself."

"He was able to partially shift?" It was rare that their inner animals surfaced to any degree before puberty.

"Yep. The footage was uploaded to YouTube. The anti-shifter extremists pounced on the whole thing, claiming Dexter is a freak that even his pride doesn't want. They said Dexter needed to be 'put down' like a rabid dog. We've been hiding him from them."

His wolf flexed his claws, wanting to lash out. "The kids have had a tough time."

"They have."

Entering the parking lot, Ryan whipped into his usual parking space. "I want to ask you something." He just hadn't been sure how to bring it up. Makenna looked at him, expectant. "Do you want to contact your uncle?" Okay, he probably should have eased her into the subject a little better.

Caught off guard by the question, Makenna sucked in a breath. "I haven't given it any thought. There's a lot going on right now. I need to concentrate on the shelter. I'll worry about my uncle at a later point." For some reason, that made Ryan scowl. "What?"

"You don't always have to put others before yourself." It was pissing him off more and more.

That put her on the defensive. "I don't *always* do it."

He grunted.

"No, I don't."

He grunted again.

"*I don't.* Look, my uncle isn't exactly going anywhere. There's no rush to deal with that. But the shelter . . . that's a 'here and now' problem." She sighed, admitting, "And maybe I don't want to deal with my past just yet. Maybe I want some time to let it all sink in. Maybe."

Ryan cupped her nape and drew her close. "That doesn't make you weak."

"I never said it did."

"You were thinking it."

Yes, she was. "*You* wouldn't put something aside temporarily. You'd deal with it straightaway and then move on."

"Because I don't feel even half of the emotions that you do. I'm numb to a lot of things."

She gave him a pointed look. "There's nothing at all wrong with you. Being reserved and logical doesn't make you—"

"Emotionally detached? That's exactly what I am." He'd accepted that.

She framed his face with her hands. "You are a good person, Ryan Conner. You take care of your pack, you have strong family values despite your childhood, and you're someone people respect and *know* they can rely on. You can't be emotionally detached; you care about people."

"In my own way. But I don't care about people the same way you do." Maybe that was why he was so protective of the people in his life—he was compensating for the things he couldn't give them. Maybe not. He didn't see that it really mattered either way. "Except when it comes to you." There were so many emotions tangled up in what he felt for Makenna—some familiar, some not. "It's different with you."

"It's the same for me, you know. Just because I have a bigger . . . emotional repertoire than you, doesn't mean I feel strong emotions for everyone." Makenna paused, nervous at revealing so much but knowing he deserved to hear it—maybe even *needed* to hear it. "You once said I step into other people's lives but don't allow them to step into mine. You were right. I don't give much of myself to people. You have all of me."

Warmth built in Ryan's chest and seemed to flood every part of him. This female . . . she could get to him in a way that no one else ever could. She wasn't just under his skin; she was inside him. She was part of him. The best part. "I'm keeping it all." She deserved more than those possessive words, deserved to hear what he felt, and it pissed him off that he couldn't articulate himself.

Sensing his internal struggle on some strange . . . almost metaphysical level, Makenna put a finger to his mouth. "I don't need words. Everything you do shows me you care. Now come on, let's go inside."

Ascending the cliff steps, they went into the mountain and strode through the tunnels. As they neared the kitchen, they found Tao and Riley having some kind of standoff. Several other wolves were gathered around, who all seemed amused.

"You're being dramatic." Riley sighed. It was very like the raven to blow off people's anger—she didn't let much get to her. Makenna liked that about her.

Tao's spine locked. *"Dramatic?"* He pointed at Savannah, who was standing behind Riley with Dexter and Kye. "She bit someone."

"She's not poisonous; she's only four."

Noticing Makenna, Savannah coiled and sprung in the air. Makenna caught her easily, smiling at the melted chocolate on the little girl's face and T-shirt. "Hey, cutie, how are you?"

Her little face scrunched up. "I don't like it here."

"Why not?"

"I'm not allowed to bite the mean old lady."

Makenna did her best to contain her smile. "Why would you want to bite her?"

"She said something mean to my Riley." Savannah was very protective of the raven.

"Sweetie, the old lady says something mean to pretty much everyone."

"Then why can't I bite her?"

Hearing Jaime and Taryn laugh, Makenna asked, "Is Greta okay?"

"She's fine." Taryn waved away her concern. "She's milking it, of course, for attention, said she could feel the poison working its way through her body and needed to go lie down."

Jaime snorted. "Savannah's little teeth didn't even break the skin—though it wouldn't matter if they had, since she's not poisonous. Tao's just worried that she'll bite Kye, and, well, he's tetchy when he worries."

Savannah shook her head, frowning at Jaime. "I don't bite my friends. I like Kye." She turned back to Makenna. "He lets me play with his toys."

Makenna smiled. "Yeah? That's nice of him."

Riley smirked at Tao. "You heard Savannah; you have nothing to worry about. As for Gretchen—"

"Greta," growled Tao.

"Whatever. I can't say the same for her."

Grace stepped forward. "Now that that's settled, how about I show Riley where she and the children will be staying? Looking at the mess they've made of themselves, I'm sure the little ones would like a bath."

She turned to Makenna and Ryan. "Have you eaten?" At Ryan's nod, she said, "Good."

Tao scooped Kye up off the floor when he went to follow Grace and the new guests down the corridor. "Not you, pup."

Zac walked over to Ryan, grinning. "Dude, I thought *you* had no tact. Tao is way worse."

Ryan grunted. While Tao didn't have a diplomatic bone in his body, he was a pretty sociable guy. But only with his pack—he didn't trust or have much time for outsiders.

Tao shook his head. "I can't believe we have a raven here."

Taryn took Kye from him. "Why? What's the big deal?"

"Do you not know anything about raven shifters?" asked Tao. "They're a lot like their animal counterparts. Cunning. Tricksters. Cheaters. Thieves. They're the ultimate masters of deceit."

Taryn's brows flew up. "Really? Intriguing."

Trey rolled his eyes at his mate. "You're just saying that because you love birds."

"Why does she need somewhere to hide anyway?" Tao said, his tone challenging. "I mean, can't she just fly away?"

Zac slapped Tao on the back. "Dude, don't worry; Riley is cool. Crazy but cool."

The Head Enforcer's expression said, "We'll see."

Taryn turned to Makenna. "Those kids are so cute. How the hell did they become loners?"

"Let's go sit down while we hear their stories," said Trey. So the pack followed him to the living area, where Makenna sat on Ryan's lap as she shared what she knew about both children.

Tao, slouched in an armchair, asked, "What about the raven?"

"That's her story to share or not to share," Makenna told him. Tao grumbled something under his breath.

"Kye's so happy to be around kids near his age." Taryn smiled. "The only other pup we have in our pack is Lilah, and she's too little for him to really play with. I think it makes him feel kind of lonely at times, even though he sees Willow a lot. Having other kids around will be good for him."

"Yeah, *if* they don't hurt him," said Tao. "Savannah might not be poisonous, but she'll still bite at the slightest provocation—it's instinct. And if Dexter can partially shift, he could *really* hurt Kye."

Makenna might have been annoyed by Tao's attitude if she couldn't see the anxiety in his expression. He was extremely protective of Kye, which was only natural considering he was the pup's bodyguard.

"And I'm not convinced it's wise having a raven here," he added.

"It's wise if we want the little ones under control," said Taryn. "Riley's the only authority they recognize."

Ryan didn't contribute as Taryn and the Head Enforcer continued to discuss the issue. It wasn't that Tao had any real prejudice against snakes, partially shifting children, or ravens. Tao's reflex reaction to strangers was to reject them. Once he got used to them, his attitude would change and he would be one of their biggest protectors.

Ryan rubbed his jaw against Makenna's temple. "You're quiet. What's going on in that head of yours?" If she was stressing about anything, he could—

"Does it bother anyone else that the Easter Bunny carries eggs?" asked Makenna, causing the room to fall quiet. "I mean, rabbits don't lay eggs."

He closed his eyes. Honestly, what was he supposed to do with a pointless question like that? He expected his pack to gawk at her. He was wrong to do so.

Jaime paused in stroking her cat. "That's a good point." The others nodded, and Rhett announced he would Google it.

Unreal.

CHAPTER EIGHTEEN

Two days. Makenna experienced two blessed days of peace. A peace that ended as she and Ryan pulled up outside the shelter, only to find Remy waiting with some of his wolves. Just the sight of him was enough to cause a deep, dark rage to unfurl in her stomach and make her wolf leap to her feet with a snarl.

Hearing a low growl build in Ryan's chest, she put a hand on his arm. "Whatever happens, whatever he says, stay calm. The council meeting is tomorrow. We've been smart up until now. Let's not fuck it up by losing our shit at the last hurdle."

Ryan grunted. "I could say the same to you." Her calm exterior wasn't fooling him for a second. Not just because he knew her well but because he could *feel* her fury like it was his own. It practically sizzled in his veins. There was only one explanation for that. "The mating bond is operating on some level." It was still psychically out of his reach, but it was somehow working.

"Or imprinting has started."

That made more sense, since a mating bond couldn't fully function unless it had snapped into place. And yet, Ryan's instincts told him this was more than imprinting. His wolf agreed.

She exhaled heavily. "Come on, let's get this over with." They both hopped out of the Chevy, and Ryan then moved to stand beside Makenna as he lifted a questioning brow at Trick. The enforcer was guarding the door with Dominic.

"He just arrived," Trick told them, arms folded.

"And he doesn't seem inclined to tell us why he's here," said Dominic, glaring at Remy.

Ignoring them, Remy pushed away from his vehicle and came toward Makenna and Ryan, exuding superiority and arrogance. "Makenna," he drawled with none of his usual charm. His gaze flicked briefly to the distinctive bite on her throat. "I heard you wore a claiming mark." Most likely from his spies. "I was doubtful about it. I hadn't actually believed someone would claim a loner."

Remy's enforcers snickered. It would seem that Remy had decided to drop *all* pretense of being a nice guy.

His eyes shifted to Ryan. "I see you're wearing a mark too. I'm curious, are you true mates or have you imprinted?"

"Why are you here?" asked Makenna, voice bland.

"I thought I'd give Dawn one final chance to join my pack before the council meeting tomorrow."

Makenna snorted. "If you wanted to speak to Dawn, you wouldn't have been waiting by your car. You're here to see us. Why?"

Remy returned his focus to Ryan. "I appreciate that you're protective of your mate and, by extension, the shelter. It's only natural." His expression hardened as he added, "But Makenna's mate or not, you need to stay out of this, Conner. This matter does not concern you or your pack. Are we clear?"

Ryan grunted. It was a sound that Makenna translated to "Fuck you."

"It would be wise of you to do as I say, Conner. After all, it's not only your mate you have to think about. That cousin of yours—young Zac—also depends on you to keep him safe. I'll bet he was a pretty child." An arrogant smirk slowly spread across Remy's face. "We wouldn't want his old pack to learn his whereabouts, would we?"

A black, bottomless rage slammed into Makenna, churning her stomach and almost causing her knees to buckle. She quickly realized the emotion belonged to Ryan, who was as stoic and unreadable as always. He'd never show any vulnerability to this sick bastard. "You're a big fan of blackmail, aren't you, Remy?" A little of her own anger leaked into her tone. "That's how you got some of Dawn's sponsors to withdraw their funding."

Remy's chin jutted out. "Blackmail is a quick and efficient way of getting things done."

"Especially since your little plan to sic the cougars on the shelter didn't work so well, huh?" The morning after Riley and the children had been moved to Phoenix Pack territory, several cougars had arrived at the shelter asking whether a young viper was staying there. Trick had replied no, had told them about Remy's hopes to get his hands on the territory that the shelter sits on.

Face tightening, Remy clenched his teeth. "I know you're hiding the viper."

"Viper?"

"Play dumb if you wish, but I've seen your records."

"When you hacked into Dawn's computer, you mean? Yeah, we know all about that." Makenna smiled sweetly. "Say, how's your mom?"

His nostrils flared, his lips flattened into a harsh line, and his fists clenched. She actually thought he'd hit her. Instead, he took a long breath and turned to Ryan. "Don't ignore my warning, Conner. For young Zac's sake."

Ryan's wolf bared his teeth, releasing a primal growl that held both hatred and challenge. The animal wanted to leap on the sick male who would do Zac harm; he had no care for the politics surrounding the situation. But Ryan's practicality won out, keeping him still and silent as he watched the Alpha return to his car and drive away. It was one of the hardest things he'd ever had to do.

Ryan turned to his seething mate, striving to control his anger so that he didn't overwhelm her with it. If the strain on her face was anything to go by, it was too late for that. He cupped her nape and drew her to him, pressing an apologetic kiss to her temple. "You okay?"

"I wanted to slit his throat." She shuddered. "He makes my skin crawl."

"His time is almost up, Kenna." Soon, Remy Deacon would die. Ryan urged his mate up the path and into the shelter. Trick and Dominic followed them inside.

Dawn was in the reception area with Madisyn and Colton, rubbing her arms. "What did Remy want?"

"To warn Ryan and his pack not to come with us tomorrow," said Makenna.

Dominic leaned against the wall. "I noticed he didn't bother acting innocent when Makenna flung accusations at him."

"Probably because he's lost his patience at this point," said Madisyn. "Most of his plans have come to nothing."

Ryan nodded, looking at Dawn. "He wants you to feel backed into a corner so that you give in to him."

Makenna draped an arm around Dawn's shoulders. "But you didn't; you fought for these people. You may have lost some of your sponsors, but you were able to attract new ones. He thought that having residents fired would keep the place full, stopping others from seeking refuge here. Instead, you were able to get them new jobs working for people who didn't care they were shifters.

"He probably also thought that getting me out of his way would not only leave you understaffed and without someone to rehome the loners, but that it would mean the Phoenix wolves would no longer care what happened here. He didn't realize that they class you, Madisyn, and the shelter as under their protection."

"*You're* a Phoenix wolf now," Ryan growled at his mate.

Makenna smiled before turning back to Dawn. "He most likely sent the cougars here in the hope that you'd feel so threatened and scared that you'd ask him for help, but all he's done is earn himself an enemy by pissing off the cougars."

"You've done everyone here proud, Dawn," said Madisyn.

Forcing a smile, Dawn patted Makenna's hand. "I wouldn't have been able to do all that without the help of *your* pack."

Ryan's pleased grunt made Makenna's smile widen.

"Still, his meddling worked in some ways." Dawn sighed. "The shelter is almost full, which means more expenses—money and supplies I just don't have. The new sponsors don't give as much funding as the sponsors that we lost. Worse, Riley, Dexter, and Savannah were forced to leave because of his actions. This place should be a sanctuary."

"It is," Colton insisted. "The residents still think of it that way or they would have left by now."

Madisyn nodded. "You heard what Riley said: she'd stay with the Phoenix Pack until the Remy situation blows over. They plan to come back."

"I'm just so worried that the council will give him what he wants." Dawn rubbed her cheek. "Loners aren't seen as people who have the same rights as other shifters. Remy's word will have more weight than mine for that reason alone. Plus, he could blackmail them or bribe them."

"It doesn't matter what he does, Dawn, or what the council decides," said Makenna. "Remy Deacon will not get his hands on the shelter. It. Will. Not. Happen."

Ryan grunted his agreement.

"I mean it, Dawn, I'll kill him before I'll let him have it."

Dawn squeezed her hand. "We can't go to war with them, honey."

"No," agreed Ryan, "but my pack can. Makenna's one of us now."

"That means Makenna's fights are our fights too," Trick stated, his tone one of total resolve.

Again, Ryan grunted his agreement. He'd always be at his mate's side.

Dawn smiled at each of the males. "You're all too good to be true."

Makenna gave Dawn's shoulder a squeeze. "Let's go to your office. We need to discuss how to proceed tomorrow."

Madisyn nodded. "Remy's going to present a damn good case. It's important we do the same."

"If he doesn't get what he wants," Dawn said, "what do you think he'll do?"

Ryan had said it before, and he'd say it again: "Dead men can't do anything."

Having finished his final perimeter check of the day, Ryan was just about to return to the caves when he heard, "Ryyyyyaaaannnn!" Turning, he saw the Alpha pair and the Beta pair relaxing at the patio with Tao, Riley, and Kye.

Waving frantically, Kye hurried to Ryan and then climbed him like he was a fence post. Not much amused his wolf, but the pup sure did. Gripping him by the back of his shirt, Ryan detached a laughing Kye with a grunt. The pup grunted back with a wide smile. Ryan headed for the other wolves, frowning as he picked up the scents of snake and cheetah. It was only as he neared that he noticed Savannah was dangling from a tree branch upside down and Dexter was smacking the tree with his shoe.

Dexter gave him a somber, studious look that told Ryan he was being sized up. Then he dug his hand into his pocket and offered Ryan half a cookie.

Taryn laughed. "Where is he getting this food?"

"He's a hoarder," said Riley. "I think it was because he was surviving mostly on scraps until he arrived at the shelter."

Ryan took the cookie to be polite. It was no surprise that Kye snatched it and ran off. Dexter gave chase. That kid was fast, even for a cheetah.

Threading his fingers through Jaime's hair, Dante tipped his chin at Ryan. "I see you changed your shifts around."

"I'm glad," said Trey. "It's about time you saw yourself as more than an enforcer."

Smiling, Jaime nodded. "Makenna's good for you."

Of course she was. She was his mate.

"I gotta say, I wouldn't have pictured you with someone like her." Taryn snuggled closer to Trey. "Fate seems to enjoy surprising us."

"On another note, Trick told me that Remy turned up at the shelter earlier," said Trey, face hard. "I'm not surprised he threatened to reveal Zac's whereabouts if you're present at the meeting tomorrow. Part of the case he's making to the council is that the shelter has no protection. But if some of our pack appear, it will cancel out that side of his argument."

"Do you think he really would contact Zac's old pack?" asked Riley, her eyes on Savannah.

"I think he'll do it whether we go tomorrow or not," replied Ryan.

Dante nodded his agreement. "We've helped Dawn and the shelter. We've screwed up his plans in a major way. He'll want revenge."

Jaime's hand fisted so hard her knuckles turned white. "We can't let Zac's old pack get their hands on him. And we can't let Remy get his hands on that shelter."

"Neither of those things will happen," growled Ryan. His wolf echoed his growl.

"Something tells me that if they did," began Tao, "Makenna would be first in line to kill them. There's a wildness in her."

Riley smiled. "There is. I like it."

Trey looked at Ryan. "You're positive she's your true mate?"

This again? "I already had this conversation with the females and Marcus."

Dante smiled. "Yeah, he told me about the female intervention." Jaime and Taryn had the grace to blush. "Let me give you some advice. I'd known Jaime since we were kids, but we hadn't once guessed that we were mates. It wasn't until Kye was born, in that one unguarded moment while she held him and both our defenses fell, that we both realized the truth."

Jaime linked their fingers. "It hit us like a two-by-four."

Ryan scowled. "Makenna doesn't have any defenses up now."

"There has to be something or you'd feel the bond," said Tao.

Not necessarily, given recent developments. "It's operating."

Dante arched a brow. "Operating how?"

"I feel what she feels. I think our scents are starting to mix." It was only a slight change, but Ryan could swear it was there.

Trey pursed his lips. "That could be the start of imprinting."

Ryan shook his head. He sensed it was more.

"I don't see how the bond could have snapped into place without you feeling it," said Dante.

Taryn held a hand up. "Let's say, for argument's sake, that it had. That would mean the frequency isn't jammed, that the bond is up and working just fine. Something is stopping you and Makenna from psychically sensing it." Taryn's shoulders sagged. "Honestly, I don't see how anything could possibly do that."

"There is another possibility," said Riley.

"What?" Tao asked her.

"It could be that the bond truly hasn't formed yet. But that it's functioning on some level because it's so very close to snapping into place."

Taryn's brows flew up. "That is possible." She looked at Ryan. "Usually when mates psychically connect, the bond isn't fully formed; it takes certain emotional steps to make that happen because the couple still has some hurdles to jump. But what if you and Makenna don't have any hurdles? What if the bond is ready and waiting, it just needs a little something to get out of the damn way?"

"Like what?" Trey asked, and she shrugged.

"Ooh," interrupted Jaime, "maybe it's an external issue. Something that isn't coming between you and Makenna—hence why the bond is ready to fully form—but something that's coming between the bond and you as a couple."

Tao waved a hand. "For example . . ."

Jaime sat upright. "If I remember correctly, Makenna went to the shelter when she was a child. Right?"

Ryan nodded.

"Was she banished? Betrayed in some way?"

Taryn gaped at her. "I can't believe I never thought of that."

"You would have eventually," assured Jaime.

Taryn smiled. "It makes total sense now."

"I know, right?"

Trey sighed. "Could you please share with the class?"

Taryn turned to Ryan. "If Makenna was betrayed by her pack, it stands to reason that part of her is hesitant about joining another. Mating with you means becoming one of us. She's done that. But maybe somewhere deep inside, she doesn't trust that we won't betray her too."

It made sense. Makenna spoke of the pack as if she were an outsider. She had yet to call herself a Phoenix wolf. Years of volunteering at a place where other people were banished and betrayed by their packs wouldn't have exactly filled her with faith about packs. "She's holding back from the pack, not me."

"Exactly," said Taryn. "She needs to see—to believe wholeheartedly—that we won't betray her."

"We've done what we can to make her feel like one of us," said Jaime. "She *is* one of us."

Taryn shrugged. "That's a realization she has to come to on her own. At least you can take comfort in the knowledge that she's not at all unsure about you, Ryan."

Smiling at him, Jaime nodded. "She loves you. We can all see that. She doesn't even try to hide it."

Riley caught Savannah as the little girl sprang onto her lap. "You're lucky to have Makenna as your mate. She's awesome."

Tao leaned closer to the viper. "What's that you got in your hand?"

Savannah smiled impishly. "It's for you." She opened her fist and offered her possession to Tao.

To the guy's credit, he did nothing other than say, "It's a worm."

"You can share it with your mean old lady."

Apparently Savannah had decided that since he was Greta's ally, Tao was her enemy.

Tao shot a silently laughing Riley a narrowed-eyed look that she completely ignored.

"I absolutely *love* this kid," said Taryn, grinning.

Dante pulled out his beeping cell phone and swiped his thumb across the screen. "It seems we have a visitor."

"Who?" Trey asked, stiffening.

"Myles is here. And he's brought a friend."

By the time Myles had parked in the lot, Ryan was waiting there with the Alpha pair and Beta pair.

Trey spoke. "Why are you here, Myles?"

The male stopped with a sigh. "Two reasons. One, Rosa's friend called and said that a huge pack has just entered Remy's territory—the York Pack."

Zac's old pack. *Bastard.*

"They're planning to invade this place with Remy in three days," Myles went on. Trey and Dante growled.

"What's the other reason for your visit?" asked Taryn.

Myles slid his friend a glance. "Well that would have to do with Grayson here. He has something to tell you. Trust me, you'll want to hear this."

CHAPTER NINETEEN

Waking to the sound of a fist thumping on Ryan's bedroom door, Makenna groaned. The male curled around her merely grunted against her nape. The fist didn't give up, however. "This is the shittiest wake-up call ever," she grumbled.

Ryan lifted his head and called out, "What?"

"We have a major situation on our hands." It was Dante.

Ryan sat upright. "Explain."

"Come take a look at the security monitors in Trey's office."

A short time later, Ryan and Makenna entered the crowded office. "What's going on?" asked Makenna. Moving aside, Dante gestured at the monitors. One look had Makenna blurting, "Fuck."

"Yes, fuck," agreed Tao. "Remy has to be behind this."

Trick nodded. "He wants the council to think we're not the right people to be guarding the shelter."

"Given that there are dozens of extremists outside the security gates, yelling and protesting, I'd say he'd make a good point," said Makenna. They were all wearing hoods to conceal their faces—most likely hoping to protect their identities from The Movement. Makenna looked at Trey. "I thought you said the extremists wouldn't come here."

"Something's got them so worked up that they don't care about the danger it's putting them in." The Alpha leaned closer to the screens. "What are they shouting?"

Jaime shook her head, worrying her lower lip. "I can't tell."

Dante took out his cell phone and keyed in a number. "There's only one way to find out." He put the phone to his ear. "Gabe, what is it they're saying?" Gabe was guarding the gate.

The room was quiet enough for everyone to hear Gabe's response: "They want 'the rabid cat.'"

Makenna met Ryan's gaze as she said, "Dexter."

"They're yelling that it belongs in hell and they want to send it there," added Gabe.

"Hey look, cops have showed up," said Tao. "Tell me they aren't part of the protest."

"They're trying to move the extremists along," Gabe told them. "The bastards are blocking the road. Can you see the news crew?"

Makenna cursed. "The council won't need Remy to tell them about this. They'll see it for themselves."

"He hasn't just done this to persuade the council we can't protect the shelter," said Ryan. "He's trying to block our exit so we can't get to the meeting."

Makenna's spine locked. "I'm not missing it."

"No, you're not," Trey assured her. "There are other ways out of here—hidden exits we have for emergencies. It will slow you down a little, maybe make you a little late for the meeting. But you *will* get there."

Taryn turned to Makenna. "I really wanted to be there today but—"

"You need people here in case they somehow manage to get through the gates," finished Makenna. "I get it."

"Jaime, Trick, and I will come with you and Ryan," said Dante. "That means you'll have enough backup without the pack being defenseless."

"Is Riley likely to flee with Savannah and Dexter, thinking it will protect them?" Taryn asked Makenna.

Tao frowned. "She won't flee." It was more of a "she'd better not flee" statement.

"Riley's smart," said Makenna. "She'll know that running off alone to protect the kids would be much worse than staying in a vast territory where there are lots of places to hide should the unthinkable happen and those fuckers get inside."

Taryn released a sigh of relief. "Good. Those kids have wormed their way into my heart."

Ryan checked the clock on the wall. "Kenna, we have to leave now."

With a nod, Makenna quickly followed him out of the room, out of the caves, and through the dense forest until they came to a camouflaged building that turned out to be a garage. Claiming one of the four SUVs, Ryan then drove them out of a cleverly concealed exit that was only accessible from the inside of the territory's perimeter fence.

After a ten-minute drive on a dirt path, they came to the highway. It took twenty more minutes to reach the territory on which the meeting was being held. Bordered by three mountains, the expansive land belonged to one of the council members, Parker Brant, who was known for being fair and impartial. Makenna sure hoped he'd be that today.

The council itself wasn't exactly "good." It would do what it had to do to preserve peace—even if that meant ending lives and wiping out packs. That was what made her so nervous. If they thought Remy having possession of the shelter would preserve the peace, they might just grant him what he wanted.

After they parked, four guards escorted them from the SUV to a building that looked like a smaller version of a courthouse. In the reception area, Dawn, Madisyn, and Colton sagged in relief at their arrival.

Madisyn hugged Makenna tight. "For a minute there, I thought you weren't going to make it."

"So did I," said Makenna.

Dawn came forward. "What happened?"

"Extremists turned up at our territory, looking for Dexter," said Jaime. Dawn paled.

"Bastards," spat Colton.

Jaime glanced around. "Where's Remy?"

"Opposing parties use separate entrances," Dawn explained.

A door at the opposite end of the room opened and a male called out, "The council is ready to hear you now."

Dawn straightened her blouse. "Let's stay calm. Dignified." She shot a meaningful look at the fidgety feline at her side.

Madisyn rolled back her shoulders. "I got it."

Urged in by the dark wolf manning the door, they walked into a partially wood-paneled courtroom. It was empty other than for the four council members, who sat behind a raised bench, facing the attendees.

At the dark wolf's direction, they all slid into a pew-style bench located on the front left-hand side of the room. A door on their right opened, and Remy and five of his wolves—including Selene—filed out . . . with Deanne, who cast Makenna an evil snarl that made her inner wolf flex her claws, wanting to take a swipe at the bitch.

Ryan shuffled protectively closer to his mate, all the while glaring at the female who he guessed was Remy's mother—making it clear that he wouldn't stand for her shit. She got the message, and she didn't appear to like it. Remy lounged on the bench parallel to theirs, his posture and smirk arrogant. But arrogance could be a downfall, couldn't it?

The eldest council member cleared his throat. "I am Parker Brant. On my left is Emilio Mendes. The two wolves on my right are Harrison Whittle and Landyn Green." Harrison and Landyn inclined their heads to no one in particular. Emilio tipped his chin at Remy but merely stared at Dawn—clearly he was one of those people who were prejudiced against loners. The male had always been a bit of an asshole. It seemed they wouldn't be getting much support from that corner.

Parker looked at Remy. "As I understand it, you wish to claim the shelter and its land as your own."

Remy straightened. "Yes. Unfortunately, Dawn is opposed to the idea."

"Before we proceed, I must ask both parties if either wishes to change its stance." When he received no response, Parker continued, "Remy Deacon, as you are the applicant, let us hear your case first."

"May I please ask that the Phoenix wolves be removed from the room? This business is not theirs."

Makenna blinked. Ho, ho, ho—what a sneaky little shit. She placed a hand over Ryan's clenched fist, feeling his aggravation flow through her.

Dawn spoke quickly. "Makenna is one of my most trusted staff members and, as such, this is very much her business."

"She is a Phoenix wolf?" asked Parker.

"Yes. Naturally, her mate and some of her wolves are here to support her, just as Remy's wolves are here to support him."

Parker inclined his head slightly. "Very well. Let us continue. Remy, please come forward."

As Remy moved to the chair that was slightly to the right of the panel, Emilio leaned forward. "Tell us, Remy, how long ago did you first approach Dawn about joining your pack?"

Remy spared her a brief glance. "Approximately seven months ago."

"And what was it that you discussed?"

"I told her that I admired what she did for lone shifters, that I would imagine she found it difficult to run the shelter without protection. I offered for Dawn and her staff to join my pack. I won't say I did it purely for selfless reasons. I made no secret that I was interested in possessing the land the shelter sits on. I wish to expand my territory."

"What was Dawn's response?"

"She turned down the offer, claimed she didn't need any protection. I wasn't happy about that, but I respected her decision. I would have stayed away from the shelter but . . ." Remy sighed. "I'm sure you all remember that local humans began a petition to have the shelter shut down."

Harrison replied, "Yes, the human court dismissed it."

Remy nodded. "But I was worried for the shelter and its future, so I went back to Dawn and repeated my offer. Again, she rejected it out of hand. I felt my only choice was to apply to the council. When I served Dawn the mediation letter, I tried one final time to convince her to accept my offer. It did not happen. In fact, the Phoenix wolves warned me away. I don't feel that such intimidation was necessary or fair. I expected better of Dawn."

Emilio tapped his chin. "I take it mediation was not productive."

"Dawn sees no gain in this for anyone—not even me. I had hoped she would change her mind at some point. I'm surprised she didn't, given the things that later happened."

Landyn's brows pinched together. "Could you elaborate?"

"As I said, I was worried for the shelter and its future. And as I hoped the land would soon be mine, I assigned some of my wolves to guard it. They reported that Dawn was having problems."

"What sort of problems?" asked Parker.

"The shelter always had a constant flow of people coming and going, but lately it seems that not many loners are moving on. The place is becoming overfull. And, according to some of her staff who actually want to move to my pack, some of her sponsors have pulled out."

The lying little fucker. Makenna clenched her jaw to stop the words from escaping her.

"I see," said Emilio.

"I have already told Dawn that I have the means to financially support and expand the building. Yet, she did not seek my help. At first, I thought the female was merely stubborn. But I've come to believe that it's not actually Dawn who's so opposed to joining my pack, it is the two females you see with her."

Landyn consulted a sheet of paper in front of him. "Madisyn Drake and Makenna Wray?"

"Yes," confirmed Remy. "They are, in a sense, her enforcers. I suppose they fear losing their position. My point was proven when Makenna insisted on continuing to work at the shelter after being attacked by extremists, even though it could lead them there. It clearly demonstrates she's selfish and not devoted to the shelter for the right reasons. I believe that Dawn is. Still, if Dawn did not insist that Makenna stay clear of the shelter until things cool down, she doesn't care for the place as much as I thought."

Oh, the asshole was seriously good at twisting things. And that was a real problem. Makenna barely resisted the urge to call him the lying, scheming, sick piece of shit that he was.

"To Dawn's credit," Remy added, "she did appoint two Phoenix wolves to help guard the shelter—something which was very helpful when a pride of cougars tried to invade the building."

Landyn stilled. "Cougars?"

Remy nodded. "They believe Dawn is giving sanctuary to someone they are seeking."

"What happened?" asked Emilio.

"My wolves chased them off. They haven't returned." Remy shifted in his seat. "As I said, the Phoenix wolves have been helpful in guarding the shelter. But the reality is that their presence cannot be a permanent thing. Their pack is reasonably small. They cannot afford to spare enforcers on a daily basis. I doubt they will spare Makenna so often either, meaning Dawn will have less help from now on."

Remy leaned forward. "The truth of the matter is the shelter needs help. It needs protection from humans, it needs more funding so that it can be expanded, and it needs more staff so that Dawn has extra support. I can ensure all of that. Dawn has worked hard for many years; she has put the needs of the shelter before her own in all that time. She deserves to finally be part of something bigger than the shelter; she deserves to have some of the load taken from her. I understand that the idea of change can be unnerving, but she would soon lose that fear and realize this is for the best."

After a brief moment of silence, Parker spoke. "Remy, you may return to your seat. Who were the wolves who chased away the cougars? I'd like to speak to these witnesses."

"They're here with me."

Selene and another of Remy's enforcers were briefly questioned. Emilio praised them for protecting the shelter.

Parker then turned his attention to Dawn. He swept a hand toward the empty chair by the panel. "Dawn Samuels, could you please come forward?" She rose and, head held high, walked to the chair.

Once she sat, Emilio said, "Remy approached you a few times with his offer of protection, yet you quickly declined without giving any real thought to his proposal."

It wasn't a question, Makenna recognized; it was a statement designed to put Dawn on the defensive. If the way Dawn narrowed her eyes was anything to go by, she saw that very clearly.

Emilio braced his elbows on the table and steepled his fingers. "I must say I'm confused as to why."

"Loners don't trust packs," Dawn pointed out. "They would never come to a shelter that is run by a pack. It's also worth noting that there are many species of shifter at the shelter, not just wolves. They wouldn't all fit in a wolf pack, and I doubt they would want to try."

Emilio couldn't deny that, but he sure as shit looked like he wanted to. "Remy has been very civil in his dealings with you. Nonetheless, you felt the need to scare him off using the Phoenix Pack."

"No words were exchanged between him and the Phoenix wolves. They merely stood with us for support. If he finds them intimidating, I can hardly help that." Dawn's response made Remy's upper lip curl back.

"So you admit that you need support?"

"Only against Remy."

Parker looked about to ask a question, but Emilio beat him to it. "Tell me, Dawn, why is the shelter becoming overfull?"

"A large number of the residents were fired from their jobs after their employers—"

"Fired? That made it hard for them to support themselves and move on, I'm guessing. Is it true some of your sponsors pulled out?"

"It is, but—"

He whistled. "Now that must have had a big impact."

Dawn's mouth tightened. "We've attracted new sponsors. And none would have pulled out if—"

"So when Remy says you need help, support, funding, and the ability to expand the building, he couldn't be more accurate. Your shelter is overflowing—"

"No one said it was overflowing," she hissed, and Emilio looked pleased to see her riled.

"—you have cougars fighting to get inside the building—"

"There was no fighting."

"—and you're lacking the one thing the shelter needs to keep going: appropriate funding."

Hissing again, she snapped, "Maybe if you'd let me get a word in edgewise, I could explain why I'm suddenly having all these problems."

Instead, Emilio looked at Parker. "I think it might be helpful to speak with Makenna Wray and hear more about her problems with the extremists."

Oh, fucking groovy. Makenna watched as Dawn's back snapped straight and alpha vibes flowed from her. Not good in a courtroom.

"Makenna does not need to be questioned," stated Dawn. "I can tell you whatever it is you need to know."

Landyn gave Dawn a pointed look. "Reign in those vibes. We will not be intimidated."

"I'm not trying to intimidate anyone, I'm—"

"Wasting time," finished Emilio. "Makenna Wray, please take Dawn's seat."

Swallowing back a groan, Makenna patted Ryan's rock-hard thigh. He didn't want her going up there, she knew; he wanted her close, wanted her where he could easily protect her. "I'll be fine," she whispered in his ear as she rose.

Grinding his teeth so hard he was surprised something didn't crack, Ryan rested a possessive hand on his mate's ass as she slid past him. With each step she took away from him, his anger at Remy and Emilio built in his system. He hated the distance between them. Emilio probably meant to toy with her and twist her words, just as he'd done with Dawn.

What Emilio didn't know was that she'd toy with him right back. Makenna would be pissed at the asshole for playing with Dawn and so she'd deliberately antagonize him. Ryan knew from personal experience how good she was at it.

"I saw the news clipping of your encounter with the extremists," Emilio said as Makenna sat. "They appeared outside your apartment building, correct?"

"I don't live there anymore."

Emilio opened and closed his mouth. "In any case, did they begin a protest outside the building?"

Makenna tilted her head. "Why would you ask if you saw the news? Were you lying?"

Emilio's eyes flashed. "No, I'm merely asking you to verify it."

"Why?"

"Why are you asking why?"

"I think it's important to question everything. Don't you?"

Taking a deep breath, Emilio gave her a brittle smile. "You must have been very frightened to see them outside the building, knowing how zealous these human extremists can be."

Makenna pursed her lips. "I was more annoyed than anything else. They were aggravating my headache."

"Clearly you escaped. Were you seen?"

"By who?"

A muscle in his cheek ticked. "Extremists."

"Well, none followed me."

"The extremists know your name and address—"

"*Old* address."

"—yet you didn't stay clear of the shelter for its safety. You persisted in going there." He paused as he caught sight of a spider crawling along the bench. He wacked it hard with a notepad, crushing the insect.

Makenna winced. "You shouldn't have done that. It'll rain now. Quick, cross your fingers."

Ryan closed his eyes, sighing inwardly. His mate was insane, and now everyone knew it. Still, he couldn't help but want to smile.

Emilio arched a brow. "Rain?"

"Yes, you killed a spider."

Emilio turned to his fellow council members with a smirk, which they didn't return. In fact, they seemed to agree with Makenna. Expression hard, Emilio turned back to her. "Why didn't you stay away from the shelter?"

She blinked. "Why would I?"

"To stop the extremists from following you there, of course."

"I already told you, no one was following me."

"I'm sure they will from here on out, considering the news showed them hanging outside your new pack's territory." So they *had* seen this morning's news.

"I don't have to physically be at the shelter to help. My main job is to find loners a new home by tracking their family members. That mostly involves using a computer. I can do that from my own territory."

"Perhaps, but—"

"They won't stick around long, though. They'll be too scared that The Movement will come for them."

"That you're so determined to continue working at the shelter makes me think that Remy is right. I put it to you, Makenna, that you have been pressuring Dawn to reject his offers of help. I put it to you that you have no true devotion to the shelter; you are too selfish to—" Cutting himself off, he stilled—hell, everyone stilled—as they heard it . . .

Tap. Tap. Tap. Tap. Tap. Tap.

It was the sound of rain hitting the window. Ryan almost smiled. Makenna blinked innocently as Emilio stared at her, jaw clenched.

Makenna leaned forward, as if about to share a secret. "Hey, do you want to know the truth, the whole truth, and nothing but the truth?"

"I know the truth. I don't need to hear your distorted version of it." He waved a hand, dismissing her. But he froze as an audio recording began to play.

"You're a big fan of blackmail, aren't you, Remy? That's how you got some of Dawn's sponsors to withdraw their funding."

"Blackmail is a quick and efficient way of getting things done."

"Especially since your little plan to sic the cougars on the shelter didn't work so well, huh."

"I know you're hiding the viper."

"Viper?"

"Play dumb if you wish, but I've seen your records."

"When you hacked into Dawn's computer, you mean? Yeah, we know all about that."

Makenna clicked "Stop" on her cell phone, enjoying the shock on Remy's face. "That's right," she told the council members. "The cougars would never have appeared if Remy hadn't hacked Dawn's computer, read her files, and then tipped the pride off *about a four-year-old child* they wanted to kill." She licked her front teeth. "See, the real reason that Dawn won't give into Remy's demands is that she refuses to allow a pedophile constant access to children." Parker sucked in a breath. Makenna snorted. "Come on, we've all heard the rumors."

"Rumors," echoed Emilio. "Rumors created to blacken Remy's name and undermine his power—nothing more. And your recording means nothing. Remy does not state that he contacted the cougars. Nor does he state that he did in fact blackmail anyone, just that he finds it an efficient method."

Makenna nodded once. "True, so I think you'll be better hearing this from someone else." Knowing Emilio would be of no help at all, she looked at Parker. "There should be two people waiting outside that door. You really want to hear what they have to say."

After a moment, Parker nodded and instructed a wolf manning the door to open it. He frowned as two males entered the room. "Who are you?"

The taller of the two, looking slick and smart in a designer suit, said, "Ravi Lamar. I'm a lone shifter and I've been sponsoring the shelter for many years. Not so long ago, I was approached by a wolf who wanted to pass on a message from his Alpha."

Harrison asked, "What was that message?"

"That if I didn't withdraw my funding from the shelter, he would expose me to my clients as a shifter. I ignored the threat. My loyalty is very much to the shelter. I was once a resident there. If it wasn't for Dawn, I wouldn't have the education, skills, or money to be the successful businessman that I am today."

Emilio's gaze narrowed. "Did this wolf name his Alpha?"

"No."

Emilio grinned. "Then why would you think his Alpha is Remy?"

"Because the wolf who approached me is sitting at his side."

That made Emilio's grin vanish in a rush.

Parker eyed the male behind Ravi. "What about you? Are you another witness?"

The blond reluctantly stepped forward. "My name is Grayson. I was a member of Remy's pack until three days ago."

Parker leaned forward, bracing his elbows on the panel. "What happened three days ago?"

Grayson balls his hands into fists. "I ran away."

"Why?"

"As I was passing his cabin, I looked into the window and caught him . . ." His eyes briefly flicked to Remy, and he swallowed hard.

Harrison pressed, "You caught him, what?"

Grayson took a deep breath. "I saw him touching a child . . . inappropriately."

"Define inappropriately," said Parker. "I need to understand the gravity of what you saw."

Grayson thrust a hand through his hair and recited an account that made Makenna's stomach churn and her fists clench in fury. He then added, "Before I could do anything, Deanne burst into the room."

Harrison's brows pinched together. "Deanne?"

At the same time that Grayson explained, "Remy's mother," the woman jumped to her feet and shouted, "That's a lie!"

Landyn gave her a hard look. "You will sit down." It wasn't until Remy hissed something at her that she actually did.

Parker looked at Grayson. "Carry on."

Grayson swallowed. "She screamed at the kid to get out. At first, I thought she was helping him. But then she turned to Remy and started crying and shouting, saying she refused to share him with anyone—including the pups; she said she'd kill them all just like she'd killed the others. She was jealous and raging, and she hit him over the head with a lamp."

"Lies!" shouted Deanne. "It's all lies!"

"One more outburst and you will leave this room," Landyn warned her. He turned back to Grayson. "Continue."

"I don't know what happened after that; I ran. I wanted to take the pups with me, but I couldn't get inside Remy's cabin without being seen. I knew that I had to go for help." Grayson's face scrunched up.

"They're both sick in the head, and neither of them should be anywhere near kids."

Deanne leaped to her feet, but Remy tugged her back down and hissed, *"Quiet."*

There was a short, pensive silence that was broken by Harrison. "This is a matter that needs to be thoroughly investigated—a case separate from the matter of the shelter." Parker and Landyn nodded their agreement. "In light of what has been said today, I'm satisfied that Remy attempted to sabotage the shelter in an attempt to help him gain what he wanted."

"Remy Deacon, your application is dismissed," declared Parker. "With regards to these allegations, an investigation will begin straightaway. I believe in being innocent until proven guilty. Even so, the pups of your pack will be relocated until the case is resolved."

Deanne gasped, but Ryan thought she didn't look very upset. The crazy bitch was probably pleased the children would be out of her way.

"My wolves will escort you back to your territory and take the pups to safety," added Parker. "This meeting is over." Each of the council members rose and left the room, and Makenna made her way to Dawn. The feline wrapped her in a hug, happy and relieved.

Remy very slowly rose to his feet, like a snake uncoiling. He glared at Dawn. "I warned you. You'll regret this. All of you." His eyes went to Ryan. "Especially you."

Ryan didn't have to ask what he meant. But if he really thought the York Pack would get anywhere near Zac, he was a dumb son of a bitch.

"You lied to me," Deanne growled at Makenna. "My son never touched you."

Makenna flashed her a taunting smile. "Didn't he?"

A crease formed between Deanne's brows. The woman was so paranoid where Remy was concerned that she had no confidence in her own convictions. "Remy, it's not true, is it?" He didn't answer, just headed for the exit. She trailed after him, repeating her question.

Dante waited until Remy and his wolves left before speaking. "I half expected him to attack."

Ryan gave a quick shake of the head. "He still thinks he has the upper hand. If he knew that we're fully aware the York Pack are his guests, he would have reacted very differently."

Grayson moved to Dante. "You'll kill Remy, right? The sick fuck needs to die."

"He'll die," Dante vowed before calling Trey and telling him the result of the hearing. Hanging up, he said, "The extremists left."

Makenna wanted to be relieved by that, but there was no saying the humans wouldn't return. Still, she'd count today as a win. She linked her arm through Ryan's. "I'm fucking ecstatic that the pups will be taken from Remy."

"Me too," said Jaime. "You know, I wasn't all that superstitious until I met you. Did you see Emilio's face when it started to rain? Priceless." Nodding, Madisyn chuckled.

Makenna looked up at Ryan. "Are you a believer yet?" He grunted. "Fine, be irrational."

Ryan just didn't understand her. "How can you call *me* irrational when *you* picked your clothes this morning based on what your horoscope told you?" Who did that?

"Well, if you remember correctly, it told me to prepare for wet weather. Turns out it was necessary. Although . . . I suppose it's worth considering that if Emilio hadn't killed that spider, it might not have rained. In that sense, maybe it wasn't fated to rain. Unless, of course, the spider's destiny was to die at Emilio's—"

"Stop, stop," Ryan told her. He just couldn't take anymore. "Let's just go."

"Always so grouchy."

Whatever.

CHAPTER TWENTY

Normally, Makenna found a bath with Ryan to be the epitome of relaxation. Hot water, bubbles, large hands sliding over her skin—total heaven. She loved feeling those hands massaging shampoo into her hair and soaping her down. Loved returning the favor. Tonight, though, the tension wouldn't leave her mind or body. Not that she'd expected differently, given what loomed ahead.

She had spent the entire afternoon in Trey's office with most of the Phoenix wolves, discussing Remy's plans to invade their territory in two days' time. It wouldn't be easy to defend the territory. Remy's pack was large and would be accompanied by the York Pack. Also, it was probable that he would top up his numbers by calling on his alliances.

A preemptive strike wasn't possible because Remy's territory was so vast. All they could do was be prepared for the attack. They would have been seriously outnumbered, but, thankfully, several of Trey's alliances—including the Mercury Pack, Dante's brother's pack, and Taryn's old pack—had agreed to join them. In addition, Myles's Alpha had contacted Trey, having heard of Remy's plans via Rosa, and offered to support them. The numbers were now pretty even.

Still, no one was feeling reassured. The other couples had retreated to their rooms, wanting some private time together. Makenna refused to even consider that she could lose Ryan in the fight. It wasn't a possibility. Nope. No way. Nu-uh.

He nuzzled her neck. "Stop thinking so hard."

She would. Nothing good could come of dwelling on the battle ahead. Her worries would only intrude on their time together. "Sorry." She forced her limbs to loosen as she leaned back against him. "Let's talk about something to get my mind off the fight."

That was the perfect opening for Ryan to reveal what was on his mind. "I know why the mating bond hasn't snapped into place."

"You do?" Makenna still wasn't convinced there was one, but she didn't want to argue.

"It's an external issue."

"What does that mean?"

Under the water, he splayed a hand on her stomach. "Deep inside, you worry this pack will betray you the way your childhood pack did."

Makenna frowned. "No, your pack is good."

"You've just proven my point."

"Huh?"

"You called it my pack." She still didn't see it as hers. It aggravated his wolf.

Squirming, she said, "I'm still adjusting to being part of one, that's all."

"Adjusting, or holding back because you fear getting comfortable here in case they turn on you?"

"I don't fear they'll betray me. I just don't really feel part of the pack yet. I can't explain why."

"I can. Your fear of being let down again is causing you to hold back." He licked at his claiming mark. "When it's gone, it'll clear the path for the bond."

"You know, I have to give you credit where it's due. At no point whatsoever have you ever doubted that we're true mates. Nothing I've said has made any difference. There's no bond, and yet you're still unwavering in your belief. It's admirable."

He linked their fingers, speaking into her ear. "Do you ever feel something pulling at you? A pressure on your head and chest? I do." He was pretty sure it was the bond.

Sometimes she thought she did. But admitting that aloud was hard; it could just be setting herself up for disappointment.

"It's there, Kenna. Waiting." He kissed her temple. "The pack sees you as one of us. None of them would ever betray you. They'd try to kill anyone who ever hurt you."

"Try?"

"I'd get there first." That made her smile. "At least be honest about one thing: you hold yourself back from the pack, don't you?"

Makenna took a moment to think about it. "I've lost most of the things that were important to me. It's hard to fully trust it won't happen again."

He got that. He got why, on one level, she was preparing herself for the disappointment of losing more. He couldn't blame her. But it was essential to him that she accepted her place in the pack. There were certain to be some casualties during the battle. He needed to know that if anything happened to him, she'd be okay; she wouldn't be alone, wouldn't be lost under the grief of losing another person. Right now, he very much doubted that she'd stay in the pack without him. "Promise me one thing."

She wasn't sure why, but the hairs on her neck rose. "What?"

"Promise me that if something happens to me—"

"It won't."

"Kenna."

"No. This a pointless conversation because you are not going to die." And she was done talking about it.

"I need to know that you won't be alone."

"I won't, because you'll be there." Pulling out the plug, she got to her feet and stepped out onto the mat. Wrapping a fluffy towel around her, she went into the bedroom. Yes, she was fleeing from the conversation. She refused to even discuss that he might—

Cutting off the thought, she grabbed her brush and began dragging it through her wet hair. Her wolf hunkered down, thoroughly annoyed with her mate for even suggesting the unacceptable. Makenna felt Ryan's energy beating against her skin before his warm, solid chest pressed to her back. She gave him a sidelong glance. "Are you done talking about morbid shit?"

Ryan took her brush and placed it on the bedside cabinet. "We could instead talk about how it would be better if you stayed inside the caves during the battle."

"You're not cutting me out of the fight." They'd already discussed that. She would *not* sit here, twiddling her thumbs, while he was in danger.

He curled his arms around her. "We need people to stay inside and protect the others."

"People have already been assigned to do that."

"The pups will feel better if you stay with them."

She snorted. "That's not going to work, Ryan. Look, I understand you don't want me risking myself. I'm not crazy about you doing it. But I wouldn't ask you to stay out of the battle. It's not who you are."

He growled, exasperated by how fair she was being. It made it hard to argue his point. "You're not trained in combat."

"No, but I can still fight. My wolf can fight."

He didn't doubt that. Her wolf was wild even when she played. Still . . . "You've never been in a battle before."

"There's a first time for everything."

"If I'm worrying about you, I won't be able to focus."

"You'll be able to focus if you don't pointlessly worry."

Ryan nipped her throat. "Stubborn."

"Yes. Now can we drop this? You're missing the bigger picture: I'm naked, you're naked, and there are much more interesting things to do when naked."

She did have a point. And honestly, talking about the battle was the last way he wanted to spend the night. "Turn around, Kenna." Once she was facing him, he fingered one of her wet locks. "Drop the towel."

Well. It would seem that the battle talk was indeed over. Makenna let the towel puddle at her feet. Her skin burned under the intensity and heat of his gaze as it drank her in. His rarely expressive eyes glittered with possessiveness and a predatory hunger that made her mouth dry up. She bit her lower lip, but his thumb tugged it free.

"Only I get to bite this mouth. It belongs to me." Tangling a hand in her hair, Ryan angled her head how he wanted it and lowered his mouth to hers. Her lips parted, and he swept his tongue inside. He tasted her. Feasted on her. Demanded everything she had . . . because it was his to take.

He snatched her head back, exposing her neck and making her spine arch. She ground against him as he licked and sucked at her claiming bite. Her little throaty moans made his cock jerk. He closed his hand possessively around her breast, squeezing and plumping. How the fuck did she get her skin this soft?

Needing to touch him, Makenna tugged off his towel and then fisted his cock—it was hot and hard and pulsed in her hand. He grunted into her neck as she pumped him, keeping her grip firm just the way he liked it. But she needed more than just to touch him.

Ryan watched as she dropped to her knees—something she hadn't done since that time when she'd tried to take control and he'd refused to allow it. There was no calculation in her gaze this time. "Are you trying to take control again, Kenna?" He didn't think so, but he had to be sure.

"No. I want to taste you."

"Then do it." Without any preamble, she took him into her mouth. No teasing licks. No nibbling or stroking. She just deep-throated him. And it was fucking amazing. Ryan had never much liked having the whole thing drawn out. He didn't have the patience for it. His mate obviously sensed that about him.

"Suck harder, Kenna. That's it." The sight of her gorgeous mouth wrapped around his cock, the scent of her need, and the feel of her sucking him deep over and over . . . *fuck*. Wrapping her hair around both fists, he took over. He needed this. Needed to fuck her mouth and come down her throat—another way to mark her as his. Soon enough, his balls tightened and he felt the telling tingle in his spine. "Swallow it." He thrust hard and came with a growl—and she swallowed it all. Masculine satisfaction settled deep in his gut. She was getting a reward for that.

He jerked his chin at the bed. "On your back, legs spread." For once, there was no defiance in her as she obeyed him. "Good girl." Ryan took a moment to just look at her, taking in her flushed face, gorgeous breasts, pebbled nipples, delicate curves, navel piercing, and her glistening pussy.

Kneeling on the bed between her thighs, he met her eyes; they were glazed over with the vicious need that he could *feel* coursing through her. That need was feeding his, making it hard to stay in control. "You're the most perfect fucking thing I've ever seen."

The gruffly spoken compliment made her smile. "So you can say pretty words."

"Not pretty words, just a fact." Slipping his hands under her ass, Ryan tilted her hips and swiped his tongue through her folds. Her taste, so familiar and addictive, thrummed through his system. He didn't tease her. He devoured her: licking, lapping, nipping, suckling her clit, and stabbing his tongue inside her.

"Ryan, I want you in me." She felt so empty. Ached to feel him thrusting deep. Instead, he drove one finger inside her. Again. Again. And again. He added another finger, curving them just right. But then his tongue replaced them, and one of those fingers circled the rim of her ass. She sucked in a breath as he worked it inside her. The dual assault on her senses didn't help. It only made her ache more. *"Ryan."* He ignored the demand in her voice. She shoved at his head to dislodge him. He growled against her flesh and thrust a second finger into her ass. Then she was coming. The orgasm took her by surprise, hitting her hard.

Ryan withdrew his fingers, released her, and tapped her hip. "Roll over." As soon as she lay on her stomach, he pulled her to her knees. "Keep your head down." He lunged deep, grunting as her pussy clenched him tight and fluttered around him. "So fucking wet. Good. I need my cock to be slick so I slide in here"—he pressed the tip of his finger into her ass—"nice and easy."

She tensed. "What?"

"You knew this was coming, Kenna. You knew I'd want to claim you everywhere."

Well, yeah, she'd expected him to do this at *some* point. Male shifters always claimed their mates in every way possible. Still, she—

"You want this." If he thought for even one second that she didn't, he'd wait. Ryan fucked her slow and hard as he again worked two fingers inside her ass. He scissored them, stretching her enough that he soon had a third finger inside. She pushed back into every thrust. "That's it."

"Ryan, I'm close."

"I know." He fucked her faster, deeper; barely resisting the craving to bury himself deep into her pussy and explode—she was just so hot and wet. "Come," he growled. She threw her head back and choked out a scream as her back arched and her pussy clamped and contracted around him. Fighting the urge to come, he withdrew from her pussy and replaced his fingers with the head of his cock.

Makenna's eyes snapped open at the feel of his cock pushing into her ass. The pressure and the burn of his size stretching her made her squirm.

He gave her ass a sharp slap. "Be still. Just push out as I push in. That's it, like that." He slowly sank into her, gritting his teeth against the temptation to pound hard and fast. "Tight," he hissed. So tight she was strangling his cock, but it felt too fucking good. They both sighed when he was finally balls deep. "You okay?"

"Sort of." She was full. Maybe too full for this to be fun. But then, as he slowly pulled back and smoothly plunged back in, she gasped as all kinds of nerve endings sparked to life. "Again." Friction built inside her as he kept each thrust slow and easy, which was very unlike Ryan. "More." His pace barely altered. "I'm not delicate," she snapped.

"No, but you're mine. And I don't want to hurt you."

"You're not. I need more."

Taking her at her word, Ryan hardened his thrusts as he pumped in and out of her. He branded her with every plunge of his cock, loving the moans and gasps she fed him. Fuck, he wouldn't last much longer. He needed to shoot deep in her ass, claiming it as surely as he'd claimed her pussy and her mouth.

Raking a hand in her hair, Ryan yanked her head back and pounded harder. "Make me come, Kenna. Do it now." For a second time that night, she screamed as she gave him what he wanted. He plunged deep and held himself rigid as he came so fucking hard that he was surprised he didn't see stars.

Afterward, as he pressed kisses along her spine, a sudden pressure built in his chest and his head seemed to throb. "Do you feel it?"

Glancing at him over her shoulder, she nodded. "What is it?"

"You know." Pulling out of her, Ryan scooped her up and took her into the bathroom. As they stood under the hot spray of the shower, he said, "The bond won't let you hold back much longer." It was too strong. Probably because, as a couple, *they* were strong. Makenna might have initially doubted his commitment, but not anymore. Like she'd told him, he had all of her. She had all of him. Mating bond or not, Ryan doubted he'd survive losing her. Even if he did, he'd be a husk. Empty. Useless. Going through the motions but not living.

Unlike the time he'd escaped from captivity, he didn't think his pack would get him through it. There would be no chance of him healing. He wouldn't *want* to heal. Everything would be fucking pointless without her—this quirky little person who made him want to smile on a daily basis, who never made him feel like he lacked or needed to change.

Makenna curled her arms around him. "Why are you sad?" The emotion trickled through her veins.

"You'll be in danger. I hate that."

"So will you. I hate that."

"You're not going to stay behind, are you?" It wasn't a question; it was a resigned statement.

She licked at his claiming mark. "I can't." She couldn't wave him off as he walked into certain danger. Hell, no. Seeing he was about to argue, she said, "When I was twelve, I watched my mom walk out of our little apartment to pick up some groceries. And I waited for her to come back. And I kept waiting. And waiting. And waiting. There was nothing else I could do. She'd once made me promise that if she was ever late, I wouldn't go searching for her. So I didn't. Two days later, there was a knock at the door. And I knew before I even opened it that it wasn't her and that I was never going to see her again. Don't ask me to wait like that again for someone I care about to come back to me. Don't do that."

Fuck. Ryan tightened his arms around her. "Why do you hold shit in?" It frustrated him that she'd give the people she cared for anything they needed, but she very rarely shared her pain with them.

"You do it too."

Okay, that was a fair point. He gripped her chin and snared her gaze. "You don't leave my side during the battle. You have to stay with me at all times." If he couldn't see her with his own eyes and know that she was safe, he wouldn't be able to focus.

"I have no objection to that." It meant she could watch his back. "You don't need to worry so hard, you know. My wolf's a badass. Why is that funny?"

"I'm not laughing."

His expression hadn't even changed, but . . . "I can feel your amusement, White Fang. My wolf is not impressed." She was very much offended.

"I'm not denying that she's tough. But she's streetwise tough, not battle tough."

"There's a difference?"

"Yes. Street fights are over fairly quickly and require a minimum amount of strategy. Battles go on for longer and require *a lot* of strategy. Not to mention stamina and endurance. No matter how tired you are, you can't afford to drop your guard or lose concentration. And your wolf . . ." He struggled for a nice way to say it. As he had no tact at all, it wasn't easy. "She's not very focused. She's easily distracted." No, Makenna didn't like that comment one little bit. He quickly added, "Not in a bad way, but . . . like a cat."

"A cat?"

Ryan inwardly winced. He was just making this worse. "You know: show her something shiny and she forgets that she's supposed to—*ow!*" He rubbed at the spot where a sprinkle of chest hair had once been. "That hurt."

"*Good.* Oh, and when my wolf saves your ass tomorrow, you *will* publicly apologize for comparing her to a cat."

The certainty in her voice made him blink. "She's going to save my ass?"

"Yes."

"You know this how?"

"I have a feeling."

Ryan closed his eyes. *Insane.* On the upside, there was never a dull moment with his mate. "Let's just get out of the damn shower and sleep."

"Always so grouchy."

Whatever.

CHAPTER TWENTY-ONE

For the second time in two days, Makenna was in Trey's crowded office. He was discussing battle tactics with Taryn, his Betas and enforcers, the Mercury Alphas and Betas, and via teleconference the other Alphas who would join them against Remy.

As Makenna listened carefully, she became increasingly aware of just how right Ryan was. There was a lot of strategy involved in battles. It was all completely foreign to her, and she was totally out of her element. Still, that didn't mean she would be anywhere other than at her mate's side when the danger came.

The door opened and Grace entered with a tray of coffee. Ryan handed one to Makenna as he said, "You sure you want to be part of this battle tomorrow?" He understood why it would drive her crazy to stay behind, and he couldn't ask it of her now that he knew the source of her determination. Still, both he and his wolf hoped that she'd change her mind. Makenna just stared at Ryan.

Jaime grinned. "Wow, you've got Ryan's serial killer look totally down." That made all the females chuckle. "You gotta teach it to me."

"Stop trying to talk her out of fighting, Ryan," complained Taryn. "She's not helpless. There might be a lot of them, but there's a lot of us too. And we have the advantage of knowing every inch of this land. They don't."

Makenna smiled, thankful for Taryn's vote of confidence. But her smile faded when an unexpected wolf walked inside. "Zac, what are you doing in here, sweetie?"

Zac rolled back his shoulders and planted his feet. "I want to be part of the battle."

Ryan had half expected this to happen. The teenager had pride, guts, and a need to face his demons. "Zac—"

"I know what you're going to say. I'm just a kid and I don't have any real training. But it's my fault they're coming—"

"Nobody put a gun to their head and forced them to make these plans," said Dante.

Ryan grunted his agreement. "You are not responsible for their choices."

"I should have stood up to the Alpha a long time ago," Zac gritted out. "I didn't."

Grace put a supportive hand on his shoulder. "What could you have done, Zac? He's bigger and stronger than you, through no fault of your own."

Makenna nodded. "You did the smart thing. You got away. I've told you before, it takes guts to run. A lot of people don't try because they're too scared to get caught. You're not weak, but you're not strong enough to hold your own against these assholes. That's shitty, but it's the truth."

Ryan grunted. He couldn't have said it better himself.

Zac rubbed a palm on his thigh. "I don't like that everyone is risking their lives while I hide here."

Dominic hung his arm around Zac's shoulders. "There's no shame in hiding if it's the smart thing to do. Do you judge Grace, Lydia, Hope, and Riley for staying behind?"

"No, of course not."

"They're not staying because they don't have guts," added Tao. "They're doing it because they know their strengths don't lie in fighting. But they can keep the kids calm and safe, so that's what they're going to do."

Zac snorted. "Riley's a fighter."

"Which is why it's torture for her to stay," began Taryn, "but she knows Dexter and Savannah are so attached to her that they'd try to follow her. Staying is the smart thing to do, so she's doing the smart thing. You need to do that too."

His shoulders sagged. "I just hate that I've brought trouble here."

"*They* are bringing trouble here," corrected Trick. "Not you."

"You have no reason to feel so guilty," said Ally. "The fault belongs only to them. They've made the decision to come here and—" Ally broke off with a gasp. Her eyes turned white, and, shit, it was the freakiest thing Makenna had ever seen. Her wolf's hackles rose and her ears pricked up.

Shaya went to their Beta female's side. "Shit, she's having a vision."

Derren drew his mate to him, rubbing a hand over her back. She didn't move or speak. It was like she wasn't even with them. It seemed to take forever before she snapped out of it with a low gasp.

Derren cupped her face. "Baby, you okay?"

She nodded, blinking a few times.

"That vision was longer than your usual ones," said Roni.

Trey sidled up to her, arms folded. "What did you see?"

"It was two visions—one right after the other." Ally swallowed, her eyebrows drawing together.

Just the look in the Seer's eyes was enough to make anxiety curdle in Makenna's stomach and cause the hairs on her arms and nape to rise.

"Something's changed," said Ally. "Something's twisted everything and changed the plans. The York Pack . . . I saw them here. They're coming now. And they're bringing at least a hundred wolves with them."

The news hit the room like a bomb. Trey went rigid. "You're certain?"

"In the vision, we were all wearing exactly what we're wearing now."

Curses rang throughout the room, and then everyone was talking at once. The Alphas communicating via teleconference said they'd leave immediately with their wolves and head for Phoenix Pack territory. Similarly, Nick called his brother to summon him and his other enforcers.

"Wait!" shouted Ally, once again gaining everyone's attention. "There was something else. A second vision. I saw Remy. But I didn't see him *here.*"

Marcus frowned. "Then where?"

Ally looked at Makenna. "He wants the children back. He thinks the council brought them to the shelter."

Makenna felt the blood drain from her face as an ice-cold dread flooded every vein. Her hand flew to her stomach, which suddenly felt rock hard. Her heart was racing so fast she was surprised it didn't explode. She turned to Ryan. "I have to get there. I have to get there *now.*"

Ally grabbed her wrist. "Wait, you have to listen to me. You can't barge in there; you have to be very careful how you proceed. Remy . . . I was in his head for a minute—that doesn't happen a lot in a vision. When it does, it's plain horrible."

Derren grimaced. "In his head?"

"He's not rational right now," said Ally. "In a strange, twisted way, having the children around kept him stable. He's known sickness and depravity at the hands of his mother. But the children . . . they're so innocent, so pure and unthreatening, and he's drawn to that. They keep away all the shame and guilt he feels even though he can't accept that he's a victim. He doesn't seem to realize what he's become. He just knows he needs them close. He'll do whatever he has to do to get them back, and he's convinced they're at the shelter, that Dawn's keeping them from him."

Makenna raked a shaking hand through her hair. "They're not there; I have no idea where they are."

"We know that," said Taryn. "But will he *believe* that?"

Ally gave a sad shake of her head. "I really don't think so. Like I said, he isn't thinking rationally. He wants the children and the shelter. He blames Dawn for everything that's gone wrong."

"I'll call her." Makenna moved to the corner of the room to make the call.

Zac hurried to Ryan. "You'll go to the shelter and help them, right?"

Feeling torn, Ryan clenched his fists. "I promised I'd protect you from your old pack."

"Dude, Dawn and Madisyn are more important to me than that. There will be hundreds of people here to side with our pack soon. No one's guarding the shelter because they all wanted to hear Trey's plans and thought Remy would come *here*." Zac licked his lips. "You can't let Makenna go alone. She will if she has to."

Knowing Zac was right, Ryan looked at Ally. "How many wolves did Remy have with him?"

"There were around twelve that I could *see*. But that doesn't mean there aren't more."

Makenna returned to Ryan. "Neither Dawn nor Madisyn are answering their phone. How long do we have before Remy arrives at the shelter?" she asked Ally.

The Seer shrugged. "Sometimes I have a vision seconds before it happens, sometimes it's longer."

Which meant there was a very strong possibility that Remy was already at the shelter. *Fuck.* Makenna turned back to Ryan. "I can't wait any longer." Her wolf was just as frantic as she was.

Taryn nodded. "You need to go. But not alone. The shelter's under our protection. Fucking nobody gets to harm a single person in it."

Dante stepped forward. "Jaime and I will come with you."

"If you're going to need to sneak inside, we're the best people to have with you," said Jaime. "We're almost as good as Ryan."

"Good idea," said Taryn. She turned to Makenna and Ryan. "I'm sorry, but I can't afford to spare more people right now." The Alpha female was right; at that moment, the pack was vulnerable against all of the wolves that would soon attack. "I'll send others to the shelter when reinforcements arrive."

Makenna gave Zac a hug and then followed Ryan, Dante, and Jaime out of the office. Minutes later, they were in the Chevy, and Ryan was speeding to the shelter. Makenna repeatedly tried to contact Dawn, Madisyn, and Colton, but she couldn't get through to anyone.

"Fuck. No one's answering their cells, the reception phone, or the one in Dawn's office." Which meant something was very seriously wrong, and it was more than likely that Remy was already in the building. Her wolf paced, anxious and filled with the same bubbling fury that was building in Makenna.

"The shelter still has wards that keep out threats, right?" asked Dante from the backseat, to which she nodded. "How could Remy have got past them?"

Makenna shrugged, rubbing at her wrists. "He could have hired a witch to unravel them." He'd known about the wards from his failed attempts to enter the building; he'd felt the magick there, just as Ryan had.

"Is there any way inside the shelter other than the front, back, or side doors?"

"Yes. There is an emergency exit for people who need to make a quick getaway."

"Then that's how we'll get inside," said Ryan.

"We'll need to enter the territory through the forest behind the shelter," Makenna told him.

"Does Dawn have a drill for situations like this?" asked Jaime, linking hands with her mate.

"Yes," replied Makenna. "The witch I hired told me that if anyone tried to disable the wards, an alarm would be sounded. Most of the residents know to grab any children and get to the bunker below the building."

Dante arched his brows. "The bunker can't be big enough for all the residents."

"It isn't, which is why women and children are the priority. Others might have escaped through the emergency exit. A lot of people will have stayed with Dawn to protect her."

Jaime worried her bottom lip. "Is there any way Remy could find the bunker?"

"The only way inside is through a hidden door in the basement. Given how well it's concealed, I'll be amazed if he finds it. He won't be able to sniff out the people hiding because the basement smells of enough bleach to throw off the strongest nose."

Ryan remembered the smell and knew she was right.

The Beta female exhaled a relieved breath. "So the children should all be safe."

"I hope so."

Ryan cast a quick look at his mate. She was pale, her lips were pinched, her body was subtly tremoring, and the wild glint in her eyes was feverish. But, since her emotions were echoing inside him, he didn't need to read her body language to know she was an emotional mess. His wolf wanted to nuzzle her. Ryan put a hand on her thigh. "Kenna, you need to stay calm for me."

"I'm calm."

He grunted. She was far from it. Her system was restless with anger, anxiety, desperation, and dread. He was just as fucking infuriated, but he knew better than to let emotion get in the way. His mate wasn't so good at that. Being one to overthink things, she was most likely imagining all kinds of awful scenarios and driving herself insane with them. "We won't let anything happen to Dawn and Madisyn, I swear that to you."

It was difficult to swallow, and the movement pained the back of her throat. "You heard what Ally said. Remy blames Dawn for everything. He's not rational right now."

"She also said we had to proceed carefully. If he hears us, if he knows we've come for him, he'll hurt as many people as he can."

Makenna blew out a long breath, knowing he was right. "Calm. I'll be calm. But Madisyn won't." And that was what worried her most of all. "She doesn't think; she reacts."

"She won't endanger Dawn."

"No, but she might try to kill Remy if he or one of his wolves harm her."

Unable to deny that, Ryan said nothing. He didn't know Madisyn well. He wasn't sure anyone other than Dawn and Makenna could claim to know her well. But he did sense that she was extremely close to those two females, that they were anchors for her. He also sensed that Dawn and Madisyn were equally important to Makenna. If anything happened to either of them, there was no saying what she'd do. That meant he'd have to keep a close watch on his mate. He couldn't afford for her to lose her shit and get herself killed.

Minutes later, Ryan turned down a dirt path and parked close to the shelter's perimeter fence. Switching off the engine, he said, "Remember, Kenna—"

"Be calm, I got it."

But she wasn't anything even close to calm. So he cupped her nape and kissed her. "You can *feel* how calm I am, right?"

She could. He was admirably cool and collected, his mind clear and objective. "Yes."

"Use it. Let it flow through you." If they could feed from each other's arousal, they could do this too.

"I don't know how."

"It's already inside you. All you have to do is cling to it. Okay?"

Nodding, she reached for that calm and held tight to it.

When some of the wildness retreated from her eyes, Ryan nodded in approval. "Let's go. Stay close." They easily scaled the fence, not making a sound. He was about to head through the trees when he heard slight rustling behind him. It was Makenna, reaching beneath a bush. "What are you doing?"

"You want to go in through the emergency exit, right?" There was a slight grating sound, and she smiled as she flipped back the bush, revealing a downward tunnel.

Jaime's brows flew up. "That's seriously smart."

"About nine years ago, a badger shifter stayed here who'd once served in the army. He was pretty paranoid. Dawn had to keep confiscating his smoke grenades—we didn't even know where he was getting them from. Anyway, he built tunnels beneath the shelter and the forest, preferred living in his animal form."

"So there's a tunnel system under here?" asked Dante.

Makenna nodded. "He also insisted on building this escape route for when 'they' finally came for him because he 'knew too much.' We never did work out who or what he was talking about." She swiftly descended the ladder and then shuffled aside to make room for the others.

Bending to fit into the tunnel, Ryan patted her ass. "Lead the way." As they advanced through the tunnels, he noticed the little red symbols on the wall that marked the way to the shelter. Makenna didn't once glance at them; she seemed to know exactly where she was going.

"Almost there." Rounding a corner, she stopped dead, causing the others to bump into her.

"Makenna!" A teenage girl grinned at the group of people with her. "See, I told you Madisyn would get word to her."

Moving toward them, Makenna said, "I thought at least some of you would have left."

A dark woman shrugged one shoulder. "My man's still up there. I won't leave without him. Besides, we figured you'd need some help when you got here."

"Help?" asked Dante.

"You want to know how many people are here and what they want, don't you? Remy brought about twenty to twenty-five wolves with him. He announced that he's the Alpha now and that this is his territory. Then he started shouting names, saying they belonged to him and he wanted them back. We have no idea who he means."

Makenna's chest clenched. "Dawn and Madisyn?"

"They were alive when we climbed down here. But I don't trust Remy not to hurt them."

An elderly male tapped his temple. "He's not right in the head." He peeked around Makenna. "You didn't bring many people with you."

"Others will come soon. Did all the kids make it to the bunker?"

The dark female nodded. "We all got moving when we heard the alarm. Everyone else huddled in the cafeteria to make it look like they were the only people there."

The teenager bit her lip. "He won't hurt Dawn, will he?"

"No, he won't," stated Makenna. Her wolf growled, backing her up. The animal wasn't interested in being calm or thinking clearly. She wanted to rip out the throats of all the bastards who'd invaded the shelter and endangered everyone in it. She kept pushing to surface, wanting to take control so she could hunt them down. Taking a deep breath, Makenna again reached for the calm echoing through her, thanks to Ryan.

"You all wait here," she told the residents before gesturing for Ryan, Jaime, and Dante to follow her past the group. That was when they came to another ladder. "Okay, this leads to a trapdoor in one of the family rooms. Don't be alarmed when you get to the top and realize you're in a closet."

Dante frowned. "The trapdoor's at the bottom of a closet?"

"Another of the badger's ideas. And a good one."

"How close is this room to the cafeteria?"

"Close enough that we have to be quiet." If they found them, they would also find the trapdoor and the people hiding below.

"I'll go up first." Reaching the top of the ladder, Dante pushed open the trapdoor and then, without making a sound, slowly swung open the closet door. She was guessing the room was empty, because he stepped out of the closet. Jaime went next, quickly followed by Makenna and Ryan.

Dante quietly spoke. "Whatever you see in the cafeteria, remember that killing Remy is the priority. We do that, we knock the others off balance."

"Remy's mine," rumbled Ryan.

"Then we'll attack anyone who tries to help him, because I really don't think these shifters have the kind of honor that would make them stand back while two wolves duel."

Makenna agreed with Dante. "How long do you think it will be before backup arrives?"

"No idea," replied the Beta male. "The battle will have already started by now. We can't be sure how long it will be before Trey can afford to spare people."

Jaime winced. "Four against twenty-five isn't great odds."

No, it wasn't. "Madisyn and Colton are good fighters. Dawn's damn vicious and capable of holding her own. Most of the residents have received combat training from Colton—lone shifters have to know how to protect themselves. If nothing else, they'll keep most of Remy's wolves occupied."

Looking into his mate's eyes, Ryan knew she wasn't quite as confident about their safety as she sounded. She had to know there was a huge difference in knowing defensive maneuvers and being trained enforcers. There were certain to be casualties.

"It might be best if we don't shift," added Makenna. "The residents won't be able to tell us apart from Remy's wolves if we're in our other form. They know our scents, but they'll be too hyped up to really take note of them."

"She has a point," said Jaime, rolling back her shoulders. "I have some experience at fighting wolves while in my human form."

Dante looked at Ryan. "Don't worry if you have to shift to fight Remy. We'll be guarding you anyway."

Makenna went to speak, but then everybody froze at the sound of footsteps in the hallway. *Shit.* The footsteps stopped a short distance away from the room.

"Did you find them?" The voice was male and unfamiliar.

"No," said a masculine voice that Makenna also didn't recognize. She arched a questioning brow at Ryan, Dante, and Jaime. They all shook their heads.

A heavy sigh. "I don't think the boys are here."

"They could be hiding."

"I haven't picked up their scents anywhere. You?"

"No, but Remy believes—"

"Remy's fucking lost it, and we both know it."

A derisive snort. "You think a guy who likes little boys has ever been sane?" That received a chuckle. *A chuckle?* Makenna barely held back a growl. How could anybody find such a concept amusing? These people knew their Alpha was twisted and they didn't care. They weren't just without honor; they were without morals.

Ryan held a finger to his mouth, opened the door a little . . . and fucking disappeared out of the room like smoke. Dante must have sensed Makenna's automatic instinct to follow, because he raised a hand and shook his head. She was about to tell him to fuck off, but then he mouthed, "Listen."

So she listened . . . and realized nobody was talking anymore. Ryan poked his head into the room and signaled for them to exit with a jerk of his chin. Her brows shot up as she spotted two males on the floor, their heads tilted at an unnatural angle. He and Dante dragged them into the room and quietly shut the door.

Well, that was two less immoral fuckers in the world.

Dante took the lead as they kept close to the wall, using the shadows as cover. She guessed he was following the voices they could hear—unfortunately, they weren't yet clear enough for anyone to understand the words.

Approaching a T-junction, Dante raised a hand and briefly glanced around the corner. He then raised his thumb and led them around it. Still sticking close to the wall, they silently hurried down the hall. That was when the voices started to become clear.

"Don't make me ask you again, Dawn," growled Remy.

"I can't tell you what I don't know." Dawn sounded cool and collected, but Makenna knew the feline would be nervous as hell.

"I know they're here, so lying to me is pointless," he spat.

"You can't truly believe that the council left them here, in such an obvious place," scoffed Dawn.

Reaching the cafeteria, Makenna found the door ajar. Staying within the shadows, the Beta pair moved to the opposite side of the doorframe while she and Ryan peeked through the gap near the hinges of the door. Madisyn and Colton were flanking Dawn while the residents and other staff members were grouped behind them; some looked nervous, others looked ready to kill.

Over twenty of Remy's wolves were present, including Selene. They had kicked aside most of the tables and were circling Dawn and the others. It was a relief to see that Madisyn hadn't gotten herself killed. But going by the way she was eying Remy with lethal precision, she sure was thinking about pouncing on him any moment now.

Pacing, Remy sniggered. "The council left them here *because* it's an obvious place, thinking I wouldn't suspect it." His every movement was jerky and awkward, like a junkie needing a fix. His recently deceased pack mate was right: he'd lost it.

"You had your wolves search the entire building, and they didn't find them," Dawn pointed out. "The second search doesn't seem to have yielded anything either. What does that tell you?"

"That you're hiding them with the others." Remy went nose to nose with her. "You think I haven't noticed that there are no children among this crowd? You think I wouldn't find that a little fucking suspicious? You've hid them somewhere, and you've hid mine with them. Tell me where!" Remy slanted a glance at Selene. With a wicked grin, the female sliced out her claws and pointed them at Colton's throat. "Tell me, or he dies."

To his credit, Colton didn't move a single muscle. He showed no fear at all. Dawn, on the other hand, hitched a breath as her eyes rounded.

Remy snickered, smug at her slight sign of weakness. "I think we understand each other now, don't we?"

Makenna shot a "We need to do something" look at Ryan. He then exchanged a look and some kind of weird hand signal with Dante and Jaime. They both nodded.

"Colton has nothing to do with this, Remy," said Dawn. "Leave him out of it."

"You've taken something important from me. I think it's only fair that I take something important from you. Of course, you can save him if you just give me what I want. So I'll ask you one more time. Where. Are. They?"

"I've told you, they're not here, and I don't know where the council took them."

"I warned you."

Selene sliced open Colton's throat. Everyone froze, breaths catching. Unable to process what was happening, Makenna watched as, eyes wide with horror and pain, her friend gurgled and dropped to his knees. Then he slumped to the ground. Time seemed to slow as ice-cold fury slammed into her core and settled heavy in her stomach while heat rushed to her head. Everything inside her screamed and bled, inflating like a balloon that was destined to burst. And that calm she'd clung to . . . it went.

Sensing the storm of emotion in his mate, Ryan made a grab for her. It was too late. She charged into the room just as Madisyn launched herself at Selene. Several things then happened at once.

A hand fisted in Madisyn's hair from behind, wrenching her away from Selene.

The residents roared and lunged at Remy's wolves, shifting into their animal forms.

Makenna jumped on Selene's back when the Head Enforcer tried to stab Madisyn, making Selene hit the ground hard.

Ryan, Dante, and Jaime raced into the room and joined the fight.

Remy made a dive for Dawn, but Ryan swiped his back, raking his claws over the bastard's skin.

Then everything and everyone pretty much went crazy.

CHAPTER TWENTY-TWO ☉

Somewhere in the back of Makenna's mind, she knew she was half feral. Knew she was back in that state where mercy had no place. A state that seemed to intensify every emotion—the raw anger, the terrible grief, the heart-stabbing pain, and the desperate need for vengeance . . . all of that curdled inside her and fuelled her every move.

Straddling Selene, she dragged her claws down the Head Enforcer's back. Makenna smiled at the sound of cloth tearing, skin splitting open, and the bitch's howl of pain. The smell of Selene's blood made Makenna's wolf bare her teeth in wicked satisfaction.

Yeah, she was half feral all right. But for now, Makenna didn't have the emotional capacity to care.

As she raised her hand to stab the bitch beneath her, someone grabbed Makenna's wrist and yanked her away. Pain rippled through Makenna's shoulder as the move almost wrenched her damn arm from the socket. Then the interfering fucker at her back disappeared with a howl of agony.

Makenna didn't check to see whom her savior was. She only had eyes for Selene, who had jumped to her feet. Selene, who had *killed Colton and tried to stab Madisyn.* She needed to die. And it needed to hurt.

Makenna snatched a chair and swung it at Selene. The bitch caught it by one leg. No matter. Makenna snapped off one of the other chair legs and, once Selene had slung the chair aside, whacked the leg across her face. It hit Selene's cheekbone with a satisfying crack.

Selene stared at her, wide-eyed in pure disbelief. "You hit me with a chair." Pure disbelief.

Yeah, yeah, shifters fought with teeth and claws. Well, Makenna fought with whatever she fucking found. She was a scrapper, not a trained enforcer. And right then, she had no care for what was fair.

"Aw, was Colton a dear friend?" taunted Selene. She kicked Makenna hard in the stomach.

The impact took Makenna's breath away and made her stumble. The backs of her thighs banged into a table and, *shit*, that hurt. Shelving the pain, Makenna went at her with an arsenal of teeth, claws, limbs, and a chair leg. All the while, shifters howled and roared and hissed around them. The scents of blood, sweat, and anger rose in the air, inciting her wolf.

Selene ducked and dodged. Punched and kicked. Bit and clawed. It hurt, it stung, and Makenna motherfucking bled. But she was beyond caring about the pain. Beyond caring that Selene was strong and well trained. Beyond caring that her own blood was flowing. Beyond caring about anything other than ending this bitch.

The female went to skirt around Makenna, no doubt to reach Remy and help him fight off Ryan. *Oh the fuck no*. Makenna blocked her path.

"You can't win this," Selene hissed. "I'm a Head Enforcer."

"Who's hot for a pedophile—go judge me for not ranking you highly." Makenna grabbed a tray from one of the tables and whipped it at Selene. It caught her head, making it snap to the side.

"He never touched those boys." With a growl, Selene copied her by snatching another tray and hurling it.

Makenna raised her hand to block the tray. It smacked the tip of her little finger, making the nail snap back for a single second. *Motherfucker*.

"Sure he did. He's a twisted fuck, just like his mother." The latter word made Selene's lip curl back. So she didn't like Deanne either. "Let me guess . . . she tries to keep you away from Remy."

"Because she knows he's my mate."

"Your mate?" echoed Makenna, shocked.

"My *true* mate. When he finally accepts that, when he's ready, we'll claim each other."

No wonder Selene was in complete denial about Remy. If Makenna weren't half feral, she might have felt sorry for her, might have pitied her for discovering that her mate's childhood had so warped his mind that he could never be the perfect match he otherwise would have been. But right then, Makenna only saw a bitch who'd killed her friend.

Selene once again tried to reach Remy. Makenna blocked her path and slashed at Selene's face, catching her bottom lip. That had to fucking sting. And now she'd be able to taste her own blood. Makenna's wolf liked knowing that. "I'm surprised you haven't gotten rid of Deanne." Makenna would have destroyed anyone who harmed Ryan that way.

"It would hurt Remy." Selene ran a finger over her bleeding lip. "He loves her. He says she never hurt him."

"Because he can't accept he's a victim."

Selene shook her head. "If he says she didn't hurt him, I believe him. Now let's get this over with so I can end you, just like Remy will end your mate." She leaped at Makenna.

Ryan used his arm to swipe away the blood obscuring his vision. The slashes on his forehead were deep and throbbed. It was no surprise that Remy, as an Alpha, was a worthy opponent. He was strong. Confident. Well versed in various forms of combat. Careful not to telegraph his movements. And his punch was like a jackhammer.

All of which was very inconvenient.

He was also a guy who liked to go for the face and chest. Ryan's jaw throbbed from the hard blows it had taken. His ear burned from when Remy had tried to bite it off. And his T-shirt was wet with blood and sweat.

Still, Ryan had been training since he was a child. He knew how to block pain, knew every weak spot on a human body, and knew how to defend just as well as attack. Remy, however, wasn't so good at defense—Ryan had pounced on that weakness. Which was why Remy was in no better shape than him.

"I don't know many enforcers who'd take on an Alpha." Remy licked his split lip. "I guess you're a little pissed that I sold Makenna's identity to the extremists."

Ryan really wasn't sure why the guy kept talking. He actually didn't mind that Remy was doing his best to taunt him. Talking meant he found it hard to keep his breathing steady. Besides, Ryan knew better than to let emotions, worries, or pain distract him. So he'd kept his anger in check. Didn't let himself dwell on how this bastard had stolen the innocence of children, or on how he was made from the same cloth of the males who had hurt Zac.

The only thing concerning Ryan, the only thing capable of distracting him, was that he could *feel* his mate was half feral. Sure, it would give her an edge. It could also make her ignore her smarts. Lead her to make mistakes. Mistakes meant losing. Losing meant death. That wasn't acceptable to Ryan.

"She should have stayed out of this," Remy went on. "That was all she had to do. *You* should have stayed out of it too. Did you know that while you're here fighting me, young Zac's old Alpha is leading an army of wolves to your territory?" His smirk fell when Ryan lashed out, carving deep grooves in his chest. "You do know. How?"

Ryan's only response was to aim a punch at his opponent's nose. Remy jerked back, avoiding the blow. Then he came at Ryan with claws and fists again. His wolf was raring to surface and tear Remy apart. He wanted to destroy this male who had put his mate in danger and led Zac's old pack right to him. The scent of blood mixed with the corruption and cruelty that wafted from Remy only increased his wolf's thirst for vengeance.

A hard kick from Remy caught Ryan's thigh. He grunted as Remy's heel raked over what was sure to be a fucking colorful bruise. Makenna would be pissed. Pumped up on adrenalin, Ryan only felt a quarter of the pain. He retaliated by snapping out his leg, booting Remy's side. Something cracked and the breath whooshed out of Remy.

The Alpha's eyes flashed wolf. "Son of a bitch." Remy tore off his jeans and shifted forms. He was fast.

So was Ryan.

The wolves crashed into each other in a fury of teeth and claws. The dark wolf had hungered for this. Longed to confront and battle this male who would have seen his mate dead. He was merciless. Vicious. Stabbed his claws deep into his opponent's sides.

The gray wolf snarled and tore a strip out of the dark wolf's flank. Blood soaked his fur, filled his nose. But the dark wolf didn't back off. He fought harder.

He sank his teeth down into the gray wolf's shoulder and shook him. His fangs tore through skin and muscle. Scraped bone. Made satisfaction flood the dark wolf. He didn't want to defeat his opponent. Didn't want him to submit. He wanted him dead. Wanted more of the gray's wolf blood on his tongue.

Chests heaving, the wolves fiercely fought again. Growling. Snarling. Clawing. Biting. Body slamming. The Alpha was strong like his human side. Ruthless and without honor. So it didn't take the dark wolf by surprise when dominant, oppressive vibes slammed into him. Vibes that tried to force him to submit.

The dark wolf shook his head in an effort to shake off the weight pressing down on him. He would not submit. He would not lose. But the pressure was heavy and thick, it—

Wolves burst into the room, growling and snarling. The dark wolf recognized their scents, knew some were his pack mates. The sight distracted the gray wolf, made his vibes ease away. The dark wolf took advantage and barreled into him. He wrestled the Alpha onto his back, pinned him there and—

"*NO!*"

A hard force slammed into the dark wolf, knocking him off the Alpha. The dark wolf slid along the floor and hit the wall with a thud. The man within the animal pushed hard for supremacy, and the wolf didn't have the strength to resist.

Ryan got to his feet, ready to fight off the crazed female baring down on him. He didn't have to. A growled, "Not a fucking chance, bitch!" was followed by Selene crashing to the ground as a weight hit her back and took her down. *Makenna.*

"This time," snarled Makenna, fisting the female's hair and yanking up her head, "you won't get up." She sliced the female's throat open, just as Selene had done to Colton.

"Selene!" The agonized cry came from Remy, who was back in his human form. He crawled to the female, slipping in her blood.

Moving to Ryan, Makenna stared at Remy. "You knew she was your mate, didn't you?"

"She should have been given someone better than me," he replied, only then seeming to realize the battle was over and his wolves were dead. Some of the residents that Dawn and Madisyn were tending to looked badly hurt, but Ryan couldn't tell if any were dead.

Makenna snorted. "I won't argue there."

Upper lip curled back, Remy leaped up. Like a flash, Ryan, Dante and Jaime were blocking his path and Ryan had a hand wrapped around the Alpha's throat.

Remy managed a pale imitation of a laugh. "You're protecting her? Really? Then you mustn't know about her past. You must have no idea what she did to be banished from her pack and forced to run for her life. I do."

It was a total bluff, Makenna knew. Clearly he had no idea that Ryan had already discovered the truth about her pack. Ryan would know that Remy was talking bullshit, but would the others? Would they give a female who was once a loner the benefit of the doubt?

Remy spat out blood. "Do you want to hear it?"

"No," said Dante just as Ryan thrust his claws into Remy's chest.

"She's a Phoenix wolf," added Jaime. "One of us. That's all we need to know."

And, for the first time, Makenna understood what Ryan was trying to tell her. She wasn't alone anymore. Didn't have to be so emotionally reliant. Didn't have to hold back. She was part of a pack. *This* pack. And being part of the Phoenix Pack meant something very special.

The breath left her lungs as pain lanced her head and chest. Then it was gone, and she could feel Ryan everywhere. In her. Around her. She felt his heartbeat, felt his surprise, relief, and satisfaction. Their mating bond, despite being new, wasn't by any means weak. It was strong. Complete. Probably because it had been ready to form for so long.

Releasing the dying wolf, Ryan turned to his mate. He'd been right. Or, more specifically, Jaime had been right. The bond had been jammed by an external issue. Now it had not only snapped into place, it was—

"Not my boy! Not my boy!"

The screech had everyone spinning to face a gun-waving Deanne. A shot fired, and something slammed into Ryan. It was like there was an explosion in the left side of his stomach. The impact made him grunt and catch his breath. Putting a hand to his stomach, he looked down. Distantly aware that Roni had disarmed and gutted Deanne, Ryan pulled away his hand. And frowned. There was no blood. No wound.

Beside him, his mate fell to her knees. His frown deepened. "Kenna?" She blinked up at him, her expression one of utter shock. Then he saw the red blooming across her T-shirt. Panic raced through him and his wolf. "Shit." He dropped to his knees and cupped her face. "Kenna, it's okay."

She nodded. But she didn't feel okay. She *hurt*. God, it was like she was burning from the inside out. Every instinct she had told her this was very, very bad. Shock gave way to panic, and she clung to Ryan's arms—as if he could anchor her. Her wolf went fucking ape shit.

"Lay her down, put pressure on the wound," Dante told him, all business.

Ryan gently eased her onto her back and pressed his hand over the fucking hole in her stomach. She winced. "Shit, I'm sorry." He shoved strength down their bond, listening as Dante called their Alpha female. "Taryn's a healer," Ryan told Makenna, unsure if she already knew. "She'll fix you."

"The bullet went straight through, so that's good," said Jaime, but there was worry in her voice. She didn't need to worry. His mate would be fine.

Ryan looked into eyes swirling with the pain, fear echoing through him. "It's okay. You're going to be fine. Say it."

Makenna swallowed. "I'm going to be fine." She wasn't certain she believed that. Her stomach burned and throbbed. She could feel warm blood on her skin and pooling beneath her. She'd already lost some in her duel with Selene. As fingers linked with hers, she looked to see Madisyn and Dawn kneeling close by. "Hey."

"Don't you die," Madisyn hissed, eyes wet and fierce.

"She's not going to die," snapped Ryan.

"That's right," agreed Dawn, voice breaking. "Makenna's strong."

Ryan kissed her gently, brushing a thumb over her cheekbone. Her eyes fluttered closed. He tapped her cheek. "No, Kenna. Look at me."

Makenna forced her eyes open. "I'm tired," she whispered. Crazy tired. She was pretty sure the only thing keeping her conscious was the iron strength Ryan was feeding her. She clung to that strength. She didn't want to die, didn't want to leave him or miss the life they could have together. But it was just so hard to stay awake, no matter how hard she fought the urge to sleep. Everything seemed to be fading. Darkening. Like she was falling. No . . . sinking.

"It's okay," said Ryan, his pulse beating frantically. "The wound's not that bad."

Her mouth kicked up into a small smile. "Liar."

He *was* a liar. No matter how much pressure he put on the wound, her blood kept seeping through his fingers. *She* was seeping through his fingers. "Kenna." The solid, vibrant bond between them flickered slightly. And he knew what that meant. "No," he bit out. "No, no, no, *no*." She couldn't die. He wouldn't fucking allow it. He glared at Dante. *"Where the fuck is Taryn?"*

"On her way," Jaime choked out, eyes shiny. She wasn't the only one crying. Many were gathered around, most of whom were residents.

Ryan dropped his forehead to Makenna's. "Did you hear that? She's coming." Makenna gave the tiniest nod. And closed her eyes. "*No*. Eyes open. Look at me. Good girl." She coughed, and he saw blood in her mouth. His chest tightened. "No." This was *not* fucking happening. It just wasn't. "Taryn's coming. Just hold on a little longer."

Makenna forced a smile. They both knew Taryn could never make it in time. "Don't die with me."

Rage flared through him and his wolf. "Don't you dare fucking give up! You live!"

She coughed again, tasting more blood. "Zac needs you."

"And I fucking need you. If you want me to live, you have to stay alive. You fight, okay. *Fight*."

She tried to, she did, but she was so tired and . . . "Cold." So damn cold. Her wolf lay down with a whine.

Ryan forced more strength down the fading bond. It made no difference. Her heartbeat kept slowing, their connection kept weakening, and the blood just kept pumping out of her. "Kenna, fight."

"It doesn't hurt anymore," she murmured.

"That's good." No, it wasn't good. He knew it; she knew it. His wolf was pacing, anxious, afraid, and wanting to kill.

"And I'm not scared anymore. Isn't that weird?" She should be terrified. She was dying, and she knew it. But she felt peaceful. "I love you." She should have told him that before. "Super shit timing, haven't I?" She heard Dawn and Madisyn sniffling, wanted to tell them to take care of Ryan. But she was sinking again, and everything seemed so far away.

Her eyes closed again, and Ryan's heart slammed against his ribs. "Kenna, look at me." She didn't. He shook her. "Open your eyes." Her sluggish heartbeat stuttered and their bond began to wink out. *"No."*

Hands yanked at him. "Get the fuck off me!" They didn't. They pulled at him, ignoring his efforts to fight them off, and dragged him away. He couldn't get back to her, couldn't fight them; he'd pumped most of his strength into Makenna and wasn't able to—

"Easy, Ryan! Just give her some room! *If you want your mate to live, give her some room!"*

He stilled, only then noticing Ally squatting beside his mate. The Seer could heal, he remembered. Derren and Dante released him, and his knees nearly buckled.

"Don't let her die," Madisyn hissed at Ally.

Hands on Makenna's stomach, Ally looked at him. "You're going to have to help me, Ryan; she's hanging on by a thin thread."

Ryan went back to his mate and held her hand, trying to push what little strength he had left into her, whether it knocked him unconscious or not. But the bond was too weak to take it.

Ally's eyes stayed closed as she did . . . whatever the hell she did. Unlike when Taryn healed, the wound didn't glow. He couldn't tell what the fuck was happening. It was only when Makenna's heartbeat steadied that hope trickled through him. He tightened his grip on her hand as her pulse quickened and their bond strengthened.

Pale as a ghost, Ally sat back. "She lost a lot of blood, so she'll be unconscious for a little while, but she's gonna be okay." Then the Seer slumped . . . right into Derren's waiting arms.

Ryan scooped up Makenna and cradled her tight against him. God, he was fucking shaking. It actually hurt to breathe. His lungs burned and his throat felt clogged up. It didn't matter that he could feel that she was alive; fear still had him in a tight grip, and it wasn't letting go anytime soon.

Breathing her in, he kissed her forehead and tucked her face into the crook of his neck. His wolf was still pacing, unable to relax in the belief that she was okay. Madisyn and Dawn, faces red and puffy, were still at her other side. Ryan knew they probably wanted to hold her, but he couldn't let go. Hearing her heart beat steady and strong was really the only thing keeping him and his wolf stable at that moment.

"Ally had a vision that Makenna would be shot," said Derren. "I'm glad we got here in time."

They almost hadn't, but Ryan wouldn't let himself dwell on that. He gave Derren a nod of thanks, unable to speak while a knot of emotion was lodged in his throat. Ryan owed Ally more than he could ever repay.

Jaime's eyes widened. "Shit, the battle on our territory!"

Dante dug out his cell phone. "In case the others are still fighting, I'll call Grace and ask what's happening." He then faded from the crowd to make the call.

"When we left, it was starting to settle down and things were going in our favor," said Marcus. "Most of the wolves actually retreated pretty quickly. They'd expected an easy defeat. The sight of us with so much backup threw them. And they started to panic when they realized there were trip wires and land mines on the territory."

Jaime inhaled deeply. "Any casualties on our side?"

"Trick nearly had his throat ripped out. Dominic came very close to dying while defending Eli." Eli was Nick's brother and Head Enforcer. "They're okay, though. Taryn healed them."

Dante returned to Jaime's side. "It was Rhett who answered. Grace was busy tending wounds. The battle's over. And Zac's old Alpha is being held captive in the hut." Dante looked at Ryan. "Everyone figured that kill was yours."

Still not trusting himself to speak, Ryan inclined his head.

Jaime let out a long breath. "Let's see who needs help here and then go home."

CHAPTER TWENTY-THREE

akenna woke to the feeling of warm lips on her stomach. Her eyelids were heavy, but she forced them open. Lying on top of her, Ryan had pushed up the long T-shirt she was wearing and was kissing where her gunshot wound should have been. But there was no wound, no bandage, not a spot of blood on her body. She frowned. She *had* been shot, right?

"Ally healed you," said Ryan, feeling her confusion. He was so relieved she'd finally woken that a breath shuddered out of him. "She had a vision that you were shot." There was no evidence of it now. Only unmarred velvet-smooth skin. He couldn't help remembering the warm blood flowing between his fingers and pooling beneath her. Fuck, she'd almost died right in front of him. When he thought about it too much, his chest would tighten and his throat would start to close.

She stroked his head, sensing his distress. "How long was I out?"

He slipped his arms beneath her and held her tight. "Nine hours." It was the longest nine hours of his life. Not once had she stirred—not even when he'd stripped and washed her before dressing her in one of his tees.

She scowled as she remembered something. "Your jaw was swollen and you had gashes on your forehead."

"They healed. None of my wounds were serious." Unlike hers. He rubbed his jaw against her stomach. "I was scared." It seemed okay to admit that to her. "You were slipping away from me. I could feel it. But there was nothing for me to grab on to." Her soul wasn't a physical thing. "No way for me to make you stay."

Her eyes stung. "I didn't want to go."

"You can't die." He wouldn't survive it.

She swallowed. "Come here."

He pressed one more kiss to her stomach, reminding himself she was alive and with him. He slid up her body, kissed her gently, and rested his forehead on hers. "I would have followed you." She tried to shake her head. "Yes, I would have. I don't know how people carry on after they lose someone." He wouldn't have had the will to keep going. Not even knowing Zac needed him. It was selfish; Ryan knew that. Still, he simply would have faded away without her. Makenna was part of him. A part he *needed*.

She cupped his face. "We don't have to test that theory. I'm fine; I'm not going anywhere." She kissed him, wanting to take away the fear and anxiety that ate at him. A change of subject could help. "Well, it seems you were right. We're true mates."

Ryan grunted. Of course he was right.

"I don't like your tone." She nipped his lip. "Our scents have mixed. I like that."

So did Ryan. Every shifter would know from just her scent that she was taken. He doubted his jealousy or possessiveness would now ease, however. He still wouldn't like other males around her. Would always be jealous, just as he'd been jealous of . . . "I'm sorry about Colton. I know he was your friend."

She bit her bottom lip before it had the chance to tremor. "Me too." He'd been a good friend to her, and he hadn't deserved what had happened to him. None of them had deserved the trouble Remy had brought into their lives. "I take it we won the battle."

"Yes." He wasn't good at telling stories. "Only the Mercury wolves had arrived by the time the attack began. Reinforcements turned up no more than a minute later, which spooked the enemies. Most of them retreated, others died. Taryn's father lost some of his wolves. Trick and Dominic almost died."

Makenna was relieved to hear their pack was alive. As for someone else . . . "Deanne's dead, right?"

He grunted. "Roni gutted her." He was a little jealous he hadn't been able to deliver that killing move himself. Then again, that would have required him to release Makenna. He hadn't been able to bring himself to do that until they were in the infirmary, where Grace had given her a transfusion. Grace had tried to usher him out, but he'd just stared at her until she gave up with a humph.

Makenna rubbed her nose against his. "You look tired. You fed me a lot of energy."

According to Ally, who had earlier called to check on Makenna, his mate would have died long before Ally had arrived if he hadn't lent her his strength. "You said you love me." Again with the blurting things out.

She smiled. "That's because I do."

He closed his eyes, letting that soothe him. "No one's ever said that to me before." He slid his hand up to span her throat, wanting to feel her pulse beating beneath his thumb.

Her brows flew up. "Never?" God, his parents were assholes. "Come inside me, Ryan. I know you want to."

He did want to. He wanted to assure himself in the most basic way that she was alive. "You've been unconscious for nine hours. You need food and—"

"You. Just you." She writhed beneath him, tempting him. "Come inside me."

He shouldn't. He should have some food brought in and—

"Ryan, please. I need this too."

Fuck it. He used his fingers to ready her to take him. Then he hiked up her leg and slid inside her, groaning as her pussy contracted around him. He took her with slow, deep, deliberate thrusts. The whole time, he kissed her—sharing breaths, groans, and gasps. And when he shoved himself deep and exploded, he buried his face in the crook of her neck and growled her name. "I love you, Kenna."

She smiled. "I know. I feel it." It was like a glow inside her.

Without leaving her body, he rolled onto his back, taking her with him.

She propped her chin on his chest as he grabbed his cell phone from the cabinet. "Who are you texting?"

"Grace. You need food. You lost a lot of blood." He put down his phone. "Be warned, the room is going to fill up. There are a lot of people waiting to see you." He'd been chasing them off, insisting she needed her rest. "Let's get you showered."

As they were dressing a short while later, a knock came at the door. "Open up!" called Grace.

Makenna held up her arms so Ryan could slip on her T-shirt. "I can go eat in the kitchen, you know."

He shook his head. "You're not at one hundred percent yet."

She couldn't deny that. But she'd be damned if she'd voice aloud just how weak she truly felt. "Okay." She sighed as she sat, lotus style, in the middle of the bed.

"I'll be back soon."

She frowned. "Where are you going?"

Hand on the doorknob, he glanced over his shoulder. "To live up to a promise."

With that mysterious answer, he left. Grace entered with a tray of food. Zac, Dawn, and Madisyn trailed behind her. Eyes teary, Zac gave her a tight hug that belied his typical teenage cool act and chatted with her for a short while. Then, complaining he had something in his eye, he left with Dawn. Madisyn stayed while Makenna ate, lecturing her for getting shot.

Each of the Phoenix wolves came to see Makenna, a few at a time. They all expressed their relief that she was fine. Rhett wanted to hear about what it was like to almost die and if she'd seen any bright lights. At that point, Grace shoved him out of the room.

Riley, Savannah, Dexter, and Kye then came inside. The kids leaped onto the bed, kissing her cheeks and showing her pictures that they'd doodled for her. Well, Dexter's was more of a balled-up piece of paper, but the gesture was still there.

As the three children ran out of the room, laughing, Riley said, "Taryn's offered to let Dexter and Savannah stay here permanently."

Madisyn took a sip of Makenna's coffee. "Really?"

Having seen how closely the children had bonded with Kye and how much Taryn adored them, Makenna wasn't actually that surprised. "How do you feel about that?"

Riley smoothed out a wrinkle on the bedsheet. "It would be good for them, right? To have a real home." Her reluctance to part with them was clear in her tone.

"I don't think they'll stay behind, Riley," said Makenna. "They're too attached to you. They love you."

"Yeah, but they love you and Zac too. You guys live here now."

Makenna patted her hand. "They love you more."

Riley shifted uncomfortably. "Taryn said I could stay with them until they feel settled enough to stay without me. She said I could have a permanent place here too—"

"She said *what?*" Greta was in the doorway with Tao, whose eyes were locked on Riley with an intensity that the raven failed to notice.

"Aw, have you come to check up on me?" asked Makenna, smiling.

Greta's upper lip curled back. "I was rather hoping you didn't wake up at all. No such luck. Now I'm stuck with you *and* her!"

Riley sighed. "Look, Gretchen—"

"It's Greta."

"I don't care."

The kids all scurried back into the bedroom, and Dexter headed right for the tray.

Riley sighed. "Dexter, don't stuff more food in your pockets." Her tone was gentle but firm. The toddler looked at her with an expression that said, "Why?" Then he shoved a slice of apple down his shirt. "Savannah, stop hissing at Gretchen. Or, at least, don't hiss so loud."

Kye chuckled and then mimicked the action, making Greta gasp in horror at her grandson. That had Savannah laughing with an evil glee in her eyes.

"That kid has a mean streak that I totally love," said Madisyn.

At that moment, Dominic strolled inside, smiling. That smile faltered when he looked at Madisyn. He cast her a mock glare. "She still won't tell me what type of cat she is, Makenna. No one who saw her shift will tell me."

Makenna just smiled at him. "I heard we both had a close call."

He waved it off and relaxed into the chair beside her bed. Then he gave her a flirtatious grin. "So, are you into casual sex or should I dress up?"

The guy really was nothing but trouble.

Minutes after he'd left his mate, Ryan stalked into the hut with Dante and Trey close behind him. The hut was where they kept any intruders they found roaming on their territory. Today, it contained a well-built male with shaggy brown hair and cruel eyes.

Despite being bound to a chair, the captive tried to stare Ryan down. When it didn't work, he sneered, "You must be the cousin. Remy told me a lot about you."

Ryan's wolf snarled. "You must be the sick bastard who hurt Zac."

There wasn't a hint of remorse in Brogan Creed's gaze. You could learn a lot about a person from their posture, tone, word choice, and expressions. And as Ryan looked down at him, he had the distinct impression that Brogan wasn't like Remy. He *knew* what he'd become, knew it and saw no reason to justify it to himself or to anyone else. For him, abusing others wasn't so much about sex as about having ultimate power and dominance over another person. "I'm glad you came here."

"Really?" he drawled.

"I promised Zac you'd die if you did." Ryan's claws sliced out. "This saves me the trouble of hunting you down."

CHAPTER TWENTY-FOUR

S tanding in the forest outside the caves, Ryan watched his mate roll back her shoulders for the tenth time in the last fifteen minutes. "You're nervous."

"Well . . . yeah."

At least she was admitting it. "You don't need to be."

"This is a big thing, okay."

Fair enough, but . . . "So was our mating ceremony. You weren't nervous then."

"Of course I wasn't. I was one hundred percent sure about you and how much I wanted the ceremony."

Warmth radiated through Ryan's chest. Their mating ceremony was short, sweet, and understated, since neither of them had wanted a huge party. Ryan wouldn't have coped well with one, and he did not—under any circumstances—dance. Besides, he hadn't wanted to share his mate on the night of their ceremony. He was too selfish and possessive for that.

He'd invited Garrett and the other enforcers from Ryan's old pack to visit the next day. They all fell hard for Makenna, which probably had a lot to do with the verbal smackdown she'd delivered to his parents when they tagged along with Garrett. She'd told them in no uncertain terms that they were shit parents and even worse people, that if they couldn't see how special Ryan was, then they were even dumber than they looked. Strangely, they hadn't argued with that.

Feeling another spurt of anxiety rush through his mate, he said, "I know you want answers and closure, but you don't have to do this now."

Makenna set her jaw and planted her feet in a wide stance. "I do." It was time to face it . . . even if her muscles were tight with tension and a part of her was dreading what was to come.

Ryan grunted.

"Well, I like being stubborn. It keeps you on your toes."

Everything about his unpredictable, quirky mate kept him on his toes. "If they do or say anything to upset you, they're gone."

"I know." She rubbed at her arm. "I'd prefer it if we didn't have an audience."

He frowned, glancing around the empty clearing. "You have privacy."

She snorted. "No, I don't. Our pack's scattered around the forest to keep a close watch on things." Even Zac.

"They're protective of you."

She knew that. It was a good feeling for both her and her wolf. Good to be a part of something. And good to know they were just as protective of the shelter as they were of her. Being equally protective, Madisyn was also hanging around the forest, even though she was still mad with Makenna for getting shot. She pretty much blamed her for it.

Makenna knew she was seriously lucky to be breathing right now. Ally was officially one of her favorite people in the world. There had sadly been some fatalities in the battle. There would have been more if Taryn hadn't arrived—too late to heal Makenna, which had pissed her off and made her feel bad—and healed those with serious injuries. The Phoenix wolves had also helped repair the cafeteria.

At the sound of low voices, Makenna and her wolf stiffened. This was it. The moment was finally here. It was time to face her past. She licked her dry mouth. Maybe she should have waited a little longer and—

Ryan briefly squeezed her hand. "You're safe. No one can harm you here."

She didn't believe her visitors would physically hurt her, but she believed the information they possessed quite possibly could. Without thinking, she hooked her finger in Ryan's belt loop. Moments later, Trey and Taryn entered the clearing with five unfamiliar wolves. The Phoenix Alphas stepped aside, allowing the visitors to move forward.

The male in the center exuded power and confidence. He was definitely an Alpha. He tilted his head as he studied her and released a shallow sigh. "You look a lot like your mom. It's uncanny. I'm Harlow Gannon, your uncle." He quickly introduced his Beta and enforcers.

It took a moment for her to respond. Uncle. He was her uncle. She'd never before met any of her family, hadn't even known that she *had* an uncle until Ryan told her. And now the guy was standing right in front of her—a guy who was also a part of her mother. She cleared her throat. "I'm Makenna. This is my mate, Ryan Conner."

At Harlow's nod, Ryan grunted. If he hadn't tracked these wolves himself, he wouldn't believe this guy was her uncle. They shared no resemblance whatsoever. He'd gotten a message to Harlow from Makenna, which had very simply read that she was sorry to inform him that her mother had died many years ago after a vicious attack. The male had very swiftly replied, asking to meet her. She'd taken a few days to think about it before agreeing.

On edge due to his mate's anxiety, Ryan's wolf wasn't comfortable with these strangers on his territory. He also didn't like that this male claimed to have a connection to her, even if it was familial. Typical of his very jealous wolf.

Harlow cleared his throat. "If I'm honest, I wasn't sure you were who I've been looking for all these years until now. I guess I didn't want to believe my sister was dead. There's no denying that you're hers."

In his position, Makenna wouldn't have wanted to believe it either. Pushing past her dread, she asked the question that had haunted her for a very long time. "Do you know what happened to my dad?" Watching the Alpha's face fall, Makenna was almost sorry she asked. Her stomach knotted.

"The old Alpha hunted your parents. He found them two years later. Your mom got away with you, but he caught your dad. Killed him."

The news was like a hammer to the chest. "You know for sure he's dead?" She tensed when he averted his gaze. "Tell me. I need to know." It would be worse than not knowing, even if it would be a painful truth.

Harlow lifted his chin. "Conrad brought back his head."

Makenna's eyes fell closed, and she was glad that Ryan moved closer. She needed his strength right then. Be-fucking-headed . . . and all because he'd loved her mother. Her parents had both suffered awful deaths they didn't deserve. Her wolf howled in mourning.

"If I'd been old enough to take him on, I would have."

"It's not your fault."

"No, but it doesn't take away the pain of knowing what you and your parents went through." He did a double take as something caught his eye. "Is that a child hanging upside down from a tree branch?"

Makenna looked up at Savannah and sighed. "Yes." The viper waved. She and Dexter were now official Phoenix Pack members. Riley wasn't yet sure if she wanted a permanent place there, but she'd agreed to stay until the children were more settled. Greta wasn't happy about that, which delighted Taryn.

Harlow shifted his gaze to Ryan. "How long have you and my niece been mated?"

In Ryan's mind, they had officially been mates since he first realized what she was to him; he'd known he wouldn't let her go. But, in reality, as Madisyn once put it . . . "She led me on a merry dance."

Harlow grinned. "I'm glad to hear it. What happened to your head?"

Makenna inwardly rolled her eyes at Ryan's "I didn't want to talk about it" grunt. "It was a Frisbee. He jinxed himself by walking under a ladder."

Harlow frowned at Ryan. "Why would you do a fool thing like walk under a ladder? It's bad luck."

Ryan turned to Makenna. "He's definitely your relation."

She laughed.

That night, Ryan sat on the edge of his bed in only a towel, watching his mate putter around in nothing more than a white partially buttoned shirt and hot-pink panties. She was talking about how nice it had been to hear tales of her mother's childhood, to know about her deceased grandparents. She wasn't fooling him for a second. Deep inside, she was hurting; mourning the father she couldn't remember.

He wanted to say something, wanted to somehow make it better. But he was pretty sure that whatever he blurted out would be far from sensitive. He was—

"What did you just say?" He had to have misheard her.

She sent him an enigmatic smile. "What do you think I said?"

"Repeat it."

"Or . . . ?" she drawled. He snagged her shirt and pulled her to stand between his legs, accidentally tugging it open. "Hey!" she whined.

"Don't play with me. What did you say?"

"You're no fun."

His heart was pounding and his wolf was stock still. *"Kenna."*

She slid her hands over his broad shoulders. "I said, we'll have to move to a bigger room when the baby arrives next year."

That was what he'd thought she said. "You're not pregnant." He'd smell it if she were.

"According to Ally, it'll happen sometime soon." Makenna was pretty happy about it. Her mate, however . . . all she was sensing from him was shock. His wolf was smug. "You okay?"

Mouth dry, he swallowed. "Yeah."

"It's okay if you're a little spooked."

"I'm not spooked." He splayed a hand on her flat stomach. "I just never thought about having kids." As such, hearing he'd soon be a father was like a sucker punch. Yet, he wasn't unhappy or scared. He oddly felt a strange urge to possess his mate so completely that neither knew where he ended or she began.

As he slipped his hands inside her shirt to span her rib cage, Makenna moved a little closer. She *felt* the change in him. Felt the shock slip away to be replaced by the primal drive to take and own. She closed her eyes as he swirled his tongue in the hollow of her throat. Considering she liked sex rough and wild, it surprised her that the gentle, sensual move fired her desire. "Ryan."

He licked along her collarbone as her soft fingers skimmed over his shoulders and chest. "I need you to get on your knees for me, Kenna."

Her stomach clenched. "Now why would I do that?"

Ryan nipped her lip. "So you can wrap this pretty little mouth around my cock." Her pupils dilated and her fingers dug into his shoulders. "But first . . ." He raked a hand in her hair and closed his mouth over hers, driving his tongue inside. He'd never get enough of her taste. He loved her mouth. Loved kissing it, biting it, fucking it. Loved knowing nobody else could ever have it. "On your knees."

Makenna thought about fighting him just for the hell of it. Instead, she curled a hand around his cock and said, "I'll get on my knees . . . but only because I want to." She slowly knelt, stroking his cock.

With his hand bunched in her hair, he drew her mouth close. "Open." He didn't have to warn her not to tease him. She never did. She just sucked him deep. And she was fucking good at it. Especially when she did that swirly thing with her tongue. "That's it. Get me nice and wet, Kenna, because you're going to ride me."

Moaning at that, Makenna sucked harder and faster. She loved tasting him, but she needed him in her. Needed his cock to ease the ache that was building and building. She winced as the hand fisting her hair tugged.

"Stop. I don't want to come in your mouth tonight." Slipping a hand under her arm, Ryan helped her stand. Her lips were swollen and her eyes were languid, making his cock throb. He pulled down her panties, waiting while she stepped out of them and kicked them aside. "Come here." She straddled him, rubbing her pussy above the head of his cock. "Who do you belong to, Kenna?" Fingers digging into his shoulders, she began to lower herself on his cock. Ryan wrapped his hand around the base, stopping her from taking it all. "You didn't answer my question."

No, Makenna didn't, because it wasn't good to always give her mate what he wanted. The defiant streak in her wouldn't allow her to anyway. So she ignored his demand and slowly rode as much of his cock as she could take. But it wasn't enough. "Ryan."

"You want more?"

"Yes," she ground out.

"You can have more. You can have it all. It's yours. But first you have to tell me who you belong to." Free hand palming her breast, he raked his teeth down the column of her throat. "Tell me." He wasn't surprised when she just continued riding him. He gave her ass a sharp slap, which made her pussy clamp down on him. "Tell me."

She snarled. "Maybe I'll just go finish myself off."

He gripped her hip. "No, you're going to make me come before you go anywhere."

"Then move your hand."

"Then tell me who you fucking belong to."

She really wished that dominant tone didn't make her pussy clench. "You, you fucking asshole."

"Good girl." Ryan moved his hand and slammed her down on his cock, forcing her to take every inch. "Now ride me."

She did. She rode him hard. His hands palmed her ass, but he didn't help her. Just held her as she furiously slammed herself up and down his cock. Friction built inside her, winding her body tighter and tighter. But no matter how hard and fast she rode him, she couldn't throw herself over the edge.

Makenna gasped as the world abruptly tilted and she found herself flat on her back. Standing at the foot of the bed, Ryan pounded into her, yanking her to him with every thrust. One of his hands splayed over her lower stomach, feeling his cock push in and out. She fisted her hands in the bedsheets, arching into him.

Ryan curved over her and parted her folds so that he hit her clit with every rough, possessive thrust. Feeling her pussy getting tighter and tighter around him, he knew she was ready to come. "Now, Kenna." He clamped his teeth over her pulse and bit.

A scream tore from Makenna's throat as her back bowed and her release slammed into her. She dug her claws into him as he jammed his cock deep and erupted; she felt every hot splash, and she couldn't help wondering if this would be the night she conceived.

When he was finally able to move, Ryan shuffled them farther up the bed. He kissed and licked her stomach. Left possessive, suckling little bites. He could feel how sated and happy she was. It was like a buzz along their connection. Now that they had this metaphysical bond, he was no longer so sure it was simply an evolutionary construct. There was something very . . . mystical about it. But he wasn't about to admit that to Makenna and receive a smug smile.

She did a languid, feline stretch. "Love you, White Fang."

"You're never going to drop that, are you?"

"It's unlikely." She braced herself on her elbows. "What's wrong? You're worrying about something."

He was. He was worried the baby would turn out anything like him. But he got the feeling Makenna would rip him a new asshole if he said that, so instead he confessed something else. "I don't even know how to hold a baby."

"I'll show you when it comes."

"I'm not good with kids."

Smiling sweetly, she said, "You're not good with people, period. Being chatty and friendly and open is not you. So what? Why does that have to be a bad thing? The baby won't care; it will love you exactly as you are. And you will love the baby just as unconditionally. You will protect it and cherish it and be a total marshmallow for it. No one will believe you're a serial killer anymore. Seriously, your street cred will be shot to shit." His eyes gleamed and his mouth . . . curved. Wow. Her breath caught. His smile was sexy and sensual and dangerous all at once. "You're smiling!"

He frowned. "I'm not."

"Always so grouchy."

Whatever. Moving up the bed, he positioned himself on his side. "Time to sleep." Fitting her to him, he kissed her throat. "Love you, Kenna."

"Love you too." She snuggled deeper into him, closing her eyes. The pain of Harlow's news was still fresh. At the same time, there was a lightness inside her. Now that she knew the truth of her past, it felt like a weight had been lifted from her chest. She had her answers. They were shit and they were too sad for words, but at least she knew. Now she could truly move forward. And she could do it with her mate.

She was just dozing off when his cell phone beeped. Ryan grabbed his cell, tapped the screen a few times, and then slung it back onto the cabinet. It skidded along, knocked her compact mirror off the surface and—

Crack.

Well, shit. They both knew what that meant.

"Don't say it."

"I wasn't gonna."

Acknowledgments

As always, thanks to my family for being the most amazing people alive. It can't be easy to have a wife or mother that follows the formula: eat, sleep, write, repeat. Your patience is awe-inspiring.

Also, a major thank you to Christopher Werner, Melody Guy, Jessica Poore, and the rest of the author team at Montlake Romance for all your help and support. You're all awesome!

Last but definitely not least, I want to say a supremely big thanks to everyone who has read any of my books. You make all of this possible, and I'm forever grateful to you for that.

If for any reason you would like to contact me, whether it's about the book or you're considering self-publishing and have any questions, please feel free to e-mail me at suzanne_e_wright@live.co.uk.

Take care,
Suzanne Wright, Author

About the Author

Author Suzanne Wright, a native of England, can't remember a time when she wasn't creating characters and telling their tales. Even as a child, she loved writing poems, plays, and stories; as an adult, Wright has published thirteen novels: *From Rags*, *Burn*, five Deep In Your Veins novels, five books in the Phoenix Pack series, and the first book in the Mercury Pack series. Wright, who lives in Liverpool with her husband and two children, freely admits that she hates house-cleaning and can't cook but that she always shares chocolate. Visit her online at www.suzannewright.co.uk.

Printed in Great Britain
by Amazon

25125151R00179